Queen
Elizabeth's Daughter

ALSO BY ANNE CLINARD BARNHILL

At the Mercy of the Queen: A Novel of Anne Boleyn
Coal, Baby (poetry chapbook)
What You Long For (stories)
At Home in the Land of Oz: Autism, My Sister, and Me (memoir)

A NOVEL OF ELIZABETH I

Queen
Elizabeth's Daughter

Anne Clinard Barnhill

St. Martin's Griffin
New York

QUEEN ELIZABETH'S DAUGHTER. Copyright © 2014 by Anne Clinard Barnhill. All rights reserved. Printed in the United States of America. For information, address St. Martin's Press, 175 Fifth Avenue, New York, N.Y. 10010.

www.stmartins.com

Library of Congress Cataloging-in-Publication Data

Barnhill, Anne Clinard.
    Queen Elizabeth's daughter : a novel of Elizabeth I / Anne Clinard Barnhill.
—First St. Martin's Griffin Edition.
        pages cm
    ISBN 978-1-250-04379-5 (hardcover)
    ISBN 978-0-312-66212-7 (trade paperback)
    ISBN 978-1-4668-4074-4 (e-book)
 1. Elizabeth I, Queen of England, 1533-1603—Fiction.   2. Queens—Great Britain—Fiction.   3. Great Britain—History—Elizabeth, 1558-1603—Fiction. 4. Great Britain—Court and courtiers—Fiction.   I. Title.
    PS3602.A77713Q44 2014
    813'.6—dc23

                                                                2013032096

St. Martin's Griffin books may be purchased for educational, business, or promotional use. For information on bulk purchases, please contact Macmillan Corporate and Premium Sales Department at 1-800-221-7945, extension 5442, or write specialmarkets@macmillan.com.

First Edition: March 2014

10 9 8 7 6 5 4 3 2 1

To all those whose lives have been touched by cancer

Acknowledgments

Writing a book is hard work. Writing *Queen Elizabeth's Daughter* was especially difficult because I wrote it while undergoing treatment for stage-three uterine cancer, a very nasty, aggressive kind. I had a radical hysterectomy, chemo, then radiation, then more chemo. It was a very tough year. However, creating this story kept me going, kept me believing in my recovery, and in myself. There are many, many people I want to thank for their ongoing support and love during the process.

First, thanks to my editor, Charles Spicer, who was incredibly patient and supportive during this time. His insightful comments and impeccable guidance make him truly an editor par excellence. I'd like to also thank my agent, Irene Goodman, for her understanding. April Osborn has been a wonderful person with whom to work on the nuts-and-bolts of the book, and Anya Lichtenstein has done a great job of sending the book out into the world. I'm much indebted to

Ragnhild Hagen for a meticulous and thorough job of copyediting. Thanks also to the artists who designed such a beautiful cover—I love that blue dress.

Next, I'd like to thank some dear friends whose consistent love and care gave me courage to continue when I was ready to quit. Becky Nestor Thacker, the amazingly talented seamstress who created my Tudor dress, was there with me every step of the way through my treatments. I simply wouldn't have made it without her. Several wonderful friends sent a constant stream of cards and phoned me frequently, boosting my spirits with their love. Thank you, Chris Povish Freeman, Jo Claire Spear, Kathryn Lovatt, Sandra Redding, Carol Lewis, and the EFM group. I'd also like to thank several people who brought me food when I was too weak to crawl out of bed: the women at St. Paul's Episcopal Church in Cary, North Carolina—Judy Crow, Jeanne de Ward, Deb Richardson, and my sister-in-law, Fran Weir. Those ladies can cook!

I'm lucky to be a member of an online writing group called Book Pregnant. Those folks have been kind and generous beyond measure as they encouraged me to keep writing and keep healing. There are almost thirty members, all debut novelists (well, we started out that way—now many of them have second and third novels!), so I will not list them here. But know, BPers, I love you all!

Thank you to my Facebook friends for their support and prayers. There are others who also supported me with their love; I cannot list them all here but I hope they know they are in my heart. I'm especially grateful to the man with the green eyes who inspired Sir John's good looks.

My three sons, Michael Smith, Jason Smith, and Adam Barnhill, offered me so much love and support during the writing of the novel and my recovery—thank you for everything. They, along with their wives, Jennifer Shy and Kristi Carswell, also cooked delicious meals for me during that time. Thank you.

To my parents, Jack and Virginia Clinard, thank you for a lifetime of unwavering support.

And to my husband, Frank, a thousand thanks for all that you do and have done for thirty-five years.

I am a very lucky and grateful woman.

God's death! I shall have their heads! To marry without the permission of one's prince is treason! I will see everyone who took part in this debacle punished—the priest who dared marry them, the witnesses who arranged the wedding, even the stable boy who held their horses—all shall pay for this insult against my sovereignty.

I have punished others before them, those fools who dared to marry without my consent. Did they believe I would be more lenient with Mistress Mary, just because she is my beloved cousin? If that is what they thought, then they are wrong! They will rot in the Tower until their stinking carcasses have turned to dust!

Parry, did she think her treachery would go unpunished? After our most kind treatment of the baggage! Oh Parry, when I think of how she came to us, not much more than a babe in arms, how her chubby arms clung to my neck for comfort—God's blood, she shall pay for her prank! All I have *given her—hearth and home! Food and drink! Satins and silks to show off her beauty! Rubies and pearls to sparkle in her hair and on her person!*

Dear Parry, I gave her my heart—you know it is true! Does she put so little value on my love that she would turn traitor? I have cared more for her than I have for any man! A purer love. For she has been the daughter of my heart, if not my body! But she tossed my love back to me! Without a care!

No! I will not forgive her, Parry! She has gone too far! Ungrateful wench! I shall see her and that new husband of hers in the Tower! They shall suffer a traitor's death. I shall send for the guards this instant.

You are right, dearest Parry. I could not bear such punishment. Even now, when I look into her dark, dark eyes, I see the poppet still, barely three years old, curtsying to me with as much grace as any grown woman, her dark hair hanging down her back, her little kirtle trimmed in lace. When I close my eyes, I can still feel her solid body seeking comfort from my own. Parry, do you recall her first night at court, how she cried until you took pity on her and brought her to me, how she fell asleep in my arms, snoring gently. I can still recollect her sweet smell, like the grasses in spring, fresh and delicate. I had not yet been officially crowned—I was young and beautiful! Ah, before the cares of the world etched themselves across my face . . .

No, Parry, I cannot send her to her death. I must keep her with me somehow. For now, it is I who cannot sleep, I who toss and turn unless she is there to comfort me. Fear not, old friend, she shall come to no harm.

But by God's teeth, he shall pay! He shall pay with his life for taking my girl from me! I will have his head!

PART I

And I hope to have children;
otherwise, I would never marry.

QUEEN ELIZABETH I,
PARLIAMENTARY SPEECH

One

*A*fter eleven years under the rule of Queen Elizabeth, the England of 1569 found itself prospering, due mainly to the peace brought by the queen's foreign policies. Through cunning use of her status as an eligible young woman seemingly eager to be wed, the queen had been able to walk a thin line between maidenhood and marriage, leading to the security and, for the most part, happiness of her people. When France threatened, she pretended to entertain the possibility of marriage to the Duke of Anjou. When Spain became menacing, she turned her romantic attentions to her former brother-in-law, King Philip. She pleased the Protestants by flirting with the royalty of the German states. By balancing her numerous suitors, Queen Elizabeth kept the rich jewel that England had become from the entanglements of war. As a result, she was able to refill the coffers of the crown, which had been emptied by her sister's previous reign when Queen Mary I had supported her foreign husband's fruitless war efforts. Elizabeth took great care not to fall into a similar trap. She refused to make war and she refused to make a domestic match.

Though she had kept her country safe from foreign entanglements, there were still problems on English soil. The religious struggles between the Catholics, who lived mostly in the rural, northern parts of the land, and the stronghold of Protestants around London continued, though the queen was lenient in her dealings with recusants as long as they kept quiet and obeyed English law. However, this delicate balance was now beginning to teeter because Mary, Queen of Scots, had been deposed by her Scottish lords due to the mysterious death of her husband, Lord Darnley, a death in which Mary herself had been implicated. Then Mary had been carried away by the Earl of Bothwell, who, it was said, kidnapped and raped her. In response to this gross insult to her person and dignity, and much to Elizabeth's horror, the Scottish queen married the man.

Such events proved too much for the lords of Scotland to endure, and Queen Mary lost her crown. In desperation, she turned to her cousin Elizabeth for shelter. Elizabeth quickly recognized the threat posed by this Catholic queen, who had as much right to the English throne as did Elizabeth, in the minds of many. Elizabeth immediately placed Mary under guard and limited her access to the outside world. However, this did nothing to stop Catholic conspiracies from springing up, intricate plans to place Mary on the throne, thereby returning the country to the rule of Rome. These plots gave Elizabeth and her guardians many sleepless nights. But few were aware of the threat, except the queen herself, Master Cecil, and Robert Dudley.

For Mistress Mary Shelton, now fifteen, the world seemed safe and secure; she attended to her studies, danced and played the virginals, embroidered clothing for the poor, chattered with the queen in the royal bedchamber, and ate as many gooseberry tarts as she could sneak past Mistress Blanche Parry.

Mary had lived at court since her parents' deaths within a fortnight of each other in November 1558. Elizabeth had become queen that very month, a young, vibrant woman of twenty-five. At that moment, she had met the three-year-old orphan and taken the child into her care. Because Mary's father had received his knighthood from King Henry VIII, any of his offspring underage at the time of his death would become royal wards. But Mary was the only one of his children under the age of fourteen; the rest had reached their majority. Mary's future was at the queen's disposal.

Mary was not only a ward, she was also Elizabeth's cousin. Mary's grandfather, Sir John Shelton, had married Anne Boleyn, sister of Sir Thomas Boleyn, Elizabeth's grandfather. They were tied by bonds of kinship and, because of their long association, bonds of love.

Mary had not yet blossomed into the promised prettiness of her childhood. Her dark hair, thick and lustrous, was her best feature, along with her eyes, the same shade. Her mouth was set too primly and her nose was too long and sharp to make her breathtakingly beautiful. Though she had not fulfilled the high hopes the queen had had for her looks, she had that fresh allure reserved for the young. With her deep brown eyes and the smile that played around her mouth, she was beginning to feel her power as a woman. Her figure was shapely and she saw how the courtiers watched her taking delicate steps in the galliard on the rare occasions she consented to dance. She could see how her smile brought the same, answering response to the lips of even stodgy old men like Master Cecil.

Being brought up as the queen's favorite had given Mary an imperious air, and when she spoke, it was to command. She was the queen's cousin and royal ward. She was no shy flower waiting to be plucked. Rather, she was almost as forceful as the queen and often at odds with Her Majesty—they argued about the low cut of Mary's gowns, the bit of rouge she put on her cheeks, and the way she flounced into a room. Few people at court had the courage to disagree with the queen. Mary Shelton was one who dared.

Two
April 1569

T he spring had been unusually cold and rainy; Mary Shelton was happy to have a sunny day at last. She walked quickly across the meadow behind the Hampton Court knot gardens in pursuit of her dog, *Tom*, a large, red Irish hound she'd been awarded on her tenth birthday—a gift from the queen for excellent progress in Latin and Greek and, of course, penmanship. She'd named him *Tom* after the devilish Tom Wotton, the boy who continued to plague her at her lessons with Master Cecil's wards. Even now, Tom Wotton would hide her quill, steal her books, and laugh at her for no reason. She despised him, though he had grown handsome and filled out his doublet nicely. She enjoyed giving her dog, *Tom*, commands. She pretended she gave such orders to the *real* Tom Wotton.

Though she'd had the dog for five years, *Tom* still enjoyed a romp in the woodlands and Mary took him there almost every day. Already, she'd loosed his leash, allowing him to run and leap until he exhausted himself. She struggled through the still-damp ground to keep pace.

"Hey-ho! *Tom!* Wait for me, fellow! You run too fast!" Mary panted as she lifted her skirts to trot after the dog. Mary was well made, with dark hair that had escaped her lace caul, long curls bouncing as she ran. Her face was flushed with her efforts, giving her a pretty blush. But it was her eyes people noticed—large and brown with long, dark lashes. They were hypnotic and, though she had a resemblance to her cousin the queen—the same small, slender frame and a similar zest for life—Mary looked more like the queen's mother, Anne Boleyn. Everyone said so, though never within earshot of Her Majesty. It had become quite clear, early on, that Elizabeth wanted no talk about her mother at court.

The dog paused, looked back at his mistress, then bolted for the nearby trees. Mary sighed. "Cursed hound! I will not give chase!" She stopped where she was and turned to gaze down the slight slope toward the castle. She was glad to be away from the doings at court and the smelly confines of the queen's chambers. Hampton Court was beautiful to look at, but after a time, the air became contaminated with horrible smells from the refuse of people and animals, not to mention the garbage and wastes from the grand kitchens. Mary understood why the queen insisted on at least one daily walk. And why she moved from castle to castle with some regularity—she was driven to it by the offensive odors of her court. Mary smiled—her queen seemed to be more sensitive in this regard than most. Yet, no one would dare mention the smells; like the queen, they pinned flowers to their clothes and pretended the air was filled with the scent of roses and chamomile blossoms.

"Now what could be passing through your addled brain to make such a pretty smile?" said a young man who seemed to have appeared out of nowhere.

"Oh! Tom Wotton, you gave me a start!" said Mary, turning to him. "How dare you creep up on me! What are you doing here?"

"Same as you, I warrant. The sun is out and so am I—bleak winter lasted past his welcome. I have been gathering the first flowers of spring!" said Tom. He handed her a posy of daffodils and purple hyacinths.

"Humph. Stolen from Her Majesty's garden, no doubt," said Mary, sniffing the blossoms.

"Not so, milady. I found them growing of their own accord at the edge of the forest. Do you like them?" said Tom.

"Of course I like them. But such a gift is a bit odd coming from the likes of you. You don't usually do *kind* things—" said Mary.

"Maybe the sun has brought my humors into balance . . ." Tom said. He rocked back and forth on his feet, his hands pulling on his doublet and fiddling with a strip of velvet that had come loose.

"Here comes *Tom*, my dog. Are you tired now, boy? Do you want some food?" said Mary, rubbing *Tom*'s fur roughly.

"*Tom*? Your dog is named *Tom*?" said Master Wotton.

Mary felt her cheeks grow warm. She and Wotton were not friends. She remembered when she'd first gotten her pup, *Tom*, the boy, had been tormenting her relentlessly during Master Nowell's classes. He made fun of her Latin pronunciation; laughed when she erred in mathematics; poked her when she tried to copy her poems, ruining countless parchments; and tripped her when they were partnered together for dancing. Worst of all, he berated her for being a girl; after all, she was the only female ward to take such strenuous courses— and Tom would not forgive her for being a quick study.

"Well, yes," said Mary, her face growing more and more warm.

"You named that wretched cur after *me*?"

"Um . . . well, um . . . yes! Yes, I did," said Mary, meeting his gaze.

"That's quite an honor . . . I suppose you did it because you have always thought highly of me—even when we were but children. I'm charmed, mistress. Do you still hold me in such high esteem?" Tom said.

"Well, no, I . . . um, rather, I did not honor you, sir . . . you have mistook me . . ." said Mary.

"I see, I see. It's plain as old Nowell's preaching—you hold me dear in your heart. I confess, mistress, I would not have guessed it— you have kept such feelings buried deep—but now that I am recovered from my surprise, I admit to a certain inevitability about your love. I am, after all, a bit older and wiser—I am by nature more intelligent. No, no, do not try to concur—I know already. It is said by the serving wenches that I am the handsomest of all the wards and, I daresay, when I look into the glass, I am not unhappy with what I see . . ." said Tom, smiling down at her.

"This goes beyond the Pale, sir! You have tormented me for years. It was not for love I named my dog after you—it was so I could call your name and be obeyed. So I could scold you and swear horrible oaths using your name! Say all the things I wanted to say, like 'Hush, *Tom*, quiet!' Or 'Sit, *Tom!*' Or 'No, *Tom!*' And now, you think I admire you! Your head is bigger than that cloud and more full of airs as well. The serving wenches may think you pretty, but one of my breeding and station does not look at you twice! I am the queen's cousin—and you? You are the ward no one will purchase because of your insufferable arrogance!" said Mary, leashing her dog once more and heading toward the castle. A ward was a child who had lost his father; his lands and any monies collected reverted to the queen at the time of the father's death. The queen was then able to sell or give away the wardship as she desired.

Tom followed her, grabbed her arm, and spun her around.

"What do you mean, the ward no one will purchase? Has the queen been made offers? Have I been denied? In truth?" said Tom, his face suddenly pale and his grip tight.

"God's blood, let me go! Yes, there have been offers, but not one has come to anything. No one wants you!" said Mary. She watched as his face filled with sorrow. He looked as if he might cry. Mary's heart moved at the odd sight. She suddenly hoped to assuage the hurt she'd caused.

"Perhaps the reason has more to do with where your lands lie. If the queen had wished to give your wardship to one of her men as an honor, if your lands lie too far, he might request a different gift," said Mary.

"Do not try to soften it, Mary. I am unwanted. My own mother has not been to London to visit me in all these years; at Christmastide, I get a letter filled with the news of the year and all the records of my holdings. She does not send kisses or warm wishes. Truly, my flaws must be manifest if my own mother detests me," said Tom.

Mary watched him and their eyes met. She was overcome with sympathy. After all, she was a most fortunate girl—the queen loved her, Mistress Blanche loved her, Kat Ashley had loved her before her death—and this boy, this poor, stupid boy, was all alone in the world. He had no one.

Mary continued to stare into his cool blue eyes until she could not tear her gaze away. He *was* handsome and had grown tall and straight. She thought of how strong his grip had been on her arm. She wanted to soothe the hurt she had done him. Before she quite knew what was happening, she reached up to him, caressed his cheek with her hand, and pulled him to her.

They kissed, a very soft, gentle touching of the lips, brief as a candle flicker.

"Do you seek to strike, then kiss away the hurt, mistress? That is a perversion of love . . . and to tarry with one so far beneath you— that, too, marks a cruel mistress. But come, let us kiss again, for I have many wounds that need soothing," said Tom, his arm still encircling her waist.

"I am not cruel. Let me go! I will not kiss you again, though truly,

I did not mean to hurt you. If you would allow your gentle side to peep out once in a while, it would be as welcome as the sun shining through the clouds . . . You should try it more often," said Mary as she disengaged herself and continued to walk toward the castle.

Tom swept the cap off his head and bowed to her backside.

"For you, mistress, I shall endeavor to do so," he said, watching her go.

"Oh, Eleanor, I was stunned by the kiss! I have never even liked Tom Wotton—he has tormented me all these years. He has hated me and I, him. I am not even sure how the kiss came about!" said Mary, sitting on a pillow near the window in the queen's private chambers. She held an embroidery hoop in her hands and pulled the bright blue thread up and through, up and through. The flowers Tom had given her lay at her side, slowly wilting.

"That is often the way with kisses—I have no idea what overtook Sir Anthony when we walked in the gardens one evening. I was pointing out the beauty of the moon that night, and before I knew what had happened, I was in his arms. Perhaps Tom has loved you all this time. You know how boys are—they tease because they do not yet know the language of love. Once they learn *that* silent speech, the teasing becomes something else," said Eleanor Brydges, newly appointed lady of the Privy Chamber.

"Perhaps . . . I cannot rid my mind of the feel of his arms . . . so strong. And his mouth, so soft. His are the first lips to touch mine—I shall never forget this day!" said Mary, putting down her sewing and picking up the small bouquet. Mary walked to the queen's bed, reached under it, and pulled out a box. She carefully placed the flowers Tom had given her within, then closed the lid and returned the box to its hiding place.

"What in the name of heaven is that?" said Mistress Eleanor.

"My treasure box—Lord Robert gave it to me when I was but a

child. Yet, even now I keep my dearest things in there, but please do not tell anyone. I would be ashamed, for some items are childish—a pretty rock from the river, a butterfly wing. The others would laugh at such trifles," said Mary.

"Have no fear—we are friends. I shall keep any secrets you tell me, if you will do the same for me," said Mistress Eleanor. "Even though you keep his flowers, you must blot Master Wotton from your mind. Have you forgotten our most recent lecture from Her Majesty? 'My ladies are to be above reproach. You represent me, and as my representatives, you will be chaste and guard your honor with your life. The unmarried state is best. However, if your carnal lusts force you to coupling, be certain you do so after I have given my blessing to your marriage. Anything otherwise is treason!'" said Eleanor, mimicking the queen's pose and facial expressions.

"Oh, stop! You are making me laugh and I shall ruin my stitches," said Mary, shaking and wiping tears from her eyes.

"'I know full well the temptations to be found at court—young ganders prancing around in their finery! But you, my ladies, are not geese! You serve the queen, who remains married to England. I have found this a most satisfactory union—give your allegiance to me and I shall find you all good husbands, those of you foolish enough to want them!'" continued Eleanor, now strutting with long, authoritative steps, moving exactly as the queen did.

Both young women were giggling so loudly in their corner they did not hear Mistress Blanche approach.

"What in heaven's name are you two laughing at? Have you nothing better to do?" said Mistress Blanche as she stood before them.

"We . . . er, we . . . we are sewing, Mistress Blanche. As the queen instructs . . . putting our talents to good use," stammered Eleanor.

"I could have sworn you were putting your *acting* talents to use. I cannot imagine two young women of the court, girls who serve the queen and are at her mercy, to have been mocking Her Majesty. Such a thing could not be possible . . . Especially you, Mary. You who have enjoyed the queen's love for most of your life," said Mistress Blanche. She shook her finger at the girls.

"Take this as fair warning—the queen is in no mood for jokes these days! The poor woman is hounded on all sides, and for the two of you to amuse yourselves at Her Majesty's expense— Well, I'm confounded, just confounded . . ." said Mistress Blanche, her voice rising higher and higher.

"Do not upset yourself. We do the queen no dishonor. We were merely talking about Master Tom Wotton and somehow we got carried away," said Mary.

"Why on earth would you be discussing Master Wotton? Isn't he the boy who has played the devil with you in your studies?" said Mistress Blanche.

"Yes. That's what we were talking about . . . oh, Mistress Blanche . . . Master Tom kissed me in the field today!" said Mary.

"Ah. Well, that explains a great deal! Sit down, child, and tell Parry all about it," said Mistress Blanche.

Three
June 1569

G iven the warm breezes, the gillyflowers and roses in full bloom, the court preparing for summer progress, Mary could not contain the fullness in her heart, a joy that threatened to burst out for all to see. It was no surprise she found herself consumed with love, dreaming about Tom Wotton, imagining herself in fantasies with him so often she lost all track of time. She'd pricked her finger more than once while sewing, her mind distracted by remembering the feel of his lips, his strong arms. She had met him many times since they had exchanged that first kiss and now fancied herself in love with him. If anyone noticed how often she walked her dog, no one mentioned it. As long as she was there of an evening when Elizabeth seemed to need her, she could count many of her afternoons free.

On this day, she had met Tom in the palace gardens and, as usual, he began kissing her, his large hands trying to rove over her body.

Thus far, she had not allowed such touches. But then he had surprised her, asking her to leave their familiar haunts for a ride in the country.

"I cannot. Her Majesty's mood is so grim these days, I fear to do anything that might upset her—if she asks for me and I am not there, there would be the devil to pay!" said Mary, her back against the scratchy hedgerow that both shaded them and provided privacy.

"Think what fun we could have! I can secure a couple of horses . . . we could ride into the countryside, smell the fresh air, and remove ourselves from this odious place," said Tom, standing in front of her, his body close.

"I would love to go, Tom, you know I would. I dare not," said Mary. She placed her hand on his chest and could feel the thumping of his heart.

"If you love me as you say you do, you'll find a way. If you love the queen better than you love me, well, I might as well return to my own lands—I shall be of age soon enough to take charge of them. Do you not see what that means, Mary? When I come of age, we can be wed in a very little time," said Tom, enclosing her hand with his own.

"God's blood! I have not given you an answer, Tom. And you have not yet spoken to the queen. Or your mother. You know how Her Majesty feels about marriage, especially *my* marriage. I do not believe she will give her permission," said Mary.

"If we are already wed, there will not be much she can do about it. If we run away, she will come around. You'll see," said Tom.

Mary broke away from him and peeked around the hedge.

"She's coming! Go! I shall send word to you later! Go, now!" said Mary in a whisper.

Tom crept through a small gap in the hedges, disappearing quickly. Mary straightened her hair and smoothed her dress. She planned to rejoin the queen's ladies as they walked by. She stood stock-still as she heard the queen approach, her voice loud.

* * *

"God's death! You are telling me the Duke of Norfolk, the premier lord in all the land, is planning to marry the Queen of Scots! Mistress Eleanor, are you certain of this?" said the queen.

"I have only said what has been said to me, Majesty. I know not the truth of it," said Mistress Eleanor.

"Tut-tut. I'll warrant there *is* truth to it—what a match they would be against me! He a Catholic, she likewise. He a duke and she a queen! If they marry, it would not be four months before *I* was in the Tower," said the queen. "Oh, how am I to manage this monstrous woman, this cousin of mine! Would she were as easy as my other dear cousin, Mary. Mary, where are you?" said the queen as she walked on, impervious to all but her own cares.

Mary hurried from behind the hedge and joined the last of the ladies-in-waiting.

"Here, Your Grace. Here!" Mary shouted as she made her way through the women to catch up with the queen.

"Where have you been?" said the queen, not breaking her stride.

"I have been here, walking with Your Majesty," said Mary, her face coloring.

"Do you think I do not know what goes on beneath my own nose? You were not here—you scurried behind yon hedge, most likely to meet that Wotton boy with whom you seem besotted. Do you deny it?" said the queen, rounding on Mary, facing her.

Mary had the look of a coney caught in a trap. She had seen how frantic a captured rabbit could become and she felt just that way. Her face paled and she looked all around, anywhere but into the queen's own eyes. She said nothing.

"God's blood, as if I do not have enough to vex me! My very own girl, my darling Mary, betraying *me* for a callow youth! Yes, yes, child—I know all about it. But it is easily solved," said the queen, a strange smile playing across her mouth.

Mary dared not move. She had observed what could happen when the queen caught lovers making plans behind her back. To the Tower! They were sent to the Tower!

"I shall have the boy return to his lands. When he arrives at Yorkshire, he shall have a wedding feast," said the queen, staring at Mary.

"You . . . will send him away?" said Mary, barely able to speak. She could not look at the queen. She could not think what to do or say. All she could feel was the queasiness in the pit of her guts and the pumping blood that coursed through her veins, a blood that called for release of the rage she felt in that moment. She raised her head and gazed at the queen.

The queen was smiling, a cruel little curl of her lips. Her black eyes had a proud look about them.

"He shall leave on the morrow. You shall never see him again, I fear. Yorkshire is far from London and I intend to keep a much closer eye on you, young woman. Have a care! You are my creature to marry at my discretion! You do not make any choices on your own!" screamed the queen, her face now turning red and her body shaking with anger.

"I am God's creature! You are my queen, not my jailer! Just because *you* find no happiness in love now that your 'Sweet Robin' has found a roost with the Lady Essex, you have no right to ruin *my* happiness! God's bones, I will never forgive you for this! I loathe you!" said Mary, running from the queen onto the brick pathway that led to the doors of the castle. The ladies surrounding the queen had become quiet; they had seen such skirmishes between Mary and the queen before and knew better than to utter a sound.

"I have not excused you! You do not have my permission to leave!" the queen shouted. Then, just as suddenly as the storm arose, the waters were calm again and the queen motioned for Mistress Blanche.

"Oh Parry, I mishandled that, I fear. Go to her. Try to explain. I shall speak with her later in the bedchamber. And, dear Parry, be gentle, as *I* was not," said the queen.

* * *

Mary stood in disbelief in the empty bedchamber. She hadn't realized tears were streaming down her face. She'd been oblivious to them, startled to find her cheeks wet, much the same way she had astonished herself when she raised her voice to the queen. Such passions always took her by surprise. She and the queen had argued before, many times, but nothing like today. Mary had shown her temper in full bloom, raised her voice to the queen, said awful things to the one who had been like a mother to her.

To scream wicked words to the Queen of England! Mary's insides began to quiver. Soon, the shivering rattled up and down her very bones. She could not tell if this quaking came from anger at what the queen had done, or if it was from fear of what the queen would do now. The queen! She had told the queen she *loathed* her. She had rubbed the queen's nose in the fact her Sweet Robin had been giving his attentions to Lady Essex, the former Lettice Knollys, another cousin to the queen. Lettice had returned to court while her husband served in Ireland and she gave Lord Robert her hand at every opportunity. The whole court was abuzz about their supposed "secret" romance. But no one had dared mention it in the queen's presence. No one except Mary.

Mary had left the queen's presence without permission and turned her back on Her Majesty! She would be in the Tower by nightfall. But she didn't care! She had told the queen what was in her heart, let her see the hurt and anger. She had done so since she'd first come to Elizabeth, though, of late, the queen seemed less than pleased by such outbursts.

She must run away! That was the only way to save herself—run to Shelton Hall, her childhood home. Surely they would take her in. Her brother, Ralph, who had inherited the lands when their father passed on, would be forced to give her the small parcel of land her father had left for her. They would *have* to take her in—they were her blood! Mary glanced around the bedchamber. Her eyes lit on a small casket on the floor near the queen's wardrobe. She could pack her few valuables in there, grab food and drink from the royal kitchens. She quickly tossed a clean shift, two pairs of her favorite sleeves, a kirtle, and a pair of woolen hose into the casket and was closing the lid when she remembered her treasure box. She pulled it from beneath the queen's bed and put it in the bottom of the casket. She didn't want anyone to find it; she would never leave it behind. It meant everything to her.

Perhaps one of the stable boys would give her a pony to ride. She ticked off a list of other items she would need to make the long journey as she reached for a bodice from the queen's wardrobe.

"Mary, dearest, what are you doing?" said Mistress Blanche.

"Leaving! I must! The queen will have my head!" said Mary, running into Mistress Blanche's outstretched arms.

"Come, come, child. Her Majesty has sent me to speak gentle words of comfort. She will not send you to the Tower, dearie. She only wishes you to know how very much she loves you. She is concerned for your welfare, as she has been these eleven years since you came to us," said Mistress Blanche.

"How could she! How could she send Tom away—he's done nothing wrong! He has kissed me a few times, nothing more. He wanted me to marry him—and I was going to say yes before the queen ruined it all. How did she know?" said Mary.

"The queen knows all and sees all, dearie. I did not divulge your secret, though I considered doing so. I understand her concern for your welfare—you are like her own child. As such, she does not want to see you hurt or used for some young man's advancement. She is wise to the ways of men and you should harken unto her wisdom," said Mistress Blanche.

"I only do what the queen herself has done. I have danced with Tom and met him secretly in the gardens. We have kissed a little and pledged our love. He has had me in his arms, but not nearly so often as Sweet Robin has held the queen thus. And Tom has never touched my dugs, as I have seen Robin do with the queen. Once, I even saw him put his mouth to the queen's nipple. I have seen much over the years, Mistress Blanche. On our picnics, when they thought I was sleeping, sometimes I would open my eyes just a crack and I watched them kiss and whisper together, fondling one another. I have never done such with Tom—so how is it she can tell me to keep my honor when she besmirches her own?" said Mary, still sobbing into Mistress Blanche's shoulders.

"No matter what you have seen Her Majesty do, she is the bearer of her own consequences. She is a grown woman and she is queen. You, however, are still a girl and you remain her ward. Granted, you are old enough for marriage, but only if the queen allows it. She wants great things for you, Mary. She has trained you as she, herself, was trained: you know the classics, you can read Latin and Greek, even French; you do mathematics and can write a splendid hand; you dance and sing and play the lute and the virginals. Why do you think the queen has taken such pains with you? Why would she bother even keeping a royal ward in her presence for all these years, rather than sell the wardship to enhance her own coffers?" said Mistress Blanche.

"I suppose no one would have me," said Mary, allowing herself to be led by the hand to sit at the window across from Mistress Blanche.

"Oh, Shelton Hall is a fine palace and your brother would have had you back within its walls years ago. He wanted your marriage rights but the queen refused him. Elizabeth wanted you here, child. She loves you. Surely you must know that," said Mistress Blanche.

"Then why would she send Tom away from me? Does she not wish my happiness?" said Mary.

"She has a grand plan for you! She intends to make you a fine match—not marriage to the son of a minor lord but perhaps to a prince! She has seen to your education and has dressed you in fine clothes and jewels. Have you not noticed that among all her ladies, you are the only one allowed to wear colorful gowns of blue and yellow? She wants your beauty to shine forth for all the court to see. And you, selfish girl, have almost ruined it," said Mistress Blanche.

Mary remembered all the nights she and the queen had spent together when Mary was a little girl. So many times, Mary had been afraid and sad, waiting for the queen to join her in the royal bed. Elizabeth would sing to Mary, funny ditties about lambs and wool and ring-around-the-rosy. Mary could still recall taking Elizabeth's long, delicate hand in her own and rubbing each nail, feeling the sleekness of the fingers and the heaviness of the rings that adorned them.

"I am sorry," said Mary. Such an admission was difficult to make, but it was true. Mary *was* sorry.

"Give your apologies to the queen. You have naught to fear—she will not send you to the Tower. Tonight, when she comes into the bedchamber after dancing, go to her and make amends. I have found Her Majesty quick to anger but even quicker to forgive," said Mistress Blanche. "Now, crawl into your trundle bed and I shall bring you some bread and ale. You need to sleep a little, methinks."

The night air was cool, as though June were some imposter and April the true month. After an evening of dancing, the queen found herself inhaling great gulps of the cold air as she caught her wind. She would not admit to being tired out from such leaping and stepping—her courtiers would never see her out of breath. At thirty-six, she was fast approaching her middle years, but no one must know the queen, Elizabeth Regina, was mortal, and time dealt with her in the same way he dealt with all—the slow decline of the flesh, even as the spirit remained ever young.

How she had needed this evening! How the weight of government fell heavily onto her thin shoulders! A night of frivolity with Robin! That always soothed her. And her Sweet Robin had never failed her—he was the best dancer at court, the handsomest man, the best on a horse. Oh, if only he'd an ounce of royal blood, she might have married him, the naysayers be damned.

But such a match was never to be—she had come to that decision long ago, when his name (and hers) had been blackened by the mysterious death of his wife, Amy Robsart. Amy's death was the death knoll for the queen and her lover. Her Majesty could never have Robin after that—her own honor would have suffered and that she could not abide.

She strolled along the familiar garden path, lit by torches and the moon. The fresh leaves on the trees shone silver in the light and the pebbles along the path glinted like the stars. She was heading for her white garden, hoping to find some early rosebuds to pin to her silk dress. Just as she was approaching this place that was wholly hers, she heard voices coming from within the garden itself.

She paused, listening.

She recognized the voices at once—Robin and Lady Essex! She could identify that tinkling, silly laughter anywhere. She stood immobile, straining to hear their love talk. Oh, he tells her she is beautiful. She laughs again, throatily this time. He says hers is a warm beauty, not like the queen's regal coldness. Elizabeth could contain herself no longer.

"Cold, am I? Untouchable? I shall teach you of coldness, milord!" said the queen as she strode toward Lord Robert. Before she could think, she slapped him hard across the face. Then she turned to Lady Essex and pushed her so that she almost fell to the ground. The shoulders of Lady Essex's dress had come down and her breasts were exposed. The queen stared and then grabbed hold of Lady Essex's hair, tugging it with great gusto.

"Out, whore! Adulterer! Go back to you husband! And do not

return to London on pain of death!" shouted the queen. Lord Robert regained his senses and grabbed the queen by her arms.

"Run, Lettie! Run while you can! Bess! Bess! Get hold of yourself!" said Lord Robert.

Lady Essex gathered herself and disappeared into the larger gardens. Lord Robert still held the queen.

"How dare you! How dare you make love to her! Oh Robin! How can you betray me thus?" said the queen, her voice cracking.

"Bess, dearest, what would you have me do? Just because you choose the virginal state does not mean I must—I am a man, Bess. I have desires you would not understand! Such women mean nothing to me, darling. You are my love—you will always be my true love! If only you would marry me, Bess, I would be your faithful knight, serving you only and always. Marry me, my love, and put me out of my misery," said Lord Robert, pulling her against him.

"Hah! Marry you! So you could rule this kingdom! That is the only reason you would marry me. I am cold and regal—nothing like the hot beauty you were holding only minutes ago. Go! Get out of my sight! Go!" screamed the queen, sinking down to the ground. "Go at once or I shall call my guards!"

Lord Robert bent down to her but she shoved him away. He turned and left her there, sitting in the damp grass.

Four

God's blood, how am I to bear it? How can I stand to look at him,
see him each day, imagining him with his arms around that
she-wolf? Does he think me a fool, that I would still cling to
him after such a display? Does he believe he can act as he pleases, that I am
so besotted with him that I will allow any sort of betrayal? God's blood,
Parry! What am I to do?

And Mary, my dear Fawn, how can I make her understand the importance of a good marriage? You remember well my own silly youth, that
terrible scandal with Thomas Seymour . . . What is it about the name
Tom? She does not see the dangers in men—how could she? I know, I know.
She is no longer a child. But she will always be my girl, the child of my
heart.

Do you remember how she first came to us? The sky over London was
bleak and gray, though the mood of my people was light, almost giddy, for
my sister was dead and I was to be crowned queen. I still recall the way my

people gathered as I rode from Lord North's city house to the Tower, the guns booming and the trumpets blaring. The bells rang constantly as the procession snaked its way through the narrow streets. Peasants threw sweet herbs in my path and children sang songs. The litter stopped at my command so I could receive the gifts from my people—an apple, a bit of fine cloth, flowers. I looked each person in the eye and I can still hear their cries of "God Save the Queen!" and "God Bless Elizabeth" ringing over the cobbles. Washerwomen and apothecaries, boatswains and carters, porters and merchants—all of London jammed the streets to see me, hoping I might favor them with a smile. So long ago and I was young.

And Mary, sweet Mary—you brought her to me while Robin and I were selecting the materials for coronation clothes and all the festivities of that day. Robin said I would empty the coffers before I was crowned; I told him how the people were taken and held by pompous shows. Then he said he knew how I had longed for such luxuries, as if I desired to please myself more than my people. He raised my ire then as he does now. I still feel the touch of his hand upon my cheek as he told me my beauty would shine forth even if I were dressed in filthy rags. How I blushed for him. By the saints, I shall blush for him no more.

Then, there you were, Parry, holding Mary by the hand, the girl's black hair and large dark eyes setting her apart from most of the children I'd seen on the London streets, children with golden curls and pale eyes. She walked so slowly toward me, I could sense how terrified she was. Her eyes were wide and she could not stop gazing at me, at my jewels . . . and when she curtsied to me, just like a grown-up woman, I smiled at her. I couldn't stop myself from holding out my arms to her and she ran into them just as if I'd been her own mother. You told me then of how her parents had died within days of each other, the sweats, you thought. Her brother, Sir Ralph, had inherited, but he was asking for Mary's marriage rights. I was ready to give him what he wanted, so busy was I with preparations. But later that night, when you brought her to me, the little thing sobbing her heart out, I made the mistake of putting her in my bed. She took my fingers in her pudgy hands and began to trace each nail, rubbing me over and over again. For whatever reason, the action seemed to calm her and she fell asleep, curled up beside me.

Ha! After that, wild horses could not have dragged her from me! We have raised her up, Parry, together. And we shall see she makes a good marriage. I will not allow her to throw herself away on some ruffian like Tom Wotton!

Five
June 1569

Most of the torches had been dimmed for the sleeping ladies in the queen's bedchamber, but large candelabra gave off flickers of light that played against the tapestries on the walls. Mary fidgeted in her nightgown, fingering the gathers at her neck. She could feel the raised threads—blackwork, the queen's favorite form of stitchery, and done by the queen's own hand. Such a style had been a favorite of Elizabeth's father, Bluff King Hal, but was somewhat out of fashion with the younger set at court. However, Elizabeth excelled at those tiny stitches and continued to create smocks and gowns for her favorites. Mary had been a favorite for as long as she could remember. But after tonight . . . after tonight . . . she could not allow herself to think about that.

Mary dreaded the confrontation to come. The queen's dark moods of late were the talk of the court. No one was immune from her lashing tongue. Indeed, Mary had seen Her Majesty strike serving girls when they spilled ale or wine onto the table. Once, she witnessed the queen pull the hair of Mistress Eleanor because Mistress Eleanor had outwitted the queen at primero. While Mary had observed the queen's temper for more than ten years, she knew Her Majesty's inner rage grew worse with each passing day. Since Kat Ashley's death, the queen seemed more prone to giving fits, as though losing Kat had freed her in some way.

Mary did not know what suffering awaited her when she gave her apologies to the queen. She had no *wish* to say she was sorry because she was *not*, at least not completely. But she knew an apology was demanded and she dreaded a long, laborious lecture. She had not long to fret over it.

The queen arrived without fanfare, her hair falling in ringlets from the coif Mary had helped build earlier in the day. Her eyes were red-rimmed and she walked as if she'd been beaten by the world's troubles. Her shoulders slumped and her face seemed pulled down— her mouth, even her eyes, seemed slanted toward sadness. To Mary, the queen looked very old.

Mary rose from her trundle bed beside the queen's large four-poster. She curtsied deeply and did not lift her head.

"Oh, child. I had forgot you were waiting to make amends. Well, get up. Stand, I say," said the queen, her voice ragged.

"Your Majesty, I am sorry. I do not know what came over me to speak to you in such a manner. Forgive me," said Mary. She tried to keep the irritation she felt out of her voice.

"Bah, you do not *sound* sorry in the least," said the queen, standing as her ladies slowly rose to help her untie her sleeves and unlace her stomacher.

The queen stood still as a statue. Mary knew she was waiting for further demonstration of Mary's sorrow at their disagreement. Mary cleared her throat, ready to try again.

"Majesty, I am truly sorry to have offended Your Grace," said Mary, her voice a monotone this time.

"Tut-tut, all is forgiven," said the queen.

The ladies fussed over Her Majesty as the queen motioned for Mary to join them. Mary carefully plucked the jewels from the queen's gown and sleeves to put away. She knew the queen loved her, had raised her for a fine marriage. But she also knew Tom Wotton loved her and she loved him. His lands were not grand, nor was he. He would be just fine for Mary, no matter what the queen thought. She felt her blood rising again and her breath coming in short spurts.

"Mistress Mary, I *said* we are finished with this business. Now, help me out of this infernal gown," said the queen. The queen sighed loudly, then spoke in a more gentle voice. "I only want what is best for you."

"I know, Your Grace. I have always known your love for me to be a true and genuine thing. My love is also true," said Mary, still not looking at the queen.

Mary untied the ribbons that secured the sleeves to the pair of bodies. The silk felt light as feathers in her hands. She was not speaking of her true love for the *queen*, but for Tom.

"Humph, love. What could one such as you know of that cursed condition?" said the queen.

"Your Majesty seems in low spirits tonight," said Mary as she unlaced the queen's stomacher and helped her step out of her kirtle. The petticoat came off and the queen could relax—there would be nothing left to bind her.

"Ah, much better, Mary. I'll sleep in the silk gown, yes, that one," said the queen as she slipped her shift from her shoulders and raised her arms over her head so Mary could slide the nightgown on. Mary noticed how thin the queen had become—too thin. She looked unwell. The queen sat on her bed so her maids could remove her velvet slippers and her silk hose.

"Begone, all of you! All except Mary," shouted the queen. The other ladies scurried about like mice. When they had all disappeared, the queen patted the spot on her bed and indicated for Mary to sit beside her.

"Mary, I would protect you from what happened to *me* tonight. Aye, and every maid at court," said the queen, color creeping up her slender neck. Mary could see the royal pulse beating there.

"What is that, Your Majesty?" said Mary, sitting beside the queen.

"Man's treachery!" said the queen, pounding her fists against the mattress.

"What treachery, Majesty?" said Mary, stretching out beside the queen.

"My Sweet Robin! He has betrayed me with that she-wolf, Lady Essex! I caught them in my very own white garden!" said the queen, her voice pinched up.

"This cannot be true—if ever a man loved a woman, Robin loves Your Majesty!" said Mary.

"He may love me—I do not doubt it. But he lusts for the she-wolf!" said the queen. "He held her in his arms and his mouth was on hers! Oh, she tried to straighten herself when I found them—but it was too late!"

"What did Your Majesty do?" said Mary.

"Well, I am ashamed to say that first, I pushed them apart. And then I pulled her hair, almost yanked it out by the roots," said the queen. She cut her eyes to Mary and they exchanged a look. They burst into nervous giggles; the strain between them vanished.

"Then, I banished the baggage! Told her never to return to my court. And Robin—I sent him away as well. I cannot bear to look upon him—he has broken my heart," said the queen.

"Majesty—I do not know what to say. I would comfort you," said Mary, rubbing the queen's shoulders as she used to when she was a child.

"There is nothing to say, Fawn. This is woman's lot. This is what I would protect you from—this emptiness, this sorrow," said the queen.

Mary could feel the shuddering of the queen's body as Her Majesty sobbed quietly. Suddenly, the queen sat up straight.

"Now you know why I sent that young cur away from you. To love a man is death to a woman—our love never holds them, Fawn. Always, some younger, prettier woman catches their faithless eyes. And then . . . and then, the betrayal starts!" said the queen.

"But Your Grace, surely this is not the same for all men and women. Surely there are some who love until death parts them," said Mary.

"No! Men marry to get heirs and a goodly portion of money and land from a dowry. They scheme and lie and keep kitchen wenches as mistresses. They dissemble and dishonor God's holy laws by making do with any whore they can find. Oh Fawn! Beware the marriage bed! One night of pleasure could bring death nine months later! Or the French pox! Or a broken heart! Look at poor Amy Robsart—I'll warrant her heart cracked ere she died. And Sweet Robin did not blink—he barely saw her during those last years of her life. She was alone and in misery. No, Fawn. Best not to marry. That way, you will be alone, but on your own terms. And you will never be miserable—there are too many handsome men to allow you to feel sad for long. From now on, I will not keep my favors for our Sweet Robin. I shall enjoy the attentions of all the handsome fellows," said the queen, her mood switching from dejection to elation.

She grabbed Mary's hands and pulled her out of bed. They scrambled to their feet and the queen clapped her hands loudly. The women, eyes bleary with sleep, hurried back inside.

"Mistress Eleanor! Call my musicians! I would dance! I would have you all dance!" shouted the queen.

Her Majesty swung Mary around in a circle, skipping and jumping in an Irish jig, humming and singing an old tune about moonlight and fairies. Mary gladly joined in, though she wondered at the queen's sudden turn of mind. The queen seemed almost frantic in her happiness, a defiant joy that frightened Mary even more than the queen's rage.

After an hour or more of dancing and drinking sweet wine, the queen finally dismissed her musicians and crawled, slightly drunk, into her grand bed. Mary fell asleep quickly on her trundle bed, listening to the queen's light snores. She considered all the queen had said.

Was it true? Could she trust no man, not even her Tom? Were they all, as the queen said, dissemblers? Or did the queen wish Mary to remain with her forever? Was that why she'd said the terrible things she'd said about Lord Robert? Mary was no longer angry at Her Majesty. She was confused. She tossed the questions around in her mind until, finally, her heavy lids could no longer remain open.

Six

A little more to the left, Parry. Ah, that's it. My dancing last night must have been too much activity—that shoulder waxes more painful as each hour passes.

So many tangles for me to set straight—trouble simmering in the north with the Catholics; the Queen of Scots charming every man I send to guard her, in spite of her conspiracy to murder her husband and her ill-conceived marriage to her captor, Bothwell; I have tweaked Spain's nose by taking over their payships last year; the Duke of Alva has all but turned the Netherlands over to the Pope; France threatens, though this is no new thing. Yet, for all that, what runs through my mind is nothing but the Earl of Leicester and his she-wolf.

And, of course, worry over our Fawn. She is becoming quite beautiful, don't you think? She may yet grow into the beauty promised in her childhood. Do not be ridiculous, Parry, I am not a fool. I have eyes! I can see she is more beautiful than I have ever been. She looks so like my mother—all dark and striking against the rest of the ladies, pale, blond maids. Like the sea at night, dark upon dark. I am not surprised the young bucks wish to take her away from me.

She was not full of shame at her outburst over that Wotton fellow. But she did make up with me, if ever so reluctantly. I fear she forgets who rules here. She reminds me of my own girlish self—so full of hope, so happy to be alive, so greedy for the future. I would shield her from making the same errors I made. Yes, I mean Seymour—who else? He almost ruined me—kept me estranged from the woman who had been most like a mother to me of all my father's wives; entangled me in his treasons; opened my young heart and played it with great accomplishment. Aye, Parry, he almost ended me ere I started.

It was easy to forgive Fawn's anger. I recall how my own youthful urges got the best of me. It took all my strength and control not to lose my temper with my sister when she was queen. Bloody Mary, they call her now, so I hear. Though then she was known only as Queen Mary. Another case where a woman's heart led her to nothing but pain and sorrow. Poor woman—no child in her womb, only desperate hope blossoming there. And Philip! Turning his eyes to me, while his wife lay in her confinement. At the time, I found such attentions flattering. Now, I find his intentions revolting.

But our Mary is so young, so innocent. I would keep her with me always, Parry. Oh, I shall, I shall. I had it in mind to bind her to some foreign prince—she is, after all, my cousin and has received a fine education. She has been groomed for such a role. But I would not wish her so far away from me.

I do not know why I have been out of sorts of late. There is the usual weight of government, but on some days, I feel the blood pounding through my veins and I growl and bark at everyone I see—even those I love. Even Robin.

My courses do not run as regular, no. But I am yet young! I shall dance and laugh and walk out under the stars for many a long year. I am yet young! And I will make Robin love me—and only me—once more. He must! I am the queen!

*T*he air was warm and growing warmer as the sun made its way to its zenith. Mary and the other ladies-in-waiting walked slowly along the garden paths of Whitehall, while the queen and Master Cecil strolled ahead of them. Mary bent to smell a red rose, her nose close to the velvet petals. She inhaled loudly. Her friend Mistress Eleanor paused to finger some nearby columbines. The two young women discussed what gown Eleanor should wear for the night's upcoming festivities. Mary had recently been made gentlewoman of the Privy Chamber while the queen had been on progress earlier in the summer. It was a great honor. Mary thought the appointment was a peace offering from the queen, a reward for giving up her hopes concerning Tom Wotton. Whatever the reason, Mary was happy for the promotion, even though it meant she would no longer be allowed to wear gowns of any color she wished. Now, she was limited to black, white, or silver, as were all the gentlewomen of the Privy Chamber, including Mistress Eleanor. The only exceptions were when the ladies were off-duty or when there was a special occasion when the queen wanted her court to sparkle with exceptional vibrancy. Her Majesty had refused her begging to wear more colorful dresses, though Mary had argued for over an hour. But on this point, the queen proved firm.

"I have a new white silk with silver sleeves and matching kirtle—I even bought a pair of shoes and have spent the morning sewing pearls on them. I hope to look ravishing!" said Mistress Eleanor.

"Which color will suit me best? Black?" said Mary, still looking at the flowers.

"Your dark hair would look lovely against silver. Do you have such a gown?" said Mistress Eleanor.

"No. My appointment has been so recent I have barely had time to learn my duties. The queen gave me this old white gown—it was one of her own. Though the moths have had it for some time," said Mary, as she put her finger on a tiny hole in the fabric. "They have eaten their fill, it seems." Both young women laughed.

"Does the queen pay you for your duties?" said Mistress Eleanor.

"Hardly. If she did, I could have a new gown made. Does she pay you?" said Mary.

"No. I do think she pays Mistress Blanche a pretty sum. But most of us are here on our own. My mother sends me money every now and then—that is how I could afford my new clothes. And, as you well know, I win at dice and cards—luckily, the queen always pays her gambling debts," said Mistress Eleanor.

"And luckily, she loses frequently," said Mary, smiling.

The young women continued discussing the advantages and disadvantages of their recent promotions. Mary was not convinced her life would be the better for it.

"You are in a position for which others would commit bloody murder. And you are now allowed to stay in the Great Hall after we sup to enjoy the entertainments, although I have not seen you there," said Mistress Eleanor.

"Come, we are falling behind the others. Let us hurry," said Mary.

The two young women walked quickly, arm in arm, across the path.

"You are dodging my question. Why have you not joined in the queen's festivities of an evening?" said Mistress Eleanor.

"Truth to tell? I am uncertain. Since Tom was sent away, I have no desire to speak with any of the courtiers—they all seem so old and . . . well, so bold. I am still young . . . I fear them, I suppose," said Mary. "It was different when I was a child and the queen sent for me to show off my dancing—I was not afraid, but proud. Now, I feel my stomach quaking at the thought of being on display."

"I am not much older than you and I tell you—there is nothing to fear. The gentlemen are courteous and witty. Some of them are marvelous dancers—Sir Christopher Hatton, for one. The queen does love a man who can dance," said Mistress Eleanor.

"That she does. But as for me, I'd just as soon while away the time in the queen's apartments, working on my embroidery or reading the Book of Common Prayer," said Mary.

"I hope you will have a change of heart. If you come, I promise I will not leave your side unless you tell me to go," said Mistress Eleanor.

"I will make you a bargain—when I have a silver dress, I shall stay for all the festivities in the Great Hall," said Mary as they joined the rest of the ladies.

"I shall hold you to your part," said Mistress Eleanor.

Mary stood as still as she could while the silk woman pinned the sheer fabric around her waist. The color set off her dark eyes, making them even more noticeable.

"How does that feel, Your Worship? Too tight?" said the woman, her mouth filled with pins.

"Not too tight—just right. But the neck seems quite low. Can you bring it up a little?" said Mary, barely daring to breathe.

"The queen gave me directions to pattern the gown after her own, Your Worship. And that I must do," said the woman. "You be a young lass—you can show your duckies if you like, long as you are no married woman. Pretty little breasts they are, too."

"I have no wish to show my 'duckies,'" said Mary. She sighed heavily. "But you must do as the queen has bid you."

Soon, the fitting was over and Mary stood in her shift in the queen's bedchamber. Several other ladies took their leisure, reading from the English Bible, sewing, playing the lute.

"I am glad you are finally to have a new gown, Mistress Mary," said Mistress Frances Vaughn. "You are such a pretty package I'll warrant even the queen envies your beauty."

"No one is more beautiful than our queen, Mistress Frances. As I am sure you know," said Mary.

"No one currently at court. Lady Essex is quite the beauty—and I am not the only one who thinks it so. The Earl of Leicester, the queen's own 'Sweet Robin,' has discovered her charms," said Mistress Frances.

"You mean *uncovered*," whispered Mistress Eleanor.

"Hush! Let us let sleeping dogs lie. I do not wish to upset the queen with such talk. She is, after all, buying me this new gown and is most happy I shall soon attend her at evening festivities. I would not spoil her happiness with talk of the she-wolf," said Mary, into Mistress Eleanor's ear.

A rustle of movement at the door and the yeoman announced, "Make way for the Queen! Make way for the Queen's Majesty!"

"God's teeth, you look like a gillyflower in full bloom—just ripe for the plucking. You were right, Fawn—the silver *is* perfect," said the queen, holding the silver material up to Mary's body.

"Oh, you shall be the envy of every woman at court! But remember," said the queen as she turned around and looked at all her ladies, "beware the men. As I have said many times, the unmarried state is by far superior to the married state. Our Lord himself told us this. Do not give way to yon courtiers. You know *I* prefer to have *all* of your attentions. Come, ladies, let us walk in the gardens before we sup. By the toes of God, I feel the need to stretch out my legs and breathe in the sweet air of England," said the queen.

The silk woman took her own time to complete Mary's new dress. A little less than a fortnight later, she presented it to the queen for inspection, laying it across the queen's bed.

"God's teeth, I refuse to pay for a dress that may not fit you well! It has cost me the salary of a yeoman for a year as it is! You must put it *on*! Mistress Eleanor, Frances—assist Mary at once. Do not stand gaping at me as if I were a madwoman! By the wings of all the angels, must I say everything twice!" screamed the queen as she kicked her foot at Mistress Frances, barely missing her.

"Yes, Your Majesty," said both young women, hurrying to assist Mary.

An hour later, Mary paraded before the queen in the silver gown of fine silk with white satin sleeves matching her kirtle. She wore a silver and white French hood studded with tiny pearls. A net of white silk, fine and delicate as a spider's web, caught up her heavy hair. White satin shoes with bows of silver velvet made no sound as Mary walked gracefully and slowly. But the more the queen and the ladies commented, the sillier Mary began to feel.

Suddenly, she skipped around the room, bowing to each maid and planting a kiss upon several cheeks. She then made mock of the Earl of Leiscester, standing on tiptoe and bowing to the queen. She said in a loud, low voice, "Your Majesty, may I have this dance?"

No one spoke. All were terrified of the queen's response. As the problems in the north continued to plague her, and the Scottish queen's not-so-secret plan to wed the Duke of Norfolk caused her to have trembling fears of losing her crown as the result of *that* union, the queen had been in a difficult temper for weeks. No one could escape her frustration. The ladies had seen the queen round on Master Cecil and her "Sweet Robin" many times, accusing them of plotting against her and trying to force her to marry. She had not laughed or been merry since the early summer. And now, Mistress Mary dared mock her favorite.

"I do not believe the earl would look quite so pretty in a dress—but I shall dance with you, Mary! It will do my heart good!" said the queen, laughing. The two women stepped lively to a galliard, the others clapping their hands and singing. Round and round they twirled, two pretty birds in flight. Finally, winded, they stopped.

"If only Leicester could make me laugh again! How I have missed a good jest! Oh Mary, you are such a comfort to me," said the queen, now sitting on her chair while Mary sat on the floor beside her.

"And you, Majesty, are the kindest mother I could have," said Mary.

"I am Mother to all of England—not only you—to all these maids!" said the queen. She smiled and motioned for Mistress Blanche to approach.

"Parry, go into my jewels and bring a pretty for each maid here—and for Mary, a pearl necklace, one with diamonds, too, so she will sparkle a little now and then," said the queen. She rose and her women followed suit. "Just remember—never outsparkle your queen!"

As Mistress Blanche did the queen's bidding, Mary waited at the back of the group. She watched as Mistress Frances elbowed her way to the front so she would receive the first "pretty" and observed the happy smile spread over her features.

"Are you not anxious to see the lovely necklace Mistress Blanche will give you?" said Mistress Eleanor.

"Not really. Though I like jewels as much as anyone, I am pondering the queen's quicksilver humors. First, she is in a rage; then, she is laughing and dancing—I cannot fathom what spurs these rapid changes," said Mary.

The two women discussed the myriad of problems besetting the queen: the continuing trouble brewing in the north, the unpredictable Queen of Scots, and the queen's personal heartbreak over her Sweet Robin's attentions to Lady Essex.

"How does she manage it? She seems to know everything that happens at court—as if she has eyes everywhere. And, though she faces a ceaseless sea of difficulties, she navigates her way through them. I am in amazement to think on it," said Mary.

"They say she has spies at all corners—from Old Catspaw, the washerwoman, to Master Walsingham, who assists Master Cecil, to Master Cecil himself. Of course, she has her 'Eyes' as well. I do not know why she does not go mad—I'd be in Bedlam were I queen!" said Mistress Eleanor, smiling.

"Oh, Mistress Blanche is beckoning us—let us see what 'pretties' she will give us," said Mary.

Mary was amazed when Mistress Blanche handed her a very long rope of pearls interspersed with diamonds, with one large diamond at the center. This was no bauble, but a jewel fit for a princess. She stood still as Mistress Blanche roped it around her neck and thought of the pleasure she would feel when she secreted it into her treasure box.

The last week in August, the court prepared to move to Greenwich as the smells and heat of the last month had made Whitehall no longer fit for habitation. Mary assisted the queen as she dressed for the night's activities.

"You will join us in the Great Hall this evening, Fawn. I have arranged for a short play to be presented, and then we shall dance. I would see your skills at conversation and your dancing feet move with great delicacy this night—I have invested much in you and wish to observe how well my efforts have been met," said the queen, as

Mary helped pile curl upon curl of Her Majesty's hair upon a wire frame, while other ladies tied the queen's sleeves onto her bodice. Still others painted the royal face with white paste and her cheeks with rouge. For upward of two hours, the ladies worked their magic, turning an almost middle-aged woman into a regal and handsome woman—a desirable woman.

"Yes, ma'am. I shall be along anon. I would like to freshen myself first," said Mary.

"Of course, of course. You must look your best. Mistress Eleanor and Mistress Frances will help you—also, Mistress Dorothy. Hand me the looking glass," said the queen.

Eight

*T*he sultry night sky was clear and the stars glittered like tiny diamonds sewn onto a black velvet cape. Mary and Mistress Eleanor walked behind the queen as she entered the passageway leading from the gardens to the Great Hall.

"You *do* look lovely in your new dress, Mary," said Mistress Eleanor. "You are the prettiest girl here, of that there can be no doubt."

"Nay. You are trying to boost my estimation of myself so I will not be clinging to the walls of the Great Hall," said Mary. "Are there many handsome gallants waiting for us?"

"Sir George Carey, Lord Hunsdon's son, is at court. He is quite handsome but has his nose out of joint because his father is risen so high. My favorite is Master Nicholas Hilliard—he is a marvelous sketcher of portraits and is fair of face! The queen favors Sir John Pakington and calls him 'Lusty' because he writes poetry and is skillful in the tiltyard . . . and *other* places," said Mistress Eleanor.

"But Eleanor, you have never mentioned Master Nicholas. Have you been keeping him a secret?" said Mary as she smiled at a group of gentlemen who had nodded and bowed as they passed by.

"He is no secret—he does not know I exist. His eyes are for the queen, as are all the eyes of the court. But, once in a while, I see him glance toward me. The last time I caught him so, he smiled at me. His teeth are white as the pearls in your new necklace," said Mistress Eleanor.

"What others are there?" said Mary.

"Well, there is the Duke of Norfolk, who disturbs our queen with rumors that he will wed the Scottish queen. He's not as young as the others—he must have thirty years or more—but he is manly and makes many beaux gestes. The Scottish queen would be fortunate to have him. Oh, I almost forgot Edward de Vere, the Earl of Oxford—he's nearest in age to you, Mary. But watch him—I fear he is as randy as a bull in spring," said Mistress Eleanor.

"I remember Oxford. When I first began my studies at Master Cecil's house, he was there. I was but eight. He seemed much older at the time—he was perhaps twelve. He studied under Master Nowell for a year, maybe less. I did not see him again. I have no idea what happened to him," said Mary, shaking her head.

"He would not have bothered you then, but now I fear he chases anyone in skirts. Be forewarned," said Eleanor.

"I shall watch out for them all. Oh, the queen leads us into the Great Hall. Do stay with me, Nora—I may faint," said Mary.

The queen walked slowly to her throne, stopping along the way to chat with one courtier or another. She held in her right hand a fan made of peacock feathers with an ivory handle studded with jewels. When she approached the Earl of Leicester, she passed by him without a word but tickled his face and neck with the fan. The earl then left the group of men with whom he was conversing and followed the queen to her throne. He knelt in front of her and she began whispering in his ear. Mary wondered how the earl could be so duplicitous—fawning over the queen after she had caught him in the arms of another woman.

"Mistress Eleanor, I have not yet had the pleasure of meeting your friend," said a young man dressed in a fine silk doublet with a green velvet cap on his head. On the cap, a white feather plume angled up, making the man seem taller than he actually was.

"This is Mistress Mary Shelton, newly made gentlewoman of the Privy Chamber and royal ward. Mary, please meet Edward de Vere, Earl of Oxford," said Mistress Eleanor as she gave him a small curtsy.

"Mistress Mary, I am charmed . . . you are the fullest blossom in this bouquet," said Oxford.

Mary felt her face warming. She lowered her head and curtsied. She was afraid to speak lest her voice betray her fear.

"My lord . . ." she stammered.

"Might I invite you to dance? Let us join the queen and Leicester—they have begun a stately pavanne," said Oxford.

"Certainly, my lord," Mary said as she took his arm and followed him to the dance floor. With great solemnity, she focused on the steps, worried that, though she had practiced this dance a hundred times in the privacy of the queen's apartments, she might make a misstep. She glanced up and noticed both the queen and Sweet Robin were staring at her. Robin gave her a wink and she smiled at him. Soon after, she began to relax.

"You are not new to court, then?" said Oxford, turning her around as they faced the opposite direction.

"Do you not remember me?" said Mary, skipping with her left foot.

"I am certain we have never met—I would not forget one so lovely," said Oxford, lifting her into a slow spin.

"God's blood, you *have* forgotten me!" she said.

His face began to turn pink and Mary could not help but smile. No doubt, he was racking his brain to recall who she was.

"Have no fear, my lord. I am not one of your quickly forgotten conquests. We were both wards at Master Cecil's house. We studied under Master Nowell—I was the only little girl in the class," said Mary.

"You are *that* little imp? The queen's special pet? And quite spoiled, as I recall," Oxford said.

"I was not! It may interest you to know I have lived at court since I was little—I was only three years old when I first arrived, a poor orphan," said Mary, lifting her skirts with one hand while he circled her around. She matched the queen's rhythm exactly and moved with much grace.

"I am sorry to hear you lost your parents at such a young age," said Oxford.

"Many children lose parents . . . I am fortunate the queen decided to keep me rather than sell my wardship to some great man far from court," said Mary.

"I am surprised she did not do so—our Bess is well known for her parsimony," said Oxford.

"You should not speak so of the queen—it is unkind and untrue. She is most generous to those who love her and whom she loves," said Mary, fingering the pearls at her throat.

"Have no fear, mistress. My bold talk is part of what the queen loves about me—I am one of her favorites, though I be young," said Oxford, laughing.

"Bold talk has been known to lower a man by a head, sir," said Mary.

"God's blood, you sound like her! Always going on about shortening her subjects when she is in an evil mood. Are you in a foul temper?" said Oxford.

"I was not until I began this dance!" said Mary before she could halt the words.

Oxford stopped where he was, turned to Mary, and began to

laugh. He did not take up the dance again but merely kept laughing. Mary realized that soon the whole court was staring at them. She felt the blood rise to her face once more.

"Oh, for the sake of all the devils in Spain, Oxford, what amuses you?" shouted the queen as she, too, stopped moving. She hushed the musicians with a wave of her arm.

"Majesty, forgive me! Mistress Mary's 'bold talk' has tickled me as surely as the feathers of your fan," said Oxford.

"Come here, my lad, and I shall give you a tickling you will not forget! You have need of a grown woman, not a shooting stalk of a girl," said the queen.

"May I obey all Your Majesty's commands with equal pleasure," said Oxford as he knelt before the queen. She took her fan and ran it round and round his neck. Then, she leaned over to him and kissed him on the cheek.

"You are far too much of a sprout yourself, Oxford, to dawdle with your queen. Return to yon girl and come back to me when a man you be!" said the queen, laughing.

Oxford, without chagrin, walked back to Mary and encircled her waist with his arm. Mary watched as Leicester gave the queen and Oxford a dark look. The queen gestured to the musicians to play again, this time la Volta. The crowd circled around so they could watch the queen and her Master of the Horse begin the dramatic leaping and lifting this dance entailed. Mary searched the hall for Mistress Eleanor and saw her standing next to a handsome man, a goblet in hand.

"Pray excuse me, milord. I am thirsty and will join my friend," said Mary, giving Oxford a short curtsy.

"A pretty retreat, mistress. Do let me know when you wish to fence with me again," said Oxford as he turned from Mary toward Mistress Frances Vaughn.

Mary made her way to her friend.

"I see you have survived the dance with young Oxford," said Mistress Eleanor. "That is better than some have done—I've seen more than one maid reduced to tears by his antics."

"That rutting goat shall never make me cry," said Mary as she took a goblet from the gentleman standing beside Mistress Eleanor and sipped.

"Well said, ma'am," said the young man, bowing slightly.

"This is Master Nicholas—the artist I told you about?" said Mistress Eleanor.

"Dear Nora, you have too high an opinion of my small ability," said Master Nicholas.

"You will find, sir, Mistress Eleanor has a reasonable head on her shoulders and does not stoop to flattery when the truth will serve," said Mary.

"Who speaks of truth at the court of Elizabeth?" said another young man as he joined them. He was dressed all in red—red doublet, red cloak around his shoulder with false sleeves, red shoes and red hose. The cap on his head was red with gold trim. He, however, had dark coloring with a large prominent nose and a thick black beard. He bowed to Mary and Mistress Eleanor, then grabbed Mary's hand and pulled her toward the dancing space.

"May I present Sir John Pakington," said Mistress Eleanor, calling out behind them.

Before Mary could respond, Pakington swung her around and around as the fresh music grew steadily faster. She could barely catch her breath as she tried to remember the steps to the country roundel. While her mind could not recall each turn and step, her feet had learned the dance perfectly.

"Methought at court a young gallant would ask a lady *if* she wanted to dance, not drag her to the dancing floor like a stubborn mule," said Mary once the music stopped and she stood facing Pakington.

"You have an overly high expectation of chivalry, ma'am. Here, we be brutes," said Pakington, reaching over to a nearby table and lifting a mug of ale to his lips. He gulped down the drink and called for more. A serving man refilled the mug and Pakington drained it.

"You have proven your point well, sir. And now, I shall return to my friend," said Mary, searching for Nora.

"You will not find her in the Great Hall, mistress. She and that silly artist have ducked out the door—no doubt to find a private cove where they might escape the prying eyes of the court," said Pakington.

"You do not know Mistress Eleanor, if you think she would put her honor at risk," said Mary.

"Oh, I don't believe there would be any risk involved. She lost her honor some time ago," said Pakington, laughing.

Mary rounded on him, her eyes full of fire.

"God's blood, you shame yourself, sir!" said Mary, unaware her voice rang out loudly over the stone walls.

The queen and her Sweet Robin had pushed their way across the crowded hall.

"Why speak you so, Fawn? Has this lusty fellow been bothering you?" said the queen, holding on to Leicester's arm.

Mary knew she blushed under the queen's gaze. She started to speak but Sir "Lusty," as she now thought of him, spoke first.

"Your Majesty, forgive me. I was merely jesting with the new maid—I had not seen her before and her beauty is extraordinary. I shall watch my tongue in the future—I did not know she was one of Your Majesty's favorites," said Pakington, bowing low to the queen.

"God's death, Pakington, you would mar a girl if she were *not* my favorite? I should have you thrown from court. But it is not this slip of a girl you want—surely, your queen, in her full maturity, could satisfy you, you great brute! Shall we dance, Sir John?" said the queen as she placed her delicate hands against Sir John's chest.

"Ma'am, the pleasure is all mine," he said. The queen gave the sign and music, tapping feet, and swirling skirts filled the Great Hall once again with sound.

Before Mary could make her way to one of the few benches set against the walls for the revelers to take their rest, she felt a tug at her elbow. She turned and faced yet another young man.

"Please, mistress, do not think all men at court are like Pakington. Some of us have proper manners and behave in ways that are suited to our station in life. I am Baron Hunsdon, George Carey. My father, Henry, is cousin to the queen," he said. He gave Mary a small, prissy bow and offered her his arm.

"Would you care to stroll in the gardens? I assure you, your virtue will be safe with me," he said. He picked a bit of lint or dirt from his doublet and drew a bouquet of flowers to his nose. He then sniffed at the blooms.

Mary thought he looked like one of the peacocks strutting around the grounds, considering himself beautiful and holding his head up as if he were above the rest of the crowd.

"You are kind to offer, sir. But I fear my feet are tired and I suffer an ache in my head. I shall ask the queen if I may return to her chambers," said Mary, curtsying and moving quickly away from the baron.

"Why did you not tell me I would be like fresh kill for those vultures?" said Mary as she and Mistress Eleanor prepared the Privy Chamber for the next day.

"How could I have explained what the evenings are like for us? You have been sheltered by the queen, sent off to bed after we sup. Her Majesty has just acknowledged your womanhood—now that you serve as one of her ladies, you must grow used to these men and learn how to handle them. You did very well, I should say," said Mistress Eleanor as she set the table for the queen's breakfast.

"I suppose with so many men and so few women, it is no wonder the court is full of romance. The odds are against us—how can we protect ourselves when there are five men laying siege to us at one time?" said Mary, folding a cloth over her arm.

"Even those with wives are not allowed to bring their spouses with them to court—the queen forbids it. She wishes to direct all manly attention to herself—things have always been thus," said Mistress Eleanor.

"They are all in love with her, no doubt. She is witty and graceful and elegant," said Mary.

"Humph. She is also beginning to show the wrinkles across her brow. She was never a great beauty, even when she was young, so my mother tells me. She never had your sweet looks!" said Mistress Eleanor.

Mary shook her head.

"Ha! My looks are anything but sweet—the queen has told me she can read my every thought because it is written across my features. My nose is too long and sharp—like the blade of a knife. My lips are not like a rosebud, but pouty, as if I were always unhappy. And my face is shaped like that of a cat. No, the queen outshines me by much. She is the great light at court. The queen is everything glorious in a woman— she dances, plays the virginals and the lute, has a melodious singing voice. She speaks so many languages and is clever in her speech. I would wish to have all her talents and abilities. Most of all, she knows how to handle her courtiers. She has kept the Earl of Leicester's interest for over ten years and he still adores her," said Mary.

"Aye, she has her mother's way about her—the same allure. She runs hot, then cold, then hot again. The poor fellows know not what to think. But Mary, you should mark *this*—I saw the queen's ill-humored looks directed toward you tonight," said Mistress Eleanor as she placed the finger bowl next to the queen's place and filled it with water.

"But why should the queen spear me with dark looks? I have done nothing," said Mary.

"When you were at the center of that group of young courtiers, she was jealous. Do not be so surprised—you are young and full of beauty. The queen is not. But she cannot abide this, so she forces the attentions of men young enough to be her sons upon herself. It is loathsome," said Mistress Eleanor.

"This cannot be. Surely the queen is not so vain! What shall I do? I do not wish to anger her against me," said Mary.

"I do not know—you are close to her heart. She will not turn against you," said Mistress Eleanor. "Come, let us sit with our sewing until the queen comes in from her walk—the good thing about serving the queen in her Privy Chamber is there is not much to be done—we shall have some time to ourselves."

As the two young women worked at their needle and thread, Mary realized she had not thought of Tom Wotton in several weeks. In fact, she could barely remember what he looked like. What she could recall was the way his lips felt against hers and the way his lean, muscled arms made a shell around her when they kissed. She thought of the courtiers she'd danced with, each with his own special charm. The Earl of Oxford was somewhat handsome, though small in stature. He was unmarried. Would he be a pleasing match for her? Would the queen allow her to marry someone like him? After all, he was an *earl*. The queen could hardly hope for a better match. Though he was an earl, something about Oxford made Mary's blood chill. Maybe it was the way he pursed his lips, or the weak look he had about the eyes—a pale blue with very light lashes. No matter. He was not the one—she did not feel anything in her bones, the way she imagined she would when she met the man she would marry.

Mary hummed a familiar ditty, a love song about a maiden and her mysterious lover from the sea. She was sad she had forgotten so much about Tom Wotton. Perhaps she was as fickle as a man. Perhaps she was no better than Oxford, who, according to Eleanor, had the fidelity of a flea.

Nine

*O*h Parry, what am I do to? Such rages roil within me, such storms, that I shall never see my way clear of them. What must those young pups in my court think of me? What must my dear Robin think? And Mary, poor Mary . . . to see the queen command the love of young men away from her?

She is a pretty thing, is she not? And her dancing quite filled with grace. How staunchly she put Oxford in his place! And our "lusty" Pakington! She sparred quite well for her first time in the field.

God's breath, do I not already see the truth of what you say? Time ticks faster and faster, it seems; the Queen of Scots intrudes on my lands and gathers men to her—there must be something divine about the Queen of Scots, something that obliges her very enemies to speak well of her! She is said to be quite lovely. And she is young, so much younger than I am.

Spain dawdles in the Netherlands and the Duke of Alva amasses a well-equipped army of men. I have no army to speak of and little money to *equip one. And Norfolk will not admit to his plan to marry the Queen of Scots—he plots against me, yet smiles and speaks with the greatest charm. My nerves are as frayed as the hem of an old shift.*

No! I care not for wine! I must have my wits about me. You think these shifting humors are related to the changes in my monthly course? But I am not yet old enough for the great cessation. I am still young—still pretty. God's blood, you would have me ready for my winding sheet!

I know not what to do with Mary—if I am not careful, one of these daring young men will woo her and she will be lost to me. I would not wish to live without seeing her smile each day or hearing her sing to me. She is full of vinegar sometimes, like you, Parry. But even so, her company is better than most. Oh, I do not doubt her love, nor do I doubt your own. Even though she is young, I know she loves me deep in her heart. She could not help doing so—I am the only mother she can remember.

Men may think me monstrous, as I show no desire for a husband or children. But they do not know Mary is mine own little lamb—she is the child of my heart.

But her future . . . what man is worthy of her? Oxford? He seemed taken with her. And he has position and wealth. He could be a good match, with the right woman. Pakington? Heavens, no! Hunsdon? That pompous peacock? Oh, so much rides upon making the right choice—Mary's entire future happiness.

What to do? What to do?

I have it! I shall summon your cousin Dr. Dee. I shall have him cast a chart for Mary. Then we shall see what the stars can tell us. Then I shall know in which direction to head. I'll find her a fine husband, a man who can give her as much comfort as she finds in my court. She shall marry well and she shall be happy. By God's teeth, I shall make it so!

*T*he queen and her ladies walked earlier than usual to escape the heat of late summer. The queen had taken Mary by the arm and insisted the young woman walk with her, leaving the rest of the maids to linger among the flowers while the queen and Mary made haste to the far end of the gardens. The sun beamed down and the green fields surrounding Whitehall already showed a hint of brown as the summer season drew to a close. Mary could smell the stench of the court, but overlaying that odor was the sweet scent of late roses and lavender. Already, Mary could feel trickles of sweat stream down her ribs beneath her shift. She hoped it would not blotch her white silk gown and silver sleeves.

"Pick up your pace, little Fawn. You must step high if you hope to keep up with your queen," said Elizabeth.

"Your Majesty sets a difficult task," said Mary, struggling with her skirts.

"Just be certain you never try to outpace me. Have no worries, child. I did not bring you with me to scowl at you," said the queen. She stopped in front of a large yew tree and sat on the stone bench beneath. She patted the spot next to her and indicated for Mary to join her.

"I have been wondering what to do with you, Mary. You are now at an age to return to Shelton Hall if that is your wish, although your brother, Ralph, is very happy there with his family. I do not know how he would feel about shouldering the expense of your care. And I fear that after growing up in my court, you would find life in the country terribly dull. No, do not speak. I would finish my thoughts," said the queen, holding up her hand as if to stop Mary by physical force if need be.

"If you choose to stay at court, which is the choice I hope you will make, I shall make a good match for you, one that will please you and raise you up. You are my kinswoman and, as such, could marry a foreign noble if you wished it. You are accomplished and have a level head—a gentle temperament, *most* of the time. But, alas, you have little ability to dissemble—you are as honest as the noonday sun," said the queen.

"Your Majesty has too high an opinion of my poor abilities, but I thank you for your kindness. If it please you, I have no desire to unsettle my brother and his family. I should like to stay here and continue to serve Your Majesty," said Mary.

"Good. I have consulted our esteemed Dr. Dee about your future and he casts a fine chart for you. Would you like to hear?" said the queen.

"Yes, Majesty, I am most interested in the patterns the stars make on our lives. I have studied some with Lord Robert—he promised to take me to Mortlake to see the stars through Dr. Dee's great glass. As of yet, he has not found time to do so," said Mary.

"And I imagine you would like to peruse Dr. Dee's library; he has more books than all of the universities. I, too, should like to do nothing but read from those great tomes of knowledge . . . but I have a people to rule," said the queen. "Here is what he saw in the stars about you, dearest Fawn."

The queen settled herself more comfortably on the bench and searched Mary's face. Mary felt herself grow warm under Her Majesty's gaze.

"First, you are born under the sign of the water bearer, Aquarius. You are friendly and would serve humanity, as would I. Dr. Dee then spoke of your loyalty and honesty, qualities Rob and I have endeavored to instill in you. I believe you to have both traits in great strength—these are characteristics I admire and need in those who would serve me. You are inventive and intellectual, not a follower but a leader like myself," said the queen as she handed Mary a fan and motioned for her to begin fanning them.

"I do not recognize myself in these words, Your Grace," said Mary, slowly moving the peacock feathers in front of their faces, stirring a small breeze that felt good against Mary's damp cheeks.

"We seldom see ourselves as others see us," said the queen, patting Mary's knee. Mary noticed a rivulet of sweat sliding down the queen's cheek.

"There is more, Fawn. If your sign is out of balance, you become stubborn and aloof, showing little emotion. You also become quite unpredictable—I am remembering when you were a child and fought with Master Wotton when he said girls had no business learning Greek. How outraged you were at his words!" said the queen, chuckling. "God's blood, I thought Master Nowell would never allow you to return to the class after you let Wotton feel the sting of your hand against his cheeks. I had to pay him a pound to let you return, for he agreed with Master Wotton—what was the point of educating a girl unless she was going to rule a kingdom someday."

The queen paused and took hold of Mary's hand.

"I hope by now you have forgiven me for sending Master Wotton away," said the queen.

"Yes, Majesty. Now that he is gone, I can see why we were enemies for so long. He held women in low regard, as so many young men do. I believe God hath appointed all to our place, but that is no reason to fail to see God's spirit within each. Some still debate whether or not we women have souls—such an attitude should not surprise Your Grace," said Mary.

"Hah! I should like to hear them say such rubbish in front of me! Well, Fawn, let us not make ourselves any more heated. My only concern regarding Dr. Dee's chart is in reference to our friendship—for he said it would be unlikely for us to endure each other's company. However, he was quick to say that the stars cannot tell us all. They are sometimes wrong. At any rate, for the most part, he confirmed what I already knew—I can trust you and you shall be of great service to this realm," said the queen.

"By serving Your Majesty, I serve the realm," said Mary.

"I have it in mind to put you to a much greater service than folding my linens. I hope to make a strong ally by marrying you to a foreign dignitary, perhaps even a prince. No, no, clamor not to know the man I have in mind, for I do not yet know myself. You may be set to soar higher than an eagle, my Fawn. You are my cousin, of my blood. You are fit for a king," said the queen.

Mary shook her head. She could not believe what she was hearing. A foreign prince? Surely the queen was joking.

"You are also levelheaded and thirsty for knowledge; you care about people and you are honest, dearest Fawn. These are the qualities of a highborn lady. Do not gape! You shall catch a fly with that open mouth. Remember, though we have spoken of many things, I have told you nothing. The words that pass between us are never to be repeated," said the queen.

"I shall never tell, Your Grace," said Mary. She did not feel she could move—the queen's words had frozen her and she shivered a little, though the sun overhead beat down on them. She could not imagine leaving England for a foreign court.

"I meet with Master Secretary this afternoon, along with Leicester and a few other advisors. I would have you come with me to observe. Later, in private, give me your thoughts. If you are to marry a foreign noble, you must still serve England. You must learn what concerns us on our little isle. Then, you can use your high position to give us aid if need be," said the queen.

"As you wish," said Mary, struggling to rise and follow the queen as she marched through the garden, a woman on a mission.

Before Mary was to join the queen and her advisors, she had time enough to take old *Tom* for a run. She had been too busy lately to attend to the dog, but she felt the need to see him, feel his welcoming licks and escape the pressures she felt at the court. She wanted time in the sun, in the cool shade of the nearby woods, so she could clear her head and digest all the queen had told her. And, though the day grew ever more warm, she hurried to the kennels, quickly soaking her undergarments. She'd made quick time from the castle, past the barns where the horses and ponies were kept, and was headed up the slight rise to the kennels. She could hear the dogs baying at her, welcoming her.

She noticed a figure walking toward her, but the sun shone in her eyes, making it impossible to distinguish any features. She could tell by the silhouette it was a man and, by his brisk walk, she guessed him to be a young man.

"Can the gods have smiled upon me? Can this be Mistress Mary Shelton, the beauty of Elizabeth's wondrous court?" said a familiar voice.

Mary shaded her eyes with her hand so she could see who addressed her.

"Milord Oxford. What has brought you to the kennels on such a hot day?" said Mary. She could not hide her lack of enthusiasm at seeing him. Something about him put her on her guard. She would rather have run into the blustery Pakington, though neither man particularly appealed to her.

"One of my bitches dropped a litter of eleven pups last week. I came to inspect them and leave instructions with the kennel boy. I am happy to say each is splendid and I shall train them for the hunt," Oxford said, pausing in front of her, blocking the sunlight.

"Oh, I should like to see them!" said Mary, gazing at him. He was barely taller than she and his body was wiry and quick.

"Then, by all means, allow me to introduce you to the little darlings," Oxford said, offering her his arm. She took it and they headed toward the kennels.

As they entered a conclave of various-sized buildings, Mary looked to find *Tom*. There he was, in the small hut he shared with two other dogs of similar size. He had seen her and was barking and leaning his front paws against the wooden slats that fenced him in.

"Just a minute, *Tom*. I want to see the puppies first," she called to him. At the sound of her voice, he jumped, eager to escape his confines.

"He cannot understand you, you know. He's just a dumb animal," said Oxford, leading her to a larger pen, one in which they could stand. The space was dark and Mary could make out four smaller cages, each roiling with squirmy pups.

"*Tom* is anything but dumb—God's blood, you ought to see him chase a pheasant! Fast and very smart," said Mary, her voice edgy.

"I did not wish to offend—I simply see no reason to become sentimental over a cur. They are a halfpenny a dozen," said Oxford.

"I paid more than that for *Tom*—I paid with a year's worth of Greek and Latin. He was my reward for good marks from Master Nowell," said Mary as she leaned over the pen and gazed at the pups. "Oh, they are darling!"

"I shall make you a gift of one if you like," said Oxford, standing very close to her.

"That is very kind but I fear *Tom* would be very jealous—I barely have time to spend with him these days," said Mary.

"I can understand his feelings of envy. I would feel that way, too, if you were my mistress," said Oxford. There was no mistaking his meaning.

Mary straightened up and faced him.

"You flatter yourself, sir. For I shall be no man's mistress. God's teeth, I should rather remain a maid!" Mary said.

"*God's teeth.* You sound exactly like our esteemed queen—I do believe she has forced her unnatural ways onto you! Surely you know a woman's best use is as a wife and mother, to be subject to her lord, her husband," said Oxford.

"I know that is preached from the pulpit, but I have also noticed that is not the true way of things—at least, not at Elizabeth's court. As I am her ward, it is only right I should reflect those ways she has taught by her example," said Mary. She turned from him and strode over to *Tom*. She opened the gate and *Tom* jumped on her. She went to her knees and hugged him around the neck, accepting his canine kisses with smiles and sweet words. She noticed Oxford still standing near the puppies.

"I shall take my dog walking now, milord. Thank you for showing me your pups," she said flatly.

"Perhaps I shall see you this evening after we sup. I should enjoy very much dancing with you again," he said.

"I do not think so, milord. I have much work to do on the queen's behalf this evening," said Mary as she tied the leash around *Tom* and sauntered out of the kennels.

A fortnight later, Mary had joined the queen to listen and observe as Her Majesty met with her councillors. That particular afternoon, Master Cecil was going on and on about how Parliament had given the queen permission to marry whomever she pleased, whenever she pleased years ago, and still the queen remained unwed. Mary sat on cushions at the queen's feet and stifled a yawn. The afternoon was hot, though the windows were open and a slight breeze drifted in and out. Cecil continued to prate about the unhappy Catholics in the north and the one beacon who drew them to her, Mary, Queen of Scots. Mary watched as his face grew more and more red, up to the very hairs of his head. She glanced up at the queen, who was also pinkish, the familiar look of a rage about to erupt on her features.

Ever since the queen had hinted she might make Mary a noble marriage, the girl had felt the weight of the world on her shoulders. Her appetite had left her and she had grown pale. At times, she felt haughty and proud; then, quickly, terrified. Now, the queen insisted she meet with these men of import and listen as the problems of the realm were discussed. Even Sweet Robin seemed more solemn than usual—he didn't wink his eye at her or even smile. The one consolation was that Mary had noticed a new young man among those gathered around the queen. He was incredibly handsome with yellow hair that hung rakishly over his forehead, almost into his eyes. And those eyes—the same shade as the aquamarine jewels in one of the queen's necklaces. He did not seem to notice Mary at all, but kept his gaze on the queen and her councillors. Mary began to imagine speaking to him, but her reverie was quickly ended when the queen erupted in anger.

"God's breath! You continue to plague me about getting an heir.

And how has getting an heir helped the Scottish queen? She sits at Tutbury all but in prison while her babe sits on her throne," shouted the queen.

Her Majesty rose and pounded the table in front of her with the palm of her hand.

"I shall seek to marry at the time God chooses—God and no other!" said the queen.

"Your Grace, if you wait for God, you will be past the time for childbearing," said Sir James Croft, a longtime supporter of the queen. An older man with thick gray hair on his head and a full, white beard, Sir James spoke in a voice that sounded like one of the desert prophets— low, deep, and resonant. And behind Sir James stood Mary's mysterious young man, who seemed to be smothering a smile.

The queen stood, silent as a stone. No one moved.

"While I am assured of your love for us, Sir James, you abuse that love we have for you! Gentlemen, He who placed me in this seat will keep me here. That is what you must believe. Let me comfort you—I will marry when God leads me to it, for I know full well the needs of my people and I do not wish bring war upon us," said the queen.

With that, she arose, nodded to Mary to accompany her, and left the men standing, their caps in their hands.

Later that night, Mary sat on the queen's bed, rubbing Her Majesty's feet with almond oil. The queen had cleared her bedchamber of all but Mary and Mistress Blanche, who was busy emptying the night stool.

"What think you of my advisors, Fawn?" said the queen, her long red curls spread out on the pillow and her pale face gaunt.

"Master Cecil is quite forceful in voicing his thoughts, ma'am. I found Sir James Crofts a handsome old fellow, kindly. Does he sing?" said Mary.

"God's teeth, girl! What has singing to do with anything?" said the queen.

"Majesty, calm yourself. His voice was so sonorous—I should like to hear him sing," said Mary.

The queen laughed. Mary joined in.

"What has the two of you cackling like geese?" said Mistress Blanche.

"Oh Parry, I wanted to see how astute our Fawn is with matters of state. But all she can think about is Sir James's baritone! If I had only such worries," said the queen.

"I have no head for state matters, ma'am," said Mary, her face flaming.

"Your head is as good as any, better than most. But the night grows dark. Let us to bed," said the queen.

Mary put away the almond oil and crawled into the trundle bed beside the queen's imposing bedstead. She still wondered about the handsome young man she had seen earlier. She decided to ask the queen about him and hoped she would be able to conceal the level of her interest.

"Majesty, who was that young man standing behind Sir James?" Mary said.

"Oh, that was his son-in-law, Sir John Skydemore. A handsome devil, is he not? I do not wonder why you ask about him," said the queen, laughing.

"I . . . did not notice how he looked—it's just that I had not seen him before and was curious as to how he arrived in the Privy Council," said Mary.

"God's blood! You cannot hide your girlish interest from me, mistress. One would have to be dead not to notice his beauty—he rivals Adonis. He is at the Inns of Court, studying law. Sir James asked if the young fellow could sit in on our meeting and I agreed. Fear not, dear Fawn—he is not for you, though you are free to gaze upon him all you like. Just do not become a fool for him!" said the queen.

Mary said nothing. She was disappointed to discover he was married and safe in the family fold, using his father-in-law's position to wheedle a place at court, no doubt. But he *was* handsome and Mary fell asleep thinking of him.

*T*he heat of August had passed, and as winter reared its icy head, fires roared in the hearths of Richmond, where the queen had come for several weeks, to enjoy her "warm box." The colder air was a relief to those at court, for the foul smells, which seemed to grow even more foul in hot weather, were not so bad once the season turned. Mary looked out from the queen's apartments to the fields below. The sun was shining and the leaves had gone from green to yellow, russet, and brown. Mary especially liked the deep purples she spied in the nearby woods.

Though autumn was her favorite time of year, this particular fall had been difficult. The entire court was worried about the restless north, whether the northern lords would rebel, as the rumors predicted, or whether reason would win out. The tension was palpable and discord rampant. Mary did not enjoy meeting with the queen and her advisors, for, no matter what point of view Mary heard, she could see no way out of the problems facing the realm. She tried to answer the queen's questions about policies, but she felt completely inadequate and often wished she could disappear into one of the tapestries with scenes from the life of Abraham, those beautiful and bright carpets purchased at great cost by the queen's father.

Though she had no head for policy, Mary had taken up a new task, the making of cordials, for medicinal use as well as for pleasure. Her interest had been sparked when Mistress Blanche brought her a draught for stomach ailments earlier in the year. She swallowed it down, surprised to discover it tasted sweet, like a mixture of fine fruits. And it quickly soothed her aching belly.

When she asked Mistress Blanche about the brew, she learned Old Catspaw was the maker. She spent many hours learning how to select the best fruits, how to cover them with aqua vitae so that they could have room enough to "swim" and remain immersed, and how to be patient as she waited the thirty days for the fruit to ferment. Then, she had to strain the large and small pieces from the liquid, bottle it tightly, and keep it away from the sun. Catspaw told her it was best to wait a year before tasting the mix, after she had added a generous amount of sugar, but Mary had a difficult time waiting. She wanted to share her work with the queen as soon as she could, so she brought samples to Her Majesty, who had been quite impressed. So much so, that she gave Mary leave to have her own cordial-making room next to the kitchen. She needed space to store the large vats filled with her concoctions, her utensils—filters, strainers, large spoons, bottles— and the bottles of wine and aqua vitae she used as a base for her brews. She learned how to distill juices and herbs, then add just the right amount of spirits to create delicious and health-inducing aperitifs for her friends.

After she had been released from the dreary meeting of the Privy Council, Mary stole a moment away from her usual duties to slip down to her cordial-making room. She loved going into the deepest recesses of the castle, hearing her feet slap-slap-slapping against the stone hallway. The heat rose to meet her, along with the wonderful smells of baked bread, roasting meat, and apple pastries. She could hear the cooks and scullery maids talking and laughing, the music of the kitchens now familiar to her—the clanging of pots, the click of wooden spoons against the crockery—and she felt at peace.

Suddenly, she felt someone grab her elbow from behind and spin her around.

"Ah, I thought it was you—I would recognize your gracious form anywhere, Mistress Mary. Well met," said the Earl of Oxford.

"My lord Oxford. You have taken me by surprise. What brings you to the queen's kitchens?" said Mary, removing her arm from his grasp.

"I was looking for you, mistress. I went to the queen's apartments in search of you and Mistress Eleanor said you were most likely checking on your cordials. I knew you to be a woman of many skills, but I did not know you dabbled in medicine," said Oxford.

"'Tis merely a pastime. I am by no means an expert. I have much to learn, but it is pleasant to sip my own concoctions. Why were you looking for me, milord?" said Mary, now walking toward her cordial-making room.

"I wanted to tell you something. Or rather, ask . . . I am not sure which," said Oxford. His manner was uneasy. Gone was his usual arrogance and in its place, uncertainty. Mary grew more uncomfortable.

"I shall do my best to answer, if you have a question," said Mary. She watched as the earl shifted from one foot to the other and bit his lower lip. He did not look at her, but instead gazed at the stone floor.

Mary waited, impatient to get to her fruit and spice mixture, to check on its progress.

"Mistress, I am of an age to take a wife. I have met, and I might add, bedded, many a likely prospect. However, none has touched my heart," Oxford said, still staring at the floor.

Mary said nothing.

"But now . . ." he said, reaching for her hand, "now I have found one I would wish to be bound to—you, dearest Mary."

Mary stood still. She could not think of what to say. She could feel the blood pulsing in her neck and her chest pounded. She did not wish to marry this man—to think of him touching her most private parts made her shiver with disdain. Yet, she could not insult him, either. He was an earl, and powerful.

"Can you say nothing to ease my discomfort?" Oxford said.

"I am . . . I am taken aback, milord. I had no idea you held such feelings for me in your heart," said Mary.

"I have been unable to think of anything else—Pakington swears you have put a spell on me. Perhaps he is right. Perhaps you have slipped me one of your potions," Oxford said, smiling.

"Oh no, milord. I would never do such a thing," said Mary, unsure of how she should respond to him.

"I wish to pay you court, Mistress Mary—to dance with you in the evenings, write poems for you, woo you with every intention of making you my wife. What say you to this?" Oxford said.

Mary continued to stand rooted to the spot as surely as if she were a great oak tree.

"The queen will make my wedding arrangements for me—I have little say in the matter. I will be happy to dance with you and listen to your poetry, but I can make no promises regarding a marriage between us without the queen's blessing," said Mary.

"Of course, of course. I shall follow the proper protocol, mistress. But I wanted to sound you out first—to see if you have any interest in me," said Oxford.

"Sir, I barely know you—I cannot say what my interests are," said Mary.

"But you do not refuse me outright—this gives me hope. I thank you, Mistress Mary. I shall pursue you, then. You shall find me a faithful knight, filled with ardor, ready to serve you at your pleasure," Oxford said. He gave her a short bow, then quickly strode up the hallway.

Mary continued to stand, her head spinning with a hundred thoughts. She shook herself as if she were awakening from a dream and walked into her private room. Her hands trembled as she lifted the lid from the fruit and smelled the sweet, sharp aroma of brandied peaches and cinnamon.

Mary, along with Mistress Eleanor, Mistress Frances, and Mistress Dorothy Broadbelt, rested after tidying the queen's apartments. Mary wanted nothing more than to tell Eleanor about Lord Oxford's conversation, but she could not with Mistress Dorothy and Mistress Frances there. Yet, to sit and wait for the queen's next command seemed impossible to her. She felt as if bugs were crawling over her body and she must move to shake them off.

"The day is fresh and clear—I should like to take *Tom* across those meadows for a long walk," said Mary as she continued to stare through the wavy glass.

"Not too cold, nor too hot—a perfect day for it," said Mistress Eleanor, sitting on one of the low stools scattered about the room.

"I shall not go with you. I intend to wait right here until Her Majesty has need of me—I danced too late last night," said Mistress Frances, sitting on one of the large pillows strewn on the floor.

"You and that handsome Oxford! He is a cocky fellow," said Mistress Eleanor, who was seated next to her.

Mary stood, but said nothing. If Oxford danced so often with Mistress Frances, perhaps his interest in *her* was not as serious as he had led her to believe. She felt a weight lift.

"You were in the arms of Master Nicholas frequently, Nora—are you going to marry him?" said Mistress Frances.

"I cannot marry without the queen's permission. But perhaps she will give it? I can only—" said Mistress Eleanor.

A commotion brought the ladies to their feet.

"Make way! Make way for the Queen's Majesty! Make way!" said one of the Gentlemen Pensioners, whose job it was to guard the queen at all times.

Several more of the pensioners entered the queen's apartments, their faces stern and their hands on their swords. Mary's heart skipped a beat and she turned to see the queen enter, her face white as death. The queen walked quickly to her desk, took a piece of parchment and a quill. No one spoke, though loud voices could be heard in the hallway. Without observing the usual protocol, Master Cecil, Sussex, the Earl of Leicester, and several other members of the Privy Council entered.

Mary saw fear in their faces and noticed her friends had stopped their chatter and Mistress Eleanor held the hand of Mistress Frances.

"Ma'am, Northumberland and Westmoreland have raised a tremendous army. I fear the Duke of Norfolk's removal to Kenninghall shall signal them to begin their march southward. You should go immediately to Windsor with your Gentlemen Pensioners and Leicester for your own safety," said Master Cecil, his voice strained.

"God's death! For what cause have these nobles risen against their queen? Have we not befriended them? Have we not been generous?" said the queen, quill in hand.

"Majesty, some prefer the Duke of Norfolk by his blood, some like the Scottish queen, some like the old religion, and some are persuaded by all three," said Sussex.

"Aye, there must be something in the northern air that makes men traitors. My father faced the Pilgrimage of Grace, my sister Wyatt's Rebellion—it is only fair I should have to fight for my crown and, by God's blood, fight I shall. Lord Hunsdon, raise an army from the Midlands and go to meet these rebels. I shall send word to Huntingdon at Tutbury to bring the Scots queen as far south as Coventry at once! If this vast army from the north should rescue the Catholic queen, we would have war upon us," said the queen as she scribbled a note onto the parchment.

"Every Catholic outside London has been predicting just such unrest. They say the stars are aligned to bring trouble upon our realm," said Sir James Croft in his melodious baritone.

"By the bones of the Virgin, it takes no necromancer to see that sixty thousand men have pledged their services to Northumberland and Westmoreland! This has been coming on since the Queen of Scots first sought refuge from us. We have housed her and even tried to get her reinstated to her throne, but she is a viper. She and Norfolk would marry and bring their armies to London. But she shall not take my kingdom from me. I have the heart of a man, not a woman, and I am not afraid of anything!" said the queen, sealing her orders with red wax that looked to Mary the color of blood.

"Bess, I shall make arrangements to move the court immediately to Windsor," said Leicester, rising from one knee beside the queen's chair.

"Anon, Robin. Do not leave us just yet," said the queen. She wrote further orders and sent the messenger off with instructions.

"Gentlemen, this is all we can do at present. We shall burrow in at Windsor and await word from Lord Hunsdon. Until then, we can pray for his success. Now, begone! And send the serving wenches for some wine and manchet," said the queen, slumping in her chair.

The chambers emptied except for the maids and the Gentlemen Pensioners. The queen rose and held out her arms to Leicester. He took her in a tender embrace.

"Bess, Bess, you shall be safe in my care. I will never let harm come to you, sweetheart," said Leicester, rubbing her back soothingly.

"Out, guards! Stand by our *doorway* this night—we do not need you in our chambers!" said the queen. The men marched out quietly.

"Oh Robin—see how I tremble. Is this the end? Has Norfolk gathered his armies to seize his bride and make way to London?" said the queen.

"Majesty, if he be such a fool, let him come. My sword shall stop him . . . forever," said Leicester.

"As much as I have given him, still he succumbs to that woman— she must have such sway with men as to drive them to madness. Monarchs ought to put to death the authors and instigators of war," said the queen.

"I fear you will have to put the Scottish queen to death, dear Bess. As long as she lives, you are in grave danger," said Leicester.

"Put my own cousin, my blood, to the block? Destroy an anointed queen? This I shall never do, Robin—for if I take such power into my hands, who shall stop others from doing the same to me? No, I shall keep her in safety," said the queen. She straightened herself and no longer leaned against Leicester. Mary noticed her color had returned a little.

The serving woman entered with a tray of manchet, cheese, and fruits along with a bottle of wine and several goblets. She poured a glass and handed it to the queen.

"Come, ladies, drink to fortify your spirits! Tomorrow we shall move to Windsor, so this night will be a busy one. You must prepare for a long stay," said the queen, taking a long swallow.

"Majesty, can you tell us what is happening? Are we to be slaughtered?" said Mistress Eleanor, her voice sounding shaky.

"We shall not be slaughtered, Nora. We are perfectly safe with yon pensioners to guard us and Lord Robert's trusty sword. The army of the north has sacked Durham Cathedral, destroying the English Bible and the Book of Common Prayer in a bonfire. Then they celebrated High Mass. They now begin their march south, probably first to Tutbury where they shall find their quarry has been stolen from them. Then, onward to London," said the queen as though explaining a geography lesson to a less-than-apt pupil.

"Is our army large enough to defeat them, Your Grace?" said Mary.

"Ha! We have four hundred men from London—most of them old

or blind or young and untried. They have no weapons except rakes, if
that. We hope Hunsdon will be able to rally many from the Midlands, but even that is not sure—so many will take to the Catholic
side. They are superstitious and ignorant and altogether blinded by
popish loyalties," said the queen.

"Bess, your people will rise to protect you—why, the citizens of
London will take to the streets to fight if Norfolk's army gets this
far," said Leicester.

"I pray you be right, Rob. I pray you be right. Now, kiss me good
night for I crave sleep above all else. Who knows what fresh hell the
morrow shall bring," said the queen. She eased into his arms and
they kissed for a long while. Then Lord Robert Dudley strode from
the queen's chambers, his blue velvet cape flowing behind him and
the matching cap bobbing jauntily with each step.

"Now, Mary, let us go to our bedchamber. Ladies, sleep elsewhere
tonight. I would have some quiet time with Mary and Mistress
Blanche," said the queen.

In the queen's bedchamber, one candle burned by the bedside; the
torches had been put out and the fire was merely embers. The queen
in her silk nightgown and cap with Belgian lace around the edges sat
on the edge of her sumptuous bed.

"Mary, I would you sleep with me this night—as you did when
you were a child. I need the comfort of your presence," said the queen,
holding the bed curtains so Mary could crawl in first.

"I should be honored, Your Grace," said Mary, climbing in. "I
have not forgotten how warm and cozy your bed is."

"Would that it were this night," said the queen, moving in beside
Mary. "Parry, close the curtains, won't you?"

As the curtains pulled tight around them, Mary felt, for the first
time that evening, safe.

"Child, will you rub my back? I ache all over," said the queen, turning with her back to Mary.

"Yes, Your Majesty. Do not fret—Lord Hunsdon will not fail you. He is your cousin, after all, and as such, he cannot fail," said Mary, her voice soft and soothing.

"I pray you are right, Fawn. Oh, that feels so good . . . yes, there, across my shoulders . . . I feel as if I have been like Hercules, carrying the world on these thin shoulders. Perhaps you should go someplace safer," said the queen.

"I shall not leave you, Majesty. My place is with you and I am safe enough at your side," said Mary, rubbing the hard knots with great tenderness.

"You are a good child. I am blessed, indeed, to have my Fawn, my Spirit, and my beloved Eyes. Even if the Queen of Scots tears my flesh to ribbons, she will never have the kind of love I have had with you and Sweet Robin—our little family," said the queen.

"Majesty, I have made a sleeping cordial—would you like to try it?" said Mary.

"That is just the thing I need—ring for the serving wench to fetch it," said the queen.

Twelve

*S*ee how I tremble—*it has not stopped since Durham Cathedral. By God's heart, I do not allow these arms to show their weakness to any but you, Parry. I hold myself still when my ministers are near—they would think me but a weak woman, should I shake thus.*

But I do have fears, fears I dare not speak to another living soul. No, not even you. They say Norfolk has not left Kenninghall—that is a surprise, yes. I would have thought he would join his army as they march from Durham, but it is rumored he has not moved.

If I were planning a rebellion, I should think it prudent to join with my army. But I am not Norfolk—who knows what evil he plans, safe in his castle . . .

I am happy to have my Sweet Robin at my side—without him, I would have given way to my terror. His sword, ready at my service, is a great comfort. Do not worry, Parry, you are a great comfort, too.

Shall my reign end now? Is this the way I shall die? Captured by the queen I now hold captive? My father would spin in his tomb to see the Tu-dor dynasty end so. I have kept England safe from war these ten years. God's blood, those advisors do not see my achievement—they think it some sort of idle luck or magic that a woman has ruled thus. Now, they will clamor more stridently than ever for me to marry, to make a tie with some great prince who should protect us against rebels.

I shall not do it! I shall not! I have no taste to marry Philip of Spain or the French king! Nor Eric of Sweden nor the Archduke Charles! I will not have any of them! If I cannot have my Rob—

I shall not give way to tears, madam, do not fear.

If the Queen of Scots should marry Norfolk and, together, they march against me, what would she do with me? Make me a captive? Never! For my living and breathing would be her death! She would send me to the Tower. Would she dare execute me? An anointed queen?

And if so, would it be the axe or would she order a swordsman from France? Think you history can repeat? Oh, my thoughts turn to death. I once said to my Privy Council that I cared not for death, for all men are mortal and I have good courage. Now, faced with it, I find I have not the courage I thought I possessed.

Yes, I have felt such fear before, once. Do you remember when Fawn was but eight and she caught the smallpox? How I nursed her myself, spooning warm broth into her mouth, her lips dry, the skin curling around the edges? She was covered with those running sores, those horrible pustules, and I dot-ted each one with a salve of aloe and chamomile. Her forehead blistered in beads of sweat and I thought she would surely die.

But she did not die. Instead, I caught the dreaded disease myself; I al-most died. I was so close to death I could feel his icy grip on my spine and, Parry, I was sore afraid. I prayed to God that I should survive, for the sake of my country and my little Fawn. How my councillors must have prayed for me, too, especially when I named Rob as Protector of England. Cecil and Hunsdon were not happy with those words but I did not care—I knew Rob was the only one I could trust with my beloved country, the only one who shared my love of peace. I knew he would see to our Fawn, as well as keep the north country in line. Oh, I entrusted him with everything and left no doubt in the world of my feelings.

Do you recall that November, after Fawn and I had healed, though we were still weak, Rob fixed a picnic for us inside the Great Hall? He had made trees of logs with green cloth for leaves, soft, mossy velvet for the grasses of the meadow, a bright yellow sun hanging from above. The whole place seemed alive; he even brought a couple of birds to settle on the branches of the trees. How we laughed! It felt good to laugh, after looking death in the face. Fawn and I played with our hair, which was hanging loose on our shoulders. I tipped my head over so she could have my red curls and then she tipped her head over so I could have her thick black locks. And then I had the idea to make rings of our hair. Rob took his knife and cut a long strand of mine and an equally long strand of hers. I wove the two together, red and black, black and red, into one tight braid, and then Rob cut it into two pieces. I made a ring for Fawn and a ring for me.

"This shall always be a sign of our bond, dearest Fawn. If ever you have need of me, send me this ring and I will come to you and I will help you," I told her. Her eyes shone as she took the ring and put it on her small finger.

I still have mine, yes—it's in the small casket along with other treasures, gifts from Rob, my mother's necklace. I do not think Fawn still has hers. Children do not keep such tokens. They are, after all, mere trifles. No, I cannot sit still. I must pace and pace until my heart stops beating like the drums of war.

No, Parry, I cannot eat or rest unless our Fawn gives me her sleeping cordial. I would rather be in the field with my brave soldiers than to wait here, pacing and waiting, wondering what is happening.

Yes, yes, I will take another cordial. Bring it to me. Dear Parry, what would I do without you . . . and those few who do love me.

Thirteen
December 1569

By Christmas, the queen's great Northern Rebellion had been quashed. When Hunsdon's army went to meet them, the rebels scattered. For some unfathomable reason, the Duke of Norfolk never joined his army, though he had ample opportunity. Without such a leader, fear of the queen's wrath ran through the rebels and they dispersed. Norfolk quickly gave himself up and was put under arrest in the Tower, the Scottish queen was safely back at Tutbury, and those rebels who could, had escaped across the Pennines into Scotland. Others merely melted back into the rough north, disappearing into the mists. However, Sussex routed several hundred and gave them a traitor's death. The rotting bodies of rebels dotted the small villages in the north, stark warning to traitors everywhere.

In London, the relief was evident in the lavish Christmas celebrations and in the usual flocking to court of lords and ladies from all corners of the realm.

"I shall be glad when Christmas Eve comes to mark the final day of our fasting," said Mistress Eleanor as she handed the queen's night-gowns and shifts to Mary, folded and stacked to go into the linen press.

"We shall have gooseberry tarts to our heart's content," said Mary, carefully placing the queen's most private garments on the shelf.

"And marchpane and stuffed peacock and manchet spread with creamy butter," said Mistress Dorothy.

"And no more fish!" said Mistress Frances.

"We can all breathe again now that Sussex and Lord Hunsdon have removed the threat against us—I thought our lives forfeit just a month ago. Cowering and hiding in these apartments, too afraid to venture a step away from the Gentlemen Pensioners and their swords, the queen ill as an angry hornet. Thanks be to God those days are behind us," said Mary.

"Did you hear what the queen said to Lord Hunsdon? She was all smiles for him when he brought her news of how he routed the rebels. 'I doubt much, my Harry, whether that the victory were given me, more joyed me, or that you were by God appointed the instrument of my glory; and I assure you that for my country's good the first might suffice, but for my heart's contentment the second pleased me.' And then she gave him a goodly portion of Northumberland's holdings. Sussex also grew in wealth for his part," said Mistress Eleanor.

A manservant entered the queen's chambers and walked toward the ladies.

"Which is Mistress Mary Shelton?" he said.

"Here, sir," said Mary.

"The queen sends for you—she is in the Presence Chamber with several of her gentlemen," said the man.

He bowed and left. Mary glanced in the looking glass on the queen's silver table and patted her hair, smoothing it beneath her

French hood. She straightened her sleeves and pinched her cheeks. She ran her fingers in the olive oil kept for such purposes and moistened her mouth.

"I will be happy when the queen no longer requires me while she is meeting with her advisors—talk, talk, talk!" said Mary, laughing.

"I cannot imagine why she calls you to these meetings—you are not going to be *queen* of anything, except the jakes," said Mistress Eleanor.

"Well, perhaps I am—you may kiss my hand now, mistress, and do a very low curtsy!" said Mary.

"I shall bow, O great mistress, but you shall have the backside!" said Mistress Eleanor, bending over so her bottom was in the air.

"Then I shall backhand it!" said Mary, swatting at her.

"I shall get you for that!" said Mistress Eleanor, giving chase. Around and around the chamber they ran, pulling the other two ladies into their game. Soon all four were batting at each other, running and laughing.

"Stop! I must be off or Her Majesty will have my head!" said Mary. She hurried out the door before the others could catch her. Walking more slowly, she fixed her hair again and straightened her skirts. When she arrived at the Presence Chamber, she told the guard who she was. He opened the door and stepped inside.

"Mistress Mary Shelton," he said in a loud voice.

Mary saw many gentlemen talking in clusters as she made her way toward where the queen was sitting. The queen saw her and motioned her to sit at the pillow near her feet.

"Oh, my Fawn, you look as if you have been on a merry chase this morning. Come. I want you to observe how I manage these," said the queen as she opened her arms to indicate the buzzing crowd of courtiers.

Mary sat on the large pillow and looked around. She recognized Sir John Pakington and Oxford. Lord Robert knelt on the other side of the queen while Master Cecil stood slightly behind the throne. Most of the men were strangers. Mary noticed Sir James Croft's son-in-law immediately as he talked with Sir James. Her heart leaped and she quickly looked down. When she raised her head, she could not help but gaze at him again. She caught his eye and he returned her stare. He did not turn away. She lowered her eyes.

"We have much for which to thank our God this Christmas, have we not, Fawn? He has delivered us from civil war," said the queen, smiling.

"Your Majesty, though we have won this skirmish, I fear the war will not be won until the Queen of Scots is given the traitor's death she deserves. She is the fount of all discontent and I fear she will remain so as long as she lives," said Master Cecil.

"Dear Spirit, let us leave off speaking of our doom this day as we remember Christ's birth. Allow us to celebrate a little, will you not?" said the queen.

"As you wish, Your Majesty—but in the New Year, we shall have much to discuss," said Master Cecil.

"Tut-tut, tut-tut," said the queen.

Mary watched as Sir James and the handsome young man— Adonis, she silently named him, remembering the queen's comment about his beauty—made their way to the queen. Sir James bowed deeply, as did the young man. Mary watched him as he leaned over. He was not as young as she had first thought, for she saw tiny lines at the corners of his eyes. His hair shone in the morning sun streaming through the windows. She still thought him quite handsome, even at a close distance. There was something about his manner—calm and assured—that she found appealing.

"Majesty, you remember my son-in-law, Sir John Skydemore, from Holme Lacy of Herefordshire. He is newly come to court to study law at the Inner Temple and is looking for rooms at the Inns of Court," said Sir James.

"Welcome to Hampton Court, Sir John. We can always use another man who knows the law," said the queen, offering him her hand to kiss. Mary watched as he did so with great grace and affection.

"Thank you, Your Majesty. Already I am dazzled by the beauty of this palace. Never have I seen the like. And your own beauty, if I may say so, matches very well your surroundings," said Sir John.

Mary had heard many men say such things to the queen. Oxford frequently discussed the queen's merits, using flowery language and overblown style. But the words from this Sir John seemed sincere. The queen must have thought so, too, because she was smiling at him.

"And this is our dearest cousin, Mistress Mary Shelton," said the queen.

Mary looked up at Sir John and found him bowing to her. His smile was like the sun breaking through clouds; it warmed his entire face and those around him. Mary discovered she was returning his happy look and felt her face flush. He took her hand to kiss, and when his lips touched her skin, she shivered. His lips were dry and soft and his kiss as gentle as the fluttering of a butterfly.

"I can see the family resemblance—two beauties set next to all this finery is almost too much to bear," said Sir John.

"Then I suggest you shield your eyes," said the queen.

"I said 'almost,' Your Majesty, 'almost,'" said Sir John, still staring into Mary's eyes.

She held his stare because his eyes were unlike any she had seen. They were a strange mix of blue and green, pale. They seemed lit from within. A darker rim held in that bold color, emphasizing it. She felt as if she could look into those eyes forever; they were mesmerizing.

"As you may recall, Your Majesty, Sir John is my son-in-law," said Sir James.

"Yes, yes, Sir James—I do recall," said the queen.

Mary realized she was still holding his hand and dropped it immediately. Though she had known of his marriage before, she felt suddenly bereft at the news. Why she should care whether or not this courtier was married was beyond her—yet, she did care. She cared a great deal.

"My dear, departed daughter left him with five young children who are at Holme Lacy with my wife," said Sir James. "I fear I shall never get over the loss."

"I am sorry to hear about your daughter, Sir James. And your wife, Sir John. The Lord giveth and the Lord taketh away. Blessed be the name of the Lord," said the queen.

"Amen," said Sir James, taking his son-in-law by the elbow and bowing once again as the queen indicated they were to make way for the next courtier.

Mary kept her eyes on Sir John. A widower with five children. Not the sort of man she intended to marry. She blocked him from her mind. The queen had plans for her; in her future lay great events waiting to happen. She refused to be bothered by a minor noble with five mouths to feed. The queen had groomed her for greatness. Yet, those eyes, those amazing aqua eyes. Mary felt goose prickles rising on her arms.

The next morning the queen and her ladies went in procession to the Chapel Royal to hear not one but three Christmas Masses. The people of London crowded in to see their queen as they did each Sunday, falling to their knees as she passed. Mary was used to this give-and-take between the queen and her people. She watched as the queen stopped to accept a bunch of dried flowers from a small child.

"Thank you, sweetkins. These are lovely," said the queen graciously.

"For when you be sick—the smell help you feel better," said the child. Others crowded around the queen, one handing her a tattered bag with a few coins jingling within, another a warm loaf of bread.

"My good people, I thank you with all my heart," said the queen, waving to them before she moved on. A little farther down the walk-way, she lifted her arms and said, still walking, "God bless my people."

The crowd responded with cheers and shouts of "God save the queen!" Mary was proud to walk behind such a sovereign and watched as the queen bound her people to her with love.

As they entered the Chapel Royal, the queen went to her private box while her ladies stood outside. The choirboys sang with heavenly voices. Mary looked out over the crowd of worshippers and saw Sir James Croft and his son-in-law. Sir John was dressed in a green dou-blet that seemed to influence his eyes, making them turn a deeper shade than they had been earlier. He was watching the queen's box and she felt his eyes on her, though she knew he shouldn't be able to see her. She immediately looked at the queen's trailing skirts and took care not to step on them. When she raised her head again, she saw Oxford across the way, smiling at her. She gave a slight nod.

The tapers were lit and the sweet smell of beeswax filled the chapel. Mary listened as the priest read from the Gospels and the Psalms. His voice droned on and on, almost putting her to sleep.

Soon, the service was over and the queen paraded back to the Pres-ence Chamber where she welcomed her courtiers. Mary stood behind the queen, while Her Majesty sat on her throne, speaking with Sir Christopher Hatton and Lord Hertford, along with Master Cecil and Leicester. When each man spoke to the queen, he knelt until she gave him leave to rise. Mary smiled, thinking they looked like the mario-nettes she had seen in Cheapside, bouncing up and down. Mary caught movement from the corner of her eye, and before she could react, Ox-ford had joined her. He stood very close, bowed, and wished her a happy Christmas. Luckily, the queen crooked her finger, motioning Oxford to kneel in front of her.

"Our dinner will be sweet this day," said Mistress Eleanor into Mary's ear.

Mary nodded. She watched as various courtiers moved about

while the musicians played. Several choristers sang and, for a moment, the queen stopped her talk to listen.

Then, Mary saw Sir John Skydemore enter with his father-in-law. He had a cloak of deep green slung across his shoulders, shoulders that looked as wide as the doorway. He carried himself with ease, met and mingled with the other courtiers quite naturally, as if he had always known them. Mary caught his eye upon her and turned toward Mistress Eleanor.

"After we dine, the queen has requested a play for us—she says she will take a part in it herself. Then, dancing and music," said Mistress Eleanor. "Will you sing?"

"If Her Majesty asks it of me, though I would prefer not to show myself among all these fellows. Singing to Her Majesty as we go to sleep is one thing—in front of everyone is quite another," said Mary.

Sir John made his way to her and bowed.

"Mistress Mary, happy Christmas!" he said.

"And to you, sir," said Mary, curtsying slightly. "My friend, Mistress Eleanor Brydges."

"Ah, Eleanor . . . that was my late wife's name," he said softly. "Master Nicholas has already sung your praises to me, lady. I find he does not jest."

Mistress Eleanor blushed and Mary felt suddenly jealous. Then, her better sense prevailed and she smiled at her friend.

"Since I am a newcomer, would you two ladies care to show me around the gardens? I have heard it said the queen has flowers even in the dead of winter," said Sir John.

"That she does," said Mary, taking the arm he offered. On his other side, Mistress Eleanor did the same.

The threesome walked from the Presence Chamber through one of the doors to the cold outside. Mary pulled her false sleeves around her, like a shawl. She placed her hands inside a warm muff made of fox fur. Sir John pulled his cap down over his head.

"This wind is blowing bitter—I fear I shall have to leave you, as I cannot bear it," said Mistress Eleanor, withdrawing her arm from Sir John's. "Do forgive me."

"We shall not be long away, Nora. For the cold is bitter, indeed," said Mary.

Mary and Sir John walked farther into the gardens. The hedges were still green but the grass was brown and tinged with light frost. They approached a small glass building and Mary indicated for Sir John to open the door. Once inside, boldly colored flowers filled the shelves of the room.

"This is wondrous! I have never seen the like," said Sir John.

"Yes, it's quite amazing, isn't it? Dr. Dee calls it a 'green house,' though I don't know why he doesn't call it a house of glass. He designed the construction of it and selected the flowers from his time traveling in Europe. He gave instructions to the queen's gardener about how to care for these delicate blooms. Some are even from the New World—like this one. Isn't the white flower pretty?" said Mary.

"I have heard of the famous Dr. Dee. Perhaps I shall meet him while I am at my studies," said Sir John, sniffing a large red blossom.

"His library holds over four thousand books—I have not yet seen it but have heard about it from Her Majesty," said Mary.

"So you like science?" said Sir John.

"Yes, especially the study of the stars and the night sky. And Dr. Dee knows about the layout of the earth and where each great country lies. He wishes for England to navigate the world and become an empire. And he is an alchemist and a scryer and—" said Mary.

"You enjoy ideas! That much is clear," said Sir John.

"Is there a reason I should not? Surely you do not believe that because I am a woman, my head should be empty of everything but children and house chores," said Mary, her face reddening. She thought of Tom Wotton and his taunts. And then she thought of his kisses.

"I believe a woman should think about what she will. I, too, am intrigued by the study of science. That is one of the reasons I have come to London—I would learn more about this world before I am called upon to leave it," said Sir John.

"You won't be leaving it soon, I hope," said Mary.

"I have learned one can never know when that moment will come—we are never ready for it," said Sir John.

Mary saw a look of sadness pass over his features.

"But this is Christmas Day and I am in London looking at flowers in full bloom with a beautiful woman! Let us make merry!" said Sir John.

"You do not have to hide your sorrow from me. I understand such grief. I lost both my parents within two weeks—the sweating sickness. But, though I lost them, my life has been blessed. The queen became my guardian—she's like a mother to me. And I have lived here with her since I was but three," said Mary, looking at him.

"Then you *do* understand," said Sir John, staring into her eyes. "Thank you."

They stood for a silent moment and Mary thought the air had become thick and too warm. She removed her hand from her muff and smoothed her hair. She smiled up at Sir John.

"Shall we return to the Presence Chamber? The queen will miss us before too long," said Mary.

Fourteen
New Year's Day, 1570

The dinner for New Year's Day filled the halls of the palace with delicious odors: roast boar, baked pastries filled with mincemeat and spices, rich cakes and confections, tarts and other sweet delicacies. The queen ate in the Presence Chamber where she entertained important guests. The citizens of London were allowed to watch the meal from special galleries installed for that purpose.

Mary and Mistress Eleanor, along with the queen's other ladies, waited while the tablecloth and salt cellar were carried into the chamber. Trumpets and kettle drums announced the entry of each dish. The servers bowed three times to the currently empty throne beneath the canopy of estate.

"Come, mistress, we must place the cloth upon the table now," said Mary as she walked to pick it up. She and Mistress Eleanor spread it over the table and then Mistress Frances and Mistress

Dorothy placed the food on the table. Countess von Snakenberg, dressed in white silk, followed Mistress Anne Cecil, who had recently been created a maid-of-honor, as Mistress Anne held a large tasting fork in front of her. The countess bowed reverently to the empty throne and then rubbed the plates with bread and salt. Then Mistress Anne offered "the assay," bits of meat from each dish, to the guards to eat to make certain there was no poison. The ladies left after their duties were completed and everyone waited for Her Majesty to appear.

Mistress Eleanor leaned over to speak in Mary's ear.

"I see Sir John Skydemore of Holme Lacy is invited to dine with us today," she said.

"And I see your Master Nicholas is not here. Did the queen neglect to invite him?" said Mary.

"He was called home—his father is ill. I hope he shall return by the Feast of the Epiphany," said Mistress Eleanor.

"I'm sorry. I know you would like to spend the festivities dancing with him," said Mary.

"There are others—there are always others. Remember that, Mary," said Mistress Eleanor.

"I find my attentions cannot shift from one to another as easily as yours do. I have not found any to my liking since the queen sent Tom Wotton from court," said Mary, suddenly aware she had been staring at Sir John the entire time she had been conversing with Nora.

"Are you certain? Your eyes seem to have found something to like," said Nora.

Mary straightened.

"Pffft! Untrue! But look, here comes the queen," she said.

The trumpets and drums played again, and this time the other musicians joined them. The guards shouted, "Make way for the queen!" and the crowd separated as if the queen were Moses and they, the Red

Sea. Lord Robert walked directly behind her, then came a few of her ladies.

"Happy New Year's Day! Ah, my good Master Cecil, how fine you look in your new suit. Such a lovely wine color, and if you make a spill, it should never show!" said the queen, laughing. Master Cecil bowed and smiled.

The queen sat at her table and selected a few choice pieces of chicken, some greens from a sallet, a thick slice of manchet spread with marmalade, and a glass of lightly brewed beer. She then waved her hands and the ladies cleared the dishes away, sending servants to bear them to the Great Hall where the court would eat after the queen had finished dining.

Meanwhile, the courtiers and ladies chatted while the musicians played a new piece written for the occasion by Master William Byrd.

"I see the queen is broad of mind when it comes to her musicians," said Sir John Skydemore as he approached Mary and bowed. She gave him a brief curtsy.

"What is your meaning? The queen is liberal with all her subjects," said Mary.

"I meant only that Master Byrd is a known Catholic and has enjoyed Her Majesty's protection upon occasion," said Sir John.

"Her Majesty has often said she has no desire to look into men's souls, sir. Are you one of those Puritans who wish to bend the world to his own way?" said Mary.

"No, mistress. I am merely surprised, after the recent unrest in the north, that Her Majesty tolerates any Catholics at all," said Sir John.

"You will find our queen is most gracious—those who were not involved in the Northern Rebellion should not be punished, no matter their religious views. Only the guilty deserve death," said Mary, her head turned resolutely away from him.

"You are a most remarkable woman, mistress. Would you care to sup with me?" said Sir John. He continued to look at her—she could feel his stare and she faced him again.

"I should be most happy to do so," she said, her heart beating fast.

The queen finished her meal and called for the subtlety, an enormous creation representing the royal arms in marchpane. Everyone applauded as three manservants carried the confection to the queen's table. Her Majesty waited for them to cut her a large piece and then proceeded to eat. She dismissed her court, indicating for Lord Robert and Mistress Blanche to stay.

Sir John offered Mary his arm, which she took carefully. She could feel his strong muscles holding her own arm easily. She caught a whiff of his scent—he smelled like yew trees mixed with a manly odor, not strong or disagreeable, just a sharper odor beneath the fragrance of yew.

A large crowd walked toward the Great Hall. Mary noticed Mistress Eleanor walking with Oxford. She was laughing and his arm caressed her waist. But his eyes, his weak, watery eyes were on Mary.

After dining, the courtiers and ladies awaited the queen for an evening of revelry. The musicians played several saucy tunes, the words of which were too indecent for the ladies to hear, let alone sing. But the men called for ale and drank, then sang and drank some more. Several played at dice while others challenged each other in chess or cards. The ladies chatted and a few were busy with their needles. Every woman was surrounded by four or five men, or so it seemed to Mary. She thought how hard it was to keep one's virtue in such a situation.

Finally, the queen arrived. She and Lord Robert led the dance, beginning with the daring la Volta. Mary watched as Lord Robert lifted the queen higher and higher, often touching her very near her most private places to get his leverage. Mary had never danced this particular dance with a man. She and the other ladies had practiced it in the queen's chambers, but only Lady Essex and Mistress Frances had performed the dance for the queen. But Lady Essex had been sent home to her husband months ago and the queen had not called for the dance since.

"I would ask you to join me in the dance, but I fear this one is beyond my skill. Would you care to walk outside instead?" said Sir John.

Mary was grateful he had not asked her to dance and she quickly assented to a stroll under the night sky.

"Look! A falling star! Make a wish, quickly!" said Mary as she closed her eyes and wished for good health for Her Majesty.

"What did you wish for, Mary?" said Sir John, standing very close to her.

"The queen's health. And you?" said Mary.

"I wished for someone to fill up the hole that is in my heart," said Sir John.

Mary gazed up at him. In the dim light, he looked young, but the sadness that hugged him like a heavy cloak clung to him, making him seem older than his years. Somehow, this made Mary tender toward him.

"How long has it been since your Eleanor died?" said Mary very softly.

"A little over two years—it seems a lifetime some days. But on others, it seems as if I heard her voice only yesterday. I am sorry. This is not what I intended . . ." said Sir John.

Mary stepped away from him and gently picked up his hand and kissed it.

"I fear there is no cure for your pain, Sir John. You put a brave face on it, but I know that ache only too well. I fear you and I have a streak of sorrow in our natures that, perhaps, was not there before we lost our loved ones. And while we may wish for the joys we could have had, now we must accept our sadness and allow it to work through our spirits. For with this grief comes compassion for others who suffer. And with compassion comes love, which Our Lord commands. There will be a happier time for you, sir. Tears may last all the night but joy cometh in the morning," said Mary.

"You are very kind, mistress. I hope this means we shall be friends. Please call me John," he said.

"We *are* friends. And you may call me Mary," she said.

Silence fell between them but there was no discomfort in it. Mary felt as if she had known this man her whole life. She felt his strength and sensed his tender heart. And she felt the pull of his body on her own, something she had never before experienced. She was actually leaning toward him.

Before she realized what she was doing, she embraced him, her arms around his neck and her face against his chest. She could feel his beating heart and hear his quickened breathing. His arms wrapped around her and they stood together without speaking.

Finally, he pushed her away from him.

"I hear them playing a country jig. Shall we give it a try? Just out here, where no one will see us," he said.

"I would be happy to attempt it," she said. They embraced and he spun her quickly around. Though they had never danced together before, their bodies moved as if they had always been joined in motion.

As winter gripped London, the Thames froze hard enough for the queen to ride her carriage across the ice and a Frost Fair was held on the river. Mary and Mistress Eleanor made their way from Richmond Palace where the queen had moved her court after celebrating the New Year. Pebbles were strewn across the slippery paths for traction but the foot traffic had worn them down and now the way had become treacherous.

"Do not let me fall. I had no idea this path would be so slick," said Mistress Eleanor as she held on to Mary's arm.

"If you fall, I'll go down, too. But smell the gingerbread baking—shall we buy a piece?" said Mary.

"That must be the stand over there—see, where all the people are lined up?" said Mistress Eleanor.

"Truly, I have not seen so many on the 'regular' streets of London—this strange Frost Fair brings them out. I suppose it is the novelty of shopping on a frozen river," said Mary.

The two ladies made for the small stand where several large ovens stood, and watched as the baker brought forth steaming gingerbread in enormous pans. He took a knife and cut the bread into large squares. A boy, his apprentice, stood at the front of the stand, singing out, "Gingerbread! Hot gingerbread!" and handing pieces to those who had given the woman in a dark blue woolen dress a farthing.

People of a humbler sort allowed the queen's ladies to step to the front of the line. Holding the hot gingerbread in their gloved hands, Mary and Mistress Eleanor walked away while biting into their treat.

"Delicious! Better than we get at court!" said Mistress Eleanor.

"Oh, it *is* really good. I am going to tell the queen about this baker—he should *be* at court!" said Mary who headed toward a small wooden crate. She picked it up, emptied it of what dirt was inside, turned it over, and sat down.

"Do you see another box?" said Mistress Eleanor.

"No. We can take turns," said Mary, finishing her food and brushing the crumbs from her hands. "I hope I haven't stained these gloves—the queen gave them to me."

"She'll give you another pair. She keeps you dressed royally. The rest of us are jealous, you know," said Mistress Eleanor.

"You aren't jealous when I must attend those infernal meetings in the Presence Chamber with all those serious old men," said Mary, smiling.

A voice thundered behind them.

"Old men? Old men? What old men?" he said.

Mary turned to see Sir John Skydemore coming to join them, his face serious but his eyes looking full of mirth.

"Old men like you!" said Mary, laughing.

"I suppose I do seem old to such a child as yourself," said Sir John. "I am but twenty-eight."

"It is your serious manner that makes you seem old, Sir John. Many of those older than you act like braying donkeys. You, however, are modest and mature," said Mistress Eleanor.

"You make me sound quite dull, mistress. Do I seem so to you, Mary?" he said.

"Well, when you *are* dull, I simply introduce a new topic for discussion—that seems to bring out the life in you," said Mary.

"I had hoped to invite you to visit Mortlake with me this afternoon, as Dr. Dee has asked me to come by to discuss astronomy, but I suppose that might be too *boring* for such a lively lass," said Sir John.

"Mortlake! Honestly! Oh John, I would love to go! You know that," said Mary, rising from the crate.

"Well, then, I shall meet you in the Great Hall at three o'clock. Do dress warmly—it is quite a walk," said Sir John.

"Have no fear—I shall wear my heaviest cloak," said Mary. She watched as he bowed to them, then walked away, almost slipping on the ice as he rounded the gingerbread stall.

"You have been keeping secrets from me—I think you care for him!" said Mistress Eleanor.

Mary said nothing. Then she grabbed her friend's hand and pulled her onto the ice.

"Let us skate, Nora! Let us slide like slippery eels," she said as the two young women slid onto the path, laughing and gasping for breath all the way to the palace.

*T*he sun glinted off the mounds of snow that had been shoveled in order to make a path wide enough for those on foot as Mary and Sir John made their way to Mortlake. Mary's cloak flowed behind her, billowing out like an ocean wave, the fine green velvet the color of the sea. Sir John walked beside her, carefully holding her elbow in case she should slip. He was much taller than she and his long strides caused her to half skip, half run to keep pace with him. Finally, they came to a long house which looked as if rooms had been added again and again.

Sir John knocked on the heavy wooden door and it opened immediately. A young serving woman looked at them, motioned them to hurry inside, and shut the door quickly against the cold air. She took their cloaks and hung them on a wooden peg next to the door. Then she brought them to a blazing fire in a large hearth. Mary stood with her back to the flames, feeling the delicious warmth crawl up to her hair. Sir John faced the hearth and rubbed his hands together.

"Ah, my friend, I see you have arrived. What? And brought a pretty girl with you?" said Dr. Dee, dressed in black robes and carrying a large book in his hand.

"May I present Mistress Mary Shelton. Mistress Shelton has an avid interest in science and I thought she might enjoy seeing your instruments and, especially, your magnificent library," said Sir John, presenting Mary.

She curtsied to the famous scientist and was rewarded with a smile.

"I am pleased to be able to show my toys to such a lovely maid," said Dr. Dee.

"And I thank you for allowing me to see them. The queen has often spoken of your work and how much she admires your great learning," said Mary.

"Shelton, Shelton—ah, yes! I remember now, the queen's cousin. I cast your chart for Her Majesty . . . and you have an interest in the sciences?" said Dr. Dee.

"Yes. I have studied all the subjects beloved by Her Majesty— Greek and Latin, mathematics and astronomy. The queen has seen that I have received a very good education—the New Learning, she calls it," said Mary.

"Though it be very old," said Dr. Dee, chuckling to himself. He turned to open a door to the hallway.

"Come along then. I shall show you my sanctum sanctorum," said Dr. Dee, leading them down a dark corridor.

"I hope we shall emerge alive," whispered Mary.

"And not be changed into frogs," said Sir John, his hand on her waist.

After much winding, finally they entered an enormous room filled with books. A large window allowed in sunshine and Mary stared, her mouth open.

"There must be hundreds, nay, thousands of books here! Look! Here is a book of maps—that is the New World, is it not?" said Mary, pointing at a large leather-bound atlas that lay open on a large table.

"That it is, and here is where I suspect a passageway might be, allowing us to sail around to Russia. We are here, in tiny little England—yet I believe that if we can rule the sea, we shall spread our great England all over the world—an empire," said Dr. Dee.

"I do not believe that shall ever come to pass—Spain and Portugal send their ships and priests to the New World and they are gaining all the booty. Poor England cannot compete with such great powers, I fear," said Sir John.

"That is true for now. However, I have seen in my glass what the future holds," said Dr. Dee. "Here are some instruments of navigation you might find of interest." Dr. Dee pointed to several strange apparatuses lined up on the long table. Mary watched as Sir John and Dr. Dee discussed and examined each. However, she did not hear what they said. She was too busy thinking about Dr. Dee's glass and how it could portend upcoming events. She wondered if she might see into her own future.

"Dr. Dee, can you explain to me about your magic crystal? The queen said you look into it to see what is to come?" said Mary, interrupting their talk.

"Yes, child, though I do not understand the workings of the thing just yet. I shall bring the ball hither," Dr. Dee said.

Mary watched as he disappeared into a dark closet. She listened as he fumbled around, then heard an "ouch." Finally, he reappeared holding a golden sack. As he walked toward her, he removed a large, clear globe. He polished it with the gold cloth and beckoned Mary to come to him.

"This is a crystal in which, if you look long enough, you shall see something—I cannot predict what, nor can I predict if what you see will be true. I am not certain as to the method by which the future is transmitted—I do know that every object exerts some sort of force on every other object. That is how the stars and other heavenly bodies influence humanity—they are large objects and thus have a large influence," said Dr. Dee. "Would you like to try it?"

"Absolutely!" said Mary.

"Absolutely not!" said Sir John.

Mary turned to him.

"Who knows what demons you might raise using that thing," said Sir John.

"If Dr. Dee deems it safe, I do not see any cause for *you* to be concerned," said Mary, her face flaming with anger. "God's teeth, you have no rule over me! I shall do as I please."

"I do not wish to be the cause of discord. I shall put the crystal back in its sack," said Dr. Dee.

"No! My dear Dr. Dee, I am cousin to the queen and have been educated in her household. I have no fear of science—I wish to see what may lie ahead for me. I have talked many times with Lord Robert about such things and he, too, has told me of the power of this orb," said Mary. She looked defiantly at Sir John. His lips pursed, he did not speak.

"Well then, let us try it," said Dr. Dee.

He carried the ball to a table on which stood a wooden stand to cradle the globe. He carefully set it in the stand and told Mary to sit across from the crystal. He then pulled the shade over the window, darkening the room a little. Mary stared into the glass.

"Do not tell us what you are thinking, but think of a question you might wish to have answered. No, do not speak! Now, relax. Let your bones relax and your mind float, unfettered. Keep thinking of your question. We shall be silent. Do not move your eyes from the crystal. Quiet and soft, quiet and soft . . ." said Dr. Dee.

Mary stared into the ball. At first, she saw nothing and wondered what the men, especially Sir John, were thinking. She concentrated on her question. She wanted to know who she was going to marry. It seemed a silly conceit, a subject which would interest any girl her age. Yet she could not help her curiosity. Who one married often meant whether or not one would be happy or miserable. She had seen enough of poor matches made at court. Leicester, the queen's favorite, had been unhappily yoked to Amy Robsart before her untimely death. Now, it was rumored he had an interest in Lady Douglass Sheffield, since Lady Essex had been banned from court; even the queen herself was miserable, unmarried, but in love with Lord Robert. Even Her Majesty could not find a suitable match.

Yes, marriage meant everything for the future happiness of a maiden.

Soon, Mary forgot about the men standing beside her. She forgot about the thousands of books lining the walls. All she could see was the globe and what she thought she saw within it.

A house, made of red bricks and standing on a little hill, meadows and forests surrounding it, a slate pathway leading to the front door. A woman. Herself? The woman seemed older, yet there was definitely something familiar about her. The woman grew clearer and it was, indeed, herself. Then, dismounting a fine steed, a man. His face? His face? He turned and Mary could see him. Pale green-blue eyes and a somber countenance—Sir John! He embraced the woman and kissed her—a long kiss of possession.

Mary jumped and the image disappeared.

"What did you see?" said Sir John. "You turned as pale as the snow outside!"

"Nothing . . . I saw nothing . . . I fear the queen will call for me soon—it is almost time to sup," said Mary, her mind in a whirl. She gave Dr. Dee her hand, which he kissed gently.

"Do not be a stranger—I like your courage," said Dr. Dee.

"Thank you, sir, for opening your wonderful home to us," said Sir John as he escorted Mary down the dark hall once again. She grabbed her cloak and wrapped it around her, barely able to contain her need for fresh, cold air—air that would shake the vision she'd seen from her mind, a vision that had frightened her to death.

Mary and Sir John headed back to the castle in silence. Twilight was falling and the stars beginning to twinkle in the darkening sky. The golden lights of fires and candles could be seen in the houses along the riverbank, great torches flaming on the outsides of the larger homes. People moved quickly, shouting greetings to neighbors and waving. Mary's foot slipped and Sir John moved to steady her, but she shook him roughly away.

"I am quite able to traverse this path by myself," she said, her words sputtering out in short, curt syllables.

"Mistress Mary, stop. Please," said Sir John, halting in the middle of the path.

"What do you wish, sir?" she said.

"Have I offended you? Have I done something to anger you?" he said, holding her by the shoulders, forcing her to look at him.

"God's blood! Did you think to contradict me as if I did not know how to conduct myself? What business was it of yours if I wished to scry in the crystal?" she said hotly.

"Dee deals with forces unknown to man. He is a scientist and has great knowledge. You do not. I was trying to protect you should any evil take place. It is only natural I should wish to keep you from harm," he said, staring at her with his beautiful aqua eyes, his mouth a small line.

"And why, sir, should you behave in such a 'natural' way? I am used to doing much as I please and will continue to do so. There are many wondrous things in this world—am I to ignore these because they cause you discomfort? I think not!" said Mary.

"I thought we were friends. Is it not a part of friendship for one to look after the other?" said Sir John, still resting his hands on her shoulders.

"Yes, as long as such care does not interfere with the other's growth. If we are to be friends, you must show me the same respect as you show your other friends. Because I am a weak woman does not mean I lack good sense. Look to our queen! There is a woman of great wisdom who rules with gentleness and mercy," said Mary.

"I agree, though the hangings in the north were, perhaps, less than merciful— No, no, she is a good woman. If I overstepped my bounds, I beg your forgiveness," Sir John said.

"Very well, I shall consider it. Look! Another falling star! Wish quickly before it goes," said Mary.

"I wish to kiss you, Mary Shelton," said Sir John.

He moved his hands from her shoulders to her waist and pulled her to him. She did not resist. He searched out her lips, cold and shivering, and covered them with his own. After a brief moment, he released her. She gazed up at him.

"I wish to pay court to you, Mary. Woo you with the idea that, as we get to know each other better, we shall marry," said Sir John.

Mary looked into those strange pale eyes. She could see his sadness, his loss. And, while the idea of him courting her was appealing, she read his heart there, in his eyes. She knew she must refuse him, though it pained her to do so.

"You are not ready, my dear friend. I would you serve only me, not the memory of another. When your heart has healed, then you may pay me court. Though I warn you, the queen has plans for me. So study law and wring out all your tears. For if I love you, I want to be the only woman in your heart," said Mary.

"How can one so young be so wise?" said Sir John, smiling at her.

"By eating gooseberry tarts!" said Mary, running away from him. He followed her.

Sixteen

Late January 1570

The rift between the Scottish Catholics and their strident Protestant brothers had grown greater after Mary, Queen of Scots, lost her crown. The Catholics assassinated the Earl of Moray, the ruling regent, in an attempt to put Mary back on the throne. James, her son, was just a boy; he could not hold his throne unless he had help—English help. But Elizabeth dared not send an army, for such an act would bring the wrath of France down upon England like the fall of an axe upon the neck of a traitor. Any interference might end with France, then Spain, then the Holy Roman Empire declaring war on Elizabeth, a war she did not want nor one she could afford. Her closest advisors, Cecil and Dudley, were in agreement for once; they both counseled war.

"God's blood, gentlemen! Can you not see the dangers? Can you not understand why we must keep the peace?" shouted the queen, her voice rough-sounding. Mary sat to the side, half listening to the ongoing arguments. Thoughts of John Skydemore crept into her mind, no matter how often she tried to shoo them away.

The queen rose and walked over to where Mary sat at the window seat observing. Her embroidery hoop hung limply in her hands, the needle tucked carefully into the linen. She had perked up, especially when the queen roared her oaths.

"What say you, Mary? You are fresh to the business of government—perhaps a new outlook is what we need," said the queen, staring at Mary.

"Majesty, I have no wisdom in these matters—everyone here knows more than I," said Mary, keeping her head down. She had seen the queen's anger before when a maid had spilled food or drink, and she did not want to be on the receiving end of such wrath. Her face burned as she felt the men stare at her.

"Now, child, we all know you are new to this game. But your queen has asked for your opinion—you must give it," said the queen, her voice coiling like a snake about to strike.

"Well . . . then, I should do nothing as of yet. I should wait to see how the wind blows. The Scottish queen's supporters may come to naught. If they act, then would be the time for Your Majesty to answer them," said Mary in a soft voice.

"Aha! A mere child gives me better advice than all the learned men in my kingdom! By God's teeth, wait I shall! Now, on to other business," said the queen, walking quickly to her throne and gesturing for Master Cecil to bring her the papers she needed to sign.

Mary pulled her sewing needle from the cloth and began to stitch. The blue thread was bright and just right for the peacock's feather she was about to create. She was relieved the queen had nothing further to ask her. She breathed a long, slow breath.

"How does one so young, so naïve, gain the queen's ear?" said a voice.

Mary looked up into the face of the Earl of Oxford, who stood before her in a fine blue doublet with white satin peeking through the slits. His cap was in his hands and he was making a slight bow. His lips curled in an odd way, as if he were making his mouth obey the command to smile.

"Believe me, sir, I have no desire to advise Her Majesty on any issue of state. My realm is determining what sleeves the queen should wear with what kirtle," said Mary.

"Why does the queen allow you, a mere girl, into meetings regarding the state? This is a new behavior on her part and, to speak frankly, the gentlemen do not like it," said Oxford.

"Her Majesty wishes for me to understand how our court works. She tells me she is going to make me a fine marriage, and I need to understand important matters so I can help my husband and England. I have expressed no interest in such knowledge of my own accord," said Mary, taking another stitch.

"Ah, such a pretty girl. Just to whom is the queen going to match you? A prince, perhaps?" said Oxford, sitting down beside her on the window seat. His leg touched hers. Mary scooted away from him. "If Her Majesty has plans for you, I should make my own desires known to her. I have much to recommend me for the position of husband: rank, money, polish. I wonder how the queen would take to the idea of you marrying me. I wonder who else she might have in mind . . ."

"I am not interested in her marriage plans, truth to tell. I much prefer science and playing the lute to thinking about marriage," said Mary. She looked at the earl. He was not as handsome as Sir John, but he was very well dressed. And he was close to her in age—not some doting old man. Perhaps he would be better than whomever the queen had in mind. However, though Oxford swore he wished to court her for marriage, he continued to flirt with the queen and every one of her maids. With those who allowed it, he went much further than mere flirtation, according to Mistress Eleanor.

"Would you play and sing for me, milady? I should like nothing better," he said. Mary could feel him staring at her as she stitched.

"If, of an evening, the queen should like to hear me play and you are in the room, then, yes, I shall be delighted," said Mary.

"I fear I shall never hear you, then. For the queen wishes to play and sing herself—she will never allow one of her maids to shine in the presence of the sun itself," said Oxford. He reached up and touched a tendril of her dark hair that had escaped from its caul. He held on to the strand, curling it around his finger.

"You hair is soft as the down of a gosling—would that I could run my hands through it," he said.

"My lord Oxford, please. You are disturbing my sewing," said Mary, though she could barely speak. She felt her face grow warm. The earl was so skilled in the ways of love—she had watched him dancing with ladies several times and admired his abilities. Could he be trusted? Did he truly wish to marry her? Or was he trying to ruin her virtue? Why was he here with her, twirling her hair in his hands?

"I hope to disturb more than that, mistress. And, if your pretty blush is any indication, I have done so," he said.

"If I blush, sir, it is because the fire has warmed the air too much. I shall ask the queen's leave to take a walk in the gardens," said Mary, standing.

"Would you like for me to walk with you?" Oxford said.

"That will not be necessary, sir. I have my dog, *Tom*, and *he* is a quiet companion," she said.

A Fortnight Later

The ground had been covered with snow for weeks, but finally, a thaw had come and the snow was almost melted except for a few piles remaining in shaded areas. The continuing gray skies and cold weather seemed to seep into the very stones themselves. In the Privy Chamber, several ladies-in-waiting busied themselves with cards and sewing. Mistress Frances strummed a lute that needed tuning while Mistress Dorothy slowly dealt cards to herself and three others. Mary and Mistress Eleanor danced together, trying to stay in rhythm to Mistress Frances's lute.

"By all the saints, I shall go mad! Let us go to Paris Gardens to see the bears!" shouted the queen as she entered the Privy Chamber with no fanfare. She had dismissed her guards and strutted about the room as if she were on fire.

"Come! Come, ladies! You shall all accompany me—it is time to show myself once again to my people. And, if old bear Sackerson doesn't kill at least one mastiff, I'll pay you all four groats! Come!" said the queen.

The women put down their cards and instruments, their sewing and dice, and quickly helped the queen put on her blue velvet cloak and heavy woolen hose, rather than the silk ones she preferred while indoors. They applied her whitening powders and rouge, lining her eyes with kohl and her lips with distilled cherry juice. They pulled her hair back into a bun and brought out her blue hat with the white feathers. Then they dressed themselves, having just enough time to wrap up in cloaks and hats.

The queen's barge pulled slowly through the Thames, which was thick with slush and greenish-gray in color. Mary and Mistress Eleanor shared one of the upholstered seats in the open air while the queen sat in a little cabin on luxurious silk and satin pillows. The queen had pulled the door shut while she and Lord Robert enjoyed a moment of privacy. Cannons boomed and bells clanged as usual, announcing the queen was on the river.

The courtyard where the bearbaiting took place was not as crowded as Mary had seen it in warmer weather. Those who wished to place bets were doing so, while a few small children chased each other around the arena. The queen, who usually watched such spectacles at Whitehall, rarely traveled to Paris Gardens to enjoy the sport. However, as on most occasions when she ventured forth in pubic, she did so with great ceremony. This day, she was content to walk next to her Master of the Horse and keep attention to herself at a minimum. Of course, everyone watched her. The crowd cheered and threw their caps into the air when they saw the queen's retinue approach. Mary was happy to see that though the troubles of the realm worried the queen, her people held her in the highest regard and seemed to have not a care.

The ladies and a few of the Gentlemen Pensioners followed the queen and Lord Robert, tramping through the dirt paths, still partly frozen but thawed enough to ruin the hems of the ladies' gowns. Mary tried to gather up her skirts but she could not prevent a spattering of mud. The queen and Lord Robert climbed to the royal box while the rest of the ladies milled around below.

"I do not like these bearbaitings," said Mistress Eleanor, as she shielded her eyes from the cold glare of the winter sun. "It seems cruel to force the creatures to fight one another."

"Yes, but at least the bear usually lives—the bullbaiting is worse for the dogs kill the bull and then he is roasted. Luckily for the bear, we have no use for his meat," said Mary, placing her hands in her muff of fox fur.

"I wish I had remembered to bring *my* muff," said Mistress Eleanor, shivering a little.

"I shall share mine with you. Look! They are bringing in old Harry Hunks—I have seen him fight the dogs before and he is very strong. One swipe of his paw can knock a dog senseless," said Mary.

A man entered the arena leading a large black bear by a chain. He staked the bear in the center and walked to a gate behind, where several Lyme mastiffs growled and snarled. He opened the gate to allow one dog to escape. The hound barked loudly at the bear, then began to circle the chained beast. Then, suddenly, the dog leaped onto the bear and bit down on the animal's nose. The dog clamped its jaws shut tight and the bear roared and tried to dislodge the dog.

"Come, Eleanor, let us weave our way through this crowd and walk a bit. I do not like to watch, either. I wonder that the queen is fond of such sport," said Mary, linking arms with Mistress Eleanor. "I suppose it is because her father, the king, enjoyed every sort of contest, whether between men or beasts."

"Do I smell hot apple codlings?" said Mistress Eleanor.

"Yes! Don't they smell wonderful! Cinnamon, perhaps a pinch of nutmeg—oh, something hot will warm us a little," said Mary, as she and Mistress Eleanor approached a woman standing in front of an oven with a tray of baked apples in pastry still steaming.

The young women stood in the small line that had formed and Mary listened as the onlookers shouted encouragement to Harry Hunks.

"Mistress Mary? Can it be?" said a familiar voice behind her. She turned to find herself face-to-face with Sir John Skydemore and he held a wooden trencher filled with hot codlings. Mary inhaled the sweet fragrance. She could not help the smile that spread across her face, nor the quick beating of her heart.

"I am happy to see you, Sir John. You have been away?" said Mary, at once shy with him, remembering their last encounter at Dr. Dee's home.

"Yes. I had to return to Holme Lacy. One of the children was sick and my oldest son needed to be reminded of the importance of obeying his tutor. It is hard to be away from them, knowing they do not have their mother's care. My own mother was recalled to her duties at home, and now I have procured a nursemaid to care for them," said Sir John, offering her and Mistress Eleanor an apple.

"Thank you—oh, they are hot!" said Mistress Eleanor, wrapping hers in the edge of her cloak.

"I can imagine how difficult such absences must be for you," said Mary, carefully biting into the apple. She tasted the warm flesh of it and the somewhat tender peel. She noticed the tops had been sprinkled with sugar.

"It is just as hard being away from court and my own studies," said Sir John. The threesome walked farther away from the crowd, finding a pocket of privacy beneath the branches of an oak tree.

"I trust you did not fall too far behind. What are you learning this term?" said Mary.

"Rhetoric and English common law. But my favorite subject is the history of the church—I find it fascinating," said Sir John, leaning against the tree trunk.

He explained how he was surprised to discover there had always been dissension in matters of religion, even among the Church Fathers. Now that dissension was fomenting again, this time among the extreme Protestants, the Catholics, and those who tried to make a middle way between the two, the Anglican Church itself, the queen's church. As he continued, Mary could see he took these questions of religion, ideas to which she had given scarce thought, quite seriously. Then he spoke the words that made her quake inside.

"If you wonder why I find all this ancient history of interest, it is because I am Catholic, Mary," he said calmly, without fear.

"Shh! Someone might hear you! Do you not know how dangerous it is for people of your beliefs, especially after the recent uprising?" whispered Mary.

"I have no reason to fear—I am the queen's true subject; she knows that. My entire family, along with Sir James, keep the old ways. Because of my service, and that of my father-in-law, she turns a blind eye to my faith," said Sir John.

"I am sure she does. Yet many of her 'true' subjects are held in yon Tower," said Mary.

"There must be other reasons. Perhaps some have spoken out in public against the English church. I do not speak against anything; I quietly go about my way, serving the queen as best I can," said Sir John.

"But how can you *believe* such things? You are an educated man! Do you truly think some splinter of wood is from the cross of Christ? That statues of the Virgin weep blood? This is superstitious nonsense," said Mary, repeating what she'd been taught by her tutors.

"Perhaps these are tricks used to persuade the ignorant multitude of the veracity of God's word. Or maybe some need a visual representation to remind them of that which is invisible. As for me, I am not opposed to new ideas or new interpretations. But I find great comfort in the familiar rituals of the Mass," said Sir John.

Mary grew quiet. She enjoyed debating these issues with her tutors and fellow students, where it was safe to take any side, knowing they were all in agreement for the most part. But in the middle of London, to talk about such things with a Catholic man who did not seem aware of the danger his beliefs brought to him was something else. The debate was frightening to her. This was not a man with whom she could dare to share a friendship. She had seen the queen in a rage over the smallest thing; she could not imagine Her Majesty's ire if Mary entertained a Catholic man who had already told her he wanted to court her.

At the beginning of her reign, the queen had hoped to allow each subject his own beliefs, so long as he obeyed the laws of the land and showed himself loyal to her. She did not want to burn pyres at Smithfield as her sister, Queen Mary, had done. But as time passed and Cecil found plot upon plot devised by Catholic malcontents, the queen had been forced to deal more harshly with religious dissenters. Mary could name a handful of devious men who had been clapped into the Tower for continuing to worship as they pleased. She shivered slightly and turned to Mistress Eleanor, who had been standing to one side to give them privacy.

"I think the poor dog has been killed. They are taking the bear out and now come the horses, with monkeys riding them! I am amazed those monkeys ride so well," said Mistress Eleanor, who had been watching the bearbaiting from a safe distance.

"Mistress Mary, I have enjoyed our talk. I hope we shall meet again soon to discuss this and other matters of interest," said Sir John. He bowed to both women and strolled over to join Sir James Croft and a circle of other men.

"We should return to the queen," said Mistress Eleanor, taking Mary by the hand.

I hear tell the queen hopes to marry one of that French queen's sons," said Old Catspaw as she brought freshly pressed linens to the queen's bedchamber. Mary and the other ladies could not believe the woman was alive after all these years, yet still able to serve the queen. Catspaw's hair was as white as the linens she carried, her body bent over so that her spine seemed to be coming into itself. The few teeth she had left were brown and ragged, chipped and rotten. Mary could not help but shiver when the old woman passed by, though she was fond of her and knew Catspaw was wise in the ways of medicines and cordials.

"The queen will do as the queen will do—it is not up to such as *you* to question or gossip," said Lady Douglass Sheffield, newly appointed to serve the queen upon the death of Lord Sheffield, her husband. She had thick blond hair that curled when she let it down. As a widow, she was required to wear her hair beneath a net or in a bun, which made her look older than her years, for she was ten years younger than the queen, a pretty twenty-seven.

"Yes, Your Worship," said Catspaw, hobbling back to the servants' quarters.

"I do not know why that woman is still serving Her Majesty! She looks quite ugly," said Lady Douglass, peering into the hand mirror on the queen's silver table. She pinched her cheeks and smiled at her reflection.

"No one presses the queen's shifts and nightgowns so well as Old Catspaw. Her Majesty has lessened her work load, so she works only two days a week. And the queen has given her a couple of young maids to assist her," said Mary, putting the items in the queen's wardrobe while Lady Douglass continued to make faces into the glass. "Perhaps you could assist me?"

"I'm sure you can manage . . . what is your name again?" said Lady Douglass.

"Mary Shelton, cousin to the *queen*," said Mary, her tone as haughty as that of Lady Douglass. Mary glanced at Mistress Eleanor, who smothered a laugh with her hand.

"Humph. I shall try to recall that name. I shall take my leave of you now. Lord Robert has invited me to inspect the stables and select a suitable mount," said Lady Douglass.

"But who shall mount whom?" whispered Mistress Eleanor after Lady Douglass had left the room.

"Ha! But she is horrid! She does not do any of the work, but when the queen comes in, she makes a great show of serving Her Majesty and is the first to meet her needs. And how she bats her eyes at Lord Robert, her voice honeyed. I like her not!" said Mary, stacking the last of the garments on the shelves and bringing out the queen's new black gown.

"I think the silver sleeves with gold trim might look well with this. What do you say, Nora?" said Mary, spreading the sleeve out on the bed so they might view the garments together.

"Oh yes, the queen will be pleased," said Mistress Eleanor.

"Have you seen your young artist of late?" said Mary, now brushing the queen's black velvet cloak to remove any dust.

"Yes, he has asked me to meet him at the Shrovetide festivities this eve. He grows more demanding, though, with every meeting. At first, he wished only to kiss my hand. Then, he wished to hold my hand. Now, he is not happy unless he has kissed me many times on the mouth. He is like all the rest, though I have learned my lesson—I keep him at bay!" said Mistress Eleanor.

"Does this mean you have not kept others at bay?" said Mary, in a hushed voice.

"Do not act surprised—surely you must know that to be at court and keep one's virtue is almost impossible. If you do not know it yet, you soon shall. For you have caught the eye of the most notorious rake here!" said Mistress Eleanor.

"I have? You cannot mean Sir John Skydemore," said Mary.

"No, no, no. He is serious and *old*," said Mistress Eleanor.

"He is not *old*—just a few years older than I," said Mary.

"Well, he acts old. No, the one who has eyes for you is my lord Oxford. He has told everyone how he shall breach your walls and conquer you," said Mistress Eleanor.

"Humph. He says he wishes to court me, with the goal of marriage. But he has not mentioned his intentions to the queen. I do not think him an honest man," said Mary.

"Oxford is one of the queen's favorites. And, truth be told, he would be a fine match for you. I suspect the queen would agree, if he asked her," said Mistress Eleanor.

"This is not good news. For, though he is of noble rank, he makes me afraid," said Mary.

"As well he should. He has deflowered many a maid at court. He is well schooled in the ways of winning a woman," said Mistress Eleanor.

The trumpets and drums announced the queen's meal was on its way to the Privy Chamber.

"Come, friend, we are needed. Let us hope the queen will sup quickly so we can clear the tables and enjoy tonight's fun," said Mistress Eleanor.

The Great Hall at Hampton Court looked even more sumptuous as the men and ladies glittered in their finery. The queen glided into the hall on Lord Robert's arm, radiant and happy. The new black gown suited her, with the silver sleeves and kirtle accenting the rich damask dress beautifully. Pearls dangled from her ears, her hair, her skirts. Lord Robert looked especially fine, his green brocade doublet a good match for his dark coloring. Mary never tired of watching the queen and her Master of the Horse. She thought if two ever loved truly, these were they.

A large table set with goblets and pitchers of ale and wine stood to one side of the room, while directly across sat another table filled with trays of bread, meats, sweetmeats, and tarts of all kinds. In the center, a creation of marchpane in the shape of a nymph commanded everyone's attention. In the nymph's chubby arms was a bow and quiver of arrows. All those married knew that tonight would be their last night for conjugal bliss as the forty days of Lent commenced in the morning. Urgency and longing were palpable in the looks men gave their women. Mary wondered what it would be like to share such naked looks with a husband. She followed Mistress Eleanor to the tables.

"The queen has hung new Turkey carpets—look. There and there," said Mistress Eleanor, pointing.

"Yes, and the courtiers are all dressed in such exquisite dresses and jewelry," said Mary, running her fingers around the small pearls the queen had given her.

"Uh-oh. Do not look. The Earl of Oxford has spied you already.

He comes this way," said Mistress Eleanor, ducking behind Mary to grab a golden goblet filled with wine.

Mary watched as Oxford strolled over to her, his walk confident and a smile on his face. His pale blue eyes stared into hers with each purposeful step. She felt her knees weaken and suddenly she realized she was afraid. She could feel her body throbbing as he grew closer.

He removed his cap and bowed low so that the feather swept the ground. She returned a curtsy, minimal and brief.

"The lovely Mistress Mary—you are a sight for my weary eyes," said Oxford, easily rising from his bow to wrap one arm around her waist and lead her to a bench by the window.

"I thank you, sir," said Mary, sitting down. The place where his arm had touched her tingled and she could think of nothing to say. Her skills at conversation seemed to dissipate into the candlelit air.

"May I sit beside you?" he asked.

He was certainly behaving more politely than he had previously. Mary liked the way he was treating her, a little like the way Lord Robert treated the queen—as if she were a precious vessel and would break easily.

"Everyone is ready to dance by the look of their faces. For on the morrow, as you must know, we give up our earthly pleasures for forty days. For some of us, that is an unwelcome thought," said Oxford.

"Ah, but then the pleasures will seem so much sweeter when we do take them. I think the season not so much an exercise in restraint as in thanksgiving," said Mary.

"What pleasures will you give thanks for, milady?" said Oxford, his voice full of suggestion.

"For good food and good company," said Mary, watching as the queen clapped her hands for the musicians to play.

"I shall give thanks for women such as yourself—women with whom I would share more than a dance," he said, reaching for her hand.

She withdrew it at once.

"You take too much for granted, sir. God's blood, I have not agreed to share even this dance with you, let alone anything else," said Mary.

"But you are angry, mistress. What have I done? Merely complimented your beauty, and now I simply wish to dance with the most lovely woman in the Great Hall," said Oxford, rising and leading her to the dancing area. The musicians played a slow pavanne and he moved gracefully toward her, their hands touching. He smiled and made no attempt to hide the fact that he ogled her body as if she belonged to him.

Mary began to feel her body flush, as if the blood would warm her all over. She did not like the earl but was not sure how to be rid of him.

After the dance, he again took her by the arm and led her to a nearby portico. The torches blazed golden and the silver moon was full. Before she could protest, he pushed her behind a tall hedgerow and kissed her on the mouth.

"I have wanted to do that for such a long time, my Mary. I have dreamed of your sweet lips, your dark eyes that would drown me if I gazed into them too long," he said, pressing against her.

"*You* may have wanted to but *I* have not!" said Mary, pushing him away. His arms were strong and she could not move far from him.

"Do not think to refuse me, now that I have you here—your lips say one thing, but your body, oh, your womanly body tells me another. See? You are trembling," he said as he brought her to him and kissed her again. She felt his tongue moving in her mouth and she grew weak, so weak that she leaned into him. "Ah, that's it, my Mary. You want me and I want you—let us become one this night. Let me show you the ways of love."

"Sir, you have mistook me. I do not crave your kisses or your caresses. You once asked if you could pay court to me, with marriage as your goal. Yet you make no move to ask the queen about a possible match between us. It is clear to me that you only wish to besmirch my honor. God's bones, man! Bother me no more," said Mary, regaining her composure, pushing away from him.

"I have not mistook you, my Mary. For I know well how to read a woman. It is you who are deceived. But I will wait for you to come to me. And I know you will. No, say nothing. I will wait," said Oxford as he put his finger to her lips, bowed quickly, and left her standing there, quite out of breath.

She smoothed her dress and her hair. She counted to ten and took a deep breath. Then she counted once more. Finally, when she felt she could face the crowd, she walked from the hedges to the stone portico. Just as she began her journey across the tiles, she saw someone heading toward her.

"Are you studying the position of the moon and stars? For what else could you be doing out here all alone?" said Sir John, his tall silhouette like a shadow moving slowly before her.

"Yes. I thought to see Polaris," she said, looking up.

"There—see? The one at the end of the Plough—do you see it?" he said, putting his arm around her shoulders and pointing.

"Why yes, there it is. I thank you, sir. I should not have found it by myself," said Mary, her mind topsy-turvy.

"I am quite sure you could have found it! Why this sudden modesty? Or are you trying out your womanly ways on me?" said Sir John, laughing.

"I did sound rather like every other lady-in-waiting, didn't I? And not myself at all. Forgive me, Sir John," she said.

"There is nothing to forgive—I often find myself sounding like my grandfather! And, since we have agreed to be friends, you are to call me John, remember?" he said.

"I am not sure we can be friends, Sir John. We differ in our beliefs and *yours* are dangerous," she said.

"Surely two people who enjoy discussing astronomy and religion can be friends, even if they disagree. I swear to you my fealty to the queen and her rule. I do not support any other. Now come—I have danced up an appetite! Would you like to join me for some gooseberry tarts?" he said, smiling. "I know how well you like them!"

"I suppose it will not hurt to share a sweet—surely there is no danger at the table!" said Mary.

Mary couldn't help but like Sir John, though she was not certain the queen was as pliant as he supposed. He was not grasping, the way Oxford was; instead, he was sincere. An honest man. A man she could not help but admire. There was something about him she had a hard time resisting—as if they were twin stars. He exerted a pull upon her, so that she was not happy unless they were touching. She found herself leaning toward him before she had had time to think about it.

He took her elbow and guided her to the heavily laden table. She was very conscious of his touch against her arm and felt a blush warming her cheeks. Mary noticed Lord Robert was dancing with Lady Douglass and the queen with the newcomer to court, Sir Christopher Hatton. Hatton was an energetic partner, a good match for the queen. As she watched the couples swirl around the floor, she caught a glimpse of Nora and Master Nicholas. Nora was smiling gaily.

She looked over the crowd once again to see if Oxford was anywhere around. He was nowhere to be found. She sighed with relief.

*I*n the Presence Chamber, the queen sat on her throne and her councillors gathered around, standing in a semicircle before her. She had had the benches removed, and the men fiddled with their capes, their doublets, the hilts of their swords, their caps in hand, and generally looked like schoolboys ready to be scolded by the tutor. Mary and Mistress Blanche stood behind the queen, Mistress Blanche with a glass of watered wine and Mary with a napkin should the queen need it.

The queen held up her hand to call them to order.

"Our right loving lords, our faithful and obedient servants, we, in the name of God, for His service, and for the safety of this state, are here now assembled to His glory. I hope and pray that it may be to your comfort and the common quiet of all ours forever," said the queen in a loud voice.

Then she proceeded to name the laws she had changed to suit

them, laws that bridled her Catholic subjects more than she would have liked. It was now illegal to speak of the queen as a tyrant or heretic, illegal to post a papal bull in England, and all citizens must attend the Church of England at least once a month. The queen then spoke of a new threat from the King of France, who, it seemed, had taken up the cause of the Queen of Scots. He was insisting Mary be reinstated on her throne and Elizabeth assist her. The queen then explained she would help her cousin regain her crown, if Mary would do three things: first, ratify the Treaty of Edinburgh, giving up all claim to the English throne; second, maintain the Protestant religion for the peace of her realm; and lastly, retain the current lords in the governing of the country.

"Majesty, if Queen Mary is reinstated, should we not make provision that her son, young James, be educated in England? That would give us some control over her actions, considering a mother's natural affection for her child," said Master Cecil.

"This is a good idea, Your Majesty. She has shown herself to be a woman of loose moral fiber, someone who acts rashly. If we have possession of her son, it might temper her decisions," added Lord Robert, who had gone down on one knee.

"Well, then, add it, Master Secretary. I trust this measure will be the last we hear from my dear cousin. I, for one, shall be glad to be rid of her," said the queen. She indicated for Mistress Parry to pour her wine and drank quickly. Then she reached for the napkin Mary offered.

"Gentlemen, I do not know what else to do—I know many of you wish to support James and the Protestants in Scotland. But with the threat of war with France, we must at least *seem* to help Mary regain her throne. After the recent Northern Rebellion, we do not wish to give our Catholic citizens any cause to rise again," said the queen.

The queen then dismissed her council and turned to Mary.

"Ah, Fawn, how lovely you look—could you be growing more

beautiful each spring while I grow old and haggard?" said the queen, her eyes appraising Mary.

"Your Grace knows you are the one who is especially lovely this day—I have selected from among your most luxurious gowns the pale blue satin you now wear. And the white silk sleeves threaded with silver," said Mary. "How can anyone outshine the sun?"

"You have learned your trade well, my Fawn. I expect those silly geese—my other ladies—to repeat such nonsense to me, but never you. You are allowed to tell me the truth, at least a little of the truth," said the queen.

"I shall tell Your Majesty the truth," said Lord Robert, easing into their conversation. He dropped once again to one knee.

"And which truth shall this be, Sweet Robin?" said the queen, her fingers tickling his neck as she had done when she made him the Earl of Leicester.

"The truth is, we three have not picnicked in some long time. Let us go now—just we three and a couple of serving maids. The sun is shining, the day is warm—ah, Bess, I would hold you again in the fresh air of the countryside where we can cast off the burdens of state and take our pleasure in each other, and our little Fawn," said Lord Robert.

"Fawn is not so little anymore, or have my Eyes been deceived? She is a young woman now and, from what I have noted, the apple of many a young man's eye," said the queen.

Mary turned red and looked at her feet.

"See how prettily she blushes—no wonder Oxford moons over her," said the queen. "Dear Rob, I think a ride in the country should do us all good. Let us be off!"

Mary blushed more deeply. Had Oxford spoken with the queen of his intentions? Was he going to woo her for marriage? Married to an earl . . . that was quite a leap from her current station, even though she was cousin to the queen. Her father had been a mere knight, nothing more. How proud he would be, she imagined, to think of her marrying an earl.

Mary helped the queen change into her riding clothes, a pale green gown of silk with white satin sleeves edged in gold and her gold cap with the green feather. Then Mary selected her own dusky blue gown with silver sleeves and a deep blue–gray cap with a black caul interwoven with silver thread. Together with Mistress Blanche and two serving women, they walked to the gate where Lord Robert would bring their steeds.

As they waited, Mary saw Lord Robert mounted on glorious Caesar, leading two other horses and two mules. Beside him rode a courtier, though the sun shielded his identity. Mary was confused. She thought the picnic was to be only the three of them.

"Mistress Mary, I hope you do not mind—I have invited my friend the Earl of Oxford to join us," said Lord Robert, smiling his most dazzling smile.

"After I pleaded with him shamelessly," said Oxford, grinning at her.

Mary thought perhaps the queen would come to her rescue.

"If it pleases Her Majesty, then his presence is acceptable to me," said Mary glumly, trying to beam her thoughts to the queen by staring at her. The queen did not seem to notice.

"The more, the merrier! Come, Fawn, let us teach these gentlemen how to ride!" said the queen, mounting her horse and quickly guiding the beast through the gates and onto the open road.

Mary climbed onto her palfrey and followed the queen. She heard Lord Robert shouting orders for the servants to assist Mistress Blanche onto one mule and tie up the baskets of food and the blankets. A serving wench was to follow on the other mule. Mary felt sorry for the beast, forced to carry a person as well as heavy baskets of food and drink.

The queen rode as speedily as possible through the narrow streets of London until she passed through Aldgate, Lord Robert close behind her. He signaled the way, and off through the meadows they galloped. Mary tried to keep up, but she was not as good on a horse as was the queen. Oxford rode beside her, pulling her horse by the bridle when a small flock of sheep, heading into the city, blocked the dirt road.

"Have a care, mistress. Think not to apprehend Her Majesty. Let us keep safe and try not to trample any lambs along the way," said Oxford.

"But we do not know where Lord Robert is leading us. We must follow," said Mistress Mary, disturbed by the bleating and sea of wool beneath her.

"I know his mind on this—if we lose sight of them, I shall still be able to get us to the spot. Besides, those mules will be slow to get through this crowd, and *they* must follow *us*," he said.

Soon enough, the flock passed on and Mary could see the women on their mules coming up behind them. She and Oxford rode at a gentle pace, out over the meadows, toward the forest beyond. The sun shone pale yellow, the first warming rays of spring. The fields had begun to come back to life, bright green blades blending with the brown of winter. Small lime-colored buds showed that soon the trees would be filled with leaves. The air smelled fresh and clean once they had moved a goodly distance from the city.

As they approached the line of trees, Mary could see the queen and Lord Robert waiting for them. The queen spurred her horse and rode toward them at breakneck speed, her hair flying out behind her in red curls in spite of her cap. She was smiling and leaning over the horse's neck. When she reached them, she pulled up short.

"Come along, slowpokes! I am famished!" the queen said as she reined in her horse to join them. Her face was flushed and the usual crinkle in her brow had eased. She looked ten years younger.

"I must wait for Mistress Mary, Your Majesty. Else I would show you how to run your horse properly," said Oxford.

"Hah! I fear you would be shamed mightily, youngster! Hurry along, Mary! Have I not taught you to be a better horsewoman than this?" said the queen.

Without further prompting, Mary spurred her horse and took off with great speed. She kicked in her heels and the horse ran even faster. She could hear the queen and Oxford thundering behind her. She did not look back but kept her body low and whispered to her horse, "Run! Run!"

By the time she caught up to Lord Robert, Oxford was riding at her side with the queen slightly behind. Mary pulled in and Lord Robert helped her down. He then took the reins and led the horse down to the stream in the woods.

Oxford dismounted and assisted the queen. He then took both horses and joined Lord Robert. The queen shaded her eyes and looked to see where Mistress Blanche and the maidservant were.

"You rode well enough when you had Oxford to chase you," said the queen.

"I only wished to show Your Majesty my riding lessons had not been for naught," said Mary.

"Clever girl . . . How like you the Earl of Oxford?" said the queen, strolling slowly toward the men.

"He is a fair poet, I hear," said Mary.

"Oh, that he is, that he is. But as a man—what do you think of him?" said the queen.

"He seems to adore Your Majesty . . . Why do you ask these questions?" said Mary.

"If my eyes do not deceive me, I believe the Earl of Oxford is very interested in you, dear Fawn," said the queen.

"Has he spoken to you? Has he opened his mind to you?" said Mary.

"No, no—he has said nothing. I just observe how he watches you—like a cat eyeing a mouse. His eyes are greedy for you," said the queen. "But I have seen Oxford toy with others. Have a care, Fawn—remember, the single state is safest for a woman."

"Your Majesty is always wise," said Mary.

"Tut-tut. I just know how a girl's young heart can betray her. You must be careful, Fawn. You have grown very beautiful and the court-iers have noticed. There will be many who wish to have you to wife. Many more who would enjoy your pleasures and sully your good name," said the queen, stopping by a large oak tree and leaning against the trunk.

"I have done nothing to dishonor Your Majesty or her court. I am still as I was born—a maid," said Mary.

"Of course you are. I merely wanted to be certain you understand how very important it is to me that you remain so until I find a suit-able match for you. Oxford might be just the man; he is an earl, no less. And he is one of *my* favorites," said the queen, looking away from Mary onto the meadow.

"I have no feeling one way or the other for the Earl of Oxford, ma'am. I barely know the man. He seems as puffed up as the tail of a peacock . . ." said Mary.

"Peacock? Did someone say peacock? Is that what we are having for our dinner?" said Lord Robert, strolling up through the woods to join them, Oxford by his side.

"Look! Here comes Mistress Blanche with our food. Where shall we have her spread out the blankets and pillows?" said the queen, sounding like a young girl in her excitement.

The maidservant unpacked the mules and, along with Mistress Blanche, arranged the meal, setting out trays of cold venison, ca-pons, bread, and cheese. They had brought along the queen's gold plate and, for the first time, Mary ate from gold rather than pewter.

The goblets, too, were of gold and Mistress Blanche filled them with sweet malmsey wine for the women. The men drank tankard after tankard of strong ale.

"I must say, Your Majesty looks especially stunning in your riding clothes. But then, Your Grace is always as beautiful as the rising sun in the pale blue sky," said Oxford, wiping the grease from his mouth with a napkin.

"Thank you, my good earl. Mary tends to my clothes and often selects what I am to wear, with my permission, of course. As a matter of fact, Mary, I have it in mind to make you Keeper of the Books of the Queen's Clothes," said the queen. "How like you that?"

"Your Majesty, I am most honored. But is this not a task for a woman of more experience? Perhaps Mistress Dorothy, who has been in your service much longer than I?" said Mary.

"Nonsense! By God's eyes, you have the gift for it—much the way my own mother set the style, you, too, have the Boleyn refined taste—I should trust you much more than any other. And, such a post will add fifteen pounds a year—you shall have your own gambling money and shan't have to borrow from Parry when you lose," said the queen, laughing.

"Thank you, Your Majesty. I am greatly honored," said Mary, smiling. She noticed Oxford watching her.

After eating, the queen dismissed the maid from her duties and allowed her to return to the palace after packing up. Mistress Blanche withdrew and sat upon a pillow beneath an elm tree, reading from her new English Bible, a gift from the queen.

"Mistress, will you join me for a walk along the stream bank?" said Oxford to Mary as she leaned against her pillow.

"Majesty, would you care to join us?" said Mary, once again hoping her thoughts would be legible on her features. She had no desire to be alone with Oxford.

"I think not, Fawn. I should rather stay here and listen to my Sweet Robin sing. He has brought his lute," said the queen, looking very content as she rested her head on the large brocade pillow.

"That shall be my pleasure," said Lord Robert.

"Well then, much as it would please me to hear your Sweet Robin, Majesty, I should rather enjoy listening to Mistress Mary tell all those thoughts rumbling about in her pretty head," said Oxford.

"Go along, children. We shall see you anon," said the queen.

The earl offered his arm to Mary, who had no choice but to accept it. He led her down to the stream.

"Such a charming brook—listen, it sings as it moves over the rocks," said Mary, hoping to stay as close to the queen as possible.

"Yes, it says 'I will brook no wall to my desires'—much the same as my own song," said Oxford. He slid his arm around her waist and pulled her closer.

"Shall we see what lies on the other side? Look, there are boulders we could step on to cross," said Mary.

"As you command, mistress," said Oxford.

They crossed the stream with no trouble and wandered toward a large rock some distance from them. When they arrived, Mary sat to rest and the earl stood above her.

"May I join you?" he said, sitting beside her.

He sat very close so that the lower part of their bodies touched from hip to knee. Mary tried to scoot away from him but his arm caught her and pulled her to him.

"Mistress, I have dreamed of this—you and I together," he said. His pale blue eyes seemed to belong to another world, but the look in them definitely was of this earth.

"My lord, I have heard that you are a writer of verse—perhaps you could recite some for me," said Mary, pulling away from him. She did not trust him in these dark woods. She did not wish to fight him off like a bear at a baiting.

"You know well how to parry, mistress, for what poet could resist such a request. I do have some verses I have composed for you—if I may be so bold," said Oxford. He reached into his shirt and pulled out a piece of parchment.

"You have not committed the words to memory?" Mary asked, smiling.

"I have not finished writing the poem yet—it is new. But let me begin."

> *What cunning can express*
> *The favour of her face*
> *To whom in this distress*
> *I do appeal for grace.*
> *A thousand cupids fly*
> *About her gentle eye.*
> *From which each throws a dart,*
> *That kindleth soft sweet fire:*
> *Within my sighing heart,*
> *Possessed by desire.*
> *No sweeter life I try*
> *Than in her love to die.*

He stopped, waiting for her response. She said nothing. He fiddled with the edges of the parchment and finally placed it back inside his shirt.

"What . . . what do you think?" he said.

"It is not finished, you say?" she said.

"No—just barely begun. I was thinking of you, your beautiful brown eyes and how I seem to drown in them each time our gazes meet. I tried to capture how you make me feel . . ." he said, sitting down beside her again.

"It seems to me the poem does not discuss so much the *lady* as he who ardently desires her—it is more about desire itself. If I were to write a poem about someone I loved, I should make the poem more about that person, less about myself," said Mary. She did not look at him for fear he might kiss her.

"Yes! That is absolutely right! I do not know why I had not thought of it before—the focus should be on the lady herself," he said. "Now, look at me so that I may memorize each thing about you."

To her surprise, rather than stare at her, he closed his eyes. Then, gingerly, he put the tips of his fingers on her face, slowly moving across her features.

"There, the shapely lips I long to kiss," he said as he traced them over and over. "And here, the nose that turns up just a little. The eyebrows, arched and thick . . . so smooth. The cheeks, rounded and velvet-soft. Ah, the ears, little conch shells, whirls within whirls."

Mary could not move. No one had ever touched her this way. Her heart beat so loudly she wondered he did not hear it. Her face blazed under his touch. When he opened his eyes, he did peer into her own. She could not look away. He moved toward her and kissed her, a gentle kiss that lingered and lingered. Then, he pulled her to him, kissing her again and again. She felt powerless against him and was surprised to discover she enjoyed it when their lips met. She tried to think but could not. Her body had a life of its own and, although reluctantly at first, she returned his kisses. This seemed to inspire him. He forced his tongue into her mouth and she allowed him to explore her completely. She could hear his breath quicken and felt his hands move along her ribs, to her breast. She gave a little gasp as he touched her nipple, tugging and squeezing gently.

He leaned her back against the rock, putting his arm under her head for a pillow. His other hand was lifting her skirts.

"No! No! This cannot be," she said, sitting up abruptly.

"Why, my dearest? I can see that you want to love me as much as

I wish to love you," said the earl, still nibbling her neck, though he, too, was now in an upright position.

"The queen frowns on such behavior. She would dismiss me from court if I lost my honor. She has managed to keep the love of good men without giving herself to any," said Mary. Now, she stood and he stood beside her. He grabbed her waist once again and brought her near him.

"But you are no queen," he said. Before she could stop him, he kissed her deeply. She could feel his manhood against her.

"And you are no gentleman," she said. "I must return at once to the queen!" She pushed him away. When he released his grasp, she ran into the woods toward the stream.

"Mary! Wait! Please come back!" he shouted.

Mary continued to run, her heart beating furiously, her face aflame. Her clothes caught on brambles and weeds but she did not care. She knew if she stayed with Oxford, she would give way to him. She did not love him; she barely knew him. What was his power over her? How could she ever learn to keep such a courtier away and guard her dignity? How does the queen, herself, manage to govern her own desires and those of the men around her?

She hurried to where she had left the queen, hoping Her Majesty could give her advice. Oxford did not seem to be following her, so she slowed her pace and stopped for a moment after she had crossed the stream. She stilled her breathing and walked very quietly to the little clearing where they had eaten. She was just about to enter the area when she heard a deep sigh. She hid behind a large tree and peeked around.

Lying on the ground in her shift was the queen, with Lord Robert hovering over her, his doublet and shirt in the nearby grass. He was kissing her and she had her arms wrapped around his neck. Mary watched as Lord Robert ran his hands along the queen's body, pausing at her breasts, which he began to knead. Then Lord Robert lifted her shift over her head and the queen was naked beneath him. Just then, the queen rose up to meet him and Mary froze. The queen saw her, saw her without a doubt. Mary moved behind the tree again and began to tremble.

What was Her Majesty thinking? Could all the rumors about her and Lord Robert be true? Could she have been his mistress all these years? Mary shook her head, trying to sort it out. They had been like a little family—Lord Robert had treated her as his own child, as had the queen. She did not doubt their love for her, nor did she doubt the love they had for each other. But for the queen to give away her virtue? Could it be possible?

Mary could not stand there any longer. Very quietly, she dipped back into the woods and walked in a new direction. The last thing she wanted was to meet Oxford again. No, she needed to think. She needed to put the queen's words against Her Majesty's actions.

She needed to run and run until she could run no more.

Nineteen

By Christ's wounds, I did not expect Fawn to find me thus. Yes, I know I was foolish—it had been so long since I had held Rob in my arms—and that harlot, Lady Douglass—no telling if she had given herself to him or not. But when I rose up to hold Rob and saw Fawn there, behind the tree—you should have seen her face! She was pale as death and clearly shocked by the sight of us. Oh Parry, what is she to think, but that I am a hypocrite? I tell my ladies to guard their virtue, and yet Fawn has discovered I do not guard my own. No wonder she will neither look at me, nor speak to me unless I command it.

I know not what to do—should I tell her that I am still a maid and there are ways to be with a man that do not include giving up one's virginity? What sort of ideas might that put into her head? I would not have these dogs at court sniffing around my Fawn! God's blood, I am her guardian, her protector. I am to act in loco parentis, in the place of her parents. I am responsible for her virtue and I must ensure she makes a good marriage.

If only she knew the torment my unmarried state gives me! If only she could realize the sacrifices Elizabeth, the woman, has made for Elizabeth, the queen! How can I demand her obedience when now she sees me as a vessel for sin? How can I command her respect when she has seen me in my Sweet Robin's naked arms?

How can she know the way I ache for Rob? Has she ever loved a man? I think not! She is but a child in a woman's body. She knows nothing and I have not been any help to her.

Yes, yes, I see how Oxford pants after her. I shall send him from court immediately. I know, I know. I cannot send every man from court. But I would protect her, Parry. God's teeth, she has no idea what rogues these men can be. I would not give a fig for any of them—even my Robin's eyes wander. No, do not think to comfort me. I know he goes to Lady Sheffield for what he cannot have from me. She gives it willingly enough.

And I do not blame him. He loves me and has always loved me. I believe he shall always love me. I have not married him, lo, these many times he has begged it of me. I allow him a few of the pleasures of my body, but not everything. Not everything. He wants an heir. That he shall never have from me. So, let him sire a baseborn son or two. Where is the harm in that?

As for Fawn, talk to her, Parry. Make her understand. And remind her of the great love I bear her. I can still remember her little hand in mine, rubbing my fingernails as she slept, cuddled against me—child of my heart.

*A*fter Mary had seen the queen in Lord Robert's arms, she found it difficult to be in Her Majesty's presence. Each time she helped the queen dress or accompanied her around the gardens, she felt her face blaze with shame. Somehow, sharing such secret knowledge with the queen made Mary feel guilty, as if *she* had done something wrong. All those lectures she remembered the queen giving her ladies seemed laughable now. And Mary did not like the feeling she had that the queen was not quite as royal, not quite as elevated as Mary had thought her. Her Majesty seemed to understand these feelings, as she called for Mary less and less. Mary imagined the queen was ashamed and did not wish to be reminded of her sinful behavior by having to look into Mary's eyes. But, though Mary was disillusioned and disappointed with the queen, the comings and goings at court continued as usual, and soon the weather was right for the royal progress.

Because she needed something to soothe her nerves as she fretted over the queen's behavior, Mary asked Catspaw for a cordial recipe that would calm her. She hoped if she could brew something quickly, the queen might also be able to use it on progress. And, though there would not be enough time for the cordial to reach its fullest potency, Mary was convinced anything was better than nothing. Catspaw knew exactly what potion to brew, chamomile blossoms and rose petals, which she swore could calm even the most nervous creature. Mary had gathered the flowers and was in her little room, where the air was cool and a fragrant aroma gathered. She heard the usual kitchen bustle, feet running back and forth, cooks and washerwomen joking as they worked. She was straining the newly washed blooms when she saw a shadow fall across the entranceway.

"I see I find you experimenting—you look like Dr. Dee, poring over his laboratory instruments," said Sir John Skydemore. He looked a bit disheveled, as if he had hurried from one place to another. Mary smiled at him and he returned her kind looks.

"I suppose I am. Since we are leaving to go on progress soon, I wanted to try this new cordial—for calming the nerves," said Mary.

"Well, I understand the queen's progress can be a bit daunting," he said.

She nodded and continued to strain the flowers. After making certain they were clean, she spread them on a white linen cloth.

"I have been looking for you everywhere, Mary. Luckily, I ran into Old Catspaw and she told me where you were. I have something I would like to discuss with you," he said, suddenly seeming nervous.

"Oh? What is it?" said Mary, pressing another cloth over the petals.

"I wish to go ahead with our courtship. I must return to Holme Lacy tomorrow to see after the rents and some other things. And, of course, to see the children . . . I shall join the progress in a week or so. And, when I do return, I would like to speak to the queen about us," said Sir John.

Mary could not help but smile. Though she was not sure Sir John would suit the queen, as she looked into his eyes, she thought he would easily suit *her*. And she could trust that he was serious about his intentions. Unlike Oxford, who *said* he was going to speak to the queen but, thus far, had not, Mary knew Sir John would keep his word. He had such a sincere manner.

"Are you certain you are ready?" said Mary.

He took two long steps to her, wrapped her in his arms, and kissed her.

"Yes . . . yes, I am ready," he said.

The queen and her entourage set out for her annual progress in late May because the weather had turned unusually warm and a siege of summer sickness took hold of the city early. Her first visit was to Nonsuch Palace in Surrey, where the queen enjoyed hunting amid the rich forests and meadows. The whole court traveled with their mistress, though the long parade of wagons and heavily laden mules precluded a quick journey. Instead, the queen and her party slowly made their way through various towns and villages where Her Majesty would be welcomed by the local sheriff, the mayor, and aldermen who dressed in their solemn robes to hand her the ceremonial keys. Then, the people would line up along both sides of the narrow road, throwing flowers at the queen, reciting poems and singing songs in her honor. Often, the queen stopped everything to hear the song of a child or to receive a bag of gold from some poor widow who could scant afford such generosity. No matter what the gift, the queen accepted it cordially, with many waves and kisses to her people.

Although the queen lived in her usual splendor while on progress, her maids did not. Often, they were crowded together with the maid-servants of the house and sometimes they were stabled in makeshift tents. The queen loved being among her people and living lavishly at the expense of her courtiers; her ladies did not.

"At least we can enjoy Nonsuch—after that, we head for Sir Francis Carew's Beddington estate. I have heard there is no room at all there for us—we shall sleep with the kitchen wenches," said Lady Douglass, brushing specks of dust from her sleeves.

"Surely things will not be that bad—the queen does have a care for us," said Mary, washing one of the queen's shifts in a bowl of warm water. The queen had spilled a little wine on the edge of the sleeve, so Mary had taken it upon herself to try to remove the stain before the washerwoman came to collect the laundry. She looked out the window at the sprawling hills below, the forests fully green and the flower gardens showing off the colors of the rainbow—pink roses, purple columbines, pale green lilies—and Mary thought she had never seen anything quite so beautiful.

Though the queen and Lord Robert continued to enjoy hunting together, rumors were circulating about Elizabeth and the Duke of Anjou, that the queen would accept him as a candidate for her hand, though he was much younger than she.

"Old Catspaw has been spreading the news to anyone who will listen," said Mistress Eleanor, folding the lawn sheets to be fitted on the queen's bed later.

"That old bird has lost her feathers; she was ever a flibbertigibbet and now she tells such silly tales. The duke is twenty years younger than Her Majesty. Do you seriously think he would consider marrying such an old woman? And, she has that awful sore on her leg! She is aging fast and none the better for it," said Lady Douglass.

"The queen's leg will heal—it is an ulcer of some sort. Mistress Blanche has been placing warm compresses on it each night and rubbing an unguent of chamomile and aloe on it. Already, it begins to heal," said Mary, scrubbing harder on the stain. She wished she were scrubbing Lady Douglass's face.

"There is to be a grand dance tonight. Lord Robert told me to dress in my finest silks. Are you going?" said Lady Douglass.

"Of course. Where else would we be but at the queen's service?" said Mary.

"I shall wear my new black gown with cloth-of-gold sleeves and a pale green kirtle. Master Nicholas has said he wishes to sketch me tonight in the candlelight," said Mistress Eleanor.

"Humph. Sketch you, indeed! I know full well what he would like to do in the candlelight," said Lady Douglass.

Mistress Eleanor flushed all the way down her neck and looked at the floor.

"Perhaps you would know of such things, having been a married woman. As for us maidens, we have no such wisdom," said Mary, staring at Lady Douglass hard.

The women finished their chores and picked up their sewing.

"I shall wear my silver dress with silver sleeves—the queen has given me a new diamond necklace to wear as well. Would you like to see it?" said Mary, suddenly proud of her kinship to the queen, at least proud in front of this haughty woman.

"I have more important things to do, mistress, than to see what castoff the queen has tossed to her little dog. Lord Robert has asked me to go along on the hunt—I must ready myself," said Lady Douglass, rising and throwing her sewing hoop on the table near the queen's bed. She then swished out of the room, her skirts twirling about her legs.

"*I* want to see it, Mary—pay her no mind. Her head is as empty as Pakington's pockets," said Mistress Eleanor.

Mary rose and walked to the linen press. She reached deep within and pulled out her treasure box.

"Oh, the special box! I have not seen this in a while," said Mistress Eleanor, squinting to see inside.

"My treasures . . . I did not want to leave them behind when we went on progress, so I hid the box in here. Look! The necklace," said Mary, pulling out a small gold chain on which tiny diamonds glittered.

"It is beautiful—not gaudy like those heavy links Lady Douglass wears. It is delicate, like you, Mary. I think it's perfect for tonight. What is *that?*" said Mistress Eleanor, pointing.

"Oh, a silly keepsake—my hair woven with the queen's. She pledged her eternal friendship with this ringlet back when I was a child. But I kept it . . . such tokens of the queen's affection are rare and it means more to me than these diamonds," said Mary, replacing the necklace and closing the lid. She hid the box once again in the cupboard.

"My hope tonight is for Master Nicholas to sketch my portrait—and I pray he asks me to marry him. He promised to speak to his father about the match and then to write my father. I can see no reason for them to refuse us," said Mistress Eleanor.

"Aye, then I shall be forced to treat you as a refined married woman—I shall not be able to stand it," said Mary, laughing. "I shall tell you a secret—well, two secrets. Before we left London, Sir John Skydemore told me he was going to speak to the queen about courting me. I believe him to be sincere."

"That is big news, indeed! He is so very handsome, though his holdings are sparse. I fear the queen may not agree to the match," said Eleanor.

"Once I tell the queen that I am not opposed, surely she will allow it. But that is not my only secret," said Mary, hugging herself.

"Well, out with it," said Eleanor.

"The Earl of Oxford has also said he was going to speak to the queen. Though he has been saying it for many weeks now, yet he does nothing. Imagine! Marrying an earl!" said Mary.

"Oh, dear friend—you have not given way to him, have you? Oxford is notorious for making all sorts of promises to young maidens, then never following through. He will play you false. Though he is an earl, he is no gentleman," said Eleanor.

"I have kept my virtue, dear Nora. Though I had not heard this information before, in my heart I did not trust him. His eyes are not honest eyes," said Mary. "Truth to tell, I am not disappointed. I find Sir John much more to my liking."

"Come, I hear Her Majesty approaching. We must set the table for her dinner. I am happy to go a-dancing this eve," said Eleanor.

Mary felt a sudden breath of freedom. It was good to share her news about Sir John, and she was glad to have her opinion of Oxford confirmed. As she thought about the upcoming evening, she remembered her glimpse of the queen in Lord Robert's arms. Suddenly, she felt a lightness in her limbs—if the queen could live freely, then so could she. She would dance with every man who asked her; she would smile and enjoy the attentions shown to her by the courtiers. She would sparkle like the diamonds in her necklace.

"Mary, you have tired me out! Three galliards in a row and still you wish to dance. Come, let us have more wine," said Oxford as he took Mary by the hand and led her to the tables filled with ale and wine. He handed her a glass, which she drank down quickly. She, too, had worked up a thirst. She watched as the earl drained his mug of ale and then poured more from a nearby ewer. He gulped that down, too. Mary quickly finished her wine and took yet another glass. She noticed the queen walking toward her. She gave Her Majesty a quick curtsy. The queen leaned over and whispered in her ear.

"Dear Fawn, take care you do not imbibe too much drink—it

clouds the mind," said the queen. Then the queen chucked Oxford under the chin. "Have a care with my ward."

Mary's face burned with fury. She was not a child! She reached for her glass, gave Oxford a bold grin.

"I shall match you drink for drink," she said. She smiled at him and quaffed down the liquid. Normally, she followed the queen's custom of watering her wine and drinking small beer, but tonight she felt free and full of her own power. She had danced with every handsome man in the hall, and now the Earl of Oxford was partnering Mary with great gusto.

"This I should like to see, mistress! Come, let us catch some of the cool night air," said Oxford, once again taking her hand and pulling her along. She followed with no protest.

"The night is full of stars—and the sweet smell of roses. Or is that you, Mary?" said Oxford, nuzzling her neck, making a great show of sniffing her.

"I smell the roses, sir—but the scent comes from yon flowers, though I did bathe with rosewater and dabbed a bit of almond oil on my wrists. And, truth be told, I stole a little dollop from the queen's musk jar and placed it just here," she said, pointing to the space between her breasts. She could not believe she spoke with such boldness. She thought about Sir John, what she would do if it were he in the garden with her, rather than Oxford. She imagined his beautiful eyes, his sculpted body. She could not help but shiver.

"You are different tonight, Mary. You tempt me on purpose," said the earl as he leaned in close to smell her bosom.

"Why should I not tempt you, sir? You are a young man, handsome and witty. Why should I forgo enjoying you?" said Mary, her head spinning a little. She did not know why she said such things to him, except she kept remembering the queen in Sweet Robin's naked arms. If the queen could dally so, why should Mary not emulate her? This thought had been buzzing in Mary's head since she had discovered the queen's lewdness. Besides, the queen thought she could control Mary's every move; Mary was a woman full-grown. And she would prove it.

"Now you begin to sound like a courtier, indeed. Come into my arms, dearest. There you shall find a heart that beats as hotly as your own," he said, drawing her to him.

He kissed her and she allowed herself to respond to him. She raised her arms around his neck and leaned into him, their bodies touching from head to toe. She felt him rise and enjoyed the sense of power she had discovered. She imagined it was Sir John who kissed her. With Sir John in her mind, she was surprised to discover her body responding. Slowly, Oxford walked her behind the hedge, never stopping his kisses and moving his hands over her bodice. She did not flinch when he began to unlace the ribbons of her dress. Soon, he had loosened her bodice completely. She was up against him, her breasts free against his strong chest. He kissed her over and over, his hands reaching beneath her shift, touching her nipples and circling them with his palms. Then, he began to kiss her neck and her ears. She leaned her head back so he could reach her. Soon, she felt him pull her bodice over her head as she squirmed out of it. He then untied the ribbon at the neck of her shift and pulled it down past her shoulders, so that she was naked from the waist up. She felt his mouth on her chest, her nipples, her belly.

He panted and began to lift her skirts. At this, she stopped him.

"Milady, what is wrong?" he said, barely able to speak.

"I fear we go too far, sir. I am not . . . I am not ready for completion of the act," she said, breathless.

"But why, dearest? I promise you will not be disappointed . . ." he said, beginning to kiss her again. She could feel his tongue trace across her shoulders, then plunge down the crevice between her breasts. His mouth, warm and wet, was on her nipple again.

Suddenly, there was a movement in the bushes. Mary pushed him away and drew up her shift to cover herself.

"What goes on here! My lord Oxford, I suggest you remove yourself at once! Before the queen comes hither! Go!" said Mistress Blanche, her face white. She hurried to Mary and helped her tie herself back together. Then, she took her, none too gently, by the elbow and guided her to a side door into the darkened hall leading to the queen's apartments.

She did not say a word until they were in the queen's bedchamber. The fire burned in the hearth and a few candles lit the room. They were alone.

"Sit!" said Mistress Blanche, pushing Mary down onto a chair by the gaming table.

Mary plopped down, then stared at her feet.

"What in the world were you thinking? Edward de Vere is one of the most debauched men at this court. Yet, I find you almost ruined right there in the queen's gardens! Do you wish to bring dishonor upon the queen? Do you wish to cheapen yourself so you can never make a good marriage? Tell me! Tell me why you were acting so stupidly!" said Mistress Blanche in a cold, quiet tone.

"I suppose I was acting as the queen acts. I suppose I wanted to see for myself what love is all about," said Mary, growing angrier as she spoke. "Why should I forgo the pleasures of the Earl of Oxford when the queen takes pleasure with her 'Sweet Robin' all the time? Everything they say about her is true! She is lustful and a disgrace to Christendom. How dare she insist on the virtue of her maids when she has besmirched her own!" said Mary.

"I see. And how old are you, mistress?" said Mistress Blanche.

"Sixteen—of marriageable age," said Mary.

"And how old is the queen?" said Mistress Blanche.

"She is thirty-seven," said Mary.

"And do you not think a woman of thirty-seven knows better what she's doing than a girl of sixteen? If Oxford had had his way with you this night, what would you have done if a babe had been the result? *No one* would have you then. The queen would put you in the Tower and I would not blame her. You will note, the queen has not had any babes, nor will she. Yes, she may lie with Lord Robert, but she remains intact. She keeps her head about her and does not allow him full possession of her person. God knows what might have happened if I had not come along when I did!" said Mistress Blanche.

"But she is false! She tells her ladies to guard their virtue, yet she does not guard her own. She plays the whore for Lord Robert!" said Mary.

Mistress Blanche drew back her arm and slapped Mary across the face.

"You listen to me, you foolish girl! The queen has sacrificed everything for her kingdom. She knows she cannot ever marry—especially cannot marry the man she has loved these twenty years. She can neither bear his children nor share his bed. She cannot even live with him and enjoy the simple things—waking together on a sunny morning, sharing the joys of domesticity, bringing a child into this world— yet she loves him. And you, you who know *nothing*, you would judge her as a wanton. I suggest you think hard about all she has done for you. How she has loved you. The many nights she sang you to sleep, though the thorny problems of the world weighed on her. She has been as a mother to you in so many ways . . . she does not deserve your scorn," said Mistress Blanche.

Mary had never seen Mistress Blanche in such a state. Usually calm and kind, comforting and full of sweet words, the strange woman who stood before her seemed to have changed before her very eyes. Mistress Blanche admonished her to stay within the bedchamber and consider her words. Then she turned without another utterance and stormed out of the room.

Mary began to cry. She cried because part of her knew Mistress Blanche was right—she had been foolish, and she was lucky Mistress Blanche had saved her. She cried because she felt sorry for the queen and ashamed of her own thoughts toward Her Majesty. She cried because she wished she had been in the garden with Sir John Skydemore. And she cried because she did not know how she would ever face the Earl of Oxford again.

Twenty-one
July 1570

*A*s the summer grew hot, the queen's progress continued west, toward Gloucestershire, as far toward the Welsh marches as the queen wished to travel. Already the ladies-in-waiting were anxious to return to London, to the easier work of moving only a small distance from castle to castle along the Thames, where each of the queen's palaces had to be sweetened after a few weeks' time. The moves were expected in London, and carried out with precision by armies of servants used to such maneuvers, unlike this progress to the wilds of the west, where few people could accommodate the queen and her court, and the cumbersome loads took longer to carry due to poor roads. The ladies were tired of sleeping in cramped quarters with little comfort. The queen, however, demanded they be energetic and ready for all the festivities to be enjoyed on progress: hunting, dancing until midnight, walking through the forests, riding horses fast as the wind, attending plays and jousts, enduring the homage paid by the poor peasants and little children. The civilization found in London seemed truly a different world from this backward outcountry. However, though her servants were less than happy, the queen herself continued to be delighted by her people and the hospitality of her hosts.

The progress finally arrived at Gloucester where Sir Norris and his wife would host them for several days before they turned back in the direction of London. After a night's rest from their travels, the queen and her ladies were ready to take their pleasures in the new day.

"What fresh entertainments must we pursue today?" said Mistress Eleanor, as she cleared away the queen's dishes from breaking her fast. It was mid-morning but the queen, as she told her ladies, was not a "morning woman" and so their day's activities never started until after the midday meal.

"I understand there is to be a hunt and picnic in the glade afterward. Sir Norris has planned a great banquet of all the queen's favorites—lots of tarts and sweetmeats with quail and boiled cabbages. They say his baker makes the finest manchet in all the land—he mills and sifts the flour twenty times before he uses it," said Lady Douglass, sitting on a chair watching the others do their work.

"I wonder if we shall be included in the hunt," said Mistress Mary, gathering the tablecloths and handing them to the laundress who stood nearby.

"I hope not. It is too hot and I am always afraid I shall be shot by mistake—I have a hard time with the bow. If she forces us, I shall wear my crimson dress—no one will mistake me for a stag," said Mistress Eleanor.

"I enjoy the hunt. Her Majesty instilled a love for a hard ride and a quick kill when I was a child," said Mary. She whispered in Mistress Eleanor's ear, "And Nora, Master Nicholas has joined us at last. You can take heart at that news."

"Come along, then. Let us finish our work and join the queen on her walk in the gardens. I have heard Sir Norris has lovely roses," said Lady Douglass.

The afternoon was dreadfully hot as the queen gathered her courtiers around her.

"My friends, we shall hunt in pairs so no one will be lost in these strange woods. Lord Robert and I shall ride out together and the rest of you find a partner. No one is to go out alone. Blow your horns if you make a kill. One of my servants will find you and assist in bringing the meat home. If we are able hunters, we shall eat well on the morrow!" said the queen, giving the signal to begin.

Mary was mounted on a gray palfrey and thought to partner with Mistress Eleanor, but then she saw Master Nicholas lead Nora's horse away. She looked around.

"Ah, the lovely Mary—would you be so kind as to partner with me?" said Sir John Pakington, his mouse-brown hair blowing in the wind, the black feather in his cap a sharp contrast. He had blunt features, was tall and large, prone to heaviness.

"I should be pleased to do so," said Mary pleasantly enough. A part of her wished Sir John Skydemore would ask for her, but she had not seen much of him since he had joined the progress. She kept hoping to catch a glimpse of him. She thought of Oxford; she had not spoken with him at all since Mistress Blanche sent him away from her. Remembering the shame of that night made Mary shudder. Oxford seemed to have harkened to Mistress Blanche's words and had not approached her again. She had seen him dancing with Lady Douglass several times while on the progress, or chatting with Mistress Frances. He had not even looked her way.

The air grew slightly cooler as they entered the woods and followed a small path that curved first one way, then another. Pakington led the way, carefully holding on to the reins of her horse and holding branches so she would not be swatted. They came to a brook and Pakington stopped to allow the horses to drink.

"Shall we rest here a moment, Mistress Mary?" he said, offering her his hand.

"Yes. I find I, too, am thirsty," said Mary, allowing him to help her down.

"I believe this stream is pure—unsullied here in the forest. Allow me," he said. He bent to the brook and filled his canteen. He took a long drink and then handed her the vessel. "I am sorry I have no cup fit for your lovely lips."

"Have no worry, I am used to such as this. Often, the queen and I, along with Lord Robert, have traveled in the forests and refreshed ourselves with such streams," said Mary, drinking her fill from the leather canteen. The water tasted sweet and was cold and refreshing.

She returned his canteen to him and stared into the creek to see if she could see any fish. Before she knew what was happening, Pakington had grabbed her and spun her around to face him.

"You are a pretty maid—and, from what I hear, one who likes a romp as well as any man," he said, kissing her fiercely on the lips.

She pushed him away from her, placing her hands on his chest. Finally, he released her from his kiss.

"What is the matter, Mary? Do you wish a jewel first? Some coin?" he said, his hands roaming over her hips.

"Sir! I have no wish for either! I am an honest maid in the queen's service—her cousin! I would suggest you unhand me immediately and apologize!" said Mary, her voice trembling.

"What's this? I do not understand. I have heard it said you are nothing but a common strumpet and will allow any man of breeding to enjoy your favors," said Pakington.

"And who told you this? Who has besmirched my good name?" said Mary. Her voice was loud in the silent forest and she shook with anger.

"Well, I . . . that is, I should not say . . . that is, it was talk among the courtiers . . . Not sure who said what . . . I'm sorry, mistress. I see now how wrong such talk can be . . . do forgive me, I beg of you," said Pakington, who had gone to one knee as he saw her draw her bow and place an arrow aimed at his heart.

"A name, sir. Give us the name of the scoundrel who defames our honor," she said, holding the bowstring taut. "God's blood, you shall tell us immediately or pay the price!"

Mary thought she sounded exactly like the queen as she heard the plural pronoun slip from her lips—commanding and powerful, which was how she felt with the bow in her hands.

"Oxford, ma'am. Oxford told us all he has made do with you, and now he has no more use for you. Told us you were still ripe for plucking," said Pakington.

Mary shifted her aim slightly and let loose the arrow. It struck a stump near Pakington's head.

"I tell you this, sir. My honor is unstained. You should do well to take this news to anyone who doubts it. And now, you shall ride back to the castle with me. We shall tell the queen I am unwell and have gone to bed. And you, sir, shall not ever speak to me again," said Mary.

She stomped to her horse and mounted. Pakington followed behind her, meek as a lamb.

After enjoying Sir Norris's hospitality for several days, the long train of wagons and supplies was ready to travel. Mary had spent many nights wondering how to undo the damage to her reputation caused by Oxford, crying in her pillow and raging at him in her imagination. The shame she felt for the dalliance *she* had allowed burned in her chest, along with indignation that he had discussed her among the other courtiers. Finally, she had spoken to Mistress Blanche about the matter. Mistress Blanche, who knew everything and was wise in the ways of the world, told her to hold herself with pride and dignity, give no further cause for gossip by behaving circumspectly, and show herself as a woman of prayer and faith. Soon, the rumors would die and she would be held in high esteem once more. Mary was relieved to hear Mistress Blanche thought such gossip would blow over quickly and she planned to follow her advice.

The caravan was ready to move out, with Mary in her place behind the queen's litter, when a horse drew up next to her.

"Good morning, Mary. I did not see you after the hunt the other day. I had hoped to speak with you at last night's dance but was told you were ill. I hope you are better now," said Sir John Skydemore.

"Thank you, I am much better. I see Sir James has kept you quite busy—I have not seen you at any of the festivities," said Mary.

"I've been going back and forth to London on business. But I shall be with you and the queen for the remainder of the progress. Which is why I wanted to speak with you. We are going very close to my modest house, Holme Lacy, and I would be honored if you would ride with me to visit. I long to see my children and I want to show you the place," said Sir John.

"God's blood! You think I would go with you to such a place without a chaperone? Sir, I know not what you have heard of me, but I shall never do such a thing!" said Mary, her anger quick in her throat.

"No, no, Mary—you mistake me. I have already arranged for Mistress Blanche to accompany us. It is but a two-hour ride from Sir Norris's and I want you to see it," said Sir John, his brow wrinkled. "I would never dishonor you, Mary."

Mary stared into his eyes, those eyes that made her think of water lapping against the shore, bluish green and beautiful. No dissembling there that she could see. He did not seem to know anything about her sullied reputation. He *seemed* sincere, though she had learned not to trust quite so willingly after riding with Pakington earlier.

"Perhaps my illness has made me testy. If the queen gives her permission, I shall be glad to make the trip with you and Mistress Blanche," said Mary.

Suddenly, they heard hoofbeats galloping up the dusty road toward the castle. The rider wove in and out of the line of wagons to stop abruptly at the queen's litter. Mary could see he was covered with sweat and his horse was lathered as well. He dropped down and fell to one knee.

"I have a message from Master Cecil for Your Majesty," said the man.

"God's teeth! Bring this man some ale—drink first, little man. Then you may give your message," said the queen, holding her pomander to her nose.

After he had gulped down two mugs of ale, the man delivered his message.

"Your Majesty, the Pope has issued a bull of excommunication against you. Master Cecil wished me to read it to you."

> Peers, subjects, and people of the said kingdom and all
> others upon what terms soever bound unto her, are freed
> from their oath and all manner of duty, fidelity, and obe-
> dience. These same shall not once dare to obey her or
> any of her laws, directions, or commands, binding under
> the same curse those who do anything to the contrary.

"Master Cecil begs you to return to London at once, ma'am. He says you are in grave danger to move in the open among your people. For now, they must decide whether to obey the Pope or you, Majesty. The Pope has also said that for *your* murder, there would be no sin on it," said the messenger.

"I thank you for this news, good sir. Rest with us tonight and on the morrow ride back to Master Cecil and tell him I have no fear of my beloved people. I shall not return but shall go onward as promised.

I shall let my people see me and receive their love as they shall receive mine. Now, Lord Robert, lead on!" said the queen. The courtiers threw up their caps and cheered. Mary saw a look of concern pass over Lord Robert's features and he called for the Gentlemen Pensioners to surround Her Majesty's litter before they progressed. Then, the long train of wagons and mules and horses and litters moved slowly through the countryside, heading now for Warwick Castle before returning to London.

Twenty-two
Late July 1570

T
he trees give good shelter from the sun," said Sir John as he rode beside Mary, with Mistress Blanche riding behind. Great branches made a green canopy above them, and birds filled the air with song. Mary could hear linnets and larks twittering in the leaves. An occasional rustling along the ground might reveal a squirrel or coney, perhaps a deer. The countryside was filled with gentle, rolling hills with fields divided squarely by hedges, and great forests offering shady comfort.

"I have not been this far west before—I had no idea it would be so very peaceful," said Mary, adjusting herself in her saddle, sitting higher so she might have a better view.

"I'm glad you like it—I have always loved these lands. We are on *my* land now and Holme Lacy will come into view in another hour," said Sir John. "How are you doing back there, Mistress Blanche?"

"I'm fine, sir. You must not keep asking after my welfare—I may be old but I am not decrepit yet," said Mistress Blanche. She shifted in her saddle, rearranging her skirts.

"How large is your holding, if I may ask?" said Mary.

"Several thousand acres, I should think. We have recently acquired a nearby farm so I am unsure of the exact number. My steward will know the precise figures," said Sir John.

They rode in silence for a while. Then, to the surprise of the women, Sir John produced a small flute from his pocket and began to play an old country tune. The women sang along. Soon, the sun had risen to its peak and Sir John reined in his horse. Mary did the same.

"There it is—Holme Lacy! I love how it looks from here. My heart always feels lighter once I see the place, and I begin to smile in spite of myself," he said.

Mary gasped and stared. What she saw shook her to her bones.

"It is the same! The same!" she said, her voice stretched high and thin.

"What do you mean, 'the same'? You have not been here before," said Sir John.

She grabbed his arm and squeezed.

"In the crystal—this is what I saw! At Dr. Dee's! Do you remember?" she said, barely aware of what she was saying.

"Yes, I remember. Do you mean to say you caught a vision of my house?" said Sir John.

"It was here. I would recognize that house, for even as I spied it in the glass ball, I found it beautiful—the red brick and the lovely windows, the stately wings on each side of the main house, the gardens. And we were there, too, John! You and I stood at the front door, talking to one another," said Mary.

"Do you remember what question you asked the crystal?" said Sir John.

"Oh, it was a foolish girl's question—silly!" said Mary, afraid and feeling light-headed.

"What was it, Mary?" he said.

"I asked to see the man I was to marry," said Mary quietly.

Neither of them spoke. The silence became thick and Mary found it difficult to breathe.

"Are we going to stand here goggling all day or are we going to ride to that great house for some food and drink?" said Mistress Blanche behind them.

They both laughed.

"We shall away with all speed, Mistress Blanche. We should not wish for you to perish for lack of sustenance!" said Sir John, spurring his horse.

Mary followed suit and urged her horse to a run. She sped by Sir John, the wind against her face cooling her. She raced to Holme Lacy, feeling as if the house itself welcomed her with open arms. Never had she experienced such an immediate love of a place. Love tempered with an eerie feeling of danger. She wondered what magic Dr. Dee had concocted and what strange forces were at work in her life.

Sir John caught up with her easily, and together they rode into the large yard. Mistress Blanche was several minutes behind them, her horse not up to a gallop in the heat.

Sir John helped Mary down from her horse and held her hand.

"Mary, you must know why I brought you here. I have told you before that I wish to court you—I would have you as my wife," he said. His eyes looked at her with intensity and longing.

"I did not believe you were ready to love again when you first mentioned the idea. Nor did I know if I was ready. I still do not know the answer to either question," she said, allowing him to continue holding her hand.

"I am not certain how to answer—I shall always love the mother of my children. But I also know that I want to see you in the mornings when I arise. I want to spend our evenings playing cards and singing with the children. I want to see you with a babe of your own.

My heart will always carry its sorrow for my Eleanor, but that is part of who I am. If you can accept a man who has known grief, one who does not play as merrily, perhaps, as other men, then I believe we can make a life together that will be rich and filled with God's blessings," said Sir John.

He spoke so simply and so truly that Mary's heart was touched. She realized she could, indeed, find love with this steady, kind man. And when she looked up into his face, his blond shock of hair hanging playfully over his eyes, those mysterious aqua eyes unlike any she had ever seen, she felt her body shiver just slightly. She wanted to be in his arms; she wanted the kind of love the queen had with Lord Robert. She did not want the shame she'd felt with Oxford and the complete humiliation Pakington had given her.

"You honor me, sir. If you wish to court me, then I will be happy to receive your attentions—with the queen's permission, of course," said Mary quietly.

"It is you who do me the honor, Mary. I shall do everything in my power to bring you happiness. And yes, the queen must give her blessing," he said. He did not move to kiss her. Instead, he walked toward Mistress Blanche, who approached them. "May I help you down, Mistress Blanche?"

Mary watched as he carefully lifted the older woman from her mount. Then he linked his arm in hers and walked toward the front door.

"Come—let us meet my children," he said.

They entered the Great Hall after servants had taken their hats and gloves and brought them refreshing light beer. Mary was amazed at the beauty of the house itself—the stone mullions and many gables. Inside, the walls were hung with arras and a few tapestries. Servants scurried to do Sir John's bidding, and soon a sumptuous meal was set before them, trays filled with fresh apples and cherries, stewed turnips and cabbages, roasted goose and pheasant, and a large boar with an apple in its mouth.

"This is quite a feast," said Mary.

"I sent word ahead . . . just in case you agreed to come," said Sir John.

Sir John called for his children and they appeared rather rowdily. Firstborn son, Henry, a lad of around nine, raced in to see his father, his face sweaty and somewhat smudged with dirt. Then in ran his two younger brothers, James and John. Two small girls followed: Ursula, perhaps a bit over four and Alice, the youngest child, almost three. The girls toddled around, while their brothers galloped like wild horses. When they saw their father, the boys settled down a little, but the girls did not seem to know him. They had the look of children who had no one to love them, though their clothes were fine enough. Mary could see their need for motherly interest and concern. She knew at that moment how lucky she'd been to have the love of the queen. The queen and Mistress Blanche had seen to it Mary had been properly bathed and cared for, educated and tenderly handled, the intimate, detailed care given in motherly love.

"Hello, little one. Alice, isn't it? Come here, child. Do you like gooseberry pies? Here, have a bite of this," said Mary as she fed the child a piece.

Mary and Mistress Blanche spent a long time with the children, playing hide-and-seek and bathing the younger ones, who, it seemed, had either become extremely dirty in a day's time or had not had a bath near often enough.

"Mistress Blanche, what do you think of Sir John?" said Mary as they watched the children run and play with two new pups in the front yard.

"He is a fine man—courteous, kind—but he has so many children.

His poor wife must have given him one each year for their entire marriage," said Mistress Blanche.

"He has asked if he may court me—he wishes for us to marry," said Mary. Her voice could barely eke out the words, she was so nervous.

"This cannot be! The queen will forbid it! He is a Catholic and holds with Sir James Croft, not one of the queen's favorites. You must refuse him at once!" said Mistress Blanche.

"But I am not sure I *wish* to refuse him—I like him. He is handsome and thoughtful—nothing like Oxford and Pakington, brutes both! I feel a different kind of affection for him . . . a friendly sort," said Mary.

"I do not care a sheep's teat for your affections! He is a Catholic—they are all suspect these days, Mary. If I were queen, I'd round them all up and send them to the Tower forever!" said Mistress Blanche, peeling an apple in her lap.

"But he is a true subject to the queen. He has declared his loyalty to me and I believe him!" said Mary.

"It matters not! The queen has her own plans for your future—she sets great store in you and will see you well matched, perhaps even to Oxford, rake that he is—he's still an earl. Enough of this foolish chatter! I do not wish to discuss it further. It is time to return to the queen," said Mistress Blanche, throwing the apple core to the ground.

"I shall never marry Oxford! He has tried to ruin me!" said Mary.

"If the queen wills it, then you shall do it," said Mistress Blanche.

Mary felt her face begin to burn with anger. Why should the queen have such plans for her? Why could she not marry where her heart led her? Why must marriage be a business arrangement rather than two hearts longing for each other? It was the queen! The queen wished no one happy! She could not marry or would not do so; she hated anyone who might find love. She was determined to see Mary miserable in some foreign country with some old man with lots of lands and money, but no warmth in his body or his heart. Well, let the queen think what she would. Mary would follow her heart, no matter where it led her, even if it led to the grave.

By the time Mary, Sir John, and Mistress Blanche had returned to the progress, the sun had set and they had missed supper. Luckily, the servants at Warwick Castle were overwhelmed by their royal guest and her entourage. The food had not yet been put away and they were able to enjoy some lukewarm chicken and manchet, washed down with the queen's light ale. After their brief repast, Mary and Mistress Blanche reported to the queen's rooms to see if Her Majesty had need of them. Mary was surprised by laughter ringing from the Privy Chamber, Her Majesty's deep-throated laugh quite recognizable. At first, the sound made Mary smile, remembering all the times she and the queen had laughed together over some silly thing when Mary was a child. Then, she remembered how the queen wanted to control every single thing in her life and she could feel the blood rushing through her veins.

The guard announced them, and when she saw them, the queen motioned them to come to her. Mary was shocked to see Oxford and Pakington seated on pillows next to the makeshift throne. Mary and Mistress Blanche curtsied to the queen and Her Majesty indicated for them to sit on two pillows between the men.

"My lord Oxford has been regaling me with naughty stories about country wenches and ladies-in-waiting and what the two have in common. If I weren't laughing so hard, I'd box his impudent ears," said the queen, resting her hand on Oxford's shoulder. Pakington took a long swig of ale and then belched, loudly. Mary thought the queen would send him from the room; instead, she laughed again. "Made room for more, did you, Lusty?"

"Always room for more, Your Majesty. And where did this pretty young thing come from?" said Pakington, playfully twirling Mistress Blanche's tendril that had escaped her French hood. She slapped his hand away.

"Neither young nor pretty, Sir John! And certainly old enough to know when a man is making himself a fool," said Mistress Blanche. Her rebuke sobered Pakington and there was a lull in the frivolity. Just then, the guard announced Sir John Skydemore. Mary's heart skipped like a stone over water. Sir John had changed his doublet and hose, the emerald color of the satin casting his eyes a deeper shade of green than usual. His hair was combed back and Mary couldn't help but notice how nicely he filled out his clothes, the muscles of his calves evident as he walked, his shoulders wide and strong-looking. She could feel her cheeks flame.

"Your Majesty," said Sir John, kissing the queen's proffered hand.

"Ah, Sir John. How were things at Holme Lacy? Do your children fare well?" said the queen in a gracious tone.

"As well as children can fare without a mother," said Sir John.

"They are lovely children, Your Grace. Three strapping boys and two little girls, all very pretty," said Mary, coming to his rescue. He could not have known the subject of motherhood was a tender spot with the queen.

"Well, Mistress Mary, you seem to have a knack for knowing how to win a man—coddle his children or, as you did in my case, coddle the man himself," said Oxford with a lecherous grin.

"Does something go on here? My lord Oxford, even you know better than to meddle with my ward!" said the queen.

"That I do, madam—but what if she meddles with me?" said Oxford, still smiling and staring into Mary's eyes.

"A gentleman would never so insult a lady, Oxford. She cannot defend herself. But if you do not take back your words, I shall defend her honor for her," said Sir John in a low, steely voice.

Mary took a sharp breath. Surely Sir John could not be calling Oxford to duel in front of the queen. Swordplay was strictly banished in the presence of Her Majesty and those who ignored the rule did so at their peril.

"Enough! Oxford, apologize at once to my ward! Sir John, take your hand from the hilt of your sword!" The queen spoke so vehemently that her voice brooked no argument. Oxford mumbled an apology, then he and Pakington took their leave. Sir John was invited to sit on a cushion while he and the queen discussed a land squabble involving one of his yeomen. Mary sat, trying to calm herself. Oxford had humiliated her in front of the queen and Sir John. How gallant Sir John had been to leap to her defense. How she suddenly was filled with hatred for Oxford and how her heart burned with shame to remember the way he had handled her in the garden. How she wished she had never gone into the garden with him. Sir John must never know of that night. He would not wish to court her if he knew that Oxford had kissed her breasts and fondled her as if she were a mere kitchen wench.

Later, after she had helped the queen prepare for bed, Her Majesty dismissed all of her ladies but called Mary to her.

"Come, dear Fawn, sit beside me," said the queen as she patted the spot next to her on her bed.

Mary obeyed and sat close to the queen, close enough to smell her perfume. The queen put her arm around Mary's shoulders and Mary rested her head against the queen's shoulder.

"You are growing up, my Fawn. I see how all my courtiers admire your beauty—I do not blame them, you have grown quite lovely over the summer. One of my courtiers has asked my permission to marry you," said the queen, very quietly.

Mary did not speak. Could Sir John have moved so quickly? She could feel her bones reverberating as her heart thumped.

"Did you give your leave?" said Mary, almost afraid of the queen's answer.

"Do you not wish to know who the man is?" said the queen, smiling.

"Of course. Who is it?" said Mary, thinking to herself how much courage Sir John must have garnered to approach the queen.

"My lord Oxford. He would be a fine match for you—you look well together. But his character is not so steady as I would like. I thought to get your mind on the matter before I answer him," said the queen.

"Oh, Your Majesty, I have no love for the Earl of Oxford. I would not wish to be wed to him. I . . . I thought another had made the request," said Mary.

The queen was silent for a moment.

"I thought as much. I see how you look at Sir John Skydemore— and how you blush when he is near. No, say nothing. I know what I know. And I would say to you, enjoy the man! Spend time with him, dance with him, walk with him in the dusk—just do not think to marry him! For you shall never marry him! He is not fine enough for you, dear Fawn. He is no earl, no prince. You are free to delight in his company. But keep your virtue!" said the queen.

Mary lifted her head.

"I intend to keep my virtue, Your Majesty. But I will not play with Sir John as if he were a toy. As for marriage, I think I should have a say in what man I shall marry—I do not wish to wed some stranger from a faraway land. I would rather follow my own inclina- tions—as does Your Majesty," said Mary.

"Ha! I do not follow my own inclinations—would that I could! And you do not have any say in your marriage rights—you are mine to command. You must trust in my love for you, child. I would not set you with someone who would be unkind to you. No, I will search for a man who will love you and be able to maintain you in a fine way—you shall be a great lady," said the queen.

Mary was silent. She did not think this was the right moment to tell the queen she had already made an agreement of sorts with Sir John. No, she would keep her secrets, just as the queen kept hers.

Twenty-three

*W*ould they not make a pretty pair? Oh, God's blood, Parry, I mean Oxford and Mary. Ah, a man like Oxford— handsome, quick-witted, funny—so much to recommend him for our Fawn. I know he is reckless—all the more alluring for it. Nothing whets a woman's appetite like the foolhardiness of men. I hear Oxford tarries far too long with barmaids and other low women. But if he had my beautiful Mary, he should be satisfied at home. He would no longer have need of tavern tarts, mark my words.

Alas, she has no use for the man. I cannot say I blame her—he is not perfect. Yes, I know his eyes are weak-looking. And I agree, his mouth is a bit prissy. But he is an earl! And he does know how to turn a phrase. Well, she has made her decision—this is not a match I shall force upon her.

Why do you mention Sir John Skydemore? What is he to our Fawn? He is nothing. No more than a poor knight who has five hungry mouths to feed. And Catholic, to boot. After the Pope's decree, I should arrest every

Catholic in the land on charges of treason. Or so my Spirit tells me. Sweet Robin agrees. But I shall not act on their suggestion. I believe in my people—even those who cling to the old religion. Let them! I am still their queen and they will not take up arms against me. You shall see, Parry. By God's knees, my people shall remain steadfast.

Yes, we do see that Skydemore has fine qualities—but a bit too dour for our tastes. Yes, he is handsome—those eyes! And yes, he seems in good health. Oh, I do not doubt he is ambitious—Inns of Court, is it? Parry, have you been hit by Cupid's dart? It sounds as though you have an affection for this young man yourself!

The queen and her court returned to Whitehall and to all the problems and difficulties they had left behind while on progress. As a result, the queen's mood was no longer merry. The men on her council were filled with ideas about how to protect the queen from the Pope's call to the Catholics of England to revolt. It seemed to Mary all they did was talk, talk, talk.

Mary stood behind Her Majesty in the Presence Chamber while Master Cecil thundered.

"Ma'am, what must I do to prove that Your Majesty is in danger? You must bind the Catholic citizens to yourself; they must not give any allegiance to the Pope. And if they will not sign this pledge, then you must hang them! Hang them all!" cried Master Cecil.

"Dear Spirit, we know you mean well—we know you have our safety and the best interests of England at heart. But we will not put such a yoke around the necks of our people. As long as they attend Anglican services once a month, they shall not be required to sign anything. If they have secret Catholic services, well, let them. Soon, they will no longer be able to find enough priests to say the Mass. Catholicism will die out of its own accord," said the queen, patiently.

"If not new laws, then the queen must consider taking a husband to help us fight against Spain and France—for they are Catholic nations and will do as the Pope commands. He has practically ordered them to make war upon us," said Lord Sussex, standing at attention.

"God's bones, man! Do you think we have not been thinking of these things? We have already opened the way for the French to press the suit of Catherine de' Medici's elder son, the Duke of Anjou. Though he is not much more than a boy and a rabid Catholic, the French ambassador will arrive shortly," said the queen.

"I am gratified to see that, as usual, Your Majesty has understood the danger and has taken action to nullify it," said Sussex, bowing to the queen.

"And, to show our faith in our Catholic subjects, we are releasing the Duke of Norfolk from the Tower. He has assured us he has no further interest in marrying the Scottish queen and is our loyal, obedient subject. This will send a message to the world that though the Pope has excommunicated us, we have no fear of our beloved people. We are no tyrants here. And now, gentlemen, you can tell the Pope that, as Supreme Governor of the English Church, *we* excommunicate *him*!" said the queen.

The men roared with laughter as the queen joined in. Mary felt a wave of admiration for her queen, amazed at how she dealt so bravely with the Pope and these men of power and prestige. She knew she would never be able to show such courage, and she would not know how to advise a royal husband if the queen found one for her. She shuddered. She did not want a royal husband. When she thought of marriage, it was Sir John's face she saw in her mind. When she thought of the marriage bed, it was Sir John's hands she imagined roaming her body. Such thoughts made her quiver and she could not wait to see him again.

October 1570

The queen was alone in her white garden, though the blooms were gone and the foliage of some of the bushes had turned russet and deep plum. She sat on a stone bench beneath a large yew tree. A couple of her Gentlemen Pensioners stood at the entrance to this small section of the gardens, waiting to escort her back to the Privy Chamber when her business here had been concluded. She heard approaching footsteps and braced herself for the act she was about to commit. She knew she would be pleasing one of her courtiers this day, and most likely making another miserable.

The queen gazed over the grounds, pleased with the sight as always. How she loved the gardens at Hampton Court Palace! She had taken great pains to see that throughout the year, there was something beautiful to look upon, planning with her "Sweet Robin" how to best utilize the space. But, enough dreaming of happier work. The Earl of Oxford approached.

"Your Majesty," he said, doffing his cap and bowing low.

"Oh, Oxford. We are glad to see you looking so well," said the queen, indicating for him kneel at her side.

"I hope you have good news for me," said Oxford, smiling up at her.

"I have seen your holdings are increasing. You have had a prosperous year," said the queen.

Oxford smiled, then shook his head.

"That was not exactly the good news I was hoping for—I meant news of a more personal nature . . ." said Oxford.

The queen watched as the color rose up his neck to his face. She regretted what she was about to do.

"Love is a funny thing, my lord. It cannot be commanded; it cannot be controlled. I realize you are of an age to take a wife and I have given this matter a great deal of consideration," said the queen.

"I thank Your Majesty for taking the time to consider my proposal," said Oxford quietly.

"I fear I must disappoint you—Mistress Mary Shelton cannot be your wife," said the queen.

"But, Your Grace, why? Who better to raise her up than myself? I am an *earl*," he said.

"Yes, yes, I know full well what you are, my dear fellow. But it does not suit us to give our Mary away at this time," said the queen.

"I would be willing to wait—she is but sixteen. I could easily wait until she is eighteen or whatever age Your Majesty chooses. I—" Oxford said.

"No, no. She is not for you. I see I shall be forced to speak plainly— she has expressed no interest in the match. She has turned you down. I am very sorry," said the queen.

Oxford blanched, but stayed rooted to the spot. The queen realized he wanted to leave, to hide his shame from her—no man wants an audience for his heartbreak.

"We do, however, have some good news to give you, sir," said the queen in her official voice.

"Thank you, Your Majesty," said Oxford.

"We have found a very fine match for you—we have already spoken to the girl's father and he is agreeable. This match will increase your wealth and your prestige," said the queen.

"That sounds promising. And who is this paragon of virtue you plan to toss my way?" said Oxford.

"Do not get peevish, my lord. We are giving you Mistress Anne Cecil, daughter of my dearest friend. And this, sir, is not a request but a command," said the queen when she saw a flash of disgust flit across his features.

Oxford did not respond. Then, somehow resolved, he wiped his hand across his face. He bowed his head.

"As Your Majesty commands," he said.

T he fires blazed at Richmond Palace as the icy winds blew outside. Mary sat in the queen's Privy Chamber, a warm quilt across her knees, the flames throwing out heat and light. The fire felt good on her feet and legs. She looked across the hearth at her friend Mistress Eleanor and smiled. They had the early afternoon to themselves as the queen was busy with Cecil and the other members of the council.

"How go the plans for the wedding?" Mary said.

Mistress Eleanor looked up from her work, an impish grin on her face.

"My father has raised the dowry and we shall be wed at Easter-time. The queen has given her blessing," said Mistress Eleanor.

"Did she put up a fuss?" said Mary.

"Well, when my father asked her, she made that little 'pup' sound she makes when she is not particularly pleased. But then she smiled at him and granted permission. They say she usually does so after a brief time of prating against marriage in general. But, her mood is good these days. I think it is because she is engaged in negotiations for marriage with the French duke," said Mistress Eleanor.

Though the Duke of Anjou had not acquiesced to any of the queen's demands yet, negotiations continued. Elizabeth had made so many demands, no one expected him to agree to them. By asking for the impossible, it would then be easy for Elizabeth to blame Anjou if things did not work out. She would seem to be *trying* to marry, yet marriage itself would be avoided once again.

"I do not think she will ever marry," said Mistress Eleanor.

"She loves to be wooed, that much is certain. And, for six months, she has had little to plague her—no uprisings, no attacks on her lands—she has been making merry with Lord Robert and the new man, Hatton. She likes *him* well enough," said Mary, her needle working in and out quickly. She was stitching gold thread around the edge of a handkerchief and it was easy work.

"They say it is his dancing! Lord Robert told her he could find a dance master who did a jig as well as Hatton. And she replied, 'I will not see your man—it is his *trade*!' Everyone laughed but not Lord Robert. He stomped away and danced the next three dances with Lady Douglass," said Mistress Eleanor.

"I am sorry to have missed such a show. But my duties as Keeper of the Queen's Clothes have kept me quite busier than usual. And, I have not enjoyed dancing as I once did," said Mary.

"You mean you are afraid to be around the courtiers after you refused Oxford. And now that he continues to besmirch your good name, you hide in the queen's apartments. I wish you would come out of your shell and show him you care not a fig for his slander. Hold your head high and ignore him," said Mistress Eleanor.

"I shall one day soon—I will not have a choice. The queen has noticed how I absent myself from her evening activities. She has told me I must appear soon," said Mary.

"How does your Sir John?" said Mistress Eleanor, pulling her thread to her mouth and biting off the end.

"He is handsome, as always—courteous and kind. He does not mind forgoing the pleasures of the evening. He says he is happier to walk in the garden with me or sing while I play the lute. Nora, I think I cannot be more in love," whispered Mary.

"Perhaps you should set your eyes on someone else. He has so many marks against him—the queen is not likely to promote the match of her favorite ward with a Catholic, and a poor Catholic at that," said Mistress Eleanor.

"I do not care about his wealth or lack thereof. He has a fine house and five sweet children. And he loves me! Surely these things count for something," said Mary.

The sounds of a goodly sized crowd moving toward the Privy Chamber caused the ladies to put aside their sewing and come to their feet.

"Make way for the Queen's Majesty! Make way!" said a Yeoman of the Guard. He stood at attention as the queen swept into the room, followed by some of her ladies and courtiers.

"Ah, Fawn, I am glad to have found you. Come here, child. And you, too, Master Cecil. I have decided, here at the year's beginning, to honor my two faithful servants. Mistress Mary Shelton, you are now a chamberer of the Queen's Bedchamber and shall, henceforth, be paid twenty pounds by the year," said the queen as she handed Mary a bag of gold and allowed her to rise from the curtsy she had immediately dropped when the queen entered the room.

"And now, Master William Cecil, it is with great pleasure that I hereby create you Baron of Burghley. Of course, a proper ceremony will follow, dear Spirit, in a fortnight, but I wanted to tell you now, in front of these do-nothings, so they would hold you in even higher esteem," said the queen, chucking him under the chin. "Now, off to celebrate my faithful servants and their good fortune. I wish to frolic in the snow—perhaps we shall make a snow queen and snow courtiers! Come all—to the gardens!" said the queen.

"Mary, this is wonderful! You shall be rich! Now you can buy all the silks and satins you want—and pay your gambling debts!" said Mistress Eleanor as they gathered their gloves and cloaks.

"I am plumb amazed! I had no idea the queen was going to do such! I cannot think clear," said Mary, tying her cloak around her neck and pulling up the hood.

They followed the courtiers and the queen out of doors where a cold wind blew. Already, Master Nicholas had made the beginnings of a snow queen. Others began to carve and create their own statues out of snow. Mary spied Oxford with a couple of his friends, Pakington and Norfolk. She watched as they laughed, piled on snow, then laughed once again. Sir John Skydemore was walking toward the group from another direction. He smiled at Mary and waved.

"What goes on here?" he said.

"Have you heard? The queen has made Mary a Lady of the Bedchamber at twenty pounds a year! It is marvelous news!" said Mistress Eleanor, scraping together a small ball of snow.

"Can this be true?" said Sir John.

"Yes! I am clean amazed! She made Master Cecil the Baron of Burghley! And now, she commands we are to play in the snow! Come, John, what shall we make?" said Mary.

"I know—let's create a statue of *Tom*, your dog. He should not be too difficult. We can portray him lying down as he does by the fire," said Sir John.

"Let us begin," said Mary, tossing a snowball at his shoulder. He scooped up some snow and threw it back at her. Soon, he, Mary, and

Mistress Eleanor were battling with snowballs over their patch of ground while the others worked steadily on their sculptures.

"I surrender, Mary," said Sir John, grabbing her arm, which was ready to fling another snowball at him. He put his arm around her waist and swung her off the ground. He whispered, "I shall always surrender to you, dearest," as he put her back on the slippery snow.

Mary felt warmth within her and a tingling in her womanly parts. Such feelings had become more and more frequent. It seemed every time she was around Sir John, she could barely contain the urge to fling her arms around him.

The afternoon wore on as the ladies and gentlemen piled snow atop snow. Cheeks were ruddy, and though most of the women wore gloves, their fingers were stiff with cold. Finally, as the pale sun hung low on the horizon, almost everyone had finished his creations. The queen clapped her hands together.

"Now, we shall judge! Each group will tell us what the likeness should be and we shall judge if it be fair or not," said the queen.

She pointed first to her own statue, which resembled Lord Robert but the legs looked remarkably like those of a hind. "It is Sir Christopher Hatton dancing la Volta!" she said. Everyone laughed.

"It looks more like Sweet Robin with a broken leg," said Oxford, slapping his hands together for warmth and chuckling.

"I daresay your own legs resemble those of a banty hen," said Lord Robert, aiming a snowball at Oxford. He ducked and the queen clapped for order.

"What have you there, you lusty young men? Is it a likeness of your queen?" said Her Majesty, trying to see what lay behind Oxford, Norfolk, and Pakington, who stood in a line blocking the view of their creation.

"No, Your Majesty. We call it 'Mary's pretty duckies,'" shouted Oxford as the men stepped aside to show a nude woman from the waist up with no head. Just breasts, correct in every detail, lovingly carved.

"Of which Mary do you speak? The Virgin?" said the queen.

"I shall not say which Mary I have modeled this great art work upon—I should not wish to cause her shame," said Oxford, staring directly at Mistress Mary Shelton.

Mary felt her cheeks burn with embarrassment. She looked at the snow in clumps at her feet.

"Do you dare to mock our dearest Fawn, Oxford? If that is your aim, I shall clap you in irons at this instant," said the queen. Her Majesty noted Mary's distressed looks and stared at Oxford.

Sir John looked at Mary, saw her discomfort, and put his hand on the hilt of his sword.

"No, madam, forgive me. I misspoke—for this is 'Merry Christmas!' the happiest of wenches!" said Oxford, trying to appease the queen.

Sir John pulled his sword from its sheath and marched to where Oxford stood.

"You said you will not insult the lady by giving her name. Now you say it is but 'Merry' Christmas. Still, you stare at Mistress Shelton. The insult is clear. I will not abide your rude jests! Defend yourself if you be a man!" said Sir John.

The queen gave Lord Robert a quick glance and he strode to stand between the two men. Oxford had not reached for his own sword, but his face had gone pale.

"Sir John, you know it is against the law to draw your sword in the queen's court. Put it away at once," said Lord Robert.

"I shall be happy to return my blade to its sheath once this cur has apologized to my lady and to the queen," said Sir John, standing his ground, his sword still pointing at Oxford's heart.

No one moved. No one spoke.

"God's blessed bones, gentlemen! Your queen commands a truce," said Her Majesty. "If Oxford is to be punished for his impudence, *we* shall have that pleasure, not you, Sir John."

Oxford stepped forward and bowed to Mary.

"Mistress Shelton, I am sorry if I have offended you. This was by no means meant to represent you," he said, his voice unsteady. Then he turned to the queen and, in a grand gesture, bowed with a great flourish.

There was a loud noise.

Unbelievably, the earl had broken wind as he bent, touching his cap to the ground. Mary watched in amazement as his face turned from pale to deep red. The entire crowd had gone silent with shock. The queen's face was inscrutable and Lord Robert covered his laugh with a cough. Oxford didn't move at first. Silence hung in the air.

Finally, Oxford mumbled something indiscernible and then, without waiting to be dismissed, he hurried away from the queen and the courtiers. No one knew quite what to do. The queen, her face a mask of seriousness, clapped her hands again.

"By the feet of Jesus, I always said Oxford was full of hot air!" said the queen, suddenly laughing. Everyone joined in the merriment, relieved. Then the queen turned to Mary and smiled.

"I see Mistress Shelton and her companions have created a fine likeness of her dog. Ah yes, quite a good likeness," said the queen.

Mary watched as the queen caught Lord Robert's eye and they both began to laugh. Soon, everyone was snickering and giggling again.

As the crowd evaluated the other carvings, Mary put her hand on Sir John's arm.

"Thank you for defending me, John. Oxford has been given his way with his bold talk—because he is highborn, he thinks he can say or do anything," said Mary. She had seen the look in Sir John's eyes when he faced Oxford, a look that had been frightening, yet oddly arousing. She felt her blood rushing through her body. She realized he had been ready to fight, maybe even die for her honor. He was a man of strong character. She wanted him to take her in his arms, kiss her deeply, and move his hands across her body as Oxford had done.

"Oxford has been saying lewd things about many of the queen's ladies. I thought it only right he should have to answer for that—and if I hear of such slander again, I shall run him through," said Sir John, quietly, without anger. Mary knew he meant his words.

The next morning, Mary watched the snow falling, the flakes as large as goose feathers. She gazed at the whiteness below. No one moved about; even the servants stayed inside where it was warm. She did not blame them; she had no desire to venture out into the cold again.

Suddenly, her eyes caught movement. A lone rider, dressed in the finest clothes, headed to the gates toward the main road. Two pack-horses and a couple of servants followed the rider. Mary recognized him by the way he sat in the saddle and by his opulent cloak and hat. It was the Earl of Oxford. He was leaving the court and Mary felt a pang of pity for him. He had humiliated himself this time; perhaps there was justice in the world after all.

Twenty-six
February 1571

*A*s winter continued to chill the land, and the snow piled high around the walls at Richmond, the court kept busy with dances, games of cards and dice, singing, and viewing plays. The queen's spirits were high and Mary often caught sight of Her Majesty dancing a little jig in the mornings on her way to her daily walk. The other maids sniggered at the sight but Mary admired the agility and grace of the queen, who was, in Mary's mind, no longer young. But she was young in spirit, Mary thought. And Mary hoped she might approach her own declining years with as much gusto.

Her Majesty kept her maids hopping as the dull, gray days passed. They fetched glasses of watered wine, cut dried fruits into small bites for the queen, and entertained her with funny stories and card playing. Mary's new duties as chamber woman did not weigh too heavily upon her, in spite of her continuing role as Keeper of the Queen's

Wardrobe. *That* job was time-consuming and difficult because Mary had to ensure all of the queen's garments remained in good repair. Mary also had to catalogue each smock, gown, kirtle, sleeve, cloak, and hat. She knew which jewels were sewn on which bodice, so that when the queen wanted them switched, Mary could easily find them.

Though she had many chores each morning, the afternoons were quiet and leisurely, as the queen met with her councillors during this time. Thankfully, she no longer required Mary to join her at the dull meetings on a daily basis, though she admonished Mary to keep up with the affairs at court and to be prepared to rejoin the councillors at the queen's command. Most afternoons, Mary spent sewing or chitchatting with Mistress Eleanor.

"Master Nicholas and I shall be wed by Easter—my father has garnered my dowry and things are all set. I shall return to my home and the ceremony will take place there. Nicholas is so pleased and, I daresay, as anxious for the banns as I am," said Mistress Eleanor.

"And I am happy for you, dearest Nora. I only wish I could see you on your wedding day. But we both know the queen will not stand for me to be away from her. Oh, look, more snow," said Mary.

"It is so beautiful coming down . . . but it gets sullied very quickly," said Mistress Eleanor.

"Come! Let us walk out and catch snowflakes on our tongues!" said Mary.

"But it's cold . . ." said Mistress Eleanor.

Mary had already grabbed Mistress Eleanor's hand and was pulling her to her feet. She lifted two cloaks off hooks inside the wardrobe and handed one to Mistress Eleanor. Thus bundled, they headed for the courtyard.

A number of people milled around the grounds. Servants with letters to deliver, men bringing in large baskets of firewood, washerwomen carrying bundles of wet clothes, all bustled in and out of the palace, like bees at the honeycomb. But their numbers were fewer than usual.

"Isn't that Sir John? He looks like he's in a hurry," said Mistress Eleanor, pointing to a scholarly looking figure in black robes.

"I think it is—it seems long since I've seen him. His studies keep him from court," said Mary, her heart lifting at the sight of him. She quickly bent to pick up snow and pack it into a ball. She tossed it at him, hitting him on the shoulder. He stopped, looked to see from where the missile had come, and, seeing, broke into a smile. He hurried to the women.

"My two favorite ladies," he said, doffing his hat and bowing to them.

Both women curtsied and smiled.

"What brings you out on such a blustery day?" he said. "I thought you would be soaking up the heat from the great fireplaces in the queen's bedchamber."

"We came to catch snowflakes!" said Mary. She stuck out her tongue and felt a large flake land there. She grinned.

"A fine endeavor. Since you are already out in this cold, perhaps you would like to walk with me in the gardens . . . er, both of you, of course," said Sir John.

"Oh, I cannot—I have too much to do in preparation for my wedding. I'm still stitching my smocks and my nightgowns. I was working some lovely silk ribbons onto my nightcap—I've had my fill of snow," said Mistress Eleanor, giving Mary an understanding look.

"I'll see you back inside, Nora," said Mary.

Sir John offered her his arm, which she took gratefully. They walked through the snow-covered paths and he steered her behind a large hedge.

"Oh, Mary, I have wanted to see you but my studies have taken up most of my time. Since we returned from Holme Lacy, all I can do is imagine you there, greeting me of an evening, delighting in the children—having one of our own," said Sir John. He stood close to her and she could feel the warmth of his breath.

"The queen suspects I have a fondness for you—she has told me we cannot marry. She suggests I toy with your affections, enjoy them. But she cautions me against loving you and warns me especially against marrying you," said Mary. She thought it only fair to tell him a marriage between them could never be.

"But why? I have a good income from my lands, though not as large as some. There are definitely richer men by far. But I have enough to care for my family and would give you a good life. Why is she against me?" said Sir John, turning to face Mary. "Is it my religion?"

"I'm sure your religion does not help matters. The queen has all but raised me. She fancies some foreign duke who would be well suited for me—and she thinks if she can use my marriage rights to secure England, all the better," said Mary, her tone bitter. She pulled away from him and began to walk fast, back on the garden path.

Sir John followed her, his breath coming in little white puffs.

"But what do *you* want, Mary? Your desires should play a part in your own future," he said.

She stopped cold.

"I want . . . I want . . . I want you. I have no wish to play the high lady on foreign soil, spying for the queen, living for her. I want my own life, my own family right here in England. I do not see why I cannot have this," she said, flinging herself into his arms.

They kissed, a long, deep kiss that stoked her desire. Though she was cold and could feel the snowflakes land on her cheeks, she continued kissing him. She could sense his muscles tensing as he held her to him. His hands began to touch her breasts, a gentle yet confident touch. She shivered.

"There must be a way we can convince the queen I am the man for you. I have friends, those who may have more sway with the queen than I do. We shall find a way, dearest. It will just take some time," he said. "Come, let us return to the palace—you are freezing."

"I hope you are right. Surely she will be reasonable—she says she loves me. That alone should convince her to give me my way," said Mary, leaning against him. "Perhaps we should just run away and marry. Perhaps that is the best way."

"As much as I would like that, my love, I do not think it prudent. We do not wish to anger the queen and I suspect any sort of subterfuge would rile Her Majesty. No, we shall go about this in a manner that is sure to please her," said Sir John.

Twenty-seven
April 1571

S pring had come early, the trees greening beneath the still
pale sky and daffodils shooting up through the ground in
great profusion. The court had recently arrived at Whitehall to find the palace sweetened with new rush mats upon the floors,
the jakes cleaned out, the rooms aired and all the linens washed and
fresh. Hyacinths and other early spring flowers and herbs had been
strewn on the rushes, and the warm air allowed for open windows both
day and night. Mary was happy to have left Richmond, for the stink
had become almost unbearable.

Morning had broken with bright sunlight streaming through the
windows and the song of the linnets and other birds lightly on the
air. The queen was just breaking her fast, though it was mid-morning.
She had worked late into the night on matters of state and Mary had
seen to it that she was not awakened by the sun, pulling the dark
damask bed curtains around her.

In her new position as Lady of the Queen's Bedchamber, Mary's duties remained almost as they had been previously, except that now Mary, along with three others, prepared Her Majesty's chamber each morning and set up to receive the midday meal. She continued laying out the queen's clean shift each day, then bringing forth whatever clothes the queen might wish to wear, being ever ready to suggest an outfit if the queen had not the mind for such slight decisions. This was often the case, with the queen wearing whatever Mary selected. One of the maids brought in fresh flowers in a vase while another set out some of the queen's jewels. One maid's sole duty was to scatter blossoms over the floor and through the corridor where the queen normally passed.

Each morning, after arising and breaking her fast with bread, light ale, and perhaps some cheese, the queen spent time in prayer and the reading of God's Holy Word. In a small closet, the queen's Bible remained on a stand and there was a pillow on which Her Majesty would kneel. She often stayed in privacy for upward of an hour. When she came forth from her closet, she would be ready to dress for the day.

On days when she did not have to meet with her council, the queen often sat in her house gown with her ladies in the bedchamber and translated ancient works into the English tongue and then back to Latin or Greek. Her ladies did sewing while the queen worked at her books.

But on this day, the queen lent her hand to sewing as well, for the Maundy services were coming soon, and after the queen had washed the feet of thirty-eight poor women, one for each year of the queen's age, Her Majesty liked to give not only a gift of coin, but a new shift. She also wished to continue her mother's tradition of sewing shirts for the poor, to distribute to those *not* selected for the washing of the feet at the Maundy services. Mary missed Eleanor's deft hands, but her dear Nora was to marry Master Nicholas on Easter Sunday, and she was away from court.

"We have not much time to make as many shirts as possible, ladies. Let your fingers fly," said the queen, her own slim fingers moving like hummingbirds at the fabric.

"I have completed ten, Your Majesty, and now work on number eleven," said Lady Douglass, her brows arched as if she alone had done any work.

"We should have thought you might have doubled that number, madam, if you had used your time wisely. However, we understand you have been spending long hours looking over our horses," said the queen.

Mary sat perfectly still. She, too, had heard rumors about Lady Douglass walking down to the stables each day with her sister. It was bruited about that both were in love with Lord Robert, each vying for his attentions. Mary had seen Lady Douglass smile and touch Lord Robert in an overly familiar way. And she knew that if *she* had noticed, so had the queen.

"It is a pastime of mine, Majesty. I hope to breed one day," said Lady Douglass. She looked directly at the queen and smiled.

"Have a care, madam. Breeding is a delicate process. You must be certain you have the right stud, one who is well matched for the dam. Otherwise, there is trouble for the dam," said the queen, her tone even but her meaning clear.

"I shall always take great care, Your Grace," said Lady Douglass.

The queen had instructed the yeoman at the door to keep any petitioners away unless there was a dire emergency. She would go soon into the Presence Chamber to handle the business of the day, but for the morning, she wished to repose with her ladies.

Because Her Majesty did not often take such time for respite, Mary did not expect any interruptions. She was taken aback when the yeoman entered and went to the queen, bowed, and whispered.

"Leave me!" said the queen to her women. "Not you, Mary—I would have you stay."

Mary remained seated while the others hurried out and Lord Burghley entered, his face flushed and his manner tense. He approached the queen and went to one knee beside her throne.

"Majesty, I have just had a message from our man Bailey in Dover. He has intercepted a letter from a Florentine banker, Roberto Ridolfi, who is currently living in London. It is a letter to the Duke of Alva," said Lord Burghley. He paused to catch his breath. Mary noticed beads of sweat sprouting across his brow.

"God's blood, Spirit! Out with it!" said the queen.

"Your Majesty, in this letter was discovered a plot upon Your Majesty's life!" said Lord Burghley.

He went on to explain that the Queen of Scots and the Duke of Norfolk had exchanged dozens of messages in which they discussed murdering Elizabeth. Then, they planned to place the Scottish queen on the throne of Britain. After Her Majesty had been killed, Mary, Queen of Scots, would marry Norfolk and make him king.

"We have discovered this Ridolfi fellow is an agent of Rome, and it was *he* who brought the papal bull, *Regnans in Excelsis*, to London. It seems he, along with Bishop Ross and others, have agreed that with your death, Spain and the Pope will send troops and arms to turn this land back to Rome," said Lord Burghley.

"By God's blood, will they never leave me alone? I have been generous to the Catholics in my land, more so than my Privy Council advises. Yet they continue to plot against me. How many are arrested?" said the queen, standing so that her sewing dropped to the floor. Mary bent to pick it up and placed it on the queen's silver-topped table.

"All the conspirators named thus far have been put in the Tower. Bishop Ross has refused to come to court and Ridolfi is on the Continent. These letters incriminate both Norfolk and the Scottish queen. They have plotted your death, Majesty. You must execute them," said Burghley.

"Not without a trial, and not the queen—I cannot execute an anointed queen. Gather the evidence and see to the trial. Bring Norfolk once again to the Tower. Perhaps he can find a way to excuse himself—I am loath to send him to the block as well. Oh, is there to be no peace for queens!" said Her Majesty. She shooed Lord Burghley away and her chin dropped to her chest. For a moment, Mary did not think she breathed.

"Fawn, what shall I do? Kill every Catholic in the land? Throw them all in the Clink? Remove them to Rome?" said the queen.

Mary stood still. She thought of Sir John. What if the queen *did* arrest those who practiced the old religion? Would she arrest good men, loyal men, like Sir John? She had to dissuade Her Majesty of such action. She slowly walked to the throne. She began rubbing the queen's shoulders.

"Majesty, your people love you, be they Protestant or Catholic. You must trust in the people of England, for therein lies your greatest strength. I have seen how they hail you when you move among them, how they send their love. They will not allow you to be struck down on account of the Pope," said Mary, massaging the tense muscles between the queen's shoulder blades.

"Do they love me? I think it is so—I know I love them. Have loved them enough to forgo marriage to my Sweet Robin—so that strumpet Douglass can dawdle with him! Have loved them better than my own self. Would they strike me down?" said the queen softly.

"They did not love your sister, Majesty. They did not love her because she burned all who disagreed with her. The fires at Smithfield are still remembered. You must not follow your sister's lead in this, for then the people will turn on you as they did her. No, follow your own gentle wisdom. For the good of *all* your people, Puritan, Protestant, and Catholic. You must find a way for them to live in peace," said Mary.

"You would make a good queen, Fawn. You have learned your lessons well and seem to have understanding that my councillors lack," said the queen.

"I have observed you, my queen. This is your own counsel returned to you. For you are a kind and generous ruler, much to your credit. I know you will continue to do what is best for England," said Mary.

"Best warn your friend Skydemore and any other Catholics you know. The Parliament will not allow for liberality, I fear. Just tell Sir James Croft and his son-in-law to be careful," said the queen.

Mary nodded and continued to rub the queen's shoulders. After a few moments, the queen stood and called for her ladies to commence their sewing.

Twenty-eight

Parry, I like not this buzzing in my bones! And around my head! My ears hum with sound. It is terror taking hold of my very body! Such panic shows me to be womanly, when I must rule with the confidence of a king! By the holy cross, this is the shaking fear that stalks me by day and paralyzes me by night. Plots everywhere! Damn the men who devise them. And damn Norfolk and his foolish pride—he's won his death with it. No, he is not yet arrested, but I fear I must give my advisors something—it may be Norfolk.

But what to do about the Queen of Scots? I cannot have her head! She is an anointed queen, as am I. And my cousin! Oh, why does she seek to take what is not hers? She lost her throne; why must she try for mine?

Look at my hands, Parry. I cannot still them. I think I shall never quell the terrors that quake within my breast. If only I knew what to do. If only I could find a way to rid my country of this conflict between Catholic and Protestant. My "Spirit" and my "Eyes" tell me to be more strict with my

Catholic subjects, punishing those who harbor priests, arresting those who attend secret Masses. As I have said before, I have no wish to peer into men's souls. But they will push me to it with these infernal plots against me. They will push me to it!

   Send for my Fawn. I would have one of her special cordials. And tell her to prepare to sleep in my bed with me—for I cannot be alone this night. There are too many monstrous thoughts in my head. I know, I know—I should turn my troubles over to God. How often I have tried, Parry. I pray for hours each morning for the wisdom to rule my people with charity. I pray for a way out of this messy business. When I close my eyes, I see Norfolk's head rolling onto the platform, landing in the straw, now the color of blood. O blessed Savior, keep me from these night visions. Help me! Dear God, help me! Maybe there is yet a way to save Norfolk from himself. I shall try. By God's ribs, I shall try!

Twenty-nine
Midsummer Festival, June 24, 1571

T he day was hot, even for June. The sun beat down relentlessly but the heat did not dissuade revelers from flocking to London for the Midsummer Festival. Mary and Mistress Eleanor linked arms and crossed from Whitehall to Charing Cross Road, chattering like squirrels. Mary was happy to have her friend back at court, and though Eleanor was now married, the two young women still enjoyed spending time together. They were going to meet Master Nicholas and Sir John; the four planned to go to Cheapside, where stalls loaded with all sorts of foodstuffs were selling their goods and there was to be a mumming. The Summer Lord reigned on his high horse, doling out gifts and causing mischief.

"I am glad the queen gave us this day to celebrate midsummer. Did you see the bonfires last eve?" said Mistress Eleanor. They had reached their appointed meeting place and she shaded her eyes to see if Master Nicholas had arrived yet.

"Yes, the queen and Lord Robert and I watched from the queen's high window. They were like fireflies, flickering here, then there. Oh look! Tumblers!" said Mary as she pointed to two men dressed in checkered hose and matching doublets. The men walked on their hands and flipped first one way, then another. One man cartwheeled across the square, while the other rolled on the ground like a ball.

"Mary! Nora! Over here!" shouted Sir John, waving to them.

The women crossed the square. Traveling minstrels meandered up to them, singing and playing lutes. Mary placed a coin in their upturned caps.

"They do sing well, do they not?" said Sir John, taking Mary's elbow and leading her to the shade of a large oak. Master Nicholas and Nora followed.

"I have brought pillows for us and lots of sweet wine, still new but tasty," said Sir John, helping Mary down to a large blue pillow. He sat beside her on a yellow one and Nora perched across from her. Master Nicholas sat across from Sir John.

"I bought some tarts—I know you love gooseberry," said Sir John, handing one to Mary. She bit into the crisp pastry and caught the dark purple juice with her handkerchief as it dribbled down her chin.

"And you, my dearest Nora, have a preference for peach," said Master Nicholas, passing the tray to her.

They ate and drank their fill while the minstrels and tumblers performed all around them. People of all sorts milled around the square: fishmongers and flower girls, gentlemen, merchants, a few foreign-looking folk, and lots of children.

"Would you like to go see the Summer Lord, wife?" said Master Nicholas to Nora.

She nodded and he helped her to her feet.

"Shall you come, too, Mary?" said Nora.

"No, I wish to rest here beneath this lovely tree. But we shall catch up with you anon," said Mary, leaning back on her hands.

She waited until they were out of hearing and then motioned for Sir John to move closer.

"I am afraid," she said in his ear.

"What dare frighten my lady? I shall topple the beast with my sword! My bare arm if need be," said John, holding her hand.

"Do not mock me! I fear for *you*, John. The Privy Council is always after the queen to punish Catholics—they want all recusants to sign a pledge that they will serve only the queen and forget the Pope. Those who will not sign, they wish to hang. I am afraid," she said again.

Since the discovery of the Ridolfi plot and the arrest and trial of the Duke of Norfolk, the mood of those in power had soured toward their fellow citizens who remained in the old religion. Lord Burghley, a staunch Protestant, and Walsingham, his right arm, both urged the queen to punish her Catholic subjects.

"Do not fear. I do not flaunt my faith, nor will I stray from it. I trust in the queen's good opinion of me; she knows I am her loyal subject and she knows my beliefs. And those of my father-in-law, Sir James. She will not allow any harm to come to us," said John.

"Still, if you would attend the Anglican services with me, just once a month, it would shield you. Or you could convert, give up your Catholic superstitions," said Mary.

"Do you hear what you are saying, dearest? You ask me to give up my faith and the faith of my fathers because I fear. Did the blessed Jesu run before Pilate and the mob? No, he just kept doing what he believed he was supposed to do. He did not antagonize, but he did not quake in fear, either. Can I do less?" said John.

"This is mere stubbornness. As our queen says, 'There is only one Christ Jesus and one faith; the rest is a dispute about trifles.' Can you not see this?" said Mary.

"Dearest, you do not understand. I will not become dishonorable in my own eyes, no matter how frightened *you* may be. I choose to trust my God and my queen. I suggest you do the same," he said. He lifted her hand to his mouth and kissed it gently several times.

"What am I to do with you?" she said, her heart melting toward him.

"Marry me. Come live with me at Holme Lacy—where we will be safe from all of this argument," he said, kissing the inside of her palm and then her wrist.

"Will you speak to Sir James about us? Perhaps he can propose our union to Her Majesty. I dare not," said Mary, gazing into his eyes.

"I would not have *you* bring the matter to her—that would be unseemly. I will speak to Sir James. He is in Herefordshire for the next few months attending to business. When he returns to court, I shall talk with him," said Sir John.

Early July 1571

The day was glorious. Clear, sunny skies and a warm breeze had made gathering herbs and flowers for her cordials a most pleasant excursion for Mary. She'd taken *Tom* with her into the nearby woods to search for ground ivy, a wild plant that often makes a carpet along the shaded floor of the forest. She wanted to try a new cordial, one which was supposed to help with digestion. Ground ivy was the most important ingredient. Luckily, she found the plant in great profusion and quickly gathered a goodly supply while *Tom* sniffed out rabbits.

After she had filled half of her basket with the pale green leaves, she and *Tom* hiked to the meadows on the other side of the small copse of trees, where she searched for tansy. That was not so easy to find, but, after a long search, she found enough to serve her needs. She and *Tom* made their way back to the castle, where Mary immediately went down to her room by the kitchens. She allowed *Tom* to settle in on the cool stones beside her worktable after giving him a large bowl of water. Soon, he was asleep and Mary busied herself preparing the herbs for steeping. She was daydreaming about John, excited at the thought of enlisting Sir James Croft to help them in their quest for the queen's permission to marry. She had gone so deep into her fantasy as she washed and picked off the bugs and bad spots on her herbs, she did not hear the gentle knock on the door.

"Mary?"

She looked up from her work and almost dropped the handful of herbs she was placing into the large jar of aqua vitae. Oxford!

"God's teeth, you gave me a start!" she said as she curtsied, her hands still full of tansy and ivy.

"Not the welcome I had hoped for, milady," he said, smiling.

"What are you doing here?" she said. She placed the herbs into the jar, making certain the leaves were completely covered by the liquid. Then, she put a heavy stone lid on top. She turned to face him.

"The queen sent for me. She has forgiven my, er, indiscretion," he said. Mary thought she could see a slight blush cross his features.

"I daresay she has forgiven much worse," said Mary. She tried not to smile as she remembered Oxford's terrible moment of humiliation.

"I have not yet been to see Her Majesty—I am certain there will be great jesting at my expense. But it will be worth it to be back at court. But this is not why I sought you out, Mary," he said. He took a step toward her, thought better of it, and took a step backward.

"I cannot imagine why you have sought me out, sir. I would have thought we had nothing to say to each other," said Mary.

He paused. She could see that whatever he had come to do was difficult for him. She could see the slight twisting of his face, almost as if he were in pain.

"I have come to beg you to reconsider my proposal. The queen informed me that you have no love for me, no interest in becoming my wife. You may not know this, but she has matched me to Anne Cecil, that horse-faced women. I cannot abide her, yet I am to marry her in December, with her great father's blessing. It seems I get part of the Cecil fortune and they get noble blood," said Oxford. The bitterness in his voice cut through the air.

"I am sorry you have those feelings. I know Mistress Anne and find her very pleasant," said Mary.

"You do not have to bed her—oh, I am sorry, Mary. I did not mean to offend," said Oxford. Suddenly, he walked toward her. She was afraid, not sure what he might do. Surely he would not accost her here, in the castle with people all around. She prepared to scream for help. To her surprise, he dropped to one knee in front of her. He took her hand and kissed it softly.

"I am begging you, Mary. Please marry me. Please speak to the queen and tell her you will accept me. I will do my best to be a good husband to you—I have never been a faithful lover but for you, I would try, I would really try," he said.

Mary was not sure how to respond. He seemed sincere and she did not wish to cause him more pain, but she knew beyond a doubt that she did not want him for her husband. She wanted John. There was no explaining it—how does one explain love? Though the earl would have been the clear choice in the eyes of the court, Mary knew life with him would be a disaster. She could not bear to look into his watery, weak eyes for the rest of her life. There was another pair of eyes she desired.

"I am truly sorry, my lord. I cannot marry you—I have no love for you," she said gently.

"But why? Why?" said Oxford.

"I love another. No, I cannot tell you who it is; there is no need for you to know. But he has my heart," she said. She turned away from him, busying herself with her work. She heard him rise.

"Then you condemn me to a hell on earth, mistress. I shall not forget this," he said. He turned and strode out of the room, covering the space in three long steps. Mary shivered. She felt as if she had been threatened though he had uttered nothing sinister. But she was suddenly afraid.

Thirty
Late July 1571

The summer progress was off to a late start because Lord Burghley and the other councillors did not believe the queen should be exposed to her people after the discovery of the Ridolfi plot. They saw traitors hiding behind every bush and tree; both duty and affection drove them to advise the queen to stay put in London, where she could be guarded completely. In London, most of the people were Protestants and very much supported her rule. But in the small villages, particularly in the north, recusants gathered in groups, hiding priests and practicing the Mass as if there were no Elizabeth. But the queen refused to hide away, shut inside the stuffy palaces in town. She told Burghley she *would* travel, as was her custom and the custom of her father before her. Now, all was in preparation to begin the journey in two days' time.

Mary and Eleanor were brushing the queen's clothes and shaking out the silk kirtles and gowns. Each piece of clothing had to be cleaned and packed with rose petals and lavender to keep the bugs away and to freshen the garments. Large wooden trunks were stuffed with items: satins and silks mostly, well suited for the hot weather. Mary took special care to make certain all the pearls and other jewels had been removed before packing the clothes.

"Oh, she does have the most exquisite wardrobe, does she not?" said Mistress Eleanor, smoothing a pair of pale green sleeves before she laid them in the trunk.

"Yes, but you should be glad you do not have to keep track of all these. She has two thousand gowns, not counting kirtles, sleeves, smocks. Sometimes I think I shall go mad with all of these garments. And she knows every single one of them. She often asks for a gown ten years old and moth-eaten. I shall be forced to find it and get it in shape for her. It is tedious," said Mary.

There was a commotion in the outer chamber and the queen was announced. She swept into her bedchamber, smiling and talking to two men who followed her.

"Ladies, look who has returned to us! My lord Oxford! And Pakington! Oh gentlemen, we have missed you—you know, Oxford, shame should not have kept you from us! We had forgot the fart!" said the queen, laughing.

Mary stared at Oxford, her face heating up. He, too, was blushing, no doubt from the queen's comment. Then he noticed her staring at him and bowed to her most elegantly.

"Mistress Mary, you are lovely as ever. Mistress Eleanor, marriage must agree with you. I have never seen you looking so handsome," Oxford said, eyeing both women with undisguised interest.

Mary and Eleanor both curtsied as Pakington bowed to them as well.

"Are you not going to welcome us back to court, Mistress Mary? You do not look pleased to see us," said Pakington.

Mary said nothing.

"Leave the girl alone, Lusty, it is your queen who welcomes you back. We are most happy to see you both. Since the Ridolfi plot, no one has made us merry. Burghley and that new man, Walsingham, look over their shoulders, certain every man in London is a conspirator. But now you have returned and I shall laugh and dance again. You will join our progress?" said the queen, smiling up at them like a young girl.

"We would be delighted, Your Majesty," said Oxford.

Oxford turned to Mary.

"You look tired, mistress. Would you like to take a break from your duties and walk with me in the shade garden?" said Oxford.

Mary could not believe he would ask such a thing after she had refused him not a fortnight ago. She remembered his horrid slur against her in front of the entire court. She certainly had no desire to walk with him.

"An excellent idea, Oxford. Do take the child out for some fresh air—the poor dear has been packing all day. She is in need of a rest," said the queen.

"But Your Majesty, I still have much work to do if your clothes are to be ready for the progress. I cannot stop now," said Mary. But the queen made that "pup-pup" sound and shooed them out into the outer rooms with instructions to enjoy some light ale while they walked.

The enormous trees and hedges in the garden made a canopy above them, blocking most of the afternoon sun. Mary wore a large blue hat to shade her face and her matching skirts rustled when she walked. Oxford had offered her his arm but she refused. They moved without speaking until he had led them far from prying eyes. Near a statue of a chubby cupid, there was a small bench. Oxford brushed it off and then indicated for Mary to be seated. She did so, spreading her skirts so there would not be enough room for him to join her. He knelt at her side.

"Mary, dearest Mary, I have not been able to think of anything but you since our last conversation. No, hear me out. I confess, I have been confused by your refusal. I can't help remembering your passion, the way you gave yourself to me that night in the garden, before Mistress Blanche disturbed us. Oh, I let my mind wander—what bliss we might have had if that woman had not come upon us when she did. Surely you, too, have thought of that night," said Oxford, his voice insistent.

Mary did not reply. His bringing up the memory of something she had tried to forget was painful. She could feel herself blushing and she could not look at him. He took hold of her hand.

"Won't you at least look at me? Am I so distasteful to you? I know I should never have embarrassed you at the Frost Fair—I am so sorry. I don't know what got into me—Pakington kept teasing me about your disdain for me. The bastard accused me of lying about our night together. It was childish of me to give credence to his words, but I wanted to show him I told the truth—that you loved me once. Can you ever forgive me?" Oxford said.

Mary could not believe he had the nerve to bring up the odious business and her anger flared at the thought of it.

"Sir, you have mistaken my feelings and my intentions. That evening in the garden which you revere as a delight was, for me, a hell. Yes, I allowed you familiarity with my person never allowed to anyone else, but it had nothing to do with *you*! Had you been *any* man, my behavior would have been the same. I was angry with someone—no, I shall not divulge the name of the person. It was someone I admired, someone I loved. Yet this person had disappointed me, had shown hypocrisy. At that moment, I cared not a fig for what I was doing—I just wanted to show her, er, I mean that person, I could manage my own life. It was complete folly on my part and I thank God Mistress Blanche appeared when she did. She saved me that night," said Mary.

Now, it was Lord Oxford's turn to be silent. He hung his head.

She removed her hand from his and looked at the branches overhead. She began to watch the birds that twittered and flew from perch to perch, almost as if they were playing a game.

"But Mary, how could you have seemed so sincere? I have thought for all these weeks that you cared for me—I have never met a woman I could not make care for me! Yet you . . . you have deceived me," Oxford said.

"Do you not also deceive, sir? You are a great dissembler, far more so than am I. I have heard from others how you promise young maids marriage, rob them of their virtue, and then disappear from their lives. And I believe with all my heart that that is what you had planned for me, too. But since I escaped, you now have it in your mind you love me. I do not think you understand what love means," said Mary. She rose. "I should like to return to the queen's bedchamber now—I have much work to do."

Oxford rose also and put his hands on Mary's waist. He tried to pull her to him, but she resisted.

"Unhand me immediately or I shall call the guards! Unhand me, I say!" said Mary in her most commanding voice.

Oxford pulled her again to himself, with greater strength than he'd used previously, and kissed her. Mary pushed him away and slapped him as hard as she could across the face. His eyes flew open wide. She could see a red spot beginning to form across his cheek.

"You shall regret that, mistress! By all the saints, you shall rue the day you dared refuse me!" he said, turning and striding toward the castle.

Mary watched him leave. She knew she should not have struck him, but the arrogance in his manner irritated her. Who did he think he was? And with whom did he think he was dealing? She was the queen's ward and cousin. As such, Oxford should show her more respect. Well, he would now, by God's blood. He would now.

Thirty-one

By God's holy wounds, did you see Oxford's face, Parry? Oh, I have no doubt it was our Fawn who gave him such a slap. Probably well deserved. He is a rake, that one. Yet, I have always loved a rake, haven't I? A man with spirit—that's what I like! And I would have given him to our Fawn had she liked him. He will be ill-matched with Lord Burghley's daughter, I fear. Tut-tut. We shall find someone else for our Fawn.

No, I will not consider Skydemore! He is a minor knight of little import. Our girl deserves better—an earl at the very least! I know she is born no better than Skydemore, except she is our cousin—this raises her immensely. And she is educated—a proper wife for a man of wealth and breeding. I shall find someone for her, have no fear. She is still young.

I know all about the Sheffield woman—Robin thinks he can hide her from me. He should know I have other "eyes" in my court, those willing to tell me all they know. Yes, Old Catspaw—she keeps me up to date on what

Lady Sheffield is doing. Oh, Lady Sheffield prates on and on about Lord Robert—how handsome he is, how dashing. If she thinks he is in love with her, she is a fool! He shall never love anyone but me. By God's blood, I know it is so!

Now, let us sleep, dear. I know how these journeys tire you, Parry. Soon, we shall return to London and settle in for the winter. Then, all the problems of the world shall tumble down upon my shoulders. No, I have not yet decided what to do with the Duke of Norfolk. Fool! His own hand has condemned him—why would he be careless enough to write letters to the Scottish queen? Well, I have never accused him of being intelligent. But come. Let us not spoil our sleep with such thoughts. Look, there is our Fawn, already asleep—I can still see the little child in her face. Oh, how I miss those days! I was her "shining lady," do you remember? She would have done anything to please me. Now, I wonder what she thinks—she rarely tells me these days. Oh, she is obedient and pleasant most of the time. But every once in a while, I catch a hateful look as it flits across her features—as if I am her enemy. She thinks she is in love with Skydemore but she knows nothing of love. She is yet young. She will understand more as she grows older. She will realize I have only her best interests in my heart. I want to keep her near me—is that so wrong? I want her to be with me forever.

T hey have arrested Norfolk yet again!" said Mistress Eleanor from her seat in the corner of a commodious tent put up at Coventry, the last stop before the court returned to London from the summer progress. She fanned herself, her cheeks ruddy with the heat.

"This time, he will lose more than his freedom, I fear," said Lady Douglass, also looking limp from the warm weather.

"I shall be happy to return to Whitehall—and soon this heat will turn to the cooler air of autumn, though not quickly enough for me," said Mary, lifting her skirts above her knees. The women chattered and fanned, fanned and chattered.

"Did you hear Anjou was wooing the queen again? I understand for the first time, Lord Robert encourages the match. When the queen complained that Anjou was nineteen years younger and would always be so, he said, 'So much the better for you!' I suspect Lord Robert no longer loves Her Majesty as once he did," said Lady Douglass, her mouth making a sneer.

"He seems the same to me, Lady Douglass. You only wish he would have a change of heart because you want him for yourself," said Mistress Eleanor.

"Can you blame me? Now that you have enjoyed the sweetness of the marriage bed, do you not agree that such a state is as close to heaven as we shall get in this world?" said Lady Douglass.

"You have not said much of the marriage bed, Nora. What am I missing?" said Mary.

"It is not seemly to discuss such intimacies—but I will tell you that I like nothing better than rising with my lord in the early morning, waking him with kisses," said Nora, blushing.

"And if you are ever a widow, God forbid, you shall miss such moments. So, yes, I would have the Earl of Leicester if he should ask me—for I long to lie in his arms," said Lady Douglass.

Mary thought of the day in the woods when she had seen with her own eyes the queen in just that position with Dudley. And she wondered how the queen would react if Dudley should remarry.

"He loves the queen—do you not see that? If he dallies with you, it is only to satisfy his lust. Have a care, Lady Douglass. Men will use you if they can—I have learned this much," said Mistress Eleanor.

"We shall see who uses whom. But I have heard that the French duke likes to dress as a woman and he, well, he takes men more often than he takes women, though he seems to take them all!" said Lady Douglass. "Can you imagine our Elizabeth married to such as that?"

"If he is as you say, I hope she will continue in her virgin state. It would be unseemly for one such as she to be yoked with a man who has more gowns than she does!" said Mistress Eleanor.

"Hush! Here comes the queen!" said Mary, who stood as the queen entered the tent, accompanied by Lord Robert.

"Ah, here you are, Fawn. I have been searching for you. Robin and

I would like to picnic and thought you should like to come with us. We have asked a few others to join us—Oxford, Sir James Croft, and his son-in-law, Skydemore. Master Nicholas and Nora, do come!" said the queen, her arm entwined with her Sweet Robin's. She stared hard at Lady Douglass, but said nothing.

"A picnic sounds lovely, Your Majesty," said Mary as she curtsied. She was thrilled the queen had invited John and Sir James. Perhaps that meant they were in high favor and the time would be right for John to mention their plan to Sir James.

Though the sun beamed down without a cloud to give respite, the party of travelers enjoyed the journey to the river, where the servants had set up food and drink for all. Mary could feel sweat streaming down her back, though one of the serving wenches fanned her and the queen with a large palmlike leaf. They sat on pillows, side by side, with Lord Robert caring for the horses at the riverbank across from them. Mary smiled at Sir John, who was talking with Sir James and Oxford. Sir John winked his eye at her when no one was looking.

"Majesty, is it true you are to marry the French duke?" said Mary, biting into a soft, sweet plum.

"We are discussing such a move—remember, dear Fawn, talk is cheap," said the queen.

Mary knew the queen needed help against the Spanish threat—the Duke of Alva, who seemed a very capable military man, was determined to take over the Netherlands for Philip of Spain and return the country to the Pope. From the Netherlands, it would be relatively easy for Alva to muster his forces and cross over to England. Since the Pope's edict, the whole of the Catholic world seemed to think England fair game.

"You don't love him, then?" said Mary, whispering. She had not asked the queen such a personal question in a very long time. Speaking so made her feel closer to the queen, the way she used to feel as a child. Then, she could ask anything, say anything to Her Majesty. Now, their talk was not as easy.

"As I have told you before, love and marriage have very little to do with each other. One marries for safety—unless one has plenty of money and courage. I have both, so I do not feel the need to marry. Better to play the maid and entertain *proposals* of marriage," said the queen, laughing.

"What if one falls into love? Would you then recommend the married state?" said Mary.

"Even Saint Paul said it is better to marry than to burn—if a woman cannot contain her natural desires, then she should marry. Why are you asking all these questions about marriage? You do not have another girlish fancy, do you? Or are you still smitten with our 'Adonis'?" said the queen, eyeing her. Mary tried to show no emotion.

"No, Majesty. I was thinking more about you and Sweet Robin. He loves you and you love him—yet you are apart. It is sad," said Mary.

"Apart? He is with me every day of my life. And so he shall always be. We eat together, hunt together, dance together, do everything except one thing—and yes, that one thing pains me, more for himself than for me. But, nothing for it—such is the life we have. I shall be grateful for it," said the queen, rising. "Enough of this dismal talk— bring out your lute, Sir James, and play us a crafty tune. Mary has been wanting to hear you sing since she first heard your 'sonorous' baritone!"

Mary blushed as they all turned to her and laughed. She caught Oxford staring at her, his look inscrutable. Something about the way he gazed at her made her feel afraid. But soon, the music made her forget that fleeting feeling and she joined in with gusto.

Before long, they were singing a madrigal. Mary stood next to John and she loved hearing his rough voice. Sir James did, indeed, sing like a chorister, his low voice clear and strong. But she liked the scratchy sound of John's voice, raspy but in tune. She felt his arm sneak around her waist as they stood side by side, and imagined them at Holme Lacy, her playing the virginals and teaching his children to sing. She could think of no greater contentment.

October 1571

The heat of summer had finally relented and the autumnal evenings were temperate and as comfortable as even a queen could desire. Most evenings found the ladies strolling in the gardens or dancing after nightfall while the queen entertained the French ambassador, who continued to tell Her Majesty how very much the French duke adored her, calling her "the rarest creature that was in Europe these five hundred years." When the queen complained this could not be so because she had heard the duke had referred to her as "that old woman with a sore leg," the ambassador had to soothe the queen's ruffled feathers, assuring her of the duke's undying love.

While the queen basked in this lover's language, Lord Burghley continued his efforts to assure her safety. He expanded his network of spies, often infiltrating Catholic groups and making certain no treason was being plotted. Weekly, he arrested some low person for disparaging the queen's good name or talking against the French alliance. Dudley was often away from court and Mary detected a strain between the queen and her Sweet Robin. The queen spent more and more time enjoying the company of Sir Christopher Hatton, while Dudley seemed to disappear for days at a time.

As London began preparations for the coming winter, storing up foodstuff and patching cracks and crevices in houses and castles, the queen seemed to want the celebrations of summer to continue.

"Ladies, tonight we shall sail up the Thames at dusk. My lord of Leicester has prepared an elegant entertainment for us, with poetry from the pen of the Earl of Oxford and music composed in our honor by Leicester himself. Wear your prettiest jewels so we will glitter on the water as dazzling as sunlight," said the queen. She motioned for Mary and Nora to help her with her clothing while Mistress Dorothy and Mistress Frances repaired her hair, weaving it in and out of the metal frame on her head.

"Fawn, you may wear your yellow gown for this eve's festivities. I would have you look ravishing for the French ambassador," said the queen quietly.

"As you wish, Majesty. But what have I to do with Monsieur Fenelon?" said Mary as she laced the queen's stomacher.

"I wish to make a favorable impression. You are young and beautiful—that should help things along. Besides, if the ambassador gets a good look at you, perhaps another Valois prince would become available—they seem to have no shortage of them. Then our countries would be doubly yoked and a better ally we could not find," said the queen.

"Majesty, you surely cannot think to marry me to a *prince!*" said Mary, her mouth open.

"Why not? You are my cousin, a blood relative of the Queen of England. You would make a fine consort for any prince in Europe," said the queen.

"But Majesty, what if I am already fond of someone here, someone sprung from England's finest soil?" said Mary, unable to stop the quaking that had begun in her legs.

"Oh, fie. You have rejected the Earl of Oxford. Who else would be suitable for you? If you think of that handsome Skydemore, I have told you he can be nothing more to you than a little toy. I gave you distinct instructions not to find love in that corner. Surely you have not! Or have you?" said the queen, her tone menacing.

"No, Majesty, no. I am Your Majesty's obedient servant. It's just . . . well, it's just that I am clean amazed at the thought of marrying a man I have never met—it is frightening," said Mary.

"I agree. That is why I will insist on Anjou traveling to England before I make my decision. And, if things work out as I might wish, you, too, may take a look at your intended before you decide yea or nay," said the queen.

The Yeoman of the Guard shouted in the outer rooms of the queen's chambers.

"The Earl of Leicester, here to see the queen! The Earl of Leicester!"

"Come, Mary—let us leave this talk of marriage and sail down the Thames this lovely eve. My Sweet Robin has many delicacies planned for us," said the queen, rising, then patting her hair into place, pinching her cheeks though they had been rouged, and then gliding gracefully into the outer room where her "Sweet Robin" stood waiting. Mary hurriedly put on her yellow gown, leaving the white sleeves and kirtle she had worn for the day. She quickly hooked her diamond and pearl necklace around her neck and ran to join the queen.

The queen's barge was lit with torches and several lords and ladies sat on pillows outside the little glass cabin where the queen rested with Dudley. Music wafted across the river and Mary watched the wherries and other small craft travel up and down the river, each lit by torches and candles. The sight was like watching fireflies in the summer night, lights blinking on and off as the boats moved on the lapping river. Several of the smaller tiltboats followed the queen's barge while groups of wherries gathered on both sides. Trumpets blared across the river, bells rang and cannon thundered, as the queen passed along. Once the noise started, the citizens of London realized the queen was upon the river and they lined the banks, waving their hats and yelling. The queen sat up in her cabin and waved back at them. Lord Leicester waved, too.

Mary saw Sir James sitting on the other side of the queen's

barge and she hoped Sir John had made it aboard as well. She could not get up to search for him, however, because of her bulky skirts.

"I wish we could traverse the river without all this hubbub," said Mistress Eleanor, arranging her dress so she could tuck her feet beneath her.

"It is always thus—when the queen moves about, the people flock to see her. I can barely hear the music—these bells and guns will make me deaf," said Mary. She was aware of movement on the deck as a small group of men walked from one side to the other. At first, she could not make out who they were, but as they approached, she recognized Sir John. She smiled up at him.

"My lady. This night is lovely but you are more so," he said, bowing to her.

"Do sit down, John. The queen is in her cabin with her Robin. Though she can see us, I do not think her *mind* will be on *us*. Have a glass of malmsey," said Mary, offering him a golden goblet she had just poured from a nearby ewer.

"Here, Sir James, there is room between Nora and me. I would not wish for you to remain on your feet," said Mary, scooting over, closer to John.

The noise eventually died down as the bells were rung only three times, the same for the cannon shot—three for the Holy Trinity—a blessing for the queen. Soon, the night's entertainments began, with Oxford reading poems composed for the queen and Dudley singing his own songs again. The smaller craft still followed the queen's barge. Mary watched as the queen and the Lord of Leicester made their way from the cabin to join her on the deck of the barge.

"Fawn, you look as though you are having a lovely time," said the queen, as everyone started to stand. She motioned for them to keep their seats, but John and Sir James stood anyway. Mary noticed that Lord Leicester, John, and Sir James were effectively blocking the queen, making themselves a wall around her.

"It is a beautiful evening, the music and food superb—even the poetry will suffice," said Mary, looking directly at Oxford, who took a little bow.

Suddenly, a loud shot rang across the water. Before she knew what was happening, all three men had thrown themselves over the queen. Another shot zinged past Mary's ear. It sounded like a large fly buzzing, and to Mary's horror, she watched John begin to sink to his knees.

People seemed to spring to life, as if they had been charged by lightning. Dudley ran toward one of the wherries and leaped across the water to land onboard. The queen stood, her elbows propped up by Sir James and Oxford.

"No harm! No harm!" she cried in a loud voice. Then she sat down beside Sir John, who was still squatting in an odd sort of way. Mary hadn't realized it, but she and Nora had ducked down behind the railing of the barge. She quickly rose and went to John, who was bleeding from his shoulder.

"Are you hurt? I see blood. Is there a doctor?" shouted Mary.

"I'm all right. Just a little wound. Caught me in the right shoulder—that's all. Do not fret, ladies," said Sir John, his hand clutching the injury.

The queen knelt over him and used her handkerchief to stanch the blood. Mary noticed Her Majesty's face was white beneath her white powder and her hands trembled as she dabbed at Sir John's wound. The boat had turned around and was heading back toward the palace. Dudley had pulled the wherry alongside the barge and had jumped back onboard, holding a terrified man in his grip.

"Majesty, this is the vagrant who took the shots. Claims his gun went off by accident," said Dudley.

The man went immediately to his knees, tears streaming down his face. He held his cap in his hands, twisting it back and forth as he tried to explain.

"Your Majesty, I meant no harm. All the cannon was a-firing and the bells was a-ringing. I just wanted to shoot me weapon to do Your Majesty honor. I swear on the body of our blessed Savior, I meant no harm. I would never hurt Your Majesty—I have loved you my whole life," said the man, his manner sincere.

"You have not harmed us, little man. But your shot has found a mark in our servant, Sir John Skydemore. It is he who must forgive you," said the queen kindly.

"Bess, I want to take this man to the Tower and rack him. That'll get the truth from his lips," said Dudley.

"No! I shall not have an innocent man racked for an accident. I believe him," said the queen.

"With the Pope's edict and the Ridolfi plot exposed, you still would trust this, this vagabond?" said Dudley.

"I be no vagabond, my lord. I am a chandler and was borned and raised right here in London. Why, I saw the queen's coronation and I bless her in me prayers each and every night," said the man, still weeping.

"Good sir, you are free to go. But when you do, tell your friends that we trust our people and we will do right by them. Go on, we have set you free," said the queen, pushing her Sweet Robin out of her way.

Lord Robert grabbed the queen's elbow and pulled her to him.

"But Bess, there were two shots fired. This fellow could have fired only one. Surely this is no accident. Surely he has a partner—allow me to rack him to discover the identity of his friend," he said.

"Whoever fired the second shot is long gone by now, Robin," she whispered. She turned to the cowering chandler. "You are free to go, little man."

"What about Sir John? He needs a doctor!" said Mary, holding her own handkerchief over the injury, pressing hard to stop the bleeding.

"Row faster, men! Get us to Whitehall!" shouted Dudley.

"I shall be fine—have no fear. I shall be fine," said Sir John, look-ing at the queen and Mary, whose faces hovered above him until his eyes closed and Mary feared he might die before they could get to Whitehall.

The next morning, Mary hurried through her duties, anxious to see Sir John, though the doctor had assured both the queen and Mary that the wound was superficial and did not endanger his life. Finally, she was finished brushing the queen's cloaks. She walked quickly to the rooms where Sir James Croft stayed when at court, knowing this was where they had taken Sir John. She knocked gently on the wooden door and a soft voice called, "Enter."

Mary was astonished to see the queen seated beside Sir John's bed, dipping a rag into water, then washing his shoulder. Strips of cloth were stacked on a nearby table and a jar filled with yellow salve sat next to them. Mary had brought one of her cordials for Sir John, one that would ease pain. She held the small vial in her hand and closed her fist around it.

"Your Majesty," said Mary, curtsying.

"I had to check on our patient first thing. After all, he saved my life," said the queen.

"I did what any true subject would do, Your Grace," said Sir John, his face pale but his green eyes lively. He was obviously enjoying the queen's ministrations.

"We disagree, I assure you. Mary was there—she saw how you bravely threw yourself across my body when the shots were fired. The bullet that hit you would have gone clean through me, if you had not done so. This shall be rewarded, Sir John. Of that, you can rest assured," said the queen.

"I desire no reward except your safety, Your Majesty," said Sir John.

"Tut-tut. Enough of talk—you need rest," said the queen.

Mary was not sure what to do. She did not wish to speak with Sir John while the queen was there, but she did not wish to leave him, either. So, she stood, shifting from one foot to the other.

"Fawn, you are as nervous as a cat. For goodness' sake, give the man the cordial you made—yes, I can see it, though you would hide it from me—and let us begone," said the queen.

"Sir, I did brew you a cordial to ease your pain. If you will take it?" said Mary, leaning over him from the other side of his sickbed.

"Mistress, I shall be pleased to take anything from your hand," said Sir John. Mary quickly pulled the stopper from the vial and poured the contents into his mouth. Then the queen ordered her to the gardens for their usual midday walk.

Thirty-three

God's teeth! When the shots were fired, I knew I was drawing my last breath! I felt the wind rush out of me and my head reeled. I fell in a swoon before the men threw themselves upon me, my dear Sweet Robin the first to land in my lap. Even Lord Burghley tried to protect me, God love him. But it was Skydemore who blocked me from the side and that is where the bullet landed, right in the poor man's shoulder. Aye, he was brave! And such a handsome fellow! I did notice a particular concern gathering itself on our Fawn's pretty face. Parry, I fear she has more interest in the young man than she lets on. She brought him a healing cordial this morning—for his wound. Luckily, I was already with him and could steer them apart. I have told her he is not the man for her—she must obey me in this. Oh, I know you want her to be happy. So do I. But we are older and wiser than she—we know the ways of the world. And, like it or not, wealth and position matter. Our Fawn has grown up at court. She has enjoyed the best music, the best food, the best dancing—if she is deprived of *these pastimes, then she shall grow unhappy. And, as her guardian, I am the one who shall decide upon her husband. I want someone who will offer her everything to which she has become accustomed, someone who will cherish her as I do. She has been like my own child. Robin has felt this, too. It is as if we make our own dear family.*

By God's blood, I know we are not truly a family—but allow me my fancies! I have so little to console me. I came this close to death yesterday, but I do not shiver. My hands are steady. Why? Because the man who set off one of the shots was a true subject—I could see it in his eyes. He was terrified, certain he was to die. Yet I could see he loved me, trusted me to do right by him even as he knelt before me. And I showed him mercy. Now, he will tell everyone he meets of my generosity and he will defend me to the death. And yes, I do believe he was innocent of any wrong. Dear man, he showed me that my people love me. They do not plot against me. It is queens and dukes who wish to steal my throne, not my people.

Yes, I know there was another shot. Some foul miscreant, no doubt. But even so, I am not afraid, for I have men such as John Skydemore to protect me.

No, Parry, I do not need a sleeping cordial. Tonight, I shall sleep with the peace of a suckling babe.

W inter blew into London with a fierceness, whipping cloaks around freezing citizens, snatching hats from heads, causing chilblains and shivering, keeping everyone indoors, huddled around hearths, sipping warming broth. Everyone except the queen. In her usual fashion, she donned heavy robes and walked in the gardens around Richmond, her favorite wintering place.

"Serving the queen will be the death of us all," said Lady Douglass, scrambling across the frozen grasses of the labyrinth where the queen was heading with Lord Burghley and her Sweet Robin.

"Her Majesty says a walk in the morning is good for what ails you. And from the look of her, the remedy works—she is as fit and spry as I am," said Mary, easily navigating the way.

"She is slim as a maid, no doubt. Yet such slenderness causes her face to wrinkle like the neck of a tortoise. I prefer a more rounded, womanly figure—such as my own. I expect nary a wrinkle until I reach the old age of forty-five," said Lady Douglass, lifting her skirts to avoid the frost.

"The queen is but thirty-eight—still young enough to bear a child," said Mary, thinking about what might happen if the queen accepted the French duke.

"She is of barren stock—her father's seed did not bear much fruit, though he scattered it far and wide. She will never live through childbirth, even if she does consent to marry," said Douglass.

"Do not say such things! If she marries, she will give us an heir and she will be fine. She is strong in more ways than in her body. Her spirit will see her through anything!" said Mary,

"Speaking of her 'Spirit,' here he comes—following the queen like a little puppy," said Lady Douglass, her face twisted in a snarl.

"I wonder why they are heading back our way? What has happened?" said Mary, still walking toward the queen. Within a few steps, she could hear the queen's voice, carrying across the cold air like the boom of a cannon.

"God's death! I will *not* execute the Scottish queen! Nor will I shorten Norfolk by a head!" roared the queen, outpacing the men behind her.

"Majesty," said Burghley, "we have letters between the Scots' queen and Norfolk, proving they planned to marry and then mount a rebellion. They have been in communication with Spain and the Pope—once Ridolfi had rescued the Queen of Scots, he was going to unite her with Norfolk, raise an army in the north, and get reinforcements from Spain—we have their *letters*, proof beyond a doubt!"

"I do not care if you racked a thousand men to condemn them—I will *not* do away with an anointed queen! Nor will I execute Norfolk! He can rot in the Tower—no more talk of this!" said the queen, still moving forward at breakneck speed. Mary and the rest of the women dropped a quick curtsy and fell in behind her.

The men stopped abruptly while Mary and the other ladies followed the queen like goslings after a goose. Mary had seen the queen in a fury many times, but this seemed more serious than usual. The queen marched straight into her bedchamber, ordered everyone out but Mary and Mistress Blanche.

"By the nails of the Cross, they shall not force me to murder those two scheming scoundrels! Keep them under guard—yes! Reduce the queen's retinue—yes! Watch their every move—yes! But kill them? Never!" said the queen, pacing back and forth, wringing her hands.

"Majesty . . . please sit down. You will have a fit of apoplexy if you do not becalm yourself," said Mistress Blanche, trying to catch the queen by her elbow and lead her to a bench beneath the window.

"I will *not* sit down! My legs tell me to walk and walk I must!" said the queen, jerking her arm away.

"Your Grace, why will you not do away with the traitors? I wish to understand," said Mary in a soft voice.

The queen stopped her pacing and looked at the girl.

"I shall tell you why, and then you shall give me your thoughts on the matter. Treachery has touched you close enough, with your friend Sir John injured in what may have been an attack on me," said the queen. She sat down on the bench and indicated with a pat of her hand for Mary to join her. "Parry, some comfits please and wine—add no water."

Mistress Blanche set about pouring wine and ordering food from the kitchens. Then she sat at the queen's feet, ewer in hand, ready to refill their glasses as need be.

Tom and the queen's dogs curled up next to them, *Tom* putting his head on Mary's foot.

"I will not take the lives of such highborn nobles because I believe God has placed us where we find ourselves. In His mercy and kindness, He put me on the throne of England. I believe it is His will that I stay here and try to keep my kingdom in security and at peace. I have brought about changes in religion which I believe are good and for His glory. But each monarch has such work to do. The Queen of Scots, though she has behaved foolishly and has lost her crown, is still God's anointed representative on Earth. How could I do away with such a person? She is my kinswoman as well. As for Norfolk, he is young and ambitious, yes. I certainly will not allow them to marry, for if they had a son, the country could easily be split into civil war—those who wanted a return to the Pope would side with their boy, and the Protestants would align with me. I cannot allow such a threat, for it is not the rulers who pay the price of war, but the people. They pay with their goods and their lives," the queen said as she sipped the wine. She paused, took a deep gulp, and then breathed more easily.

"I want my people to have happy lives. God knows, they have enough to plague them—droughts, bad crops, illness, poverty—to add war seems most unkind," said the queen, her breathing settled into a more regular rhythm and her voice calm.

Mary mulled these thoughts over, wondering if she would ever understand the woman who sat next to her. The queen seemed the most loving, considerate, and wise ruler a people could ever hope to have. Yet, she could change into a selfish, cruel mistress if the mood took her.

"So, dear Fawn, what think you? Should these traitors die?" said the queen.

Mary considered her words carefully.

"I agree that to execute a fellow queen would rouse the Catholics all over Europe to arms. Such an act would give the Pope a reason to gather his forces and attack England. I do not believe we could withstand the arms of Spain, France, and the Hapsburgs, though we be separated by the water. In my heart, I think the taking of any life is God's right, not ours," said Mary.

"You are well reasoned, Fawn. You see to the core of it. What of Norfolk?" said the queen.

"I would preserve him if I could. But I have seen how angered the men of the realm are against this treasonous plot. If Parliament finds him guilty, I fear, as head of the state, you would have to give him the same as all traitors get—death. Though I would not like it, for he is young," said Mary.

"These are my own thoughts, Fawn. Parliament will have to force me to execute him—then the blame goes to them. You have a good head for government, dear one. You have learned much from your tutor and from listening to the Privy Council. You shall be a real asset to your husband—whoever he may be. Ah, here is the food! I have worked up an appetite—" said the queen as she reached for a comfit filled with cherries.

Early December 1571

"Dr. Dee is kind to invite us once again to Mortlake," said Mary, leaning on Sir John's arm for support as she slipped and skidded across the icy cobbles on the road.

"He likes you—he has told me it is rare for a woman to take an interest in science. He says it is because you are of the queen's blood; such tendencies are communicated in the blood, he believes. Much like hair and eye color—he says even our capacity for faith is carried on in our blood," said Sir John, shielding Mary from a cart that seemed, momentarily, out of control.

"Whew! I thought that load of wood was going to run us down!" said Mary, clinging to him, her arms tight around his neck.

"If *this* is the result of such a scare, I would wish carts to run at us *every* day," said Sir John, holding her close.

She looked up at him, his wavy hair moving slightly in the wind, his aqua eyes staring into her own. Before she thought, she kissed him, there, in the middle of the street. They had avoided each other in public places. Rather, by assignation, they had met a few times, talking about their plans and stealing kisses and caresses. Mary found it more and more difficult to restrain herself from him.

"My dearest, there are eyes everywhere," he said gently as he broke away from her.

"I do not care—it has been too long since I kissed you. When will you ask Sir James to approach the queen about our marriage? I long to be in your bed!" Mary whispered.

"Oh, my love, you tempt me so! I have spoken to Sir James, but he says the time is not yet ripe—after all, my family is Catholic. Now is a bad time for Catholics," said Sir John, leading her to Dr. Dee's doorway.

"But you saved the queen's life! You took a wound upon your own body for her. Surely this proves your loyalty," said Mary.

"Perhaps. But I shall trust Sir James on this—he has a wise head upon his shoulders. Look, we are here, my love," he whispered.

Mary felt a tingle of desire when he called her his "love."

They entered Mortlake and were led to the dining room where a modest repast was set for them. Dr. Dee welcomed them and urged them to eat their fill.

"The Earl of Leicester may join us later. He is interested in the stars and what they can tell us of the future," said Dr. Dee, his long beard now almost to his waist.

"I am always happy to see Lord Robert. He has been somewhat absent from court these last few months. I think he steals away to Leicester House to avoid the queen's foul temper," said Mary, reaching for a thick slice of wheat bread smeared with marmalade. "This is delicious—so much more hearty than the queen's manchet."

"I have found the darker breads more tasty as well as better for my health," said Dr. Dee. "What questions do you have for me this night?"

"As you may have already surmised, Mary and I wish to marry. I would like to hear what the stars say about our union. I would also like to know when it would be safe to approach the queen to ask for her blessing," said Sir John.

Mary was surprised he would confess their plans to Dr. Dee and sent him a questioning look. He smiled back at her as if to say, "Do not worry—it is safe."

"I had guessed as much. The looks of love are difficult to hide," said Dr. Dee.

After they had supped, they entered Dr. Dee's laboratory with all his charts and machines and books. While Dr. Dee and John discussed various subjects, Mary wandered around the enormous room, picking up books and leafing through them.

"We are ready, Mistress Mary, if you will join us?" said Dr. Dee, spreading out a scroll of parchment across his long desk.

Mary moved quickly to see what Dr. Dee had discovered.

"You, as I told the queen a long while ago, Mary, were born under the sign of Aquarius and you, Sir John, under Libra. Your match is an excellent one—you are both honest, naturally kind. The only possible problem I can see is that Mary is a bit unpredictable—but then, she is a woman, is she not?" said Dr. Dee with a smile.

"Decidedly so," said Sir John, smiling at Mary.

"Though I see the match will be a good one, there are some shadows at the beginning. I have done a little scrying in the crystal and have seen a large dragon swooping down upon the two of you—I am not sure of the meaning of this, but you might wish to postpone your marriage for a year or so. To avoid whatever evil may be dogging your steps," said Dr. Dee.

"A year? Oh no, we could not possibly wait that long," said Mary, blushing.

"Well, these are just suggestions, dear. Just suggestions," said Dr.

Dee. "Yet I also saw danger when I checked the stars—there is the ominous shadow of death hovering over you both at present. As I said, you would be smart to wait a little while."

Mary could not help feeling discouraged by this news and her body slumped against John's. He put his arm around her and bowed to Dr. Dee.

"We thank you for taking such time for us, sir. May I repay your efforts?" said Sir John.

"Only by becoming the godparents of my expected child who, I hope, shall enter this world in exactly six months, five days, and seven hours—according to the stars," said Dr. Dee.

"Doing such would be our pleasure," said Mary. "And congratulations!"

"I have some very interesting studies of plant life, if you should wish to see them," said Dr. Dee, rising from his desk.

"Nothing could please us more," said Sir John.

Late December 1571

The Christmas celebrations were proceeding with gusto, with dancing, music, theatrical performances, and great feasting. There was even a wedding, one of the most spectacular events in the land. Lord Burghley's daughter, Anne, married Edward de Vere, Earl of Oxford. Mary attended the wedding. Mistress Anne looked as pretty as Mary had ever seen her, the joy on her features making her plain face lively, a smile on her lips and a light in her eyes. She wore a pale yellow brocade dress with cloth-of-silver sleeves and a kirtle of matching yellow silk. Her reddish-blond hair looked pretty against the matching French hood. Mary was happy for her.

Oxford, on the other hand, was somber. His mouth drew down

and his eyebrows bunched together as if he were in deepest thought. Mary caught him staring at her as he and his new wife walked down the aisle together. If his stare had been a sword, she felt she would have been stabbed in the heart. She knew, at that moment, Oxford would do her harm if he ever got the chance.

PART II

In good time I'll banish from this place
all wicked ones; keeping none of such race.

LINES FROM A POEM
BY ELIZABETH I

Thirty-five
March 1572

The blustery March winds had rattled their way into Richmond Palace in spite of the efforts of the serving men to keep the fires burning brightly. The queen had caught a chill and was coughing and sneezing frequently. She complained to Mary that her head hurt and she was too ill to leave her bed. Mary promised to prepare a special cordial for Her Majesty, Rosa Solis, a bright yellow draught that promised to strengthen and nourish the body. Mary had not made this medicine before and needed to procure the main ingredient, sundew, a carnivorous plant that gave the brew its golden color, from the stores in the royal kitchens. She also needed to restock her supply of cinnamon, nutmeg, and ginger.

Mary hurried from the queen's apartments to the royal kitchens. The halls grew more and more cold the farther she walked from the queen's rooms. Though the walls were hung with tapestries and arras, these coverings could not keep out the icy wind, and Mary wondered if there would come yet another snow. It was dusk and the torches were slowly being lit as she quickly walked to her destination. She loved going to her little room; it was a place where she could daydream to her heart's content as she mixed spices, fermented fruits and flowers, and created delicious cordials. Most of the time, she used time-honored recipes from Catspaw, but sometimes she experimented as her knowledge of herbs and plants grew. She enjoyed taking a pinch from the large amount of sugar she kept in a locked chest, as it was almost as valuable as gold. She also had a dozen jars with stoppers in which she kept herbs and spices. She used wine as the basis for most of her cordials and had a vat halfway full. For stronger drinks, she used aqua vitae. She was ticking off the list of her needs in her mind when she became aware of someone walking close behind her. The hall often bustled with servants going about their duties, but decorum demanded a show of proper respect by maintaining a certain distance. Surely none would be so bold as to dog her steps. But she could feel a presence, almost sense the warm breath of whoever it was. Well, this could not be tolerated! She turned to give the offender a good talking-to and found herself facing Oxford, with Pakington not far behind.

"Milady, you seem in a hurry. Where are you going in such a whirl?" said Oxford, leering at her. He seemed unsteady on his feet.

"My errand is no concern of yours, sir," she said, taking a step away from him. She used the same tone she had heard the queen use with her servants—haughty and in command.

"Perhaps you would enjoy our company . . . Pakington and I have nothing better to do," said Oxford, moving toward her.

"I have no need of your company, gentlemen. As you can see, I am quite capable of managing my own affairs," Mary said, again speaking as if she were addressing a yeoman rather than an earl. She couldn't help it; Oxford frightened her. He was unpredictable and unstable—and she did not like the way he was looking at her.

"It is obvious the lady does not want our help, Oxford. Let us return to the Presence Chamber and wait for the queen—I have some land issues I wish to discuss with Her Majesty," said Pakington, putting his hand on Oxford's arm in a restraining gesture.

"Nonsense! I know Mary better than you do, Lusty. Aye, that should be *her* name—I remember well how she kissed me in the gardens, how she let me touch her private places and how she sighed with desire when I did so. Didn't you, Mary? You liked it, did you not?" said Oxford. He came close enough so that she could smell the wine on his breath. She realized he was drunk and was teetering toward her.

"Sir, you are a knave and a liar!" she said with as much disdain as she could muster. She blushed because she knew *she* was the liar, not him. But she wanted to make sure Pakington would not believe Oxford's drunken ramblings. As he stumbled toward her, he reached for her with both hands, grabbing hold of her waist.

At that moment, she heard the sound of boots upon the stone floor and, to her surprise, Sir John approached them.

"What goes on here?" he said, shoving Oxford away from Mary and pushing him into Pakington.

"None of your bloody business!" said Oxford as he tried to maintain his balance.

"When I see a man bullying a helpless woman, I make it my business," said Sir John. He stepped in front of Mary, standing between her and Oxford.

"He's been in his cups today—let me take him to his rooms. Maybe I can get him to sleep it off," said Pakington, trying to get hold of Oxford's arm.

Oxford jerked away and started toward Mary again.

"She's nothing but a stewed whore! Leads a man on—till he can think of nothing else! But I'll have her yet! By all the gods, she'll be mine!" said Oxford, launching for Mary once again.

Sir John put his hand on the hilt of his sword and pushed Oxford away. He pulled out his sword and placed the point at Oxford's throat.

"Leave her alone! If you come near her again, I will run you through. That is a promise, sir," said Sir John.

For a moment, they stood still. Then a gaggle of serving women walked toward the kitchens. When they saw the drawn sword, they stopped and stared. Oxford's face had turned red and his arms shook with rage. He looked directly at Mary.

"I won't forget this, Mistress Mary," he said.

Then he turned to Sir John. "How dare you draw your sword on me? You will pay for this affront—of that you can be sure. Come, Lusty. Let us be away from here," said Oxford, turning to his friend. Together, they stumbled away from the kitchens and headed back the way they had come. The serving women moved along, very quietly going about their business.

"I am glad you came along when you did, John. What are you doing down here anyway?" said Mary as she took the arm he offered.

"I was looking for you. I was told the queen was unwell and Old Catspaw told me you were going to make her one of your cordials. I knew where you would be. What in the world was Oxford doing down here?" said John.

"He followed me, I guess. Ever since that night in the garden, he has been after me," said Mary.

"Night in the garden? What night in the garden?" said John, following her into the small room. He noticed she had made the place cozy. A small stool with a brocade pillow atop was near the table so she could sit when she cut her herbs. Several vases were filled with dried flower arrangements, two in the windowsill and one on the large wooden table where she worked. Fresh rush mats covered the floor and various utensils hung on hooks. Though the small hearth was dark, there was kindling already set to start a fire.

"Can you tell me what happened?" he said.

"I would rather forget all about it," said Mary. She began to gather the materials for the healing cordial. She did not want to tell John what had happened between her and Oxford. She was afraid if he knew, he would not wish to marry her. Yet, if he was going to be her husband, perhaps he should know this.

"Is it something you can forget? Oxford seems to be having trouble forgetting it. I wish no impediments to our marriage, my love. You will find me an understanding friend," said Sir John.

"I suppose you have a right to know," said Mary.

She took a deep breath and began.

"Oxford kissed me one night, after we had danced together. I was . . . I was upset with the queen and feeling strange. I . . . I allowed him more freedom with my person than I should have. Do not worry; my virtue is still intact. But he thinks me a wanton because of that night. And I was," said Mary. She looked down and felt shame flush her face.

"Were you . . . were you in love with him?" said John quietly.

Mary gave a short laugh, then looked up at him.

"No! I was angry with the queen—it's all so complicated. I don't understand quite why I did what I did—but Oxford will never let me forget it. I wish he would turn his attentions to his poor wife," said Mary.

"I will see that he does not pester you again, dearest. You have my word on it," said John.

"Can you forgive me for my folly?" Mary said, looking at him. She was not sure she wanted to hear his answer. She feared her indiscretion would make him love her less.

"Do you think you are the only person who has ever acted unwisely? Believe me, I have seen every kind of foolishness at court. Yours was a minor thing, quickly forgotten by all except Oxford. He is a strange man," said Sir John. He put his arm around her and hugged her to him.

"Yes, and a frightening one," said Mary.

"But you shall not have to worry about him again. Feeling my steel against his throat should dissuade him of further action," said Sir John.

"There is one more thing you should know. Oxford asked the queen for my hand in marriage. She told me and wanted to know whether or not I would wish such a match. She reminded me of Oxford's prestige and how fond she was of him," said Mary. She leaned into John and his steadiness gave her strength.

"And how did you answer Her Majesty?" said John quietly.

"I told her Oxford was not the man for me. So she gave him my refusal. Before his marriage to Mistress Anne, he begged me several times to reconsider," said Mary. "I fear I have made an enemy."

Sir John kept quiet for a moment. Then he turned Mary to him and kissed her, a deep kiss that possessed her.

Thirty-six
April 1572

T ime once again brought spring weather to London, with lambs and ducklings crowding the already bulging alleys and streets, birds nesting in chimneys, and hoards of kittens squalling for milk. The sun, no longer pale as in winter, shone down, and its warmth was welcomed by one and all: from undercooks to scouring maids to porters and clothiers, the people welcomed spring. Many a lad's fancy turned to lust, if not true love.

Mary and the queen were not immune to the charms of more pleasant weather and Mary found herself out and about more often than not. The queen played tennis and bowles, rode out to the countryside with Sir Christopher Hatton, danced, and tried to put the decision of whether or not to execute the Duke of Norfolk off for another day. Mary missed Lord Robert, who had run afoul of the queen over the question of the duke, and was licking his wounds at Leicester House.

On this fine morning, Mary and Mistress Eleanor were tidying up the queen's bedchamber when Old Catspaw hobbled in with fresh sheeting, folded nicely, though the stack was quickly slipping from Catspaw's grip.

"Allow me to help," said Mary, jumping to save the linens before they hit the floor. She stacked them in the linen press. She then saw Catspaw about to fall into a swoon, ran to her, caught her underneath the arms, and helped her to Mary's own pallet.

"Are you all right?" said Mary. "Nora, bring a cup of wine, will you?"

Mistress Eleanor quickly poured a glass of wine and handed it to Mary. Mary brought the rim to Catspaw's lips and the old woman sipped a little.

"Getting old . . . too old to carry such a load," sputtered Catspaw.

"I shall speak to the queen when next I see her. I shall ask that you be excused from all duties, old dear. I think the queen will grant my request," said Mary.

"If it be you who ask, she well may. Now, if Lady Douglass were to beg for it, Her Majesty would spit in her eye," said Catspaw.

"And why would that be?" said Nora, who had joined them on the pallet.

"Surely you know. Lady Douglass will be Lady Leicester ere long," said the old woman.

"What? This is just another of your gossips—you should know better than to pay such tales any mind," said Mary.

"Shows what you know—I heard them a-talking in the linen hall. Lord Robert told her he couldn't marry her, and if she expected such, she should break off with him. She said *that* she would never do. And then they played the beast with two backs," said Catspaw with a grin. Her mouth looked like a gaping hole, so many teeth were gone from it. Mary turned away.

"I have a cordial which will give you ease from your pains and also revive your energy a little. Would you like some?" said Mary.

"If'n it ain't poison," said Catspaw.

"Have no fear—I know of no foul cordials. The taste is good and sweet. There, drink it down," said Mary. She allowed Catspaw to rest on her pallet until the cordial had taken some effect. She helped the old woman to her feet. Once she was certain Catspaw was steady and able to walk, she sent her to the servants' quarters, promising to speak to the queen about lessening her duties. When she returned to the queen's bedchamber, she found Mistress Eleanor waiting for her.

"Do you think her story is true? Do you think Lord Robert means to marry Lady Sheffield?" said Nora, rising from the pallet.

"Fie, Catspaw is always spreading tales—like jelly on manchet. I give her words no credence. Lord Robert loves the queen, of that I am certain," said Mary.

"I have no doubt of that, either. But I have seen how Lady Douglass chases after him, like a hound on the hunt. She *is* pretty in a common sort of way," said Nora.

"Yes, and younger than the queen. But the queen is a rare jewel. None can compare with her," said Mary.

"I hope you are right in this—I would hate to see what would happen if Lord Robert ever married again!" said Nora.

The queen called Mary and Mistress Eleanor to her in the Presence Chamber where several courtiers had gathered. It was late afternoon, before time to sup, but after the queen had finished her business of the day. Sir Christopher stood on one side of Her Majesty while Lord Robert knelt in front of her. Mary was surprised and happy to see Lord Robert there, taking his rightful place as the queen's favorite. Lord Burghley stood behind the throne, talking with Sir James Croft.

Next to him stood Sir John, looking at Mary. Mary gave him a slight smile. The queen crooked her finger at Mary and Nora.

"Mistresses Mary and Eleanor, welcome. This is a special day, for on this day I will recognize and reward my faithful servants. First, the Earl of Leicester is to be commended for his efforts on my behalf in my marriage negotiations—this is a difficult task for him, for the love he bears me. Yet he is doing a superb job. The French duke is still asking for my hand, though I do not think to give it to him just yet," said the queen to much laughter.

"I give the French duke my sympathy, for I, too, know what it is like to serve a fickle mistress," said Lord Robert, staring at Sir Christopher.

"Have no fears, Robin—I shall always need my 'Eyes,' but my 'Lids' are important, too," said the queen, nodding to Sir Christopher, "so I can be blind to what lechery I know goes on at my court." The queen's mouth curled down. "And now, Sir John Skydemore, please step forward."

Mary watched as Sir John walked to the queen, bowed deeply, and stood waiting.

"For your courage on the Thames, I am making you one of my Gentlemen Pensioners. You will bear, with all of them, responsibility for my safety. You shall be paid fifteen pounds a year," said the queen. "You will have little time for your studies, I fear."

Sir John knelt on one knee and thanked the queen graciously. Mary thought he looked handsome as he gazed into the queen's face. Of course, most of the Gentlemen Pensioners were tall and fair of countenance. She was not surprised John would be selected for such service.

"And now, I would have music and dancing before we sup. Come, good fellows, by God's breath, play a happy tune!" said the queen, clapping her hands at her musicians, who were ever ready to please Her Majesty. "Now, Sweet Robin, you may have the first dance!"

Mary watched as the queen and Lord Robert took the floor in a spritely galliard. The queen's feet moved as lightly as fairies' wings, fluttering here and there. Lord Robert jumped and lifted Her Majesty effortlessly, so it seemed. Soon, the room was awhirl with swirling skirts and lords a-leaping.

Sir John made his way to Mary, held out his hand, and led her into the mayhem.

"Congratulations, milord," said Mary, smiling at him.

"Thank you, Mistress Mary. Follow my lead and we shall escape this crowd for a more intimate celebration," said Sir John, twirling her across the floor and behind a large pillar into an alcove hidden from most of the dancers.

"You had better twirl me right back into the crowd. Someone will see us, surely," said Mary, looking behind her.

He embraced her, checking first to be sure none could see, and then he kissed her.

"We must stop this at once—we are under the queen's nose!" said Mary.

"She is dancing with her 'Sweet Robin.' Believe me, she takes no notice of who is on the dance floor. But you are right—we must be very careful. Kiss me once more and then we shall rejoin the crowd," he said. He pulled her to him and she felt his tongue in her mouth, a passionate kiss to which she responded without thinking.

"You are in such high favor, John. Should we not ask Sir James to speak for us now? Is this not the perfect time?" said Mary, her head spinning.

"Sir James will let me know—the queen is not happy with any of her advisors at present. They want her to rid herself of the Scottish queen and the treacherous Duke of Norfolk. They are at odds. Give it time, dearest—you are not yet old," said Sir John.

"I have turned eighteen—old enough, sir. Many are married by the time they reach this age," said Mary.

"But many are not—you must trust me on this, sweetheart. I would do what is best for us—we want to avoid the 'dragon' Dr. Dee warned us about," said Sir John.

"Then kiss me again so I will not forget that for which I wait," said Mary, pulling him to her.

The Parliament met and argued all summer about what was to be the fate of the Queen of Scots and her intended husband, the Duke of Norfolk. Finally, after the queen refused to execute her kinswoman, her advisors pressured her into ridding the realm of the duke.

"Majesty, you must know the lords are grumbling because you have allowed this female to be a snake at your bosom. Mark me, she will cause trouble for you as long as she lives. She is not one to sit idle while you rule. Since you have decided to allow her to live, you must determine against Norfolk. The Lords and Commons are calling for blood and blood they will have," said Burghley, kneeling at the queen's throne. Lord Robert knelt on the other side and added his thoughts.

"Lord Burghley and I are in complete agreement on this matter, Majesty. The duke has proven several times now that he cannot be trusted. He signed an oath pledging to have nothing more to do with the Scots' queen, yet we find him plotting and planning with her, much as before. Your Majesty is merciful by nature, being a weak woman, but now you must play the man," said Dudley.

"How dare you speak to me thus! All right! All right! I shall sign his death warrant. But by God's breath, I shall blame you both for it and shall put it about in the public square that the duke's blood is on your hands!" said the queen.

The queen rose abruptly.

"Come, ladies. I would retire for the day," said the queen, stalking out of the Presence Chamber with Mary and Mistress Blanche behind her.

The queen stormed into her apartments, routing those ladies who sat sewing and playing cards. She paced up and down the rushes, scattering debris as she went. Her fingers were restless, twisting and clenching together.

"I do not wish to have him killed! Why do they force me? I do not wish to marry, yet they would force a husband on me as well. Aye, there is need for an alliance with France, yes. But since when did an alliance include a marriage? The devilish de' Medici woman seeks to solidify our friendship in blood—I know her machinations. I will not! I will not!" said the queen.

"Majesty, please be seated. Let us take your mind from these troubles—shall we play at cards?" said Mary.

"Tut-tut. Cards do not solve problems. Remember when you thought gooseberry tarts could fix anything!" said the queen, slowing down and smiling.

"I still believe a good gooseberry tart can work miracles," said Mary, scratching *Tom*'s head behind his ears. *Tom* had grown old. His muzzle was gray and he no longer had the energy to run across the fields. Now, they walked.

"Oh my Fawn, how long ago it seems since you were that sweet child who showed up all alone on my doorstep . . . now you are a woman, and always a comfort to me. Whatever shall I do when you marry and leave me?" said the queen. Mary looked into the queen's face and saw sadness in her dark eyes. Her heart moved in sympathy for this woman, who, by the condition of her birth, was forced to be more than a woman and, yet, less.

"I shall always be near you, Majesty—for I love you as well as you love me," said Mary.

"And our love is true. Unlike the love of men, which is as changeable as the winds. My Robin does not think I know where he goes, when he sulks about Sir Christopher. I know full well he runs to the arms of Lady Douglass, who is bound to give him the comfort I cannot. Yet, I must dissemble—act as if I do not know of his treachery. And allow him to advise me, for I *do* trust in his good judgment. But his faithlessness rankles in my heart, Fawn. And I grow colder and colder to him," said the queen.

"Have you told him thus?" said Mary, removing the queen's slippers and rubbing her feet with almond oil.

"No. What can I say? That I love him but will not marry him? That he must not be a man because I will not be a woman? Oh Fawn, better never to marry than to face the inevitable death of love that marriage brings with it. If I were to marry Robin—he would not be true to me. He would still dally with my ladies, just as my father dallied. I think there is not a good man in all the world," said the queen.

"I hope Your Majesty is wrong in this. For I hope to marry one day and I would have my husband be true," said Mary.

"Humph. Men have little honor in such areas. But enough of this foolish talk—let us send for gooseberry tarts, lots of them!" said the queen, motioning for Mistress Blanche to get them.

"And while she's bringing them, let us remember days gone by. Do you recall how you got your name, dear Fawn?" said the queen, finally relaxing as Mary continued to rub her feet.

"No, Majesty. I only know you have always called me 'Fawn,' though I did not know why. Except that you have special names for those you love—I was happy to have such a name. How did I come by it?" said Mary.

"Do you remember the picnics we used to go on—you, Robin, and I?" said the queen.

"Of course. I always loved going! We were like a little family then. You and Lord Robert would laugh and play with me—those are some of my favorite memories," said Mary, smiling at the thought of those days.

"Well, you had just come to us, barely three years old. Such a beauty you were! We'd run and played all day and you were tired, so we spread out a coverlet and the three of us lay down upon it. You were sleeping in just a few minutes. Robin and I were looking at you, admiring your beauty—he said you looked very much like my mother's people. Your dark eyes and hair . . . and then, he said you reminded him of a little fawn, such a delicate creature with those soft, brown eyes. And ever since, you have been my Fawn," said the queen.

Mary looked at the queen. Was she imagining it, or were there tears in the queen's eyes? They fell silent until Mistress Blanche brought in the tarts with some light ale.

As they enjoyed the food and drink, Mary remembered Old Catspaw.

"Majesty, there is one small favor I would ask of you—it is not for myself," Mary said.

"What is it, Fawn?" said the queen.

"Old Catspaw has served Your Grace well for so many years. She almost fainted the other day while carrying clean clothes to Your Majesty's bedchamber. I had hoped Your Majesty could lessen her load. Perhaps give her more time for rest?" said Mary.

"God's blood! I told her months ago she could work when she liked and retire to her room whenever it suited her. I thought she would quit her duties immediately. But she told me she saw no need to stop doing what she'd been doing her whole life. I made her promise to rest more. She seems determined to keep going—I hope I shall be as determined when I have a head of gray hairs," said the queen.

Mary smiled at the queen. She realized she should have known that Good Queen Bess would know everything about those who served her. She should have known the queen would have the best interest of her servants at heart.

June 2, 1572

The Duke of Norfolk paid for his folly with his head this day. The queen was melancholy and spent most of the day in her bedchamber.

Mistress Mary stayed with her and tried to distract her with cards and music. But nothing could assuage Her Majesty. She spoke bitterly about the foolishness of men and the scheming of those close to the throne.

Thirty-seven
August 28, 1572

God's death! The world has gone mad, indeed! The French king has massacred his own people—men, women, and children—slaughtered in their houses! Ten thousand Huguenots met their death on St. Bartholomew's Day! Laid low in the very streets of Paris! How can Madame de' Medici think I would ever align myself with the house of Valois? She is as mad as her ganymede son!

Our friendship with France is ruined—how can we expect such a vile people to honor their treaty? Oh Parry, I had thought to marry Anjou—I shall never marry now.

Yes, I know he was not a prize but I still hoped . . . one day . . . God's blood, it matters not! I cannot marry the man I love, though he vexes me with his clandestine romances, conducted in the dark, secret passages of my own palace. Under my very nose.

He expects me not to notice how Lady Douglass bats her eyes at him, *smiling at his every glance, looking at him as if he were a god! What man can resist such adoration? Such obvious desire?*

I see the man himself, the man in all his parts, not just the noble elements of his nature, but I see his lesser qualities as well. And still, I find that man worthy of my love. I do not seek to win him with elevated praise—that I love him should be praise enough. Douglass has lasted longer than some, I'll give her that. Between her and her sister, my Sweet Robin has his fill while I waste away in endless negotiations and ceaseless longing. My own womb remains empty while he gets who knows how many children on lesser women. I have made him jealous with Hatton. Oh, it is so true— Hatton moons over me like a schoolboy. But he is not my Rob! He is not my love!

Forgive me, Parry. This business with the French has me overwrought. I believe Catholics must be a bloodthirsty lot—the Inquisition in Spain, the massacre in France, attempts on my own crown! Perhaps my ministers are right. Perhaps I should draw up a list of all the known Catholics and keep a steady eye on them. Maybe I should hang them all!

I know, I know—then I would be no better than the French king! And Madame de' Medici is right in one thing—I will not be safe until I marry and get an heir. Yet, I would marry for love if I could—or kindness. I would have a husband who was fond of me and I, him. Is that so much to ask?

Robin, oh my Sweet Robin! I cannot live without you by my side, yet I must. I must allow you your manly sport with Douglass, with anyone you may like. Yet, I will always love you, only you.

Parry, it is a hard thing to be a woman and be queen.

Thirty-eight
April 1573

T he Earl of Leicester used to take me on picnics with the queen and himself, a few serving women, and Mistress Blanche. We would walk along the riverside, far from the prying eyes of the court. I would nap, and while I did so, the queen and her Sweet Robin would kiss and speak delicious words of love to one another. Sometimes, we would play hide-and-seek or bowles—I have such fond memories of picnics! I am happy you agreed to take one with me," said Mary as she pulled Sir John by the hand through the meadow grass to a small pond shaded by a large oak tree.

"I find when it comes to you, my dearest, I cannot say no. The day is lovely—blue sky filled with puffy clouds. Look! Here is a forget-me-not," he said, leaning over to pluck the tiny blue flower from the new grass. "I have always loved these little buds—see the yellow star at the center? So delicate and small. I hate to think of our big boots crushing such beauty."

"Then we shall be careful not to do so. Step here—now here. And see, we have arrived at the tree with its mossy skirt," said Mary. She slipped the flower into her sleeve to put into her treasure box later. Then she turned to see how far behind they had left the pony packed with vittles. Mary could see the serving girl unloading the food. Mistress Blanche told Mary she would ride out later, as she had duties to perform to help the queen prepare for Easter. She said Mary would be perfectly fine in the company of Sir John and the serving wench—no need to worry about her reputation so long as *someone* was with them.

Sir John leaned against the tree trunk and Mary stood beside him. Their fingers were entwined and she could smell ambergris and his clean, manly odor. She loved the smell of him and often, when they kissed, she pressed her nose into his neck to inhale him as they embraced.

"You should know—you are with a dangerous man," said Sir John, smiling down at her.

"What do you mean?" said Mary.

"The queen has made a list of Catholics considered 'dangerous to the realm.' And I am on it. My uncle wrote me of it recently—our entire family is listed. Are you certain you still wish to become my wife?" he said.

"I am not afraid of this 'dangerous' man—I am intrigued by him," said Mary, placing her hands on his chest.

"You had, perhaps, better fear me a little—I am not sure I can control myself here, under the wide skies. Brings out the beast in me," he said, kissing her, lifting her almost off the ground.

His kiss took her breath and her heart pounded.

"Perhaps *you* should fear *me*—for I would have you right now!" said Mary, kissing him back.

"Just in time—here comes our food!" said Sir John, breaking away from her to help the serving girl, who was balancing a load in her arms. They spread a cloth over a mossy spot and John placed two large pillows side by side. The girl poured ale and set out the food.

"Your Worship, have you any more need of me?" said the girl with a quick curtsy.

"No, Daisy. You may take the pony to the pond for water and then ride a little if you would like," said Mary.

John gave her a startled look.

"Do not worry, my lord. Mistress Blanche will arrive anon. Until then, we shall eat, drink, and *I* shall be merry," said Mary.

"Droll, my love, droll," he said.

They watched as Daisy took the pony to the other side of the pond, mounted her, and trotted off toward the woods. Then they consumed shepherd's pie, strawberries in cream, and several mugs of ale.

After their repast, Sir John cleared away the food and eating implements, returning them to the basket. He shook out the cloth and spread it again on the soft moss. He sat on one side and patted for Mary to sit next to him. She quickly acquiesced.

"It is lovely to be alone, is it not?" said Mary, relaxing against him.

"It is lovely to be with you, dearest," said Sir John, encircling her with his arms. He kissed her, a long deep kiss that quickened her breath as well as his. He began to move his hands over her, and she could feel the heat from his touch following her womanly curves. He had never touched her with such a sense of possession, as if they were already wed.

She had come to trust him, knowing he would stop himself before their kisses grew too hot and out of control. Such trust allowed her to enjoy all that he did, rather than worry about having to put a stop to things herself. And so now she gave herself to the moment, not thinking of anything but where his hands and lips were and how they felt against her skin. Suddenly, she realized he had moved his hands beneath her shift and was touching her womanly parts. He worked there for a long time until she felt herself opening, opening, opening. He kissed her again and again and she felt his member against her, then inside her. Her eyes flew open and she saw him above her, his blond hair falling onto his forehead and his aqua eyes fixed on hers. Their eyes linked and their bodies moved together as if by magic. She grabbed him and pulled him to her, her hands guiding his movements. Suddenly, she could feel her heartbeat along her entire body and she shivered with pleasure. Then, she felt him tremble and heard him sigh. He collapsed onto her, then his mouth found her own and they kissed tenderly.

"I told you I was dangerous, my love," he said, fiddling with her hair, which had come loose and lay spread across the cloth.

"And so you are—what are we to do? I fear if I get with child, the queen will throw me in the Tower—you know I speak the truth," said Mary, the implications of what had happened beginning to dawn on her.

"I will speak to Sir James on the morrow. There is no reason the queen would wish to stop our marriage. She loves you—I am sure she wants you to be happy," he said.

"I hope you are right. She does love me, but I think she wants me to be happy living forever with *her*," said Mary.

"'Tis true—she does not like for any of her ladies to marry. She becomes too jealous of their happiness, I fear," said Sir John.

"Yes. And she has such high aspirations for me. She has mentioned several times that I should make a fine marriage to a foreign duke to help secure our relations with his country. Or that I might marry here, to one of the premier peers in the land. She thought Oxford would have been a wonderful match for me. I have told her I want not such high marriage, but she has it in her mind—she said she wants me to live in splendid surroundings, just as I do at court. I do not give a fig for such things," said Mary, her face clouding more and more as she thought about the queen and her lectures about marriage.

"Her hopes for you will never be satisfied with the likes of me," said Sir John.

"Dearest, you know *my* hopes are *very* satisfied," said Mary, smiling.

"Give me but a moment and I shall see to your satisfaction once again," he said, kissing her gently.

"We should ready ourselves for the arrival of Mistress Blanche— she will be here soon, I'll warrant," said Mary.

"Let me help you, milady," said Sir John, pulling Mary to her feet.

"I hope we shall not rue this day," said Mary, brushing off her skirts and fixing her hair.

"We shall never regret this moment, this day, my love. We shall wed as we planned and the queen be damned!" said Sir John.

Early May 1573

Sir John and Mary walked quietly to the Presence Chamber in the hope of meeting Sir James there. Sir James had just returned to court from Herefordshire and this would be their first opportunity to ask him to approach the queen on their behalf. Mary wore her white silk dress with yellow sleeves and matching kirtle. The light colors looked well with her dark hair and eyes. She had smeared a little kohl on her eyelids and blushed her cheeks and lips with cherry juice. She wanted to look pretty so that Sir James would be pleased with her as a possible wife for John. And a possible mother for Sir James's grandchildren. John had dressed with special care as well, wearing a dark blue doublet with slashed sleeves that showed a deep red silk within. Never had he looked so handsome, and Mary noticed several of the ladies gazed at him with interest.

Sir James conferred in a corner with Suffolk and Leicester. They were in quiet conversation, serious by the look of it. But seriousness

was the order of the day for those with business in the Presence
Chamber.

"Ah, Sir John and the pretty Mistress Mary—what brings you
here this fine spring day?" said Sir James, smiling at Mary.

"Sir, we have some business of a private nature to discuss with
you when you are free," said John easily. No one could have guessed
the true nature of their business from his casual attitude.

"Certainly, certainly. I'll be finished here in a moment. We were
just discussing the French situation. The queen has sent for Walsingham to return to London. The King of France has issued a decree to
allow the Huguenots to worship as they wish, and Madame de'
Medici wishes to reignite a romance. This time, she offers the
younger brother of Anjou, Alençon. Our poor most royal queen! How
many sons does Madame de' Medici have? Will she offer all of them
to our queen?" said Sir James.

"Who knows? All I can say is, here we go again," said John with
a smile.

"I hope Her Majesty will truly consider this match," said Lord
Robert. "She has much to gain with such an alliance—Spain continues to roar against us and I fear if Her Majesty does not make an
alliance soon, King Philip will consider sailing his navy from the
Netherlands, where he continues to make trouble. The Duke of Alva
is a formidable foe."

Mary said nothing but listened as the men continued discussing
the issues facing the nation. She was surprised Lord Robert would be
so eager for the queen to marry, something he had sought to block at
every turn until now. He seemed relaxed and happy in a way she
could not fathom. Finally, the conversation broke up and John took
her by the elbow, leading her and Sir James to a small alcove where
they could not be overheard.

"Why the secrecy? You two aren't planning to get married, are
you?" said Sir James, laughing.

"Well, sir, that is exactly what we are planning . . . with your help," said John.

"I do not blame you one bit, John. Mistress Mary has all the qualities a man could wish for in a wife—she is beautiful and kind, and obedient," said Sir James, looking her over as if she were a fine horse.

"I would not be so certain about the 'obedient' part, Sir James. Thus far, she knows her own mind well and is not afraid to speak it," said John, his arm around her waist.

"And I must insist that you gentlemen cease talking about me as if I were deaf! I can hear and contribute as well as any," said Mary. Though she smiled when she spoke the words, both men understood she meant what she said.

"'Tis a fine match. You have done well for yourself, John, to win the cousin of the queen," said Sir James. "I shall speak to Sir Nicholas Bacon on your behalf. As Lord Keeper of the Great Seal, he will attend to such business. We can only hope the queen will be amenable to the idea."

"We thank you, Sir James. We look forward to the day of our wedding with much enthusiasm," said John. Sir James gave a quick bow to Mary and excused himself.

"Do you think he was surprised?" said Mary, reaching for John's hand.

"I think he might have been stunned! I am surprised he did not volunteer to go directly to the queen himself. But I trust him in this matter. If only I could trust myself," said John, pulling her to him.

"We must not! We cannot be seen before the queen gives her approval. She will throw us into the Tower as she has others. I fear her wrath!" said Mary.

"Do not fear, dearest. She has no reason to object—I have proven my loyalty with my body," said John, still holding her close.

"Reason will have nothing to do with it. You are a Catholic and your name is on the 'dangerous' list," said Mary. "And you threaten to take away her 'Fawn.'"

"I am also a Gentleman Pensioner and the man who saved her life, remember?" said John.

"*I* remember, but will *she*?" said Mary.

Thirty-nine
July 1573

The queen's progress was heading to Lord Burghley's lavish home, Theobalds, in Essex, where the queen hoped to be entertained in grand style. The caravan of wagons, carts, litters, horses, and pack mules snaked its way along the road at the pace of a snail. And very like a snail it was, the queen taking everything she would need for her comfort: her gold plate, her dresses, her looking glass, her state papers, even her bathtub. Carrying her house with her was hard work, though others took care of the details. Most of the court was forced to accompany her, though the ladies often complained of the irritations of such travels. Mistresses Mary and Eleanor had left their mounts in order to stretch the kinks out of their legs and enjoy the fresh air, unimpeded by the odor of horse.

"Have you heard anything yet?" said Eleanor as she walked beside Mary.

"Not a word. Sir James has been busy, but I would hope our

request would be quickly and easily granted," said Mary. She stopped for a moment to catch her breath.

"Her Majesty has not mentioned it?" said Eleanor.

"Again, not a word. Her manner toward me is ever the same—if the idea displeased her, she would let me know," said Mary.

"Of that you can be certain—Her Majesty is not one to keep her feelings inside," said Eleanor, pausing to wait for Mary.

"I cannot imagine what is taking Sir Nicholas Bacon such a long time to ask . . . I have not seen him for weeks," said Mary. "Do you think he is avoiding me?"

"He is Keeper of the Great Seal—a busy man. Do not worry—you saw how easily the queen agreed to my wedding, though she continues to keep me near to her. I rarely get to see my husband. Luckily, she maintains him at court to paint miniatures; otherwise, I would never have any time with him," said Eleanor.

The women continued to walk, following the wagons loaded with the queen's clothes. Mary's job included making certain the queen's favorite summer gowns were ready for her to wear and to see the garments remained in pristine condition on their travels over the dusty, often muddy roads.

Mary tried to see John, who was riding with the Gentlemen Pensioners surrounding the queen. But the sun was in her eyes and she could not make him out.

"I cannot believe Catspaw is making this progress," said Eleanor.

"Poor old dear—she told me this would be her last. I do not think she will live beyond another year or so," said Mary.

"People have been saying that for years and yet here she is! She must have some sort of magic," said Eleanor, laughing.

The two women walked with others along the road. As they approached a village, townspeople lined the roads for a glimpse of the great Elizabeth, their golden queen. The farmers in their simple clothes cheered at the sight of the caravan, and children crowded around, knowing that a view of the queen would make the memory of a lifetime.

Upon their arrival at Theobalds, the queen took refreshment in her apartments while Mary and the other ladies unpacked the items they would need in the crowded servants' quarters they were forced to share with Lord Burghley's staff. They slept two or three to a bed and barely had enough room to change their clothes. To Mary's dismay, Catspaw had been given no special treatment due to her age. She was to room with Mary and Eleanor, along with several others.

"The queen's man's got hisself married, did ye know?" said Catspaw, as she shuffled into the room and plopped down on what Mary had thought was to be *her* bed.

"What are you talking about, old dame?" said Eleanor, unfolding her dresses and trying to find a place to store them so they would not become soiled and wrinkled.

"Leicester, he married Lady Sheffield over a month ago—I heard all about it. They say she was with child but the babe came early and died. And now, he's scared to death the queen will find out about it! If she does, he'll be lower than a shit-shovel man," said Catspaw.

"You have told us this tale before—'tis mere gossip. When will you learn, old woman? You should not meddle in the affairs of your betters," said Eleanor, taking a comb from her bag and coaxing the snarls from her hair.

"Just keep yer eyes open—you'll see. Lord Robert looks at Mistress Douglass different. And she is moon-eyed over him more than ever. Just hope the queen don't find out—there'll be hell to pay," said Catspaw.

"Well, she won't hear such tales from *me*," said Mary. "Her Majesty has enough to vex her without upsetting her humors with tittle-tattle."

Mary and Eleanor finished arranging their things. Mary pulled her special box from a velvet bag she had been carrying and hid it in the trunk holding her undergarments. As always, finding a safe place for her treasures was first in her mind. She opened the box for a quick peek inside as she riffled through the shifts and smocks. She always checked to be certain all her treasures were there. She saw the forget-me-nots she and Sir John had picked, the stones she had collected from her picnics on the river when she was a small child, the ringlet of the queen's hair braided with her own, Oxford's poem, her other items. Everything was in its place.

A page knocked on the door of the ladies' quarters.

"Mistress Mary Shelton—the queen is calling for you! Mistress Shelton!" he shouted, his voice cracking.

"Here, boy! I'm here. Nora, I shall see you at the entertainment later this evening. Rest while you can—I fear our travels will tire us," said Mary as she gathered her skirts and followed the young fellow. She had been to Theobalds before, but to her, the mansion seemed similar to every other great house they visited on progress—rooms upon rooms upon rooms. She continued following the page, though it felt as if he were leading her *away* from the queen's apartments, rather than to them. Suddenly, she felt someone grab her arm.

"Mary, I have news," said Sir John, pulling her into a small, damp room off one of the servants' corridors. He slipped a coin into the boy's hand and shooed him away.

"What is it, my love? You look unhappy," said Mary.

"Sir James finally spoke with Bacon. Bacon said our motion will go slowly, for he will not break the matter to the queen until he speaks with you. I fear this means he has little hope the queen will give her consent," said Sir John.

"I feared as much—her temper is foul these days. And she has told me many times to have a care where I cast my heart," said Mary, a heaviness forming in her throat.

"My religion cannot help my suit—she grows more suspicious of her Catholic subjects daily. Lord Burghley does not make matters any easier—he sees conspiracy behind every bush," said John, his voice tense, yet quiet.

"Also, I am a man of modest means—not high among the nobility. You are her cousin—you have already said she wants to marry you off to some duke. Perhaps she already has someone in mind. We must bide our time—more waiting, my love," said Sir John, grabbing hold of Mary's hand.

"I do not wish to keep waiting—after tasting the fruits of love, I would have more," said Mary, caressing his face.

"It is not easy, staying away from you. But we cannot take another chance—we were lucky once. If I should get a baseborn babe on you, she would never forgive that," said Sir John.

Mary leaned against him. He seemed so steady, strong like the great oak trees of the forest. She wanted to stand against him forever, allow his calm good sense to shelter her.

"I should warn you, my love—I have heard Oxford will be joining us at Theobalds. I know this is not the news you had hoped for—but have no fear. I shall make certain he does not bother you. It is said he continues to try to make the queen forget his, er, well, his body's indiscretion," said Sir John, a smile flushing his features.

"Just remembering his gaffe makes me laugh! Oh, I am a poet, too, like Oxford!" said Mary, giggling at her rhyme.

"Come. We must get to our duties before the whole court begins to wonder where we are," said Sir John, leading her out of the cramped room into the summer light.

Forty
Late July 1573

*E*ven though the summer heat was at its zenith, it seemed the queen would never tire of her revelry: hunting, taking brisk walks through the many gardens surrounding Lord Burghley's beautiful home, dancing and singing in the evenings, and traveling to nearby villages where the simple people paid the queen homage. The queen kept her ladies busy accompanying her on her adventures, allowing them little time to rest. Even at forty, the queen's energy was greater than that of most of her ladies, though many were much younger. It was almost as if the queen refused to show any indication that time was marching on, or so Mary thought. Her Majesty seemed to laugh more heartily and dance with more enthusiasm than ever before, kicking up her heels with Sir Christopher as well as Lord Robert, holding each man in thrall, one moment selecting one to chatter with, the next choosing the other to walk her to her private rooms. Though Lord Robert paid the queen the usual amount of attention she required, Mary thought his heart was not in the chivalrous game. He seemed to be going through the motions of love, but without the ardor he had shown earlier. Mary wondered if there was any truth to Old Catspaw's gossip.

She and Sir John had little time together, for the queen kept the Gentlemen Pensioners busy, too. Sir Christopher had been made captain, so he and the others escorted the queen wherever she went. The men looked handsome in their uniforms, tall and young and fit. Mary sometimes caught Sir John's eye when they rode behind the queen and he winked at her when he thought no one was looking. Such tender moments were all she had to remember that this was to be her husband, the man she had chosen to love.

Mary, Eleanor, and Lady Douglass had been granted an afternoon's rest while the queen hunted deer in the nearby forest. The three young women had tidied up the queen's rooms and were mending some of the queen's shifts or working embroidery on the queen's sleeves. They kept cool by having one of the servants fan them and bring them ale and wine. Every once in a while, Mary would sprinkle water over their faces to keep the heat at bay. They had put their hair up with pins so the long locks did not hang heavy and sticky on their necks.

"I will be glad to see September come," said Lady Douglass, sewing pearls onto the queen's sleeves of green silk.

"Yes, it will be a relief to feel the cool air after such hot days. No wonder these are called the 'dog days'—the Dog Star lends his heat to the sun and there is little relief for forty days," said Mary, pulling a thread through the shift she was mending.

"I fear I shall not be here in September," said Eleanor with a small smile.

"Why on earth not?" said Mary.

"It is a secret but I shall have to tell it soon. I may as well let the cat slip out now," said Eleanor in a small voice.

"What is it?" said Mary.

"I am with child! About two months along! We have asked the queen to release me from my duties for one month to prepare for the babe, and she has said yes. Of course, I must return to court immediately in October and remain until I go into my confinement. She has also agreed to be the godmother. Nick is so happy, as am I," said Mistress Eleanor.

"This is wonderful news, Nora! I shall begin a christening gown for the babe at once!" said Mary, flinging down her sewing and hugging her friend.

"Yes, wonderful," said Lady Douglass quietly.

"I am especially pleased Her Majesty has agreed to be the godmother—it shows she has blessed our marriage. You know how she can be, sometimes, when one of us weds. But for whatever the reason, she has not given Nick and me much trouble," said Nora.

"I wonder how she will react when *I* marry," said Lady Douglass, a strange smile playing about her lips. "I fear she will like it not."

"If you seek her permission and go through the proper channels, she is most agreeable," said Nora.

"Oh, I do not think she will be very agreeable to this," said Lady Douglass, plucking up another pearl to stitch onto the silk.

"Have you someone in mind?" said Mary.

"Very much so, but it shall be my secret—at least, for a little longer," said Lady Douglass.

"The queen returns from the hunt—I hear the yeomen marching outside. Let us put away our work and prepare ourselves for the evening—these summer nights are all too fleeting when we can dance with those we love," said Eleanor. "Especially for me—I shall not dance long, for the babe will not allow it."

The queen entered her rooms, her hair damp with sweat and the curls escaping her hunting cap. Her face blazed and she took a seat immediately, motioning for her women to bring refreshment. Like worker bees, they buzzed around the queen, securing her comfort.

The night was, thankfully, cooler and gave everyone a welcome respite from the heat. The sky was deep blue and as clear as Dr. Dee's crystal, with more stars twinkling than Mary was used to seeing in London. Here, in the beautiful countryside, everything pulsed with life, even the heavens. After supping on a light meal of goose livers with thick gravy and bread, the queen's ladies busied themselves dressing Her Majesty, from her clean smock to her sumptuous green silk dress with the kirtle of cloth of gold and matching sleeves. As usual, the women worked for a solid two hours helping the queen bathe and dress, lacing up her stomacher, tying on the sleeves and attaching the small ruffs at her wrists and the larger one at her neck. The queen's hair had to be washed and set up high atop her head with a few curls framing her face. Her white makeup was applied, along with kohl for her eyes and cherry juice for her lips. Mary dabbed the queen's favorite perfume, sweet marjoram, on her neck, wrists, and décolletage and then took a soft cloth and cleaned her teeth with honey and vinegar. However, the final effect was worth the effort; the queen looked elegant and attractive, a comely woman with pale skin, dark eyes, and a slight hook in her nose—regal.

After working on the queen, who left with a few ladies for the Great Hall, the rest of the women readied themselves, helping each other lace, tie, and squirm into their bulky garments. The stomacher and farthingale were the most difficult; it took at least three women to help one shimmy into the contraptions.

Mary's dress was the usual silver, which set off her hair and eyes. She, too, had bathed after the queen had finished with the water, and felt refreshed.

"Come, Nora, let us go—you look so lovely, like a ripe peach.

Your condition suits you, methinks," said Mary, grabbing her friend by the hand.

They could hear the music and the scuffling of dancing feet as they approached the Great Hall. Mary saw Sir John standing near the queen and gave him a quick bow. She and Nora headed to the table laden with fruits, comfits, tarts, and pastries. Mary selected a gooseberry tart and turned in time to see Oxford entering the Great Hall.

He was more handsome than she had remembered, his doublet a lovely blue and his eyes lively. He had grown a slight beard and it suited him well. She remembered his kisses, the way he had fondled her. She felt her cheeks begin to burn. She did not like him, and she wished she could see him at court without feeling discomfort.

"Ah, Oxford, welcome!" said the queen, laughing.

He bowed graciously, this time without emitting any offending noises, and the queen motioned for him to come closer. He bent his knee at her throne and they spoke together for some time.

Mary danced with several courtiers, including Sir John. He, too, looked as if he had taken great pains with his appearance for the evening, and he was as gallant as ever. After a spritely galliard, Mary took her leave of her partner and walked outside for some air, catching Sir John's eye as she headed for the outer porch. She was looking up at the sky when she felt arms around her waist. As she had hoped, Sir John had caught her look and followed her out into the darkness. She leaned into him.

"So, you *have* missed me," said Oxford, pulling her more tightly against him. She could feel his breath hot on the back of her neck.

She broke free and faced him.

"I . . . I thought you were someone else," she said.

"Oh? And who might this mysterious lover be? Is it Pakington? He told me you rebuffed him, but things change, yes? Perhaps that scoundrel Hunsdon? But no, I suspect it is Sir John Skydemore, your hero. He is always meddling in our business," he said, staring into her eyes.

"It is none of your concern. I must return to the queen," said Mary, starting toward the door.

"Wait but a little. The sky is dark, the breeze is cool. We are young and one of us is quite lovely," he said.

"I dare not think *which* one of us you think lovely!" she said, jerking her arm away from him.

"Lady, you wound me. As you must know, I continue to think of you—your eyes, your hair, the shape of you. My hands remember, did you know? They remember every curve," he said, taking her elbow once more.

"Sir, you are mistook if you think I have any interest in you. You are married and treat your poor wife terribly—you are no gentleman," said Mary.

"'Tis true, 'tis true. But I do not love my wife," said Oxford, his arm snaking around her waist.

"Nor do you love me. You love only yourself—even the queen knows that," said Mary.

"What has love to do with anything? You and I, we want each other—there is nothing of love in it. We are like rutting pigs. Come in the mud with me, lady. You will like it there, I promise," he said.

Mary could hear the music wafting over the summer air. Then, out of the corner of her eye, she saw Sir John heading toward them, scanning the darkened gardens to find her.

"No, milord. You must find another to rut with you. For I am made of better stuff. And I have learned that when love is involved, mere rutting turns to something else, something pure and true. Leave me," she said.

She backed away from him, hoping Sir John would notice the movement and come to her. Her ploy worked. Sir John was walking toward them.

"Oh, Mistress Mary, I've been looking for you. Oxford," Sir John said, giving a small bow to the earl. Sir John strode to Mary's side and stood next to her. She immediately took his arm.

"I am so glad you have come—I hear them playing a pavanne and I wish to dance. If you will excuse us, my lord Oxford," said Mary.

"Certainly," said Oxford, himself giving a small bow.

As Mary and John headed for the dance floor, he paused before they entered.

"Is everything all right? Did Oxford bother you?" said Sir John.

"Everything is fine now that you are here, dearest. I will say Oxford is not one to give up his ambitions easily—but I managed him," said Mary.

"We have an enemy there. But my blade will make him think twice before he tries you again. Let us dance, my love—for I long to hold you, even if for a mere moment," said Sir John.

He led her into the hall where they joined the other dancers.

Forty-one

Early August 1573

*M*ary was tired of the constant travel required of her when the queen went on progress. For two months, she and almost the entire court had made a circle around the Midlands, staying at various locations for a few days to a week at a time. Though each gentleman did his utmost to entertain the queen and her retinue, after a while, the festivities seemed forced. Mary imagined a great sigh of relief being heaved as their hosts watched them ride away.

For Mary, it seemed her work never ended while on progress. The queen's wardrobe had to be kept in excellent condition in spite of dusty roads, jostling wagons, overstuffed chests, and sometimes careless handlers. She was forever brushing and shaking out the queen's dresses, trying to remove a new stain, sewing on pearls from one pair of sleeves to another, until she thought she would scream if she had to look at another garment. Her dismay must have been written across her face because when they arrived at Warwick Castle, the queen beckoned her to her side.

"Ah, Fawn—you seem overwrought. After we get settled in, I insist you take the afternoon away from your duties—tut-tut, I will brook no argument. I do not wish to work my ladies into an early grave. You should ride out into Warwick's forest—I hear there is good game to be found and a beautiful little river. Perhaps Mistress Eleanor could go with you—though I suppose she will be tired, given her condition. Now, off, girl!" said the queen.

Mary curtsied to the queen, thanking her profusely. Her heart lifted at the thought of enjoying the summer sunshine, an entire afternoon away from the queen and the bustle of court life. She immediately wondered where Sir John might be found and if, somehow, he could steal away with her. She hurried to the small room she shared with Eleanor to change into her riding clothes, selecting a hat of blue satin with a long, white feather sticking up, giving her just the jaunty look she was hoping for.

As Mary walked to the stables, she kept her eyes open for Sir John. She saw several of the Gentlemen Pensioners in a huddle in the hall that led to the queen's apartments but Sir John was not among them. Then, just as she was about to turn toward the stables, she saw him walking alone up ahead of her. She ran to catch him.

"Where are you going, sir?" she said as she caught up to him.

He turned, surprised, and then smiled.

"I thought it would be a good idea to check the duty schedule with Sir Christopher—he has not yet told us who shall guard the queen by day and who by night," he said.

Mary could barely restrain herself from holding on to his arm as they walked. She noticed he held himself stiffly away from her. She knew he, too, wanted to touch, to be reassured of her love.

"And where are you going, milady?" he said.

"I have the afternoon free—the queen has sent me out riding for my own pleasure. I was going to have one of the stable boys saddle a horse for me," said Mary.

"I shall be happy to assist you," he said.

Mary looked up at him, shading her eyes from the sun that beamed down brightly.

"I would like it if you could come with me—we could enjoy this lovely place in the quiet hours of the afternoon," she said.

He paused in contemplation. Then he bowed to her.

"If my mistress commands I accompany her—for her protection, of course—I do not see how I can refuse," he said.

"I suppose we should ask someone else along, just so there will be no tittle-tattle about us. Nora isn't feeling up to a ride these days. Who can we invite?" said Mary.

"Not a soul. For if you ride out first, and I follow in a little while, who is to know we plan to meet? You can be certain to tell the stable boy the queen has commanded that you ride this afternoon for your health's sake. I shall tell him I am sent on an errand for Sir Christopher. With all the court settling in, I do not believe our doings will be noticed at all," said John.

Mary considered what he said. She was nervous about such a plan, but it had been three long months since they had lain together and she longed to kiss him once again. They had promised each other they would refrain from acting as man and wife. They knew they could not take the chance of a babe coming before they had gained the queen's permission to marry.

"I shall do as you say. I will take the horse beyond the eyes of Warwick Castle and will meet you at the edge of the forest. We shall have hours together, my love. This is a great gift!" she said.

Never had a wood seemed so beautiful, so perfect. As Mary and John rode side by side beneath the shady trees, she felt as if she had entered the land of the fairies. The sun filtered through the leaves, creating shadows that danced and moved as if by magic. She could hear the skittering of small creatures in the undergrowth and she imagined hedgehogs and rabbits, birds and snakes, field mice and deer, all living their lives out of her sight as if they inhabited a different universe.

Beyond the brushy comings and goings of the animals, there was a deep quiet in the forest. The silence made Mary feel as if she were in a cathedral of some kind, the trees acting as the great arches, and the varying shades of green, the stained glass. They had come to a holy place and Mary could feel the sanctity of it. They remained quiet as they rode through the forest, and Mary knew John felt it, too—the rich spirit of the woods, the blessedness of the earth.

There was no trail they followed, but Mary could tell the land was rising and they were climbing a hill. As they came to the end of the tree line, there was a meadow of tall, fragrant grasses littered with daisies and wild red flowers for which Mary had no name. John reached over and pulled her horse to a halt.

"Shall we walk a while?" he said.

She nodded and he helped her down. They stood together for a moment and then he took her in his arms. He did not kiss her but simply held her, their bodies molded together. She could hear no sound but the steady rhythm of his heart, the in and out of their mingled breath.

"When I was a boy, there was a hill much like this at Holme Lacy. My brothers and I would wage battles over who could hold the top. We would often lie in the tall grasses and roll down to the bottom, trying to tumble anyone we could on the way down," said John, still holding her.

"I have never rolled down a hill—though the queen was relaxed when we took our picnics, she was never *that* relaxed! I cannot imagine her doing such a thing or allowing me to do it, either," said Mary. "I suppose I missed out on lots of things, growing up at court."

"Well, we can't have that! Come on!" he said, pulling her down beside him. He wrapped his arms around her and off they went, rolling one over the other, over and over, gathering speed as they tumbled. Mary saw the grasses and flowers in a great swirl against the blue sky and felt the soft earth beneath her. The ground was punctuated every now and then by a rock that poked her in the back, though not uncomfortably. She could not help but laugh as they spun down the hill, arms entwined, John taking his weight on his elbows so as not to squash her. Finally, they landed at the bottom of the hill, both giggling. She felt free. She had no one to correct her behavior or tell her to remember her position. She was there with the man she loved, the earth, and the sky. She rolled over onto him and kissed him, a kiss full of all the longing she had ever felt. She could not have named that which she desired—it was ineffable, as indistinct as fog. Yet her entire body was filled with it.

John returned her kiss and they continued their lovemaking, freed beneath the warming sun as they had not been before. She knew before he even touched her private places that they were going to join again as one. For a brief moment, she wondered if they were testing fate by taking another chance. But then he was inside her and she thought of nothing but how she felt, the way they moved together, his mouth on her neck, her earlobes, moving slowly to nibble at her breasts. He untied the top of her smock and pulled the material aside so he could kiss her everywhere. She felt the still-new sensations pulsing deep in her belly, radiating out, the pleasure rippling through her body the way lake water ripples when you toss a stone into the center. She could not stop the sounds tearing from her throat, animal sounds, fierce and guttural. She heard him sigh and then felt his whole body shudder. He collapsed on top of her, still breathing heavily.

"Oh, my love, I cannot keep myself from you . . . I cannot," he said. He nuzzled her neck and she held him to her.

"Nor can I keep from you. What are we to do? We have taken

another chance, though I promised myself I would not. Let me stand up—perhaps that will help keep a babe from forming," she said as she pushed him from her. She stood and felt the wetness between her legs. She wiped at it with the skirt of her smock, saying a prayer that such quick action would save her. As she tried to clean herself, she began to cry.

John stood beside her and put his arm around her.

"Do not weep, dearest. We shall marry—you have my promise on it," John said.

"But the queen! We do not have the queen's permission! From what Sir James said, we never will! What shall we do?" said Mary, now sobbing uncontrollably.

"Do not fear, my love. We shall marry. I will put the question to Sir James once again. Perhaps he can hurry the Keeper of the Great Seal along. Do not fret," said John.

Slowly, they got dressed and returned to gather their horses who were standing beneath a large oak tree. Mary was shaking as she thought about what might happen. She did not wish to consider the queen's evil actions if Mary was discovered suddenly with child. She shook her head to clear the image from her mind. She would not cry any more. She had chosen to be with Sir John, chosen him above the queen. It was unforgivable from the queen's position, but, as for herself, she would make the same choice a hundred times.

T he end of the plague season brought the queen back to London, to Whitehall, to attend to state business and return to a more settled life. Already the leaves had begun to lose their vivid green, and hints of yellow and brown peeked through the foliage. Mary and Mistress Eleanor kept busy bringing out the queen's fall and winter clothing, seeing that the silk women and seamstresses repaired spots the moths had eaten, airing the gowns to remove any musty smells. Keeping the garments Her Majesty owned in good condition took a great deal of time and employed the services of a dozen or so skilled laundresses and sewing women. Mary, as Keeper of the Book of the Queen's Wardrobe, was responsible for cataloguing and maintaining the articles in good order. Each change of season set a monumental task for her.

"What about this lovely pale blue gown? I have noticed of late the queen has not worn the pastels as often as she was wont to in her younger years. There are a few light stains on the skirts . . . should this be given to one of her women or should we keep it?" said Mary to Eleanor, who sat on a stool, rather than remain on her feet in her condition.

"Do you have leave to make such a decision?" said Eleanor. "From what I have observed, the queen is loath to rid herself of any finery, whether she uses it or not."

"I asked her last week if she wanted me to give those items away that were sullied or no longer to her taste. She told me she was too busy listening to Lord Burghley's lectures about having a care for her person to bother with such decisions. She wanted everything old or worn removed," said Mary.

She leaned over to whisper into Eleanor's ear. "From now on, everything she receives, even perfumed gloves and nightgowns, must be thoroughly examined for poison. Burghley fears another attempt on her life."

Mary lifted the gown in her hands and folded it, placing it into a large trunk.

The women worked in silence for several minutes.

"How are you feeling, Nora?" said Mary.

"Well enough, though I am happy to have a seat while I work. I shall be happy when Her Majesty releases *me*—old and worn-out as I am," said Eleanor, smiling.

"She does demand much of us. But she also rewards us—well, at least sometimes," said Mary.

"Is someone knocking on the outer door?" said Eleanor.

"Who could be here at this time of morning? The queen is in the Presence Chamber with her councillors—thank goodness she cares more about me keeping her clothes in order than having me observe the machinations of the Privy Council," said Mary. "Enter!"

A young page dressed in the queen's livery approached the two women and bowed. He went to one knee.

"Mistress Mary? The queen wishes to see you in the Presence Chamber immediately," said the boy.

"Oh, I had so hoped to escape," said Mary. She placed the stomacher she'd been examining across the queen's bed and smoothed her hair into place. Then she followed the boy down the long corridor to the Presence Chamber. The Yeoman of the Guard announced her as she entered.

"Ah, Mary, come here," said the queen, motioning for her to join her as she sat at her writing desk. The queen arose and Mary curtsied to her.

"Your Majesty," said Mary.

"Come, let us walk together in the garden," said the queen, shooing away the others who started to accompany them. "I would have a moment alone with Mistress Mary. I shall return anon."

The queen hooked her arm in Mary's and together they entered the herb garden. The smell of lavender and roses made the air pleasant, and though the weather was still warm, a small breeze hinted at the change in seasons.

"God's blood, it is a lovely day—makes me wish we were still on progress. I should like to hunt on a day like this—much better than listening to Burghley prate on about this and that," the queen said as she stopped near an ornately carved bench. She sat and indicated Mary was to sit beside her.

"Dearest Fawn, we wanted to speak with you because Sir Nicholas Bacon has come to us with a suit for your hand in marriage. Sir John Skydemore is quite taken with you and has obtained permission from his father-in-law, Sir James Croft, to woo you. As we are sure you recall, we have forbidden this match," said the queen.

Mary did not like it when the queen spoke to her using the royal "we" because it meant she was speaking as the monarch, not the woman. And the meaning was clear—she was displeased at the request and would employ everything in her power as queen to stop the match.

Mary remained silent.

"We are sorry to refuse Sir John in this matter. We distinctly remember warning you about dallying with him—we were afraid you would break his heart. He has already lost one wife. We are sorry for his disappointment in losing another," said the queen.

Mary rose from the bench and dropped a deep curtsy directly in front at the queen and remained in that position. She raised her head to look at the queen.

"Your Gracious Majesty, I beg you—please allow Sir John to press his suit. I . . . I love him as he loves me—I very much wish to marry him," said Mary in a clear voice.

"Love? Love? What do you know of love? You are but a child! We have already given our answer and it was no," said the queen, turning away from Mary.

"But why, Your Grace? You gave your permission for Eleanor and Nicholas Hilliard—they are quite happy together. You are godmother to their babe," said Mary, her voice quaking slightly. Her heart pounded and she felt anger building within her. "Why would you put her happiness so far above mine?"

"Why? Why? Must we have reasons—we are queen!" said Her Majesty, her voice strident. Then she took a deep breath. Another, then yet another. Her body slumped forward a little.

"Dearest Fawn, do not be sad. There will be other loves. I have told you for years I would see you married, but married to someone worthy of you. Sir John is a widower with five children for whom he must provide. He is from a good family, yes, but not the nobility. You are cousin to the queen! You could marry a prince! I have made you fit for any royal court in Europe!" said the queen.

"Forgive me, Your Majesty, but have you once considered I might not wish to marry a prince—I might want to settle away from court and live a simple life with my family. I am not like you—I have no wish to rule, nor do I want to rise above my station. I aim for just a taste of happiness in this vale of tears. Not the veneer of happiness, danced out in frenzied leaps and jumps. But genuine joy in the everyday things of life—a husband who loves me, perhaps children to comfort me, the scent of roses on the wind—things that touch my heart," said Mary.

"Sir John is a Catholic! As is all his family! A recusant! For all I know, he could have plans to do away with me! God's death, after a morning with Burghley, I should be suspicious of every one of my subjects," said the queen.

"I know what he believes and I respect his courage for adhering to his beliefs. I do not think his loyalty to you is in question—he saved your life, if I may remind you," said Mary, rising from her curtsy.

"You do not have my permission to stand! How dare you say you respect a man who breaks my own laws! How dare you imply that my court is bereft of joy! You shall not marry a man who will not convert to the religion of the state—*my* religion! By the feet of God, you shall marry whom I decide, when I decide, if I decide!" said the queen, herself now on her feet, pacing in front of Mary.

"May I have leave to return to my duties?" said Mary, her voice full of fury.

"Yes! Return to them at once! We shall not speak of this again—the business with Sir John Skydemore is finished!" said the queen.

Mary curtsied and walked away from Her Majesty as fast and furiously as her feet could carry her. Her head was spinning. What to do now? What could she possibly do?

Forty-three

G od's blood, that child will be the end of me! Thinks she is in love with a man not good enough to clean her boots. I try to protect her from making such a mistake and what do I get for my trouble? Dark, angry looks and sulky silences. Oh Parry, I know she is young—I was young, too, once. And had it not been for you and your wisdom, I might have met my end at the block. Yes, Tom Seymour almost led me astray, almost led me to my death. She does not understand that these forces with which she is toying have serious consequences. It is no longer the case of a scratched knee or disappointment at losing a game of bowles. If she marries rashly, she could end up spending her life in poverty. She, who has never known want, could starve if she married some ill-considered lout.

I know Sir John is not completely without means—but I want so much more for Fawn. I do not wish to see her merely scrape by; I want her to fulfill her potential. She can be so much more than what she dreams for herself.

Or, God forbid, she could die in childbirth—plenty of women do. I would not see her die, Parry. I could not bear it.

Do you recall when she had the smallpox? Of course you do. I was so afraid. Yes, I remember how hot she burned. I nursed her myself, stayed by her side for days. But we got her through it, though I did come down with the cursed disease a couple of weeks later. Yes, thanks be to God I survived, too. And you would not allow either of us to go outside for weeks afterward. I grew so agitated, Robin brought the outdoors in to us and we picnicked in the castle. I can still feel her hair and my own as I plaited the strands together; mine, red and very fine, like silk—hers, more coarse and curly, and dark, so very dark. Woven together forever.

No, Parry. You are right. We do not choose whom we love. We simply love. I have loved Fawn since that first time when you brought her to me and she called me her "shining lady." I think I knew, somewhere in my heart, I would never have a child of my own. Whatever there is of the mother in me, those feelings have gone to Fawn.

I shall not allow her to ruin her life! I shall not!

Forty-four
September 1573

W hat are we to do, my love? Her Majesty is against us and I cannot see any way past that," said Mary as she cried against Sir John's chest. They had arranged to meet in the laundry hallway while Mary was supposed to be working on the queen's wardrobe. Mary sent Sir John a message through Mistress Eleanor, fearing the queen's wrath if she and John were to be seen together.

"We shall find a way, dearest, we shall find a way," said Sir John, holding her close.

"I am ruined! I am no longer a maid! Even if I wanted to find a husband, who would marry a woman whose honor has been plundered?" sobbed Mary.

"I would gladly marry just that woman," said Sir John.

His remark caused more weeping.

They stood still for a few moments.

"Have your . . . have your courses returned?" he said softly.

"Yes, just yesterday. I had a very hard time for the last week, worrying myself almost ill, fearing the worst. But yes, we have escaped the danger for a second time. We shall not tempt fate again," she said.

"Oh, would that I could have you in my arms, though," said Sir John, lifting her chin so he could look into her eyes.

"I *am* in your arms," she said, smiling a little.

"You know my meaning," he said, his breath growing husky.

"I do, sir. Your wish is my own," she said, wrapping her arms around his neck.

They kissed and Mary's breath came in quick gulps. She felt his hands around her waist, then moving to her buttocks to pull her to him. They had not seen each other in weeks except to glance and smile when they thought it safe enough to do so. Mary had thought of him night and day, remembering their time together.

"Has she spoken to you of late? Any word at all?" said Sir John.

"No. She gives me her commands regarding what she will wear, but she has barely said anything else. She is waiting for me to beg forgiveness for our quarrel. She has ruined my life, yet *I* must beg *her* for forgiveness!" said Mary.

"Such is the way at court—she will rule here, of that there can be no doubt. But we will be wed, dearest! I promise you," said Sir John.

"How? How can you promise such a thing when the queen herself has forbidden it?" said Mary, tears filling her eyes again.

"If my lord Robert can marry in secret and keep such matters from the queen, why should we not do the same?" said Sir John.

"Have you gone mad? She will throw us in the Tower to rot!" said Mary.

"I am not so sure. Others she has forgiven—even Dudley seems to have gotten away with it," said Sir John.

"That is because she does not know about it!" said Mary.

"Do you forget? Her motto, 'I see all and say nothing,' is close to the truth—she has spies everywhere. Very little gets by her. She must know about Dudley's marriage and she chooses to turn a blind eye to it. She would do the same for her 'Fawn,' surely," said Sir John.

"But are you willing to bet our lives on it?" said Mary.

"I would rather marry you and be in heaven for a few short moments than to live in hell without you—for that is what my life would be if you were not in it," said Sir John.

Mary turned from him. The serious, wounded man she had first met seemed gone and before her was the gallant lover, ready to risk everything for her. If he was willing to gamble, she must rise to meet his courage.

"All right, sweetheart. All right. We shall marry in secret and pray for the queen's mercy," said Mary, turning to him once more and kissing him tenderly.

As their kisses grew hotter, Mary heard footsteps in the corridor. Around the corner hobbled Catspaw, a stack of the queen's shifts in her arms.

"What goes on here?" the old woman said. "Oh, I know better than to ask—you've been discovered, young lovers. Have no fear, Old Catspaw will say nothing—I never tell tales."

"Please, Catspaw, please do not tell this tale. Here, let me carry those for you! John, give her a coin—go rest a while, old dame. I shall finish your work this day," said Mary, her face pale.

"I thank you, my pretty. Me old legs is tired, 'tis true. I'll keep yer secret—my lips are sealed as with wax," said Catspaw, retreating back down the long hall. "I know how to keep my mouth shut, I do. Never tell nobody nothing . . . no, I can keep mum . . ."

"Should we worry about her?" said Sir John.

"I do not know—she is a notorious gossip but she likes me, I think. It matters not. We shall continue with our plans," said Mary, squeezing his hand.

"Yes, my love—we shall be married as soon as I can arrange it," said Sir John.

Forty-five
January 1, 1574

*H*e gave me a fan made of white feathers with a golden handle, engraved with my lion and his bear. How I smiled my pleasure at him as he presented it to me—his dark, gypsy eyes staring into my own. How I dissembled, as if I knew nothing about him and that empty-headed Sheffield woman. And how I shivered when he kissed my hand, nothing discernibly changed in his manner to me, but I knew the difference. Oh yes, by all that is sacred, I knew.

I am undone. He has killed me as surely as any of Burghley's Catholic assassins. I have known and loved him all my life and have given him more of myself than was prudent. I have rejected suitors for his sake, though I knew I could never marry him—not after the scandal with his first wife. I know, I know, Parry—I have used him as well. Used him to avoid a marriage I did not want, used him to comfort me when there was no other comfort. I have called him my "little dog," shaming him in front of lesser men. We *have been through so much together . . . I cannot believe he would betray me thus, yet it seems he has done so.*

I am too filled with despair to be angry, Parry. The anger will come later. I shall, perhaps, banish him. But that would punish me as much as it would him. I shall banish her—that would be better. She can give birth to her bastard in the Tower. Others have done so.

Yes, I have heard that rumor, too. Surely, he cannot have married *her—behind my back. Bad enough to have given her a babe. Even Dudley cannot believe I would forgive such treachery. Do you believe it true?*

Oh Parry, you stab me to the heart! Why say you thus? She lives with him in Leicester House? There were witnesses? It is done?

By God's wounds, I shall not have it! He is mine! He is mine!

Is there no single person I can trust? Will they all betray me? Oh yes, they flatter and cajole. They pretend love where there is only ambition. I am not blind, nor am I stupid—I know how privilege works. But I had hoped, oh how I had hoped, that with Robin, things were different. I dared believe he loved me just a little, a true love that had nothing to do with my queenship. I dared believe he loved Elizabeth the woman!

A fool! I have been a fool for this dark-eyed man, the handsomest in my court, they say. He is handsome still.

I shall do nothing. I shall watch and wait. She will not win him—what woman could win him from me? I am the queen! She will not keep him for long.

And what of our Fawn? She still stares at me as if I were not of this world, as if I were some demon sent to torment her. Yes, she curtsies and obeys. But there is not warmth between us, none of the closeness we once shared. It seems the little family I sought to create has turned to dust in my hands.

No, I have not sent Skydemore from court. They have my word on the matter—that should be enough to stop them from doing anything foolish. If my wishes are not strong enough to dissuade them from pursuing this matter, then to the Tower with them both! By God's blood, I will be obeyed. I have flung higher born folk in the Tower when they disobeyed me. My other cousin, Katherine Gray, found out the hard way—I will be obeyed!

Forty-six

Late January 1574

The night was bitter cold, with snow falling thick and fast. The wind howled and Mary pulled her cloak tighter. She shivered as much from fear as the icy weather. She hurried along the castle wall, heading to the courtyard where she was to meet Sir John. He had a horse ready for them to ride to a small chapel where he had arranged for a priest to marry them under the rites of the old religion. She would convert to Catholicism after their marriage and bring up their children in the popish church. It was what he wanted and she desired to please him above all else.

She looked behind her as she half ran to the gate. She could barely see, the snow fell so thickly. She imagined she heard footsteps and wondered if the queen knew, even now, where she was going and what she was planning to do. She had escaped by feigning illness, gagging herself in the jakes and allowing the spittle and bile to stain her dress. Swearing she did not wish to infect the queen with what she called the flux, she talked Her Majesty into allowing her to sleep in the common room where the ladies-in-waiting slept. She had generously shared her sleeping cordial with them and then waited until she heard them all breathing steadily, some snoring softly, before she slipped out into the winter night.

A strong hand grabbed her and pulled her behind the wall.

"Mary—the horse is here," said Sir John, already boosting her up to the pillion where she would ride behind him.

"I do not think any heard me escape—I waited until they were all asleep," she said, clambering onto the horse.

"It was the devil finding a man willing to marry us—I finally sent word to our old priest in Herefordshire and paid him a princely sum to ride to Southwark where he will meet us at St. Bartholomew's Chapel. Do not fret, sweetheart. All will be well," said Sir John.

"I am shaking—I cannot help it. I cannot imagine Her Majesty's actions should she discover us," said Mary.

"She will not, my love. Have no fear. Once we have accomplished the act, she will forgive us and we shall be happy—you will see. She is, at heart, a good woman. And she is kind to those she loves. I have seen the care she takes with you, Mary. She loves you very much—have no fear," he said, spurring the horse to great speed.

The horse wove in and out of the narrow streets as quickly as possible. Sir John urged the animal on, in spite of the swirling snow. Mary could barely see anything and she wondered how the horse managed to get them to Southwark without injury. Sir John reined in, though the chapel looked deserted.

"Wait here. I want to check it first," he said.

Mary could hear his boots crunching along the snow-covered pathway. She watched as he opened the heavy wooden doors and disappeared inside. Her hands shook and she felt the cold air travel down her spine to the small of her back, causing her to shiver. She looked around her to see if they had been followed. There was a man across the cobbled street, leaning against the wall of a tavern. He was huddled in a hooded cloak and she could not see his face. Was he one of Lord Burghley's men? A spy sent by Walsingham? Or a mere cutpurse?

What was taking John such a long time? Had someone been inside waiting for him, someone with a sharp knife? Perhaps the priest had not yet arrived. Mary continued to glance in different directions, looking for anyone or anything suspicious. The horse sensed her uneasiness and pawed the icy ground, puffs of foggy breath shooting from his nostrils. Mary felt the cold air enter her own lungs and realized her whole body trembled. She was cold; she was terrified. The night was dark and dreary. Where was John? How long could he possibly be?

Just as she felt tears threatening, the great door opened again and John walked toward her with long strides. He mounted the horse and guided their steed away from the chapel.

"What's wrong? Where are we going? What's happening?" Mary whispered.

"The priest will not marry us in that chapel—he says it is too dangerous, too public. He has told me of another location three miles hence. At the crossroads, we shall find the Body and Blood Tavern. They will be waiting for us," said John, softly.

"What a horrid name! I hope we are not to be married in such a place," said Mary.

"I shall be happy to marry you anywhere, my love. Do not be disheartened—such a name denotes a certain friendliness to Catholics. We shall be safe there, dearest. And by tomorrow morning, we shall be husband and wife. I cannot wait to hold you again," he said.

His confidence was contagious and Mary began to relax. She glanced behind them as they rode from the city into the countryside. She could see no other horses on the road this snowy night. Most people were huddled warm in their beds on such a night as this.

Mary thought about spending cold nights at Holme Lacy, wrapped in the arms of her husband, her love. She smiled and listened as the wind whistled through the few buildings and trees that lined the road. The steady rhythm of the horse's hooves gave her comfort and she tightened her hold around John's waist.

A small inn sat directly ahead on the right. Two large torches lit the place and Mary could see it was a modest establishment, certainly not the sort of place she was used to visiting.

Sir John pulled on the reins and quickly hopped down to assist Mary as she dismounted. The snow continued to fall and she almost slipped on an icy spot. Sir John caught her by the elbow and led her to a rough door where he knocked three times, then two times, then once. Slowly, the door opened and a woman welcomed them inside. No one said a word. The woman put her finger to her lips, shushing them. Mary saw a few travelers lounging at a crude table, eating something steaming from their trenchers. They gave her a quick look, no doubt surprised by her velvet cloak and her fine dress. She wished she had thought to dress more unobtrusively. Surely they would remember her, wonder what she was doing at such a place on such a night. It was too late for worry now, however. She pulled the hood over her head and tried to hide her face as best she could. She followed the woman down a long, deserted hall. Mary saw a full-sized painting of a fisherman holding a large fish. She gave a little gasp as the woman pushed against the painting, and it moved, opening to reveal a secret room. The woman bade them go inside.

Mary was surprised at the closeness of the room. Two tapers burned at a small altar where a golden cross bearing the suffering Lord stood. Incense filled the air and Mary saw the priest, blessing the sacraments in preparation for the ceremony. She saw someone stir to one side and was shocked to see Sir James standing there with Master Nicholas Hilliard at his side. There was also a woman she did not know.

Sir John spoke with the men, who had agreed to come as witnesses. The priest called them to silence and quickly, with a lifetime of experience behind him, he performed the rite of marriage. It was over in just a few minutes and Mary could not believe she had defied the Queen of England for the love of the man standing beside her.

After the Mass was taken, those who had gathered in that small room clustered together and began talking. The unknown woman turned out to be a neighbor of John's and Sir James's, Mistress Katherine Blakely. She had been in charge of John's children and she was very interested in helping Mary with her new duties.

"They are wonderful children—I should hate to be parted from them," said Mistress Katherine.

"I do not believe you will be asked to leave them, Mistress Katherine. I shall need all the help I can get with five young ones to tend to—I welcome your assistance," said Mary, smiling at the older woman.

"I hope you will not regret this rash action, my dear. But John is a good man and those five grandchildren of mine need a mother. I am glad you are one of us," said Sir James, hugging her.

"Thank you for your kindness, sir. We shall not forget your courage," said Sir John. He then bowed to them all and led Mary away, through the same secret passage.

"I am sorry you will not have the joyous celebration we would have had if we'd been wed at Holme Lacy. We would have lit the fires, had the cooks make a delicious feast, danced with our neighbors until we could not move. They would have bedded us properly, with the priest blessing our marriage bed and our friends leading us to the bed itself and throwing us in. Then, they would have sung ribald songs, raised the glass to us many a time, and finally, left us to our wooing," said Sir John as he bundled her to the outer door.

"Perhaps we can still have such festivities when we return to Holme Lacy—if the queen allows us to live," said Mary.

Sir John stopped and took hold of her by the shoulders.

"Sweetheart, you will live, I promise. If anyone, and I do mean *anyone*, tries to harm you, they will have to get through me to do so. You shall be safe—I will make it my life's work to insure that," he said, kissing her. "I have found a room for the night—let us get ourselves to it."

"But I cannot be gone all night. The queen will call for me first thing," said Mary.

"Yes, I know. But we can take the room for its proper use on our wedding night," he said.

She smiled up at him. Maybe things would work out. Maybe the queen would see reason.

The room was warm with a small hearth and plenty of faggots in the nearby basket. The bed looked somewhat clean and Mary checked for bedbugs and any other sort of vermin. She found nothing.

She began to remove her cloak when Sir John's warm hands stopped her.

"I shall assist you this night, dearest, as if you were the queen herself. I have brought some sweet oil and I will begin with your feet," he said as he removed her cloak and hung it on a hook.

He moved her to the bed where he bade her sit. Going down on one knee, he carefully removed her shoes and woolen hose. He rubbed the oil onto her feet. It was warm and smelled like spicy fig pudding. At first, she was ashamed for him to handle her in this way, and tried to hide her feet beneath her skirts. But he insisted and began to massage the oil onto the soles, the heels, and finally, between her toes. She leaned back against the pillows and sighed. Slowly, he pried the toes apart so that he could insert his finger, rubbing the oil around and around. He spent so many minutes warming and rubbing her feet that she lost track of time. She had not realized her feet could be so sensitive to his touch. Soon, he worked his way to her ankles; then he worked the oil up to her knees. He untied her sleeves, unlaced her bodice, and removed these. He took off her kirtle, which she stepped out of with trembling legs. She stood before him in her petticoat and shift. Before she knew it, he had whisked the petticoat from her and she was in her soft lawn shift edged in Belgian lace.

"If you will allow me to remove this, you may crawl under the covers and I will apply the oil," he said.

She helped him lift the shift away. She stood before him in the firelight. She could hear his intake of breath. She hurried under the covers. Soon, she could feel him pour the oil on her stomach, her breasts, everywhere. His hands seemed to multiply and she could feel him on her legs, her belly, her breasts, her hair.

For what seemed like a long time, she watched as he removed his clothes. Then he came to her, his manly smell mixed with the sweet oil. He gave her a wedding night to remember, though no one celebrated the occasion but husband and wife.

Forty-seven
February 1574

The deep winter chill showed no sign of relenting. In Richmond Palace, the queen kept her ladies busy with sewing for the poor and dancing for Her Majesty's amusement. Mistresses Mary and Eleanor spent most mornings attending the queen's wardrobe, preparing the spring dresses and keeping the heavier winter gowns smelling fresh and brushed. As far as Mary knew, her marriage to Sir John was a well-kept secret. Every member of the wedding party had sworn a solemn oath never to breathe a word about it, not even to their dearest ones. At first, Mary had been afraid Master Nicholas might let it slip to his new bride, but thus far, Eleanor seemed unaware of Mary's dangerous actions. That was what she wanted, of course. Their lives depended on such secrecy. But part of Mary wanted desperately to tell Mistress Eleanor about the clandestine wedding, how exciting it had been, how terrified she'd felt, tiptoeing into the hidden chapel, meeting the forbidden priest. And then, the beauty of her wedding night, where her husband had ravished her completely, using his hands, his tongue, and, of course, his manly parts. She had never expected such actions and, at first, had been shy. But John was patient and his tender persistence had been amply rewarded with her little cries of pleasure. She was curious as to whether Mistress Eleanor had experienced similar delights in the marriage bed. But Mistress Eleanor would not be around the palace for much longer—it was almost time for her to go into her confinement. Mary had sewn several gowns for a gift. She had even embroidered some clouts for Eleanor's babe. There was excitement in the air around Mistress Eleanor these days. Mary found it difficult to wait for the child's arrival. And she worried for her friend's first birth, an event fraught with danger.

This morning, the queen had sent Mary and Mistress Eleanor back to her bedchamber to search through her casket of jewels for a large pearl brooch surrounded by blue sapphires. Her Majesty wished to bestow the treasure upon Sir Christopher Hatton, who was quickly outshining Lord Robert as the queen's favorite. Mary liked Sir Christopher but she felt sorry for Lord Robert. She knew the queen was displeased with him because of his relationship with Lady Douglass. And though there were certainly rumors of their marriage, nothing had been proven, except that Lady Douglass was with child and living in Leicester House. All of this, the queen chose to ignore. Mary could only hope that if Her Majesty ever got wind of her own marriage, the result would be the same.

Cold winter light shone through the windows of the queen's bedchamber. No one was in sight, as Mary quickly checked the room. This would be her chance to talk to Eleanor.

"The fire does not burn too brightly for us this morning. It is freezing in here," said Eleanor.

"The queen tries to save money where she can—why pay for wood to burn when no one is in the room?" said Mary.

"*We* are in the room," said Eleanor.

Both women laughed.

"You know well enough that *we* do not count!" said Mary, rubbing her arms for warmth.

They walked over to the large casket where the queen kept her jewels. Mary turned the key which the queen had given her and lifted the lid. She never ceased to be amazed at the beautiful things contained in the box. They began a careful search for the pearl brooch.

"How would I look in this?" said Eleanor, as she placed a small golden crown upon her head.

"Take that off! What if someone comes in? We would lose our positions!" said Mary.

"You fret too much. How many chances do you think we'll get to try on the queen's jewels?" said Eleanor, adding a long rope of pearls to her ensemble.

They continued to search for the pearl brooch with the blue sapphires, slowly sifting through the hundreds of pieces of jewelry.

"I have it! Finally! Oh, it is quite lovely," said Mary, holding the brooch in her hand, admiring the delicate gold work around the stones. The pearl looked especially white in the morning sun.

"Thank heavens—I would *hate* to be forced to keep looking and trying on the queen's things. Such finery! Have you ever seen the like?" said Eleanor, now adding a bracelet of gold beads to her arm.

Mary laughed and helped Eleanor remove the items from her person. She noticed Eleanor's ever-ripening belly and knew that soon her friend would leave court to give birth to her child. Mary hated thinking about that time—she would miss Eleanor. If ever she was going to share her news with her dear Nora, now was the time.

"I . . . I have something to tell you, Nora," said Mary in a whisper.

"Well, then . . . go on," said Eleanor.

"It is a great secret, and before I tell you, I must have your pledge of silence," said Mary. She kept her voice down and took Eleanor's hands in hers.

"My goodness! It must be quite a secret," said Eleanor. "You are not with child, are you?"

"No, thank God! But it might be worse," said Mary, taking a deep breath.

"What could be worse?" said Eleanor.

Mary paused. It was harder than she had imagined, telling her secret. She feared the very walls were listening.

"Sir John . . . we are, well, we are married," said Mary, tightening her grip on Eleanor's hands.

"What? How did you? When? Oh, you're hurting me!" said Eleanor.

"Oh, I am sorry. Last month. We slipped away from court in the dark of night. I just knew someone would catch us, though we had planned our escape well enough. But no, the cold wind, the snow, and the late hour kept everyone close to the hearth or snuggled in their beds. We rode out past Southwark to an inn. There, a priest awaited us. And we were made man and wife," said Mary.

"Man and wife . . . man and wife . . . the queen's ward and Sir John, man and wife," cackled a voice from within the wardrobe press.

"Who in the world?" said Mary as she rose to fling open the large door. There, curled up on the bottom shelf, beneath the queen's warm shifts, lay Catspaw.

"Married, is it? I have been married three times—let me see. The first man was . . . well, his name was . . . I think it was Arthur, named after the late king's brother. Could have been Edward, though . . ." said Catspaw. She continued mumbling to herself, what sounded like gibberish to Mary.

"Catspaw! Catspaw! You must listen to me," said Mary, grabbing the old woman by her thin shoulders and forcing her to look into Mary's face.

"Catspaw listens—hears everything! She will not like it, mistress! She will not like it one bit!" said Catspaw.

"I know—that is why we must keep it a secret! Oh, she will be very angry—she might throw us all into the Tower! Even you, Catspaw! You will not tell anyone, will you?" said Mary.

"My lips are sealed, even as with wax, Your Worship. No one will get the word from me, of that you can rest assured. I never gossip, no, never say a word. All secrets are safe with me—even the one about Lord Robert and Lady Douglass—they was married, too, you see. She done all she could to bring him to the altar and she finally got her way. She's in a way, too—a *family* way, if you get my meaning," said Catspaw.

"Nora, what am I going to do? She will never keep this quiet!" said Mary, close to tears.

"No one will listen to her—she mumbles to herself all the time—everyone thinks she's touched in the head. Pay her no mind—if she slips and tells, no one will believe it," said Eleanor.

Catspaw grew quiet for a moment and then began murmuring to herself.

"No one believes . . . pay her . . . slips," said Catspaw, clutching at the soft lawn beneath her, her hands crooked as claws, the fingernails yellow against the crisp, white shifts.

Mary looked at the old woman and offered to help her rise.

"Would you like one of my sleeping cordials? It will ease your aches and pains for the night," said Mary.

Catspaw stared at her and smiled. She nodded her head and Mary led her to a stool by the hearth. She helped her sit down and then left Mistress Eleanor with Catspaw while she went to the alcove where she stored her cordials. She retrieved the sleeping draught and carried it back to the women by the fire. Catspaw tipped the small vial back and drank every drop. Then, Mary and Eleanor helped her return to the servants' quarters where she had a small, cold room she shared with three other women. They saw to it she went to bed immediately.

*M*ary kept her ears open during the weeks after Catspaw had overheard her secret, trying to ascertain whether or not the old woman was keeping mum about what she had discovered. Thus far, there was not even a hint of gossip. No one stared at Mary or wagged their tongues when she walked past. She began to sigh with relief and looked forward to the warming weather of spring, though no such weather had come yet. The cold wind still blew almost every day and piles of snow littered the corners of the gardens. Mary had not had a chance to be alone with Sir John since they returned from their wedding night. She had to content herself with a few stolen glances and the occasional brush when they passed each other as each attended to the duties demanded by the queen. Thankfully, her courses had come on schedule and, from the way things were going, she would not have a chance for her condition to change any time soon. Each night before falling asleep, she thought of her wedding night. The memories sent shivers down her spine, and one night the queen had an extra coverlet brought to her, thinking she quivered from the cold.

Mistress Eleanor had gone into her confinement in London, at her husband's father's house. It was a modest but nicely appointed home where Master Nicholas could visit when he was not busy limning at court. His work was becoming more and more popular, especially among the young courtiers, who often gave a miniature painting of themselves to the women they wished to stir. The queen also sat for him several times, impressed with his abilities. Mistress Eleanor had high hopes for their future, though Master Nicholas had little money at present.

Though Mary was lonely without her friend and without more than casual contact with her husband, she passed the days pleasantly enough. She looked forward to the evenings when she and John might steal a dance together with no one being the wiser. When they did so, they were both very careful not to look at one another for too long, or give each other lingering touches. Mary had to use all of her restraint to keep from caressing Sir John, and she could tell by the stiff way he held himself that he, too, struggled to maintain their ruse.

Mary thought she would wait until she and the queen had a quiet moment together, perhaps with Lord Robert, just the three of them, to tell Her Majesty of the wedding. She knew the queen would be furious, but she hoped, with Lord Robert present, he might be able to reason with her. If anyone could do so, it would be he. While she waited, Mary made a special point of being agreeable and pleasant to the queen.

"Married, married—all the folks is married. Lord Robert and Lady Douglass, Mistress Mary and Sir John, Mistress Eleanor and her Nick—all is married, all is married," sang Catspaw as she carried a stack of clean shifts and bedclothes from the laundry to the queen's apartments. She walked, as usual, up the servants' stairs. No one used this passageway except the washerwomen, though Catspaw had caught lovers hiding there in years past. Lord Robert and the queen had been known to take their time in the lavender-scented hallway. Catspaw laughed under her breath when she thought of those two together.

"Love, love, love! Queens forgo it, courtiers show it, poets know it, and . . ." she sang out again.

"What have we here? What are you singing about, old woman?" said Oxford, coming up behind Catspaw. He, with Pakington behind him, stepped forward to block Catspaw's path to the queen's rooms. The old woman cowered and tucked her head as if she were afraid of being hit.

"We shall not harm you, old woman—we heard your song. You've been singing it for days now, all along the halls of the castle. A lovely song it is—about love and marriage. We decided to follow you so you could spill your stories to us. Tell me, about whom do you sing?" said Oxford, leaning his arm against the wall so that it made a sort of bridge across the hallway.

"Oh, just old songs—Catspaw knows many old tales," she said.

"I'll wager you do, you old gossip. But we heard you name someone—someone who had married? Who were you singing about?" said Pakington, towering over her.

"I wasn't singing about nobody—just words, that's all. Catspaw keeps her secrets, she does," said Catspaw.

"What secrets? If you value your life, you better tell me or I'll have your tongue cut out—then you will not be able to carry your torrid tales," said Oxford, standing very close to the old woman.

"Not supposed to tell—it's a secret—Old Catspaw can keep a secret for the nice lady. Yes, she can," said Catspaw in a singsong voice.

"Which nice lady? Lady Douglass? Do you know something about her? And Lord Robert? Oh, Pakington, would it not be advantageous to have something on my dear Earl of Leicester? Think what prizes we might win for keeping his secrets," said Oxford.

"Tut-tut, nothing nice about Lady Douglass. The other one, Mistress Mary—she gives Catspaw cordials, she does," said Catspaw, slowly pushing against Oxford's arm.

"Not so fast, old woman. Do you mean the queen's ward, Mary Shelton? What do you know about her?" said Oxford, a smile spreading across his features.

"She never did marry that Sir John in the dark of night . . . no, she did not! And she never found a priest in a secret place! She never did!" said Catspaw.

"Could this be true?" said Oxford to Pakington. "Could the queen's ward have run off with someone?"

"She would be arrogant enough to defy the queen. She has been spoiled by the queen's favor, if you ask me. Impudent little bitch," said Pakington.

"But who? Oh, I do not really have to ask—I have seen the way Skydemore looks at her. And how he jumps to protect her from any possible harm," said Oxford.

Oxford thought for a moment, then lowered his arm.

"You may go, old woman. Speak nothing of this, do you hear? Nothing!" he said.

"Catspaw says nothing—she never tells tales. No, she keeps her secrets . . . all the secrets . . ." mumbled the old woman as she walked away.

Both men watched as Catspaw hurried up the hallway, teetering from one side to the other. She looked back at them once, then slowed her pace when she realized they were not following her.

"What are you going to do with this little tidbit of information?" said Pakington.

Oxford paused, then smiled.

"What any humble servant of the queen would do—I shall inform

Her Majesty of this news at once! Skydemore is a Catholic—it will not take much to paint him as a traitor. Oh, this promises to be rich, Lusty! Rich!" said Oxford as he turned back the way he came and trotted down the narrow hall, with Pakington following close behind him.

Several days later, the queen was walking in her garden, strolling briskly ahead of her ladies, when the Earl of Oxford and Sir "Lusty" met her.

"Good morrow, Your Majesty. Such a lovely spring morning," said Oxford, smiling as he bowed. Pakington bowed also but said nothing.

"I am surprised to see you gentlemen out walking—I usually have the gardens to myself," said the queen, smiling.

"I hope we are not intruding, Your Grace," said Oxford.

"Not at all—I am glad for the company. My ladies have trouble keeping pace with me," said the queen, leading the way.

They walked in silence for a while, occasionally stopping to watch a bird or comment on the budding trees.

"Your Majesty, I wish to offer my congratulations," said Oxford, during one of their pauses.

"Oh? For what?" said the queen.

"I understand your cousin and ward, Mary Shelton, has married Sir John Skydemore. I heard it was a small affair, though I would have thought the queen's ward would have had a more elaborate service. But I suppose Skydemore's religion might have had something to do with such a subdued ceremony. After all, he makes no secret of his popish ways," said Oxford pleasantly.

The queen did not speak. She turned pale. She faltered and both Oxford and Pakington reached out to steady her.

"This cannot be true—who told you of this so-called marriage?" said the queen.

"I will admit we got the information from a well-known gossip, Your Grace. But one who seems to know everything that goes on at court. Old Catspaw," said Oxford.

The queen stood still and closed her eyes, as if she were suddenly weary. Finally, she uttered a whispery "Can this be true?" to the men.

Both men nodded. Without another word, the queen turned and headed toward the palace. Oxford looked at Pakington and smiled.

Forty-nine

P arry, bar the door. I have come to the chapel to be alone. Let no one enter.

God's blood! Is it true? Can my Fawn have been so foolish as to marry that Skydemore man? I cannot believe it! No, it cannot be.

Rumors about Rob. Rumors about Mary. Who instigates this war against my heart? Are the rumors true? Could those two, whom I love above all others, could they have betrayed me? By God's bowels, I shall find out! If I have to tear out the tongues of every man, woman, and child in London, I shall have the truth!

No, Parry, give me no cordials! Give me no wine! Where is Fawn? Tell me, I say! Tell me at once!

Sewing? In my Privy Chamber with the other ladies? How obedient! How docile! I shall go to her immediately! No, no, I will not wait until I am calm—I shall never be calm again! Out of my way, Parry! Out of my way or I shall knock you out of my way! She shall pay for breaking my heart! She shall pay!

M ary and several of the other ladies sat in the Privy Chamber, each engaged in needlework. Mary was sewing the hem of a shift of coarse linen for the upcoming Maundy where the queen would distribute such items to the poor. She was taking particular care as she wanted the garment to be as fine as she could make it.

"I do not know why we must work our fingers to the bone sewing for the poor. Do you think they care if they have a new shift for the Maundy?" said Mistress Frances.

"Of course they care—they have little enough as it is. This seems the Christian thing to do," said Mary. "Do you know what has happened to Lady Douglass? She is a good seamstress."

"Lady Douglass has been excused to nurse her sister, who, according to Douglass, lies at death's door," said Mistress Frances.

"We all know where Lady Douglass lies," said Mistress Margaret, one of the queen's new ladies.

"She's married Lord Robert and is big with his babe," said Catspaw.

"I didn't hear *you* come in, old dame," said Mistress Frances.

"How do you reckon I live so long, missy . . . I come and go and no one knows I've been," mumbled the old woman.

"Is it true then? Has he married her?" said Mistress Margaret.

"True as the blue sky—I know a scrub woman who works for the man what married them," said Catspaw, walking slowly to lay her stack of linens in the linen press.

The women continued to chat, speaking of lords and ladies, the queen's new favorite, the Earl of Oxford's abominable treatment of his wife, and the dozens of priests crossing the Channel into England, with the Pope's edict to reconvert the English people to the true church.

Suddenly, a disturbance in the outer hall startled them. Without warning, the door opened and the queen stormed into their midst. She strode to where Mary sat stitching, knocked the work from her hands, and grabbed her arms. She yanked Mary to her feet and Mary found herself face-to-face with Elizabeth. Her Majesty's black eyes were icy and her cheeks blazed. Her reddish-gold hair had come partially undone and wild curls sprang around her head, making her look like the Medusa of Greek legend. She was, indeed, a terrible sight to behold.

"Is it the truth? Is it? Speak!" screamed the queen, her face just inches from Mary's own.

Mary tried to curtsy and bowed her head.

"By God's bones, look at me!" yelled the queen.

Mary gazed into the queen's face and felt her knees grow weak.

"Is it true?" said the queen in a whisper more frightening than her screams.

"Is what true, Your Grace?" said Mary.

"That you have married that Catholic! The man we expressly forbade you to wed!" said the queen, her hands still gripping Mary's arms with a strength Mary would not have imagined coming from so slight a woman. Her arms ached.

Mary paused. She did not know what to say. If she lied, and the queen did, indeed, know the truth, things would go much worse for her. She took a deep breath.

"Yes, Your Majesty. I have wed Sir John Skydemore," said Mary.

The entire room fell silent.

No one spoke.

No one moved.

"How dare you defy us?" shouted the queen.

Before Mary could answer, she felt a sharp slap to her face. The blow made her see stars and the stinging of her cheeks felt like a hundred bees were attacking her. Before she had a chance to recover from the first blow, a second landed on the other side. She fell back against her chair but the queen did not allow her to crumple. Her Majesty pulled Mary back to a standing position and continued beating her about the head and shoulders.

"I have raised you up from a poor orphan child—given you my love and anything you desired. I have prepared you to be fit to marry a prince! But no, this was not enough—you would marry for *love*! As if such a baggage could understand anything about love!" said the queen as she slapped Mary everywhere she could land a blow.

Mary tried to avoid the hammering attack of the queen's hands and feet, but with little success. She finally covered her face with her hands and was surprised to find tears on her cheeks.

"I have loved you as mine own child . . ." said the queen, continuing to kick and hit Mary, her eyes blazing.

"But you are *not* my mother! If you were, *my* happiness would be important to you! You would care about *me*, not your *dreams* for me!

If you were truly my mother, you would be happy I had found love in this sordid world you have made around yourself!" said Mary.

"Why you impudent, monstrous . . . You are no better than a stewed whore—marrying without my permission means there is no legal marriage at all! I shall have it annulled!" stormed the queen, once again raining slaps and kicks onto Mary.

"Well, then I would be truly *your* daughter—a cold, untouched woman! A woman with a withered-up heart, a heart shriveled and dry as an oak leaf in autumn! A woman no one could ever love!" screamed Mary.

The queen grew silent. Then she reached for the nearest object, a large gold candlestick on the small table next to Mary. She threw the object at Mary as hard as she could. Mary raised her hand to deflect it, but the candlestick hit her hand with great force. She felt a bone crack. She screamed as pain seared through her. The candlestick fell with a clatter and Mary screamed again, a long, loud shriek.

She looked at her finger, which was poking out at a right angle from her hand.

"You have broken my finger!" Mary said as the digit began to pulse.

"You are lucky I have not broken your bloody neck!" said the queen as she turned to leave. "You and your man are banished from this court! Begone immediately! Take nothing with you! You shall never return! You are lucky I do not throw you both in the Tower!"

Fifty-one

N o, I am finished. I have ranted and raved enough for one day. Yes, I banished them. I've been told they have already left the palace. No, I gave them nothing. I will give them nothing. I have been betrayed by everyone I have ever loved. First, my father when he took my own mother from me. Then my dear brother, who changed the succession to exclude me. And do not forget my sister, keeping me in the Tower, blaming me for any rebellion that took shape during her reign. Now, Robin lives with another woman and my Fawn, my dearest girl, has married a Catholic, an unimpressive man with little to offer. Well, she has made her bed and now she must lie in it.

I know you have not abandoned me, Parry. If you were to turn against me, I should not know what to do. Oh, I am tired of it all. Endless scheming, dissembling, manipulating. Fawn was right—it is a sordid world at court. I can almost understand why she might believe she would be happier away from all this—yet, to leave me! To choose that man over her queen!

After all I have done for her, after the love I have given to her. She has struck a blow to my very heart!

Yes, Parry—you are right. This grief is the price we pay for love. But it is too costly—I would not wish to feel this bereft again. The cost is too high.

D oes it hurt very much, dearest?" said Sir John as he rode with her toward Holme Lacy.

"I fear it does. But not so much as when the apothecary put it back into its place. I was glad of my cordial at that moment for I fear that without it, I should have fainted dead away," said Mary, pillioned behind him. A mule carried the few things they were able to take with them, Sir John leading it with a rope.

"It shall heal in time—it may be crooked, but then you can tell our grandchildren it was made so in the service of Good Queen Bess," said Sir John.

"How can you joke? She was furious—as angry as I have ever seen her. And all those horrible things I said! I cannot believe I said such to an anointed queen! I am clean amazed she did not throw both of us into the Tower," said Mary, leaning her face against Sir John's back, her eyes still red with crying.

"She is displeased, to say the least. But I know she loves you and her banishment will not be forever," said Sir John.

"I do not care if I am gone from court the rest of my life—I have all I need, you, my treasures—" said Mary.

"Do you mean to say you took the time to fetch that old box!" said Sir John.

"Of course! How should I leave my home without the sweet memories captured in the box? I had not thought it before, but the court is the only home I have ever known. I shall miss it—and the queen. How we used to laugh in her enormous bed when I was her sleeping companion—all those years spent knowing I was safe when I was with Her Majesty. I suppose I did get the royal treatment from everyone, once they saw how she loved me," said Mary, suddenly sad and wishing she could have at least said good-bye to the queen. Tears rolled onto her cheeks once more.

"Do not cry, love. Think no more about those times. We shall make happy memories for ourselves at Holme Lacy. And I shall keep you safe, sweetheart. We have no need of the court to bring us joy—we bring that to each other," said Sir John.

On through the snowy road they trudged, the wind howling as if in anguish and the cold seeping into Mary's feet and legs until her whole body shook with it. After three difficult days of such travel, Mary caught sight of Holme Lacy, the beautiful, sprawling manor house on the hill, torches blazing, welcoming her home.

She was beginning her new life. She wondered what the queen was doing at this moment. She wondered if Her Majesty missed her at all. She wondered if the queen would ever forgive her.

Birdsong filled the spring air as the queen walked along the garden path, Lord Burghley, Dudley, and Walsingham strolling beside her, her gaggle of ladies following behind. The air was still cool and the queen wore a shawl of green silk over her house gown of simple white lawn. Her ladies were fully dressed for the day but the queen preferred to walk, have her prayers, and break her fast before adorning herself with the royal garb.

"Majesty, Walsingham has news from France that will not please you, I fear," said Burghley, struggling to keep pace, his words punctuated by puffs of breath.

"God's teeth, what now?" said the queen, easily outpacing the men, except for Dudley, who matched her step for step.

"If I may, Your Grace, the Pope has trained a militia of God's soldiers—Jesuit priests who are already sailing for our land. They shall endeavor to win the people back to the Pope and then Spain and France stand ready to invade. As we must save our land from the superstition and ignorance of the Roman Church, Your Majesty, you must allow me freedom to intercept these men—some are trained assassins, I am told—to keep the Protestant cause alive," said Walsingham.

"I thought you were supposed to keep *me* alive," said the queen.

"Your Majesty, they are one and the same—you are the champion of the Protestants around the world. If only Your Majesty would consider sending more aid to the Huguenots . . ." said Walsingham.

"Enough! We have done all we can. Now, what of these priests who are coming to our shores?" said the queen.

"We shall do everything in our power to protect Your Grace. You must not go on progress this year—in the public eye, your person is vulnerable. If you stay in London, we have much more chance to shield you from harm," said Burghley.

"Does this perambulation around the garden kill you, Spirit? I see you are tired. Come, let us return to the Presence Chamber," said the queen, stopping to examine her man.

"Forgive me, Majesty. I am not as young as you, nor as spry," said Burghley.

The queen and her councillors turned back to Whitehall Palace and continued their discussion.

"As to the progress, I shall head this summer to the west of our land—I have not been that way in some time and it will do the people good to see their queen," said the queen.

"Majesty, I beg of you, do not go away from London this summer—it is too dangerous," said Burghley.

"You fret over me like a mother hen, Spirit. It is the love of my people which sustains me and my love for them which shall keep me safe from harm. However, do not fear. I shall send our good

Walsingham to search out these foreign Jesuits and to find which of the recusants are to be trusted and which are under our suspicions. Now, gentlemen, I shall break my fast and see you later in the Presence Chamber," said the queen, shooing them out as if they were children.

The men turned to go.

"Walsingham, you may stay. I should like for you to come with me to my Privy Chamber so we may discuss these threats over ale and manchet," said the queen.

The Privy Chamber was set with a sumptuous meal of ale, bread, strawberries in cream, and a variety of tarts and other pastries. After the queen had nibbled on a few of these, she offered some food to Walsingham, who declined. Then she sent the food to her ladies and cleared the chamber.

"I have a few names to give you, Walsingham. I want these families investigated thoroughly. In Herefordshire, the family of Sir James Croft—" said Her Majesty.

"Surely Sir James is not suspect! He has served you faithfully, lo, these many years," said Walsingham. "Even *I* recognize Sir James's loyalty, I, who suspect everyone."

"Do you think I give you these names lightly? I have suspicions of him, just a feminine feeling that he might be up to something," said the queen, wiping the corner of her mouth.

"I shall look into it, Majesty. If you would but execute the Scottish queen, you could rest easy in your bed at night. She is the source of all the discontent in the realm. The Pope wishes to place her on the throne in Your Majesty's place and that is why he sends his army. He knows France as well as Spain will come to the aid of the Scottish queen, once the people have been turned back to Rome," said Walsingham.

"There is another family in Herefordshire—the Skydemores. That whole clan is Catholic and, I fear, not likely to convert, though it be law. I wish you to locate a Sir John Skydemore—he is the one on whom my suspicions fall," said the Queen.

"He is Sir James's son-in-law, is that correct?" said Walsingham.

"Yes—they are plotting together, I fear," said the queen.

"Was not this Sir John one of your Gentlemen Pensioners? Did not he save your life?" said Walsingham.

"Yes, that is the man. But we have heard rumors since then that we have lost his love. He married our dear cousin Mary, without our permission. We banished them from court. For this, he plots against us. He thought to use Mary to gain more promotions from us. But his plan has returned him to the penury from which he came. We fear he wishes to do us harm," said the queen, her face inscrutable.

"I shall turn my full attention to this matter, Your Majesty. My spies will begin digging in the dirt this very day," said Walsingham.

"Your spies are diligent and clever—I am sure they will find something, enough evidence to bring Sir John to the Tower. That is what I would like, Walsingham, to bring that recusant to the Tower and show the people of England what happens when they do not obey the law of the land. You will bring him forth?" said the queen.

"Yes, Majesty. I, too, wish to rid our land of the Roman vermin," said Walsingham.

"Then we understand each other?" said the queen.

"Perfectly, Your Majesty," said Walsingham, kissing the hand she offered him, then, bowing, setting to his task with his usual fervor.

Early May 1574

"You have not been this fidgety since you were under house arrest when your sister was queen," said Mistress Blanche as she rubbed the queen's shoulders with almond oil. "Then, you had good reason to lose sleep. Tell me, dearie, what is the matter?"

The queen lay in her bed, Mistress Frances on the trundle bed beside her where Mary used to sleep. The queen turned away from Mistress Frances and whispered.

"All of Christendom wishes me dead, Parry. The Scottish queen plots and plans to steal my crown. My Sweet Robin has married that dreadful Sheffield woman, or so I hear. The Protestant cause is suffering from bickering among its own. Why should I not be over-wrought!" hissed the queen.

"This is as it has always been. I thought perhaps there was some-thing else on your mind—I have missed our poppet, and I know you well enough, dearie, to know you have missed her as well," said Mis-tress Blanche gently.

"Poppet be damned! She has brought this banishment upon her-self. If she thinks to soften my heart by not writing me or asking forgiveness, such a ploy will not work! She must beg on her knees before I will allow her back into my court," said the queen.

"I remember when she first came to court, all those years ago. You had just been made queen and she called you the 'shining lady,' remember?" said Mistress Blanche, warming the oil by rub-bing her hands together quickly before applying it to the queen's back.

"That feels wonderful, Parry. Yes, I remember my little Fawn—those dark eyes and that beautiful long black hair. How she loved me then!" said the queen. She started to cry.

"There, there—our Fawn will come back to us. Why don't you send for her, tell her all is forgiven—things can be again as they once were," said Mistress Blanche.

"No! She deliberately went against my wishes and she shall pay. And that recusant husband of hers shall pay as well. Then, after he is gone, I shall bring her to me, and she shall help me sleep with her soft singing and her special cordials," said the queen.

"What do you mean, 'after he is gone'? What have you done, Your Majesty?" said Mistress Blanche.

"Nothing. I have done nothing," said the queen.

Fifty-four

Most gracious Lord, forgive me, for I do not feel any guilt whatsoever for what I have done. I have merely set the wheels of justice in motion. Sir John Skydemore stole what was, by all rights, mine. Dear Lord, as Your representative on this earth, it is my queenly duty to bring him to task for his misdeeds. That is all I am doing.

I do ask that You bless my Fawn and turn her heart back to me. Once the blush of love has faded, as it surely will, after her husband has been removed from her, she will come back to me. And we shall continue as before, she and Rob and myself—my own little family. Already, my Sweet Robin shows signs of tiring of Douglass Sheffield. He would never agree to marry such a woman, not when he hopes, still, to marry me. I want his hope to grow. Forgive my womanly pride. But I would know his love for me is true, in spite of everything.

I know restoring my "family" to me must be Your will, Lord, for it is what is in my heart. Steer me aright, if I am mistook. Or if I act from anything other than the best of intentions.

The weather at Holme Lacy was warm and sultry. The freshly cut hay from the surrounding fields gave a sweet smell to the air. The flowers and herbs from the gardens at the back of the manor house bloomed in a variety of colors and the sound of bees humming made a kind of music. Mary and one of the gardeners were pulling weeds in the early morning before the sun rose too high for such work. Since coming to Holme Lacy, Mary had discovered she had a love of the domestic life and a gift for managing the affairs of a large house.

"Shall I gather some of these daisies, mum? They'd look pretty in your bedchamber of a morning," said Thomas, the head man in charge of the vegetable and herb gardens.

"That would be lovely. Maybe you can bring in a few of those red roses—the daisies and roses would look well together," said Mary, tugging at a stubborn weed.

"Here comes the master," said Thomas, pointing to the far field where Sir John walked toward them. He had gone fishing at the nearby pond, and from the look of his lively step, he had had a successful morning.

Mary rose and waved to her husband. She walked to him, anxious to see what he had caught.

"You are as pretty as those roses, milady," said Sir John, dropping his pole and the pail filled with fish, and then hugging her. His eldest son, Harry, lagged behind and was just leaving the edge of the woods. She smiled at him as he approached.

"Did you catch some, too, Harry?" she said, leaving her husband to go to the boy.

She saw him blush with pleasure as he lifted his bucket to show her two large bass crowded around each other in the water.

"Those are enormous—why, you've given us supper for a week!" she said, linking her arm in his. He was not quite as tall as she and he had his father's blond hair and pale, green-blue eyes.

"Father caught the most, though his are not as big as these," said Harry.

"Well, I think I shall come next time to try my own luck," said Mary, laughing.

"Only if you promise to pack some of those delicious tarts you helped Cook make," said Sir John, putting her arm around her. The three of them walked thus linked all the way to the main house.

"Harry, take these to Cook and tell her I wish for fish for supper this day," said Sir John, handing the boy his pail and pole.

Then he and Mary entered the beautiful brick house and Sir John took off his muddy boots, changing into his slippers. He noticed the flowers on a table by the window and smiled at his wife.

"You have made Holme Lacy truly a home, sweetheart. Little Alice adores you and I think you are winning Harry over, too. Flowers throughout the house, tarts and other pastries made from the recipes of the queen's own kitchen . . . We have our own little court right here," said Sir John.

"I never dreamed we could be so happy—it seems I have found the family I have longed for all my life," said Mary, leaning against him, smelling his manly odor. She could not get enough of him.

"And I have a wife I truly love . . . I am fortunate, indeed, to have found two such women to marry. Do not fear, wife. As you know, I shall always love my Eleanor but my heart is large enough to love you, too. And love you I do," he said, pulling her closer and kissing the top of her head.

"Shall we sit for a while beneath the large oak in the front lawn? I'll have Constance bring refreshment," said Mary. The tree in front of the house was very old and filled half the yard. Mary had grown quite fond of it and spent many hours relaxing in its shade and quiet beauty. She grabbed a cloth and some pillows and led Sir John by the hand. She stopped by the nursery to ask the new governess, Mistress Jane Ballard, to bring the children outside to join them. Mistress Katherine Blakely continued to care for the younger ones, just as Mary had promised.

Mary and Sir John spread the cloth and put the pillows on it. They sat as Constance, the serving girl, brought out mugs of light beer, some mutton, and bread, along with a bowl of almonds and berries. The younger children ran to them and crawled over Mary, talking to her all at once. Harry and James, the two older boys, tossed a ball between them.

Suddenly, Mary felt the ground shake and heard the thundering of hooves on the road. She shaded her eyes with her hand and could see at least half a dozen horsemen heading their way. She blinked a few times. The men seemed to be wearing the uniform of the Yeomen of the Guard. But that could not be—why would the queen's men be racing toward Holme Lacy?

As they drew closer, Mary saw they were, indeed, the queen's soldiers. She sent the children inside and stood as the men rode into the front yard. She noticed the men were armed and Walsingham led them. He was the first to dismount. He strode over to where she and John stood.

"Sir John Skydemore?" said Walsingham in an official voice.

"Yes, Sir Francis, you know it is I," said John.

"I have a bill of attainder for your arrest for plotting against the Queen's Majesty. I am to take you to the Tower at once," said Walsingham.

"What? This is a lie! Sir Francis, you know my husband is the queen's staunch supporter! What madness is this?" said Mary, her heart beating fast. She could taste bile rising at the back of her throat. She looked at John, who seemed stunned and unable to move.

"Lady Skydemore, please stand back. We must take Sir John immediately!" said Walsingham.

"But he has no change of clothes—no food or money. Wait and I shall pack him a bag," said Mary.

"My orders were to bring him directly to the Tower. I am sorry, my lady, but there is no time for such things," said Walshingham.

Mary turned to her husband, who was being led to a horse by two of the guards.

"I'll bring your things, John. I'll come as soon as I can," said Mary.

"I am sorry, my lady, but the queen has forbidden you to attend court. She gave me express orders to tell you to stay at Holme Lacy. You come to London on pain of death," said Walsingham.

Without a word, he remounted and led the men away, John riding between the two guards. Her husband did not turn to look at her as she waved to him, tears streaming down her face.

The next morning, Mary had packed a bag with Sir John's clothing, some gold coins, and writing implements with a roll of parchment so he could communicate with her from the Tower. Though she had been forbidden to go to her husband, she had cajoled Thomas, the gardener, into making his way as quickly as possible to London and taking the bag she had prepared to Sir John. Thomas was to bring her word about what was happening. She could not imagine what was going on, why her husband, who seemed the best of men, should be arrested. She knew the queen was angry about their marriage, but after her initial outrage, surely Her Majesty's wrath had died down. The queen was not one to sulk and moan about a spat—she was usually as anxious to mend friendship as the courtier who had offended her. Mary would write to Her Majesty at once, begging her forgiveness and her help.

"Do be careful, Thomas—London is a dangerous place full of thieves and cutpurses," said Mary, handing him some coins for the journey.

"Don't worry, mum. I may not have been to London afore, but I know how to take care of meself—I'll send word as soon as I'm able," Thomas said, riding one of Sir John's horses.

"Godspeed, Thomas," said Mary, saying a silent prayer for him and for her husband. She turned to go back into the house, where she would soothe the children and keep them busy so worry would not nag at them, though it gnawed at her already, her head aching and her hands trembling as she made her way into the front hall.

The long days of summer seemed even longer than usual as Mary awaited word from Thomas. At first, she sought to comfort the children, but they were so used to their father's absence that they did not seem particularly worried. Even Harry, at ten, was busy being the man of the house, a role to which he had grown accustomed during the long months while Sir John had been at court. He did not seem to be concerned that soldiers had taken his father away, only that the household affairs run smoothly so Sir John would be proud of the job he'd done when he returned.

Seeing the children nonplussed, Mary was able, at first, to keep fear at bay. Besides, running the household and seeing to the children's needs took up a great deal of her time. When night darkened the earth, she found herself falling onto the mattress, exhausted and going to sleep almost immediately.

She had written to the queen the day after John had been taken away, making abject apologies for her marriage, her disobedience, her lack of proper gratitude to Her Majesty, anything she had ever done that might have irritated Elizabeth, from the time she had arrived at court until her banishment. Thus far, there had been no response.

She busied herself with sewing, mending the children's clothing, and making a new shift for little Alice, taking particular care with the blackwork she embroidered around the edges. The flowers and butterflies were designs she made herself to please the youngest child, the one who had grown to toddling age without a mother's care. Soon, a week had passed. No word.

Another long week passed before Thomas returned. Mary was in the kitchen discussing menus for the next day when she heard Thomas greet the other gardeners as he entered the kitchen. His face was smeared with dirt and his hat covered with dust. When he saw her, he bowed.

"What news, Thomas?" she said, handing him a mug of ale. He drank quickly before he spoke.

"I got into the Tower and gave Sir John his package. Had to bribe the jailer just to do that. Oh, mum, the news is bad, very bad," said Thomas, taking another gulp of ale.

"What is it? Speak, man," said Mary.

"They say Sir John has been in a plot to put the Scots' queen on the throne—him and others as well. They have all been sentenced to death at the queen's pleasure. He's to go to the block on the twelfth of July—I'm sorry, mum," said Thomas, his eyes glistening.

"But how? What proof? I do not understand . . ." said Mary, her mind unable to stay on one thought, but skipping willy-nilly, as if it were playing a game of hide-and-seek with itself.

"That Walsingham fellow had papers, ciphers he said they was. Them Jesuits have been coming into the country to rile folks up and Sir John was a-helping them. Walsingham had letters between Sir John and a Jesuit priest. Said Sir John was to gain the queen's trust so that when all was in readiness, he could get at her, kill her if need be," said Thomas.

"That cannot be true. He . . . he saved her life," said Mary, staggering onto a stool.

"To gain her trust, they say. It all come out in them papers—why, they say he even married you to get close to Her Majesty. Said he picked you because the queen loved *you* best," said Thomas.

"Is there anything else?" said Mary, her voice dull.

"No, mum. I think I told it all," said Thomas. He drained the mug and turned to go to the gardens. "I'm sorry, mum. I wish I knew how to help you."

"Thank you for all you have done, Thomas. At least I know what's happening. I shall be in my bedchamber if need arises," said Mary, slowly rising and shaking her head as if to make sense of the world.

She walked slowly to her bedchamber, the room she had shared with John, the room where they had made such sweet love that she shuddered even now with remembering. Could his lovemaking have been an act? Could a man dissemble so? Was it possible her John was mixed up in treachery? Had she been so deceived?

She moved from the large window to the bed, ran her hands along the heavy coverlet of silk, and then hugged herself. She could not cry. Tears refused to come. She felt completely baffled by all that had happened. Her injured finger was throbbing as it often did. The pain made her remember the queen's anger. But Her Majesty had been angry with others and had eventually forgiven them. She was merciful in so many cases. Even the Duke of Norfolk was released from the Tower after nine months for his first treasonous offense. Her Majesty had finally executed him but he had driven her to it: Norfolk had had treason in his heart. He was going to marry the Queen of Scots, and together they would have toppled the queen. Or at least tried.

Could it be that John was truly guilty? Had he courted her to reach the queen? Could he be a Catholic traitor? His name was on the list of dangerous Catholics. She had thought the list was made of *all* Catholics, seeing as how Lord Burghley considered them all untrustworthy. But Burghley was a Protestant and Walsingham an even hotter variety, a Puritan. Walsingham had spies everywhere and knew all that went on both in England and the Continent. If Walsingham had evidence, could that evidence be wrong?

Back and forth, back and forth, she went. Before she realized it, evening had come. She had been pacing in her room all day. Constance knocked on her door gently, asking her if she would like a tray brought up. She could not imagine swallowing anything but knew she would need her strength. She would need it because she was going to London to find out the truth. She was going, even if it meant she, too, would end up in the Tower. She was going to beg the queen for her husband's life, even if it meant losing her own.

Mary rode next to Thomas in a cart filled with vegetables from the garden: cabbages, corn, asparagus, and radishes, three sacks full, the allotted amount for country farmers to bring to Cheapside for sale. She was surprised at how comfortable she felt, dressed in Constance's cotton gown, an apron tied around her waist and a partlet at her chin. Though the bodice had been stiffened, most of the stiffness had worn out and she breathed easily. She had not realized how much her fine clothes confined the body. She found she moved more gracefully when wearing a garment that moved with her, rather than one that forced her figure to its own straight lines.

Though the cotton was a rough weave, it was cool. She wore Constance's straw hat. Thomas rode beside her, holding the reins and guiding the horse and cart with expertise. She was glad to have him with her.

"If you don't mind my saying so, mum, this idea of yers is a bit ninny-brained," said Thomas.

"You must have faith, Thomas. You live up to your name—for you are surely a doubter," said Mary. She had argued with him all morning before he had finally agreed to accompany her to London, posing as her husband.

"I don't doubt our Savior, mum, but this unsound plan of yers might just get us both killed. Forgive me if I have my doubts," said Thomas.

"The plan is simple, really. I do have some friends in London. I will go to Lord Robert and beg his help. If I can see the queen, I believe I can persuade her to release John," said Mary.

"And what makes you think she will let go a traitor?" said Thomas.

"He is not a traitor! She will release him because I ask it of her. She loved me more than a little once. I have asked for nothing. She will grant me this one request—she must!" said Mary.

"As you say, mum, as you say," said Thomas.

The road was dusty and Mary wrapped the cloth Constance had given her around her mouth so she could breathe. By the time they had been traveling for three hours, her entire dress was covered in dust. Insects buzzed around her head, flies following the horse. The cart bumped and tossed her every which way, up against Thomas and almost onto the ground a few times. With each jostle, her determination grew stronger.

It took three days to reach London. Mary had brought a bag of gold coins, enough to carry them through until she had accomplished her mission. They made their way to Cheapside and Thomas set their produce under one of the tents provided. She helped him put the vegetables on a table for display.

"I shall go to the Tower first to speak with Sir John. After that, I will decide what to do," she said, once again pulling the cloth across her mouth.

"Have a care, mum. If you ain't back by nightfall, I'm coming fer you," said Thomas.

"I fully expect to be back by then. Thank you, Thomas, for everything," she said, giving his hand a squeeze.

She made her way through the crowded streets to the Tower. The sun bore down upon her like a heavy weight and she could feel sweat dripping from her shoulders to her waist. She must have looked worn out, exactly like a servant. No one gave her a second glance.

Suddenly, the Tower loomed above her. She wanted to get inside; she needed to see John and find out for herself whether he was a traitor or not. She thought she could tell by merely looking at him. A certain cock of his head, a look in those aqua eyes—such things would give him away if he were deceiving her. Surely she could not have been duped so easily. Surely the love he bore for her was true.

She saw a guard walking past, likely off duty by the way he slumped.

"Sir! Good sir!" she called in an imitation of Constance's speech.

"What is it, woman?" said the guard, hardly slowing his pace.

"I would see one of the prisoners—how do I get in?" she said.

"Depends. Is he a nobleman? If so, I can get you in—for a price," he said.

"Yes, he's a Gentleman Pensioner, least he *was*. How much?" she said.

"How much you got?" he said.

"Half a crown. Will it do?" she said.

"Nicely," he said, holding out his hand.

She gave him the coin and followed as he headed back to the Tower.

The smell in the stone corridor was musty and damp and foul. Mary pulled the scarf more tightly around her face to block the odor. The jakes for the prison must have been nearby. She followed the guard as he climbed up and up and up, the stairs circling about like a cork-screw. Finally, they reached the third floor and the guard opened a heavy wooden door.

"This is the nice part of the Tower, miss. Where all the gents stay. Some even have full apartments, though I think this Sir John of yers has merely two rooms. Go all the way to the end of this hall and his door is second on the right. If anyone asks, tell them Captain Alexander let you in," said the guard.

"Thank you so much, Captain Alexander," said Mary.

"I ain't the captain—just be sure to mention his name," he said with a wink.

Mary heard his steps circling back down the stairs. She walked forward. It was quiet for the most part, but she could hear an occasional roar from the royal menagerie. She and the queen had visited the exotic animals there when she was a child—it had been one of her favorite places to go, even if the beasts were housed in the dreaded Tower.

She came to John's door and knocked. There was a short pause and then the door opened.

"Oh John!" she said when she saw him. His hair was mussed and his face bruised and beaten. He moved slowly and she could see his body was also hurt. She hurried into his arms and felt him flinch when she touched him.

"Mary! What are you doing here? Have you gone mad?" said John, putting his arms around her.

"I had to come, my love. I had to see you!" she said, sobbing against his chest, which seemed thinner than when she had last been in his arms.

"You should not have come—it is too dangerous!" he said, pushing her from him to look at her.

"I should have let you go to the block without trying to save you? What sort of wife would that be?" she said.

"A smart, safe wife," he said, pulling her to him again, kissing her.

He put his arm around her and led her farther into the sitting chamber.

"Allow me to welcome you to my humble abode—not as commodious as Holme Lacy but it has served well enough for a traitor," he said.

"Are you a traitor, John? Please tell me the truth—I have played our lives over and over in my mind. I admit, it is possible our whole marriage has been part of a plot. No, say nothing. Let me finish. I must know the truth, even if it hurts me. I will still try to save you because I love you. But you must tell me everything; it's the only way for us to come out of this alive. We must be honest with each other," said Mary.

"Well, I shall not have to be honest for long—a week at most," he said, smiling.

"Do not joke. I have been eaten up with worry, and now, now that I finally hold you in my arms again, you make light of this disaster," she said.

"Better that than moaning away, wishing for impossible dreams to come true. You were my dream, Mary. I should have known something so good could not last," he said.

"You have not answered my question. Are you a traitor? Were you involved in a plot against the queen?" she said, standing away from him.

"Look at me, my love. Look into my face. I tell you God's honest truth—I have never been, nor will I ever be, a traitor to Her Majesty. I do not know why they think I am. I heard the evidence Walsingham presented. He told me about letters and ciphers he had found, all in my hand. He was convincing; I almost believed him myself. Yet, I knew nothing about any letters. I did not write a letter to a Jesuit priest, much less the dozens Walsingham held. As you can see, they tried their best to get a confession from me. But I had nothing to confess," said John.

Mary looked at him, studied his face, his eyes. She looked again at the bruises and bloodied spots on his face and neck. She said nothing.

"Dearest, I swear to you on the lives of my children that I have done nothing against our queen," he said quietly.

She knew, then, that he was innocent.

And she knew what she must do to try to save him.

She went to him and kissed him more fully. He responded quickly and his hands began to rove over her.

"You look beautiful even dressed in cotton and dust," he mumbled, nuzzling her neck.

"I imagine I look a fright . . . but we have no time for kisses— I must be about my business. I shall speak with Lord Robert—if anyone has a way to the queen's heart, it is he," said Mary.

"He is not in the highest favor at present. I heard the Lady Sheffield delivered him a fine son," said John, still caressing her.

"If that is true, things might be better than I had hoped. If I know Lord Robert, he will have sent Lady Douglass to the country for her lying-in. And soon, he will ignore her and his baseborn son. For he knows the queen is the source of everything he holds dear—Kenilworth, his fine clothes, his power. And though he takes other women for his pleasure, it is the queen who has his heart," said Mary.

"I hope you are right in this, my love. For if you are not, I fear for both of us," said John.

"Kiss me once again for luck, dearest. Then I shall be off," said Mary.

Mary and Thomas found rooms at Cross Keys Inn on Gracechurch Street. Mary had bundled her clothes along with her treasure box in an old woolen cloth, scratchy and moth-eaten. She did not know exactly why she had brought her special box with her, except she never went anywhere without it. Having it gave her comfort and courage. It reminded her of all she had been through as a child: the loss of her parents, the frightening journey to London, the terrifying bustle of people at court. But the contents also spoke to her of the good things from her childhood: gifts from the queen, pretty rocks she had gathered with Lord Robert, flowers from Tom Wotton, memories she cherished. The box reminded her that, even though she was without parents, she was loved.

As she placed the box on a rough-hewn table, she remembered the ring the queen had woven from their hair so long ago. Why had she not thought of it before? She imagined them on that picnic, Lord Robert cutting the strands of hair, the queen laughing as she made them each a ring. The queen had told her if she ever needed help, show the ring to Her Majesty. No matter what the problem, the queen promised to do all in her power to assist Mary.

Mary quickly snatched the box from the table to make sure the lock of hair was still there. Carefully, she opened the painted lid. Inside, the contents were jumbled together. Slowly, she searched through her treasures and there, at the very bottom of the box, was the ringlet of black and red hair, braided long ago on a summer's day. She picked it up and held it to her heart. Surely the queen would remember this! Surely if she begged and showed her this ring, the queen would relent and John would be saved. Mary carefully replaced the ring at the bottom of the box and laid the other items on top of it. Then, feeling more hopeful than she had in weeks, she began her nightly ritual: rubbing her teeth with a cloth, washing her face, and making use of the nearby chamber pot. Then, hope blooming in her heart once again, she crawled into the clean-looking sheets of the inn, happy she had the means to pay for a nice place to stay and glad she did not have to share her bed with a stranger, or even worse, Thomas. She'd had to pay highly for that privilege and she was thankful she'd been able to afford such luxury.

The next day, Mary left Thomas once again at Cheapside, selling the few vegetables he had left over from the day before. She was on her way to Leicester House to speak with Lord Robert. When she finally arrived, she was disappointed to find he was not there, but at Whitehall Palace with the queen. Mary began the long trek to Whitehall.

As she approached the palace, she wrapped her scarf more fully over her face, looking like a woman who had suffered from the smallpox and was trying to hide her disfigurement. She knew if anyone recognized her, she would be hauled to the Tower herself. She first entered through the kitchen gardens where the herbs and flowers grew in their full abundance. The kitchens were filled with bustling cooks, stirrers, bakers, and others who went about their business quickly, shouting out instructions or telling humorous tales as they created food fit for a queen. Mary ducked through and had almost made it when one of the big men who turned the spits pulled her arm.

"What are you doing in here, lass?" he said roughly.

"I'm lost sir, looking for the laundry," said Mary, her voice shaking.

"Looks like you could do with a washing—go out that door yonder, then straight down the hall to the left. The laundry will be at the end. Now, get out of here!" said the man, swatting her bottom as she turned in the direction in which he had pointed.

She hurried down the corridor and found the large washroom at the end, just as he had said. It smelled of lye and lavender, and enormous crocks were filled with water of various colors. Next door was the folding room and Mary could see women pressing the clothes into neat piles. She then followed the back hall that led to the queen's apartments, the hall she knew Catspaw would take to bring the queen's clean shifts. That is, *if* Catspaw were still alive and *if* she were still able to work. Mary hid in a small alcove and waited, saying the same prayer over and over—God help me, God help me.

After most of the day had passed, Mary heard slow, soft footfalls coming toward her. She peeked out to see if it was Catspaw.

"What you doing in there, girl? Like to scared me into my grave," said Catspaw.

"Do you remember me, Catspaw? Mistress Mary Shelton?" said Mary. She saw the old woman's eyes were covered with blue and wondered if Catspaw could see at all.

"You should not be here—the queen banished you! Are you mad?" said Catspaw.

"Here, let me help you with those. Yes, she did banish me, but my husband, Sir John, is in the Tower. I hope to get him out," said Mary as she took the bundle from the old woman's arms.

"How? Nobody gets out of the Tower unless they be carried out," said Catspaw.

"I shall ask the queen to help me," said Mary, leading the way to the queen's apartments.

"Her Grace does not love you, mistress. I never saw her so furious as the day she found out about your marriage! They say she broke your finger. Is it true?" said Catspaw.

Mary turned to face the woman and held up her hand to show her little finger, which was slightly bent in comparison to the surrounding digits. She nodded at Catspaw.

"I'll be . . . I knew she had a temper—I've gotten swats on the head enough when she didn't like the way I washed her night shifts—but never thought her strong enough to break a bone," said Catspaw.

"She's stronger than she looks," said Mary.

They were coming to the door of the queen's apartments. Mary stopped.

"I need to see Lord Robert. As soon as possible. Can you get him that message? You don't need to tell him who I am—just say a young lady is desperate to speak with him in the laundry passage. Tell him I'll wait until he comes, even if I have to spend the night here. Can you do that, Catspaw?" said Mary.

"I'll do it. But you mustn't go anywhere—for if I send an important man like Lord Robert to you, you should be here. Else he'll have my head!" said Catspaw.

"Thank you, oh, thank you. I have a half-crown for you—but I do not have it with me. I promise, though, once I see Lord Robert, I shall bring it to you," said Mary, hugging the old woman.

"I don't want any coins—the queen is generous to me in my old age. You are young—you'll need the money," said Catspaw.

With that, she was gone.

Fifty-seven
July 4, 1574

Mary had no idea she would have to wait in the laundry hall for two days. She hid in an alcove whenever she heard footsteps and slept fitfully while the palace grew quiet at night. Luckily, Catspaw had a kind heart and brought her chunks of bread with light ale a couple of times. But, even with such generosity, Mary's stomach growled and complained that it needed more sustenance. She feared it might make such a noise as to give away her presence but, luckily, most of the grumbling took place after everyone had gone to bed.

Finally, just when Mary was ready to give up all hope, she heard heavy footsteps followed by lighter, slower ones.

"She's in here, Your Worship, just as I said. I'll be on me way now," said Catspaw as she ushered Lord Robert into the alcove.

Mary's hands went immediately to her hair—she had not combed it and it was still dusty from her drive to London. She felt her face grow warm as she thought about how she must look to Lord Robert, himself one of the best-dressed men at court. She curtsied and remained bowed low.

"Oh Fawn, what has happened to you?" said Lord Robert kindly.

She had not expected gentleness, but rather consternation at what she had done. She couldn't stop the tears from flowing as she ran into Lord Robert's arms.

"My dear girl, let it out—that's it. Let those tears flow. I know what has happened to your Sir John. And I know what it feels like to be banished from court, away from the one light in our land—our Elizabeth," said Lord Robert, cradling her as if she were still a child.

She wiped her tears with the back of her hands and stopped her sobbing. She had not come to cry but to ask his help. She would do that with as much dignity as she could muster.

"I know we have done wrong in marrying without the queen's permission, milord. And we are very sorry. But I swear to you, upon my honor and all that is holy, my husband is no traitor. Yes, he is a Catholic, but he loves the queen. Of this, I am certain," said Mary.

Lord Robert remained silent, staring intently at Mary.

"How can you be so sure, Fawn? Walsingham found letters, very compromising letters between Sir John and a Jesuit priest. How do you explain that?" said Lord Robert.

"I cannot explain it. I only know that John is innocent. He has sworn his innocence to me on the lives of his children. I believe him," said Mary.

"That is not very factual, dear. And I fear you are not unbiased in this case," said Lord Robert.

"Is there no hope then?" said Mary.

"As long as there is breath, there is hope. I believe the best way for you to help your husband is to speak directly to the queen. Her Majesty often relies on her womanly instincts to make decisions of guilt and innocence. She may see more in your words than do I," said Lord Robert.

"But how can I see her? She has forbidden me to come to court," said Mary.

"Ah, that is where I come in. Let me see what I can arrange. I make no promises—I do not have the sway with the queen I once enjoyed. But there may be a way, yet. I shall call for you few days hence. Be ready, little Fawn. Be ready," he said.

"I shall be at Cross Keys Inn. I shall wait for you there," said Mary.

"I will send my man, Rogers, for you. He wears a cap with a black feather—that is how you shall know him. Until then, watch yourself. London is full of scalawags," said Lord Robert as he turned to leave her. She listened as his footsteps grew softer and softer, then stopped altogether.

Mary sighed and waited until her heartbeat returned to normal. Then, she slipped out of the palace and back to her room at the inn.

You have not met me in the laundry hall for many years, Rob. What is this all about?" said the queen, leaning against the cool stones.

"I thought you might enjoy remembering our dalliances here, Bess—it seems so long ago," said Lord Robert, putting his arm against the wall and moving closer to face the queen.

"It was long ago—before your *other* dalliances came between us," said the queen.

"I confess it—I have made love to others. I had to make do with coarse bread because I could not have manchet. You know, it was only gossip about my marriage to the Sheffield woman—we were never legally wed. She spreads it about because she wishes it were so. But I have loved *you*, Bess. I can never marry another. I still love only *you*," he said, his face so close his beard tickled her nose.

"Oh please . . . enough of this foolish talk. Why did you bring me here?" said the queen, pushing him away.

"Is it so foolish? To speak of a love that has lasted these twenty years? Longer than many have lived," he said. He pressed into her.

"When you have had a baseborn babe with another, yes, it is foolish to remember our own youthful enchantment. Yet, I am happy to learn the rumors about your wedding Mistress Douglass are untrue. I can forgive a bastard or two, I suppose," said the queen, smiling ruefully at him. "Why have you brought me here?"

"Because I love you. And I would save you from your lesser nature," he said, moving away from her.

"What do you mean, 'my lesser nature'—I ought to box your ears for such insolence!" said the queen.

"Bess, dearest, you have done violence enough to those you love, have you not?" he said, grabbing her hand before the blow could land.

"I suppose you speak of the poppet," said the queen.

"You know I do. You have had Sir John arrested for treason. He is set to die two days hence. Will you not stay your hand? There was scant proof Skydemore was involved—and I do not believe he was. As much as I applaud his efforts to root out every plot against you, I fear Walsingham has been overzealous in this case. I cannot believe you do not see this as well. Your queenly judgment is usually so keen," said Lord Robert.

"I take Walsingham's word—you have been happy enough to see me execute Norfolk and almost daily demand I try the Scottish queen. Why are you not happy to see these plotting recusants go to the block?" snapped the queen.

"Those who are guilty deserve death. But I do not think Skydemore is one of these. I think you wish to rid yourself of him so you can have Mary back at court," said Lord Robert.

The queen turned to him, her finger wagging at him.

"And what if I do want her back! Is that so wrong? He has taken her from me as surely as the hand of Death would. And he shall die for it," said the queen.

"Bess, sweetheart—this is unworthy of you. Can you not remember when we were young? How we loved? The chances we took so we could be together? Why, right here in this very corridor—do you not remember?" he said. He walked to her and wrapped his arms around her. She leaned against him and began to sob softly.

"Yes, Sweet Robin, I remember. We thought we could love and rule the world," she said.

"I would that I had whisked you away as Skydemore did our Fawn. How happy we might have been," said Lord Robert.

"Would we? Would you have been happy without your power and position? Would I? We cannot know what might have been. We must live with what is," said the queen.

"Then let us live in such a way as we first started—with honor and fighting for what is right. Will you see our Fawn? She has come to London to beg your forgiveness. Will you see her?" said Lord Robert, still holding the queen close. He kissed her gently on the mouth.

"God's blood, Rob. Send her to me. I shall see her. Now, kiss me again, won't you?" said the queen.

Fifty-nine

*B*y all the saints in heaven, how is it I have agreed to see her? What magic does the Earl of Leicester possess that causes me to throw away my perfectly reasonable ways and take up his own? If I did not know better, I would say Dr. Dee has given Leicester some sort of potion to bend me to his will. God's blood!

Now that I know she is coming, what am I to do?

Yes, Parry, I will be glad to see the urchin. I know what she wants— that husband of hers released from the Tower. I shall not release him—he has been proven a traitor! I had nothing to do with it, Parry. And what if I did! It is my right as queen, is it not, to suggest possible traitors to my spymaster! I am queen! I will be obeyed!

I wonder if these weeks away from court have changed our girl. Has she gained some creases across her brow? Is she wasting away from worry? Does she miss us? Has she shed tears because she has displeased us?

Well, I have. My heart aches without her to calm me. I cannot sleep—and no, Mistress Frances does not help as our Fawn did. I miss her! I admit it. And now, I am to see her once again. Will she be sincere in her apologies? For I know she will ask my forgiveness, which I would easily give if I thought she meant it. Do you think she will mean it from her heart? Or will this be another example of a courtier trying to get a favor from the daft old queen?

Yes, I have missed her. And I have missed my Sweet Robin, too. Perhaps it is time to forgive him, as well. I have treated him coldly for a very long time. Now, I shall welcome him to my arms. After all, he has sent Lady Douglass to the country and he has sworn to me that they never married. That was a tale she told to force him to it, but he was having none of it. He said if he could not marry the woman he truly loved, he would never marry. I do believe him, Parry. I truly do.

I shall wear my finest clothes. I shall even wear my small crown. She shall see me in all my splendor. By God's teeth, then we shall see her cower before us! Come, Parry, we have work to do.

*M*ary spent a long time preparing to meet the queen. She bathed and perfumed herself with the rose water she'd had Thomas buy at the apothecary's shop. The yellow gown she had packed was wrinkled and smudged with dirt but she brushed it as best she could. She wore the matching French hood and put her long black hair beneath the snood. She slipped on her velvet shoes with the seed pearls sewn all over and wore the necklace the queen had given her years ago, the one with diamonds and pearls, having been all this time in her special box. She took the ringlet of hair and placed it inside her sleeve. She drank a tall glass of wine before heading for Whitehall.

This time when she went abroad, people noticed her. Out of the plain dress of a serving girl and into clothes fit for the court made all the difference. Men nodded to her as she passed and women stared at her fine dress. Such looks gave her confidence.

Lord Robert had told her to be in the Presence Chamber at noon and he would see that she got an audience with the queen. She had never been more nervous—it was much like the first time she'd been led into the queen's presence by Mistress Blanche.

She entered the palace halls and walked with purpose to the Presence Chamber. The yeoman announced her and she strode through the door as if she hadn't a care in the world. She saw Nora, who smiled at her, and Pakington, who did not. Nora looked healthy and thinner than she had been before her pregnancy. Being a mother must suit her.

Mary saw Oxford, who stared at her as if she had a second head growing from her neck. She nodded to him, but did not speak. She found a spot beneath the window and waited. She did not want to contaminate Nora by talking to her—who knew what trouble *that* might cause. After all, she was banished, in the queen's bad graces. The best thing she could do for her friend was to ignore her.

Soon, the bell tolled twelve and many of the courtiers left the chamber, tired of waiting or having other appointments to attend. Mary settled in, expecting another long wait. She gazed at the fine furnishings around her, the tapestries and paintings. How different from the inn where she'd spent the last few days. How different from her beloved Holme Lacy. Suddenly, she wished she could run, leave the court and return to that peaceful house on the hill, return to the children she was just beginning to love. But it was too late for that. The door to the queen's Privy Chamber opened and Lord Robert beckoned her in.

She rose and smoothed her hair. She walked as quietly as she could and saw the queen sitting on her throne, waiting. Never had the queen looked so regal. Mary noticed she was wearing her crown, something she rarely did. Her dress was covered with pearls and the sleeves were cloth of gold slashed with white silk. Her Majesty looked more like a goddess than a mere mortal.

Mary immediately went to her knees. She stayed in that position for a long moment. Then, she slowly began to creep toward the throne. The room was long, very long and narrow. Already, she felt pain as her knees scraped along the hard floor. The rushes were filled with foodstuff, spittle, and she could only guess what else, yet she hobbled through the muck, still on her knees. The smell of refuse and urine almost gagged her but on she crawled. She hoped that by humbling herself in this way, she could move the queen's heart.

Finally, she arrived at the throne. She stayed on her knees, glancing up very quickly one time only. She saw Mistress Blanche standing behind the queen on one side, with Lord Robert on the other.

The queen did not look at her.

She did not know whether to speak or not. She kept her head bowed and waited.

Still, there was nothing but silence.

The silence grew until it was unbearable. This woman, who had been kind to her for most of her life, now refused to look at her. Suddenly, Mary realized how much she had missed the queen, how she had longed to share the day's events with her as she brushed Her Majesty's hair. Mary felt a tear trickle down her face. She had not realized she was crying. The queen must have noticed it, too. Finally, Her Majesty spoke.

"Why are you here?" the queen said.

"Your Majesty, I have come to beg your pardon. You took me under your wing as a mother hen does her chick. You provided me with all good things, especially your love. I betrayed that love by marrying without your permission. I am here to beg forgiveness and to ask for your love once again. I have been lost without it," said Mary.

Again, the room grew quiet.

Mary began to lose hope as the silence continued. She thought she could hear the beating of everyone's heart. Or maybe it was just the thudding of her own.

"These are sweet words. What proof do I have that you mean them? As I know better than most, those at court learn to dissemble so well, the truth is hard to find," said the queen, her voice like ice.

"Your Majesty," said Mary, raising her face to look into the queen's black eyes, "you know me better than anyone. You have been with me since I was but a child. You know I love you and I am telling you what is in my heart."

"Have you come to try and save your husband?" said the queen.

"Yes. I am begging you to spare him—he is no traitor, of that I am certain," said Mary.

"I see. So now you tell me my courts misjudge? There is not justice in my realm?" said the queen, her voice rising.

"No, Your Grace. I just tell you I know this man and I know he loves Your Majesty. He has proven his love with his body," said Mary.

"I am not given to executing innocent people. If Walsingham finds him guilty, then guilty he must be," said the queen.

Another silence filled the room.

Mary did not know what else to say. She slipped her hand up her sleeve and pulled out the ringlet of hair.

"Your Majesty gave me this many years ago. I have kept it in my box of treasures. Do you remember it?" said Mary, handing the hair to the queen.

The queen held out her long, delicate hands and carefully received the lock. She took it close to her face to examine it.

"I cannot believe you have held on to it this long—it was just a silly fancy. But you have kept it all these years," said the queen, her voice softening.

"Those who love Your Majesty often keep trinkets to remind us of your love," said Lord Robert. "And those who have loved you long, those are the ones you can trust."

"As she who rocked your cradle, Your Grace, I concur with Lord Robert—you can trust those who have been as close as your own family," said Mistress Blanche, smiling at Mary. Lord Robert gave her warm looks, too.

The queen fingered the strands of hair, one black, the other reddish-gold. She slipped the ringlet on her finger. She spun it around and around. The minutes ticked by. Mary dared not move. Finally, the queen looked into Mary's face. She did not smile but she did utter a soft sigh.

"All right, Fawn. I shall spare your husband. Because of the love we have shared, I will give you his life," said the queen.

Mary could not stop the tears that ran down her cheeks.

"Do not shed tears of joy just yet. There is a condition," said the queen.

"Anything, Your Majesty," said Mary.

"You are to stay at court with me all of your days. You will not be given leave to return to Holme Lacy. You will not leave me again," said the queen.

"I shall stand by Your Majesty until I die," said Mary.

The queen called for Sir Nicholas Bacon and the Great Seal. She told him to write out a pardon for Sir John Skydemore and bring it to her immediately to be signed. She then sent word for Sir John to be released.

"Your Majesty, I thank you with all my heart," said Mary. The queen motioned for her to rise. The queen also rose and stepped forward to hug Mary. Lord Robert and Mistress Parry also linked arms around their Fawn. The four of them stood together for several minutes, laughing and crying, then laughing once again. The queen called for malmsey and gooseberry tarts. She then clapped her hands to signal the musicians to begin playing.

"La Volta!" shouted the queen. She took Lord Robert's arm and led him to the middle of the floor. Mary and Mistress Blanche watched as the Queen of England pranced and leaped with her love.

Sixty-one

At first, I did not know if I could bring myself to forgive Fawn for her treachery. She looked so young and beautiful when she entered my Privy Chamber—ripe as a plum, ripe with love fulfilled, ripe in a way I shall never know. Yes, Parry, I was jealous—of her youth, her beauty. And of the fact that she had married the man she loved, something I could never do.

Ah, but when she fell to her knees and began to crawl toward me, I felt my heart shift in its cage. I could see the child once more, the sweet loving face of the little girl who had adored me. I remembered her chubby arms clinging to me, the feel of her body against my own. I remembered the smell of her breath while she slept, the sweetness of our waking together. I remembered the time she reached up to touch my face, the gentlest touch I have ever felt. She said, "I love you, Your Majesty." And the words were so pure and so real they made my eyes water.

I knew, then, I would give her anything she wanted.

Yes, I made her promise never to leave me. Do not worry. I shall reinstate Sir John as a Gentleman Pensioner—they shall both live with me. I am not a cruel woman. I would not keep them apart. Well, I would not part them forever.

Now, Parry, help me into bed. This day has been long and I wish to rest.

Epilogue
April 28, 1603

She who has been our queen for, lo, these many years is no more. I am well enough to attend her funeral this day, though I was not at court with her when she died. She had allowed me, finally, to return to Holme Lacy, for she could see Death had his fingers around my throat. This happened before she grew ill herself. I wish I could have been with her in those last moments when the soul parts from the body. But it was not to be. Perhaps the fresh air at Holme Lacy strengthened me a little. Whatever the reason, Death released his grip so that I am able to escort her to her final resting place.

But I shall see her again. Indeed, I shall follow her soon, perhaps before the harvest. For I feel the cold fingers once again tightening around me.

She would have loved the English sky on this day as her people lined the funeral route to Westminster Abbey. The heavens are blue and filled with white clouds, soft-looking as Her Majesty's finest silks and satins. Earlier in the day, many Englishmen paid her tribute, all silent, hats off in respect.

Four horses arrayed in black velvet pulled the hearse which carried her body encased in lead. Atop this coffin, a full-sized effigy of Her Majesty, holding her orb and scepter, lay dressed in her state robes. Six earls held the canopy of estate over her. Her Master of the Horse led a riderless palfrey behind the hearse, followed by the Marchioness of Northampton, chief mourner.

I followed, a dark drop in the sea of black, over a thousand lords and ladies of the realm, councillors, courtiers, the Lord Mayor, and every person of import in London. I watched the citizens, hanging from windows, climbing on rooftops for a better view, all of us mourning and crying for our Good Queen Bess.

I mourned for more than my queen. She had become my family and I, hers. From the time I was allowed to return to court until her death, John and I served her unfailingly. We were both rewarded: John with high positions and I with gifts of coin that exceeded my dreams.

As time passed, those who had been with the queen since her youth grew more powerful. I was considered one of a trinity of ladies able to work miracles for those who petitioned us. The others were Mistress Blanche and the Countess of Warwick, Lady Jane Russell. One courtier called the three of us the "triumvirate of evil" that surrounded Her Majesty.

It was true, I suppose, if one was trying to petition the queen for something or other. Her Majesty did listen best to us and, as she grew older, she depended upon us to help her remember the details of government. We did our best to protect her from those who would use her. She trusted me implicitly with her clothing, allowing no one else to select and care for her gowns. I made certain she remained regal and beautiful.

But beauty, like everything else, fades in this earthly life. They say at the end, she insisted on hours of prayer, reaching for her priest again and again when he tried to rise to give relief to his poor knees. The comfort of prayer must have helped her. I am only sorry I could not have been there with her, sorry she had to make that last journey without me.

She was the kindest yet the cruelest of mistresses. When I was sick with any small illness, she would treat me with her own medicines and spoon broth into my mouth from her own hand. She never struck me or anyone else again. At least, not that I know of.

Yet, she kept me with her at all times. I could not return to Holme Lacy unless I begged and pleaded. Rarely, she would give in to my pleas and allow me a fortnight with the children. On those occasions, I loved being surrounded by the peace and beauty that was Holme Lacy. But, more often than not, she recalled me to court before even one week was out. She said she could not sleep without me.

I believe her. She had enough difficulty resting and, in her later years, kept a rusty sword by her mattress, fearing an assassin would break into her apartments and do away with her. I knew how to soothe her, bring her lids closed and help her relax. Sometimes, I gave her one of my cordials. Other times, I would sing or rub her back. She was almost like a child then, and I, the mother.

John and I never had children of our own. I blame the queen. He and I were rarely together, though we were married. She kept us both too busy for our own love to engender a babe. Though I did not have children of my own body, I tried to raise John's children as best I could. I saw to their education and made certain they had proper clothes to wear. I kept in close contact with their governess, and when I was allowed a little time with them, I tried to make up for my frequent absences. Sometimes, they would come to court. The queen was kind to them and seemed to favor them above the children of her other subjects. Somehow, they grew up, the way children do. They are now busy with their own lives.

As time passed, I devoted myself more and more to the queen.

There is a strange scent permeating London this afternoon. It smells something like sweet marjoram. I want to inhale it, remember it, this sweetness. For I am convinced she is here, still here in the very bricks and mortar of the castles, in the cobbles and in the shops and alleyways. She is in the river, traveling to and from her houses, sustaining her people in their daily jaunts.

She rises like the mist from the water and permeates everything. She is in the very air of this England.

I go to join her soon. Already, I feel cold, as if my blood is no longer able to warm me. I shall be happy to see her again, to feel her hand on my face and hear her whisper, "My Fawn."

Author's Note

Once again, I have shaken the family tree to find a story about one of my ancestors. In *At the Mercy of the Queen*, I wrote about Lady Margaret Shelton, first cousin of Queen Anne Boleyn. In *Queen Elizabeth's Daughter*, I've written about Lady Mary Shelton, who served at Elizabeth I's court and was her second cousin.

After reading a historical novel, I want to know how much of the story is true. I suspect this response is pretty common among readers. Folks want to know which part of the story is fact and which part the writer made up. Here are some facts about Lady Mary Shelton.

First, Lady Mary was born around 1550–1551, according to various sources. She was, indeed, an orphan. Her parents both died on the same day, November 15, 1558, the same month Elizabeth became queen. This made Mary a royal ward of the court because she was the queen's second cousin. Her older brother, Ralph, was of age and inherited the various family properties. Most likely, he would have kept Mary in his care, though the final decision about her fate would have been in the hands of the Court of Wards and, ultimately, in the hands of the queen. Mary's marriage would have been of great importance, given her close proximity to the queen, and the queen would have retained Mary's marriage rights. This would have enabled the queen to make a political match, using Mary's position either to strengthen her own or to reward a faithful courtier.

I changed Mary's age when she was orphaned, making her three years old, rather than eight. I thought a three-year-old would appeal to Elizabeth's maternal instincts more strongly, with the child's need for care being greater. Although Mary would have been a little older than Elizabeth was when she lost her own mother to the executioner's sword, perhaps Mary's bereft state would have touched Elizabeth's sympathies. A younger child would also allow the attachment between them to have been stronger, more like a mother/daughter relationship.

Mary's rise in position occurred as it appears in the novel and she did become one of the queen's favorites; she exercised a great deal of power and persuasion, especially in the queen's later years. She was rewarded handsomely for her service, and the meticulous records she kept of Queen Elizabeth's wardrobe have given us a thorough look into the clothing of the day (see *Queen Elizabeth's Wardrobe Unlock'd* by Janet Arnold).

Mary married Sir John Scudamore (also spelled Skydemore, Skydmor, Skidmore, and other ways) without the queen's permission. Sir John was a widower with five small children. He was also a Catholic from an old church family in Herefordshire, where the family estate, Holme Lacy, still stands (only portions of the original remain, as the house has been destroyed and rebuilt several times). The queen did, indeed, break Mary's finger in a fit of anger over the marriage. Mary, Queen of Scots, mentions the event in one of her letters and says Elizabeth tried to pass off the incident as the result of a falling candlestick. The information about Mary's unfortunate "accident" most likely came to Mary, Queen of Scots, from Bess of Hardwick, who was her "keeper" for a while. The episode is corroborated by Eleanor Brydges, one of the queen's ladies-in-waiting.

The queen did eventually forgive Mary's indiscretion, making Sir John one of her Gentlemen Pensioners. However, she continued to demand Mary's presence as one of her sleeping companions as well as one of her ladies-in-waiting. She did not allow her ladies to leave her side very often, and Mary was no exception. Mary and John had no children. My own bloodline comes down through Mary's older brother, Ralph.

In the early months of 1603, Mary was allowed to go to Holme Lacy to die. However, when the queen passed away in March, Mary also attended the funeral. Mary followed the queen to the great beyond on August 15, 1603.